BARON AND BARONESS VON TAUCHNITZ
Of Leipzig.

_____

As a record of rare conjugal attachment, this Tale
may be appropriately inscribed to you, my good
friends; than whom I have never known a more
fondly-united couple.

Were I the Donor of the FLITCH, I would bestow
it upon you. As it is, I must content myself with
offering you this simple Chronicle of a good 'ld
English Custom—something akin to which may, perhaps, exist in your kindly Fatherland.

Accept it as a slight testimony of the great regard
in which you are both held by

Yours very sincerely,

W. HARRISON AINSWORTH.

PREFACE.

"AMONG the jocular tenures of England, none have been more talked of than the BACON OF DUNMOW." So says Grose, and truly. The Dunmow Flitch has passed into a proverb. It is referred to by Chaucer, in a manner which proves that allusion to it was as intelligible in his day, as it would be in our own.

The origin of the memorable Custom, hitherto enveloped in some obscurity, will be found fully explained in the course of this veracious history. Instituted by a Fitzwalter in the early part of the Thirteenth Century, the Custom continued in force till the middle of the Eighteenth—the date of the following Tale. The last delivery of the Flitch occurred on the 20th June, 1751; and I possess a very curious print, quite Hogarthian in its character, from a drawing taken on the spot by David Ogborne, representing (apparently with great accuracy) the Ceremony and Procession on that occasion. This print has furnished me with a few hints for my Story.

A Custom, almost precisely similar to that of Dunmow, existed at Whichenoure, in Staffordshire, but is much less generally known. Pennant, who visited Whichenoure House in 1780, states, that it was "remarkable for the painted wooden Bacon Flitch, still hung up over the hall chimney, in memory of the singular tenure by which Sir Philip de Somervile, in the time of Edward the Third, held the Manor." The Oath ran as follows :—" Hear ye, Sir Philip de Somervile, lord of Wichenoure, maintainer and giver of this Bacon, that I, A., syth I wedded B., my wyfe, and syth I had her in my kepyng and at wylle, by a Yere and a Daye after our Marryage, I would not have changed for none other, farer ne fowler, richer ne powrer, ne for none other descended of gretter lynage, sleeping ne waking, at noo time; and if the said B. were sole, and I sole, I would take her to be my wyfe before all the wymen of the worlde, of what condytions soevere they be, good or evyle, as helpe me God, and his Seyntys, and this flesh, and all fleshes." If the claimant were a "villeyn," corn and a cheese were given him in addition to the Flitch, and a horse was likewise provided to take him out of the limits of the Manor—all the free tenants thereof conducting him on his way with " trompets, tabourets, and other manoir of mynstralcie." In respect to the Whichenoure Flitch Pennant remarks, that it has " remained untouched from the first century of its institution to the present;" adding, jocosely, " we are credibly informed, that the late and present worthy owners of the Manor were deterred from entering into the holy state, from the dread of not obtaining a single rasher of their own bacon."

Our Dunmow Flitch was in greater request. Despite the difficulties of the conditions annexed to the gift, it was thrice successfully claimed before the Dissolution of the Monasteries; and thrice subsequently to that period." Of late years the Custom, I regret to say, has been discontinued. " Some persons having demanded the Flitch," observes Grose, " it has, as is said, been refused, probably from conjugal affection not being now so rare as heretofore, or because qualification oaths are now supposed to be held less sacred."

Many years ago I planned this Tale; but it is only now that my long-meditated design has been accomplished.

CONTENTS.

THE FLITCH OF BACON;

OR,

THE CUSTOM OF DUNMOW.

— ◆ —

Part the First.

THE OLD INN AT DUNMOW.

———

I.

FROM WHICH IT MAY BE INFERRED THAT PERSEVERANCE
IN A GOOD CAUSE WILL MEET ITS REWARD.

A GOOD Old Inn was the Dunmow Flitch. None
better in Essex.

The house had known better days, and wealthier
inmates—though not merrier, perhaps—than it did,
since it had come into the occupation of Jonas Nettlebed: "Jovial Jonas," as he called himself,—or "Friar
Bacon," as some of his customers styled him: and who,
out of his exceeding love and respect for the time-
honoured custom of the Manor of Dunmow, had
adopted the Flitch as his sign, and underneath the
great gilded daub, supposed to represent a side of fatted
bacon, that hung before his door, had caused these lines
to be written:

> Painted in gold,
> The FLITCH behold,
> Of fam'd Dunmow the boast!
> Then here should call
> Fond couples all,
> And pledge it in a toast!

This sign caused much laughter, and provoked much
rustic wit, chiefly at the landlord's expense; but as it

lured most of the jesters into the house, it perfectly answered its purpose.

Though Jovial Jonas had prospered in his calling, which he richly deserved to do, seeing that he brewed the best ale in Essex; the one grand wish of his life was still ungratified,—namely, the possession of the Flitch—not metaphorically, but literally. He coveted the prize more than any other worldly honour, and though often disappointed, he had not given up the expectation of gaining it.

Hitherto he had not been able to take the Oath prescribed by the Charter, which was rather strict in its conditions, requiring that any married couple claiming the Flitch, should swear that they had lived together in perfect amity for a Twelvemonth and a Day, and never for a single moment, whether sleeping or waking, in bed or at board, had repented them of their choice, or wished themselves asunder. This was more than Jonas could conscientiously affirm of any of his unions. Any, we say, for he had been thrice married, and in each instance the match was so ill-assorted, that both parties often sighed for freedom from their fetters. Jonas's first wife was a shrew, and never allowed him a moment's peace; his second was soft-spoken enough, but a sad flirt, who drove him nearly distracted with jealousy; and his third cared more about the bottle than she did about him. Nothing daunted, and animated by the same ambition as before, Jonas married again, in the full belief that this time his effort would be crowned with success. And the odds seemed now rather more in his favour, for his fourth wife, Nelly, was not only by far the prettiest of the bunch, but very amiable, and apparently very much attached to him. Moreover, Nelly was as anxious to gain the Flitch as her husband; and that was something. The

worst that could be said of her was, that she was a
little disposed to coquetry, and liked flattery; " but
this," Jonas said, " was quite natural in a pretty
young woman." As to her personal graces, he had
been known to sum them up thus:—" There is not too
much of Nelly—not half so much as there was of my
last wife, Chloe—but, what there is, is good, and of
the right sort. Her eyes are brighter than my first
wife's, Kate—you recollect Kate's black eyes, eh, neighbour?—and her waist is trimmer, and her ankles neater
than Jane's—my second—you remember Jenny, neighbour—a fine woman, but rather too free in her manners
—in short, Nelly's worth 'em all three put together.
I'm a lucky man, neighbour—by the marry maskins!
I am. I envy no man his wife—not even you—and I
care not if any man envies me, seeing I'm now as sure
of the Flitch as I am that my name's Jonas—Jovial
Jonas—ha! ha! I mean to claim it when the time of
probation is over. So look out for rare doings, neighbour—rare doings—ho! ho!"

Sam Orpint, the village chum to whom these remarks
were addressed, though he agreed with the uxorious
landlord in his estimate of his wife's beauty, was by
no means so sure that Jonas would win the prize.
However, he kept his thoughts to himself, and merely
nodded his head, as if in assent. He was married
himself, and knew the difficulties and dangers of the
case.

The claimant of the Flitch in expectation was by no
means an ill-looking little fellow—in his own opinion.
We are compelled to qualify the description, since most
people thought him too short, too stout, too red in the
gills, too puffy, too snub-nosed—too anything you please
—except too handsome. But Jonas viewed his own
figure and face in the glass in a very different light

and thought himself an extremely personable man. He was rather a lady-killer too; persuading himself that the women doted upon him—and he had some show of reason for the belief, since he had obtained four wives; but other explanations of his good luck had been given. Howbeit, he took considerable pains in the adornment of his person; wore flowered waistcoats, and coats of showy colour; was particular about the tie of his wig, and the nice sit of his hose. Nor could any innkeeper boast a whiter apron than he.

In a conspicuous part of the house, placed there for the edification of his guests—for he knew it by heart himself—and fairly copied out and framed, was the Oath, administered to the claimants of the Flitch, which had always hitherto appeared so formidable to him, but which he now hoped to be able to enunciate without any omission, or the slightest mental reservation. And as this singular formula will be frequently referred to in the course of our story, it may be here recited in full.

The Oath.

You shall swear by Custom of Confession,
That you ne'er made nuptial transgression ;
Nor since you were married man and wife
By household brawls or contentious strife,
Or otherwise at bed or at board
Offended each other in deed or word:
Or since the parish clerk said Amen
Wished yourselves unmarried again :
Or in a Twelvemonth and a Day
Repented not in thought any way ;
But continued true and in desire
As when you join'd hands in holy quire,
If to these Conditions, without all fear,
Of your own accord you will freely swear:
A whole Gammon of Bacon you shall receive,
And bear it hence with love and good leave ;
For this is our Custom of Dunmow well known :—
Though the pleasure be ours, the Bacon's your own.

No Brawls. No Regrets. No Transgressions. Con-

stant Love and Devotion. Twelve Honeyed Moons; and
One Day over, to make all sure. The conditions were
so hard, and so little applicable to the cases of married
folk in general, and those of Dunmow in particular,
that they were never accepted.

An old custom this delivery of the Flitch. Its institution is attributed to Sir Reginald Fitzwalter, who,
appearing in a rustic garb before the good Prior of the
Convent of Dunmow, received a side of bacon from him
as a reward of his constancy. But this legend will be
more fully narrated hereafter. The earliest claim on
record was made in the seventh year of the reign of
Edward the Fourth, and the guerdon of rare conjugal
love and truth was bestowed upon Steven Samuel and
his wife. Twice again in monkish times was the prize
won : at long intervals indeed, for the second successful
application occurred in the reign of Henry the Sixth,
and the third at the commencement of the Eighth
Harry's rule. But the good old custom was continued
long after the dissolution of the monasteries; in fact, it
could not be dispensed with, being part of the manorial
tenure. A portion of the venerable fabric, which had
once sheltered the old Augustine canons and their superior, was still standing; where those, who had lived
and loved as few love and live, had come in days gone
by, to make their claim, and hold themselves up as a
bright example to their fellows; the very stones beneath
the porch were left—sharp-pointed flints they were, and
little worn—on which three proud and happy couples
had knelt to verify their faith, and receive the priestly
benediction and reward : the ancient and curiously-
formed oak chair was still preserved in which those
worthy folk had sat together, and thus placed had been
borne upon men's shoulders round the precincts of the
sacred edifice, to the sound of rebec, psaltery, and lute,

and amidst joyous shouting from admiring crowds ; the
Flitch of Bacon being carried before them on a lofty
pole. All these forms and ceremonies were yet observed,
or ready to be observed, save that Squire Monkbury,
the present Lord of the Manor of Little Dunmow,
together with his steward, Mr. Abel Roper, and other
officers, were substituted for the prior and his white-
robed brethren. But alack ! and well-a-day ! Wedded
love and faith would seem a fable. Only two more
claims were made with success in two centuries. It was
now the middle of the third—that is to say, in 1750—
and though a Flitch of Bacon was regularly salted and
dried at Monkbury Place, and proclamation constantly
made at the Court Baron of Little Dunmow that it
was ready for delivery—*secundum formam donationis*
—to any applicants, on due fulfilment of the conditions
annexed to the gift—the prize was never won. The
applicants were numerous, but the conditions were too
hard.

We have seen who conceived themselves entitled to
the prize. Jonas and Nelly fully expected to be Number
Six on the list of winners.

Many years ago, the Old Inn had been the most important habitation near Dunmow ; in fact, the Hall.
Abandoned by its owner, Sir Walter Fitzwalter, an
eccentric personage, about whom strange tales were
told, though none to the effect that he had much
chance of gaining the Flitch, for indeed he behaved
very cruelly to his lady, who destroyed herself, it was
said ; and in the end sold, and for an old song, for like
most deserted houses, it was supposed to be haunted,
and for some time no one would inhabit it ; it was, at
last, converted into an inn, and was taken by Jonas Nettlebed immediately after his first marriage.

Of late years, the ghost of the unfortunate Lady

Juga Fitzwalter (for she it was who was said to "walk at midnight") did not disturb the place so much as heretofore; but there was one particular room, in a deserted wing of the house, in which whoever slept was sure to be scared by a female figure in white. With this exception, the Old Inn was quiet and comfortable enough, and the general accommodation excellent Good ale, clean sheets, civil host and buxom hostess: what more could any reasonable traveller desire?

Look at the old house. Assuredly, it is picturesque, and rich enough in elaborate architectural detail. What a fine façade it presents! high roof, quaint gables, twisted chimneys, and bay-windows, still full of stained glass. And what a large and hospitable porch! Note those noble elm-trees growing near it. To an arm of one of the largest of them is suspended Jonas Nettlebed's gaudy signboard. But for that, and the circular bench embracing the tree, and the watering trough for horses, and some other matters, you would never have taken the house for an inn. The promise without is not belied by what we find within. Here is a spacious and lofty room, capable of accommodating any number of guests; and here no doubt the old Fitz-walters—a hospitable race, save the last of the line—must often have feasted their friends, and held their Christmas revels. Is it much changed since their time? We think not. Witness that high carved mantelpiece, amongst the ornaments of which you may discern their many-quartered shield: and you may also find their armorial bearings in the blushing panes of the bay-windows. The wainscots are of oak as in days of yore; and that ponderous table of the same dark material, and that massive carved sideboard, can never have left their places. They must have belonged to some Fitzwalter in the days of good Queen Bess, when

the Hall was built, and that fine oak staircase was
reared, which you see leading to the railed gallery
above.   Many a light foot has tripped down those
polished steps : many a heavy boot clanked up them.
Rich silks have rustled in the gallery above : fair faces
have looked down upon the gallants below, when
beards were wagging at the board, and the damsels'
names were on their lovers' lips as they raised the cup
to them.   Many a swift couranto has been danced
upon the floor : many a song has echoed from the
vaulted roof : many a Yule log has crackled upon the
hearth : many a sport and pastime has been held
round it.   All are gone now.   No wonder there is a
ghost in the house.   It must mourn over past splen-
dours—over the buried joys of other days.

There are four doors opening upon the gallery, easily
discernible from below.   One of them must belong to
the Haunted Chamber.   No.   They are all too public.
A ghost requires seclusion.   There is a dark corridor
on the left.   It must lead to the lonesome room, where
the guest's slumbers have been broken at dead of night,
and his blood frozen within his veins by a ghastly apparition.

II.

HOW JONAS NETTLEBED COUNTED HIS CHICKENS BEFORE THEY WERE HATCHED.

THE Old Inn looked unusually cheery.

Not that it ever looked dull or uncomfortable, but
just now it wore a particularly bright and lively aspect.
A good fire was blazing on the hearth, roaring up the
wide-mouthed chimney, and shining on the black wainscots, on the twisted legs of the black oak table, and on
the carved doors of the black oak sideboard.   The good

fire was needed, for it was bitterly cold without: a
black frost of a week's duration. All the ponds and
watercourses about Dunmow were covered with ice, and
even the Chelmer, which flowed within a hundred yards
of the inn, encircling the grey and mossy walls of its
once stately gardens, was partially frozen.

It was close upon Christmas time, and the season
promised to be more seasonable than the winters we
now usually experience. Green Yules were rarer in
the last century than in the present. It was cold
enough in all conscience; and as Jonas Nettlebed
brought his snub nose into somewhat too close contact
with a frozen pane, he seemed to have scorched it.
He was employed at the time, together with Dolly, the
fat cook, and Peggy, the pretty chambermaid, in
decorating the bay-windows with sprigs of holly and
other evergreens. At the same moment, Peggy uttered
a cry. In handling the holly rather incautiously, the
thorns had run into her fingers and made them bleed.

"Plague on't! how it pricks," she cried.

"Burns you mean, Peggy. Oddsheart! I declare I
thought half my nose had been left sticking to the
glass," Jonas said, rubbing the injured feature.

"And that would be a pity indeed, master, for you
haven't got too much to spare," Peggy replied, with
affected commiseration, but secret entertainment.

"My nose is certainly not as long as your tongue,
saucebox," he rejoined—"nor as sharp; but whatever
it may be, I don't want to lose it. A little more bay,
Peggy. Just fill up that corner with a sprig of holly,
and mind you don't prick your fingers again. Now
a bunch of laurel—now some box—now some more
holly. We shall rob the poor thrushes of all their
scarlet berries. What's that?—a branch of yew.
That's unlucky, so put it back. Why, the basket's

almost empty. Hark'ee cook, go fetch the Yule Log,
while Peggy and I finish the job."

Dolly did as she was bidden, and presently afterwards returned with a huge and knotty log of wood,
which she laid down by the fire.

" By the marry maskins ! a bouncing log !" Nettlebed cried, contemplating it with satisfaction—" and
will make a rousing Christmas fire. Oddsheart ! we'll
have a merry time, Peggy. All the old games shall be
played. We'll 'Shoe the Mare,' and 'Hunt the
Slipper.' We'll have ' High Jinks,' Peggy. And mark
me, Dolly. There shall be roast pig, and currants;
fat capon and ham ; brawn and mustard; stuffed
goose and apple sauce; mince pies and plum porridge;
plum porridge, and plenty of it, d'ye mind, Dolly?
The strong ale shall be broached, and the black jack go
round. There shall be hot elder wine with toast and
sugar and nutmeg—and stewed cheese to relish it—d'ye
mind, Dolly ? Nor shall the lemons and 'rack be forgotten, nor the big punch-bowl. By the marry
maskins ! it shall be filled to the brim, and every Jack
and Jill shall have a glass."

"Oh ! cook, won't that be nice ?" Peggy cried.

"I wish Christmas cum'd twice a year instead of
onst," Dolly rejoined.

"Then you'd get twice as fat as you are now, cook,
and that would never do," Nettlebed remarked. " But
we've finished decorating the windows, and very well
they look, I'm sure. There's only one thing wanting."

"Lawk a daisy ! what can that be ?" Peggy inquired
with affected simplicity, though she knew well enoug
what was meant.

" Can't you guess, hussy ?" Jonas said, with a sly
look at her. " I warrant me, you can. There's not
a maid, above sixteen, in Dunmow but knows the use

of the Mistletoe Bough. That's what's wanting. Go
see whether Carroty Dick the ostler has gathered one
as I bade him."

Carroty Dick saved her the trouble. At that moment he emerged from the back part of the premises
bearing a large branch of the beautiful epidendron in
question, covered with silver berries.

"Here it be, mester," he cried. "I climbed t' owd
oak to get it, and drove a' the hungry ousels away. I
well-nigh broke my neck i' getting down. Ben't it
pratty, Peggy?"

Jonas took the branch from him, and it was speedily
suspended from a hook, to which a lamp had been once
attached, at the top of the deep recess of the window.

Somehow or other Peggy found herself beneath it.
The temptation to the amorous Jonas was irresistible.
The girl was too pretty—the situation too provocative.
A smacking sound was heard.

Yes, it was heard! and very distinctly, too.

"Good gracious! there's missis!" Peggy cried.
"Here'll be a pretty to do! How could you?—for
shame, sir."

"Hold your tongue, Peggy. I dare say she didn't
see us," Jonas said, internally blaming himself for his
rashness, as he reflected upon the Flitch, fearing he had
endangered his chance of obtaining it.

"What are you doing there, Mr. Nettlebed? And
what noise was that I heard?" Mrs. Nettlebed inquired
rather sharply.

"I've just been decorating the windows, my dear,"
Jonas replied, coming out of the recess, and putting on
a demure look—"but I do not remember hearing any
noise."

"It sounded like a kiss," Nelly rejoined. "Like a
very loud kiss!"

" Did it, indeed, my dear! Perhaps, it was Carroty
Dick trying the effect of the Mistletoe Bough with the
cook. We've just put it up. I declare the rascal's at
it again—and with Peggy this time," Nettlebed cried,
pointing to the recess, where the red-polled ostler was
detaining both the women under the bough. "Go
about your business, sirrah."

"Axe your pardon, sir," red-poll said, "but I was
only follering——"

"About your business, I say, directly," Nettlebed
interrupted.

And Dick and the others disappeared, leaving the
landlord alone with his wife.

" Charmin' effect, haven't they, my dear?" Jonas said,
pointing to the evergreen in the windows. " Quite an
arbourified look."

" Charming, indeed," she replied. " But don't think
to deceive me, sir. I saw you."

Perceiving further evasion would be useless, Nettlebed stammered out—" Well, my love, I'm sure I meant
no harm. All's fair under the mistletoe."

"You think so. Then you wouldn't object to anybody taking the same freedom with me—eh?"

"Certainly not, my dear, certainly not. But perhaps you had better not permit it—merely for appearance sake. As we mean to claim the Flitch, one can't
be too particular—before people. Not that I should be
in the least degree uneasy—but—you understand me,
my angel."

" Yes, I perfectly understand you, Mr. Nettlebed.
So if Frank Woodbine *should* come in, and I *should*
chance to be near the mistletoe—and he *should*—eh, my
dear—what would you say then?"

" Say!—Zounds and the devil!" the landlord ejacu-
ated.

"Oh fie! an oath, Mr. Nettlebed—a shocking oath. I declare you look quite in a passion."

"Nothing of the kind, my love. Never calmer in my life."

"You look very red in the face, for a calm person. Do keep your legs still. One would think you were jealous of Frank Woodbine."

"Jealous!—impossible! I know what a treasure I possess. And though Frank is accounted the best-looking young man in the neighbourhood, I know my darling has eyes only for me."

"There you are right, duck. And you are safe on Frank's side as well. For is not he married? And can he have eyes for any one except his lawful spouse?"

"One would think not. Few women can compare with Rose Woodbine in point of beauty."

"Indeed, sir. You always thought her prettier than me."

"I never said so, my dear, whatever I may have thought. But you know she was called the Rose of Dunmow before her marriage."

"Yes, I know that. And I know likewise, that you popped the question to her, before you popped to me. And she refused you."

"Fortunately she did, my dear."

"Fiddlestick's end! I dare say you preferred her. I wish Frank Woodbine had popped to me."

"Don't wish that, my love, or we shall never win the Flitch. It was a hasty expression on your part, and I forget it. In fact, I've never heard it. I know your real sentiments too well."

"You do, indeed, ducky. No one could seriously suppose that I should prefer a young gamekeeper, however good-looking he may be—with nothing but his gun for his maintenance and a cottage for his home—

to you, a comfortable well-to-do, nice little man—with plenty of money in your pockets, and a house like this above your head. Yet they do say Frank and his wife are very happy, quite a model pair; and that they might claim the Flitch, if they liked."

" Oh ! they say that, do they ? I know a way to stop Master Frank's mouth, if ever he attempts to pronounce the Oath."

" A secret about him. Oh do tell it me, ducky. I should like so much to hear it."

" Excuse me just now, my dear."

" Has it anything to do with the letter which was left here for him, by the mail post, this morning ?"

" I'm sure I can't say."

" Let me look at it. Perhaps I can give a guess."

" Well, there it is, my dear," Jonas replied, giving her a letter.

" The direction is plain enough," she rejoined, reading it—"'FOR FRANCIS WOODBINE, GAMEKEEPER TO THE LORD MAYNARD. TO BE LEFT WITH JONAS NET- TLEBED, AT THE SIGN OF THE FLITCH OF BACON, IN DUNMOW, ESSEX.' Odd, a letter should be addressed here and not to his own house ! That looks suspicious. Yet I don't think it's a female hand. I wonder what's inside it," she added, trying to peep under the folds. " How provoking ! I can't make out a word. Yes, I can. There's a capital J. Oh ! I see—it's only from a John. I don't care about it. You may take it back."

" Very well, my dear," Jonas replied, putting it into the table-drawer, and locking it up. " There it rests till Frank comes for it."

" And you won't tell me the secret ?"

" Don't press me, I beg. I know what I know. And that's enough to settle Frank, if he makes any pre- tension to the Flitch. That dainty dish is reserved for us, Nelly. By the marry maskins! we won't allow any interlopers. Oddslife! how I wish the eventful day were come, on which we could claim it. What a grand sight it will be! What crowds will throng to Dunmow from all parts of Essex—for I've already given notice of my intention to Mr. Roper, the steward, and he will cause it to be proclaimed at the Court Baron, so that all the world will know it, and all the world will of course come to see us—for it is a sight not to be witnessed elsewhere. Squire Monkbury, and Mr. Roper, and the officers with their white wands, and Doctor Sidebottom, the Vicar of Dunmow, in his cassock and bands; and Parson Bush, the squire's chaplain, and Roger Bowes, the clerk, and Timothy Tipcat, the beadle, with his staff, and the drummers and the fifers, will all be ready to receive us at the door of the old Priory. And there will be the Jury of Bachelors and Maidens, six of each to decide upon the justice of our claim. And there will be the Flitch of Bacon itself ready to be delivered. The church bells will ring joyfully and the musicians play lively tunes to welcome our arrival. Then we shall march up to the Priory, dressed in our best, and passing through the crowd, which will draw aside respectfully, to allow us passage, we shall enter the porch, and kneel down upon the stones. Uncommonly sharp stones they are, Nelly, for I've tried them, and therefore, my dear, we'll take the precaution of having our knees well padded. Mr. Roper will then, with all due solemnity, pronounce the Oath as follows——"

"Don't trouble yourself to repeat it, dearest, I know it perfectly."

"Suppose it uttered, then. Profound silence will of course prevail during this part of the ceremony. But as we arise to receive our prize, the music will strike up again, the bells ring forth their loudest peals, and shouts from the assembled crowd will rend the air. The ancient arm-chair will then be brought forth. We shall enter it. I sitting on the right, and you on the left."

" Exactly the reverse, ducky—you on the left, and I on the right."

"No such thing I tell you, Mrs. Nettlebed. I've inquired the particulars and ought to know."

"You may know what you please, Mr. Nettlebed. But I sit on the right if I sit there at all."

"Well, well—my dear, that's not material. I dare say it can be managed. We are seated together somehow; and the procession sets forth, headed by Will Crane, the chief huntsman, carrying the Flitch. Will bears it aloft on a tall pole that all may see it. Then follow the musicians strumming away; then Squire Monkbury, Parson Bush, and Doctor Sidebottom."

"Lord bless us! I fancy I see the doctor! How his fat reverence will waddle along, and mop his round face, if it happens to be a hot day! And how he will stare at me to be sure."

" Everybody will stare at you, Nelly. You'll be 'the observed of all observers,' as the poet says. But to go on. Close behind Doctor Sidebottom we shall come ; borne on the shoulders of six able-bodied men, and seated together as I have described."

"But you haven't settled how we are to sit?"

"Oh, yes, I have. How elated we shall feel as we look around, and gaze on the shouting crowds, the little boys in the trees, and on the gates, and the country folk in the waggons and carts."

"I shall be thinking of the fine company in the coaches. I don't care about trumpery in carts, and little boys on hedges and gates. I dare say it will be a pretty sight—especially if Sir John Grubham, or Sir Gilbert de Montfichet, or some of the other handsome young squires should happen to be there."

"Hang the handsome young squires! Let me proceed. In our rear will come the Jury. The six maidens on my side, and the bachelors on yours."

"That won't do at all. If the bachelors come behind me, I sha'n't see them."

"And what matters it if you don't?"

"A great deal. It must be as I wish, or I take no part in it; that's certain."

"Well, I don't mind giving up any little point if that my principal aim be attained. So the bachelors shall follow as you desire. In this way we shall be taken round the boundaries of the old Priory, and to the Priory Church, amid increasing crowds, and continued shouting, and so home—where we shall end the day in feasting and revelry. By the marry maskins! it will be a grand day! I'm sure you'll do your best to bring it about. We must both be very cautious, and never give each other a cross look, or utter a cross word—before people. Ah! here's the Saffron Walden and Chelmsford waggon. I hear the jingling of the bells. I must go and see if any one alights from it. Recollect, my dear. Always keep watch upon yourself before people."

III.

OF THE STRANGE GUEST WHO ARRIVED AT THE FLITCH.

Jingle! jingle! jingle.

Blithe music make those tiny bells. No sound so pleasant. It awakens all Dunmow, and the gossips of the place issue forth to gaze at the huge lumbering waggon, as it moves slowly along, grinding the ice and frozen mud to powder. The powerful team that draw it are well shod, and keep their feet stoutly upon the slippery road. Six strong black horses ; the leaders with bells on their collars, jingling merrily and tunefully. Children shout ; dogs bark, and Ben the waggoner cracks his long whip.

At length, the mighty vehicle stops at the Old Inn. The little bells are mute, unless one of the leaders of the team chances to snort and shake his mighty neck. Simultaneously with the stoppage Jonas Nettlebed and Tom Tapster issue from the porch. Carroty Dick is already there, attending to the horses, while Ben the waggoner informs the landlord, that he has got a customer for him : an old gentleman named Plot, whom he took up at Saffron Walden. "That's the name on his portmantle anyhow, so I s'pose it be his'n," Ben said—"he's a cur'ousish sort of chap, he is. There that be he a-callin' out."

"Here Dick—here Tom—go fetch the steps—and help the gentleman out," Jonas cried, as an elderly personage, wrapped in a large blue roquelaure, with his hands stuffed into a muff, a comforter round his throat, and an extra pair of woollen stockings drawn above his knees, got out of the waggon. And not without some difficulty, for his numerous wraps rather impeded his movements. However, he and his portmanteau were safely landed at last.

It then appeared that the old gentleman was lame —very lame. Perhaps he had a club foot, for his right leg appeared shorter than the left. He had a keen grey eye, and so far as could be seen of it, an irritable looking countenance, and when he pulled down his comforter to speak to the landlord, there was a nervous ιwitchıng about the mouth, that confirmed the general expression of his face. His manner was testy, and his mode of speech interjectional and impatient. His first order was that some refreshments should be given to a soldier's wife and her children, inside the waggon, with whom he had travelled ; and he would not enter the house till he had seen the injunction obeyed.

While Tom Tapster went for the ale and cold viands commanded, a young man crossed the road and walked briskly up to the landlord. He had a fowling-piece over his shoulder, and carried a pouch apparently well filled with game at his side. He was dressed in a green velveteen shooting-coat, and wore stout laced-boots, and buff leathern gaiters mounting above the knee. A broad-leaved hat covered his luxuriant brown locks. Above the middle height, remarkably well-formed, with a light but athletic frame, he looked the very model of a gamekeeper. His countenance was frank and open, and manly in expression, as was his bearing altogether. At his heels followed a noble retriever.

"A Merry Christmas to you, landlord," he said, "and a Happy New Year when it comes. This being the season for presents, I've ventured to bring you a couple of wild ducks for your own eating, and a wood-cock for your dame," he added, taking the birds from his pouch, and offering them to Jonas.

"The Compliments of the Season to you, Master Woodbine," the host replied; "and many thanks for the birds, on my wife's part, as well as on my own. But oddslife! I've got a letter for you. Where is it ? Oh, let me see—I locked it up in the table-drawer for safety. Ah! you're a sly rogue, Master Woodbine—a sly rogue—to have your letters addressed to me. I'll bring it to you instantly."

"Don't give yourself the trouble, my good host,"

Frank Woodbine rejoined—" I only wished to ascertain that the letter had arrived, for it is of importance, though not in the way you hint. I'll just step home and get rid of my dog and my gun, and then return for it. I've promised to meet Mr. Roper, the steward, at your house, on a matter of business this evening; and if he should arrive before me, beg him to await my coming."

The young gamekeeeper then shouldered his gun, and whistling to his dog was soon out of sight.

By this time, the hungry family inside the waggon had disposed of their viands; the old gentleman had slipped a guinea into the poor woman's hands and received her heartfelt blessings in return; Ben the waggoner had drained his pot of ale, and promised to buy some ribands in Chelmsford for pretty Peggy, the chambermaid, who came out to flirt with him; the long whip was cracked; the strong horses gave a vigorous pull; the huge vehicle was again in motion; and the little bells once more jingled tunefully and merrily, till the pleasant sound was lost in the distance.

Meanwhile, the host ushered the old gentleman into the house, and proceeded to relieve him of his roque-laure and some of his wraps. At the same time, Carroty Dick brought in the portmanteau, and laid it down near the table.

Sure enough, there was the name, marked upon it in large characters—DOCTOR PLOT.

" Welcome, sir, welcome to the Dunmow Flitch," quoth Jonas, as he busied himself about the old gentleman—" welcome to the best inn in Essex; ay, though you pit against it the Cock and Pie at Colchester, the Razor and Hen at Harwich, or the Axe and Bottle at Braintree By the marry maskins! none can compare with it.

Without fear I assert it, and make it my boast,
That no one can meet with a civiller host,
Nor a hostess more buxom his sight to bewitch,
Than he'll find, if he halts at the sign of the FLITCH.
Derry down.

Foi I'm proud of my kitchen, I'm proud of my cellar,
I'm proud of my wife, as I frequently tell her;
And there is not in Essex a hostel more rich
In comfort than that which is known as the FLITCH.
Derry down."

While Jonas was singing, the old gentleman manifested great impatience, and at last he burst forth:

"Don't split my ears with your screeching, landlord. Fancy yourself a nightingale, I dare say; but you've more of the raven or the goose about you. Fetch me a glass of brandy—the oldest and best you have."

Quite taken aback at the unexpected rebuff, Jonas proceeded to obey the order, while Doctor Plot limped towards the fire, and stood warming himself before it, till the brandy was brought him. The liquor seemed to please him, for he grunted forth something like an expression of satisfaction.

"That'll do, sir, eh?" Jonas said. "Soft as silk and mild as milk: fifty year old, if it's a day. Why, sir, that brandy's part of the old stock. It came out of Sir Walter Fitzwalter's own cellar, and it must have been his father's, for the baronet was too stingy to buy a bottle."

"Humph!—give me another glass. Think I recollect the flavour."

"Indeed, sir—then mayhap you were a friend of the family?"

"What's that to you, sir?" the old gentleman exclaimed, rather fiercely. "How dare you put questions to me? But since you must know, you inquisitive fellow, I *was* a friend of the family—the family physician—Doctor Plot. Did you ever hear of me?—eh!"

"Can't say I have sir,—but I'm proud to make your acquaintance, doctor—extremely proud."

"Fudge! Nobody need be proud of knowing me Hate flattery, even from an innkeeper. Despise it, sir. Won't have it. Folks call me an eccentric man. Dare say I am. Consult my own convenience and tastes; not theirs. Came here in the waggon because I prefer it to a chaise, the stage-coach, or the post-horse. Better company, and cheaper. Shouldn't have met that soldier's wife and her brats in the coach. Cost me more, though, in the end—now I think of it."

"A strange old gentleman, indeed!" Jonas muttered "What can I do to please you, sir?"

"Please me—nothing. Yes, you can. You're married, you say?"

"Married, sir—yes, sir," Jonas replied, wondering what was coming next.

"Send your wife to me, then. More sense than you have, I'll be sworn."

"Mrs. Nettlebed—Nelly, my dear, you're wanted," the host shouted.

"Coming, my dear," Mrs. Nettlebed rejoined, as she issued from an inner chamber. "What's your pleasure, sir?" she added, dropping a curtsey to the old gentleman.

"My pleasure, madam—I have none," Plot replied crustily.

"Your will, then, sir?" Nelly rejoined.

"I've neither will nor pleasure. Mean to stay here for a few days. That is, if you give me a good bedroom and clean sheets, and make me comfortable."

"We've only one room disengaged, sir," Nelly replied, not much liking her customer—"and that's haanted."

"Haanted!" he rejoined, mimicking her—"so much

the better. I like a haunted room. Never saw a ghost
in my life. Want to see one."

"Perhaps you may be gratified, sir," Nelly replied.
"And since you have no objections on that score, we
may manage to accommodate you."

"It's the largest chamber in the house, sir, and has
the best bed in it," Jonas interposed—"such an ancient
piece of furniture; such a high tester; and such stiff
old hangings. You'll fancy yourself in a hearse. I've
heard say it was Sir Walter's own bed; and his great-
grandfather, Sir Alured, may have slept in it for aught
I know. It's more than we could, though—eh, Nelly?
We thought we saw a female figure come out of one of
the closets, and glare at us."

"I'm sure I saw it," Mrs. Nettlebed rejoined. "It
was bright moonlight, and the figure was as pale as any
shroud. Jonas can't speak so positively, because he hid
himself under the bed-clothes."

"Mere delusion—trick of fancy," Plot cried. "White
figure—fudge! reflection of yourself in a glass—nothing
more. Hobgoblin stories frighten children and women.
Men laugh at them. Get ready the haunted room
for me, ma'am. Make a good fire. Air the bed well,
and I warrant me, I shall sleep soundly enough within
it, in spite of ghost or ghostess—ha! ha!"

"I hope you may laugh in the same way to-morrow
morning, sir," Nelly said, looking as if she expected
otherwise.

"Never fear, ma'am—never fear. Harkye, landlord,
who was the young fellow who gave you a woodcock for
your wife?"

"A woodcock for me, Jonas? You never told me
about it."

"Doctor Plot's arrival put it out of my head, my
dear. Frank Woodbine is the young man's name, sir.

He brought me a couple of wild ducks, and you a wood-cock, my dear.''

" I thought it must be a present from Frank," Nelly cried.   " A nice, dear fellow !"

" Don't praise him too much, my dear, — before people," Jonas whispered.

" And who may Frank Woodbine be ?" Plot inquired.

" That's more than I'm able to inform you, sir," Net-tlebed replied.   " He's a stranger in these parts—that is to say, he *was* a stranger some eighteen months ago, before he came as gamekeeper to Lord Maynard."

" He deserves to be something more than a game-keeper," Nelly said.   " Anybody can see he's above his situation.   He never keeps low company like the others, and when dressed in his best, he looks just like a young squire.   Indeed, for the matter of that, there's not a young squire hereabouts to compare with him— not even Sir John Grubham, or Squire Chipchase.   He rides as well as Squire Monkbury ; shoots a great deal better than Sam Snipe, the head keeper ; and as to dancing, you should just see him foot it in the Hay, sir. Nobody like him.   You've seen him yourself, sir, and can judge of his good looks."

" Pshaw ! good looks are all a woman cares for," Plot rejoined.

" Law, sir !"   Nelly cried ; "I'm sure you can't say that of me.   I didn't choose my Jonas from outward appearances."

" Rose Woodbine's a treasure beyond all price ; that's all I know," the landlord rejoined, rather nettled.

" All women are treasures—so much beyond price, that one can't get rid of them," Plot observed, drily.

" You never beheld such a charmer, sir," Jonas pur-sued, with a side look at his wife.

" A rustic beauty — cheeks red as apples, and as

round," Plot cried. "Picture of rude health, no doubt
—fine animal—but coarse and clumsy—not at all to my
taste."

"Nor to mine," Nelly said. "You've hit her off to a
nicety, sir."

"Knew you'd think so. Women never praise each
other too much. Your husband now would contradict
all I've asserted—all you've confirmed."

"Tastes differ, sir, and opinions are free," the landlord replied. "According to mine, there's not a lovelier
creature in the land than Rose Woodbine. As to manners, there's nothing low-bred about her, if I may be
allowed to judge. Many a fine lady might take a lesson
from Rose."

"Bless us! you're very warm in your praises of her,
Mr. Nettlebed," Nelly observed.

"Not half so warm as you were in praise of Frank,
my dear," he replied.

"And this paragon of perfection, who would put all
our ladies of quality to shame, is some farmer's daughter,
I suppose," the old gentleman remarked.

"An orphan maiden, brought up by Mr. Leslie, the
old curate," Jonas answered—"a niece of his wife's I
fancy she may be, sir—but I know nothing for certain.
Rose Mildmay, for such was her maiden name, was well
brought up. Good old Mr. Leslie, though poor as a
rat, did his best for her, and instructed her himself;
but after his death it was as much as the poor widow
could do to keep things together, and support herself.
So Rose married."

"How came she to throw herself away on this young
man? Had she no other offer?"

"Many a one. Some that most women circumstanced
as she was,—ahem!" with a look at his wife, "would
have jumped at. One that would have raised her to a

rank as high as that of any lady in the county. Young
Sir Gilbert de Montfichet, of Stansted House, one of
the finest places in the neighbourhood, offered her his
hand. But she preferred the humble gamekeeper, to
whom she had plighted her troth."

A shade of emotion flitted over the old gentleman's
sardonic countenance; and the nervous twitching about
his mouth became sharper than usual. But he soon
repressed it.

"More fool she!" he cried. "She'll repent having
thrown away the chance."

"I don't think she will," Nelly said. "She's not
like any other woman. She seems quite blind to her
own interests; and as to proper pride or spirit she
hasn't a jot of it. She's so wrapped up in her husband
that she can think of nothing else."

"And he pretends to be just as fond of her," Jonas
added.

"Pretends! why, isn't he?" Plot demanded.

'I'm sure I can't say," the landlord replied, evasively.
"It's no business of mine."

"Neither is it your business to make insinuations
without warrant," Plot rejoined. "I should like to see
this fond couple's love put to the test. It's easy to
make professions—not so easy to act up to them. I'm
no believer in such rare conjugal attachment. I've
seen too much of the world. All outside show—mere
make-believe. Men neglect their wives—after a time,
at least; and women console themselves as they best
can: some in one way, some in another. All women
try to govern their husbands, and most succeed in the
attempt."

"You've but a poor opinion of our sex, sir," Nelly
said.

"A very poor opinion indeed, ma'am. My own

experience has unfortunately brought me to that conclusion."

"Sorry to hear it, sir," Nettlebed said—"but you
mustn't judge all the world by yourself. For example,
I am an instance to the contrary. My slightest wish is
law to Mrs. Nettlebed. She would never dream of
governing me. Would you, my angel?"

"Oh no, ducky, I know my duty better."

"There, sir, I hope you're convinced. At last, you've
met with a fond husband and an obedient wife:—
a couple so perfectly happy and united, sir, that they
conceive themselves qualified to claim the Flitch. But
here comes Mr. Abel Roper, Steward of the Manor of
Little Dunmow. Give you good e'en, Mr. Roper. A
merry Christmas to you, sir."

As the host advanced to welcome the new comer,
Nelly withdrew to get Doctor Plot's room ready for him,
and great was Peggy the chambermaid's astonishment,
when she heard her mistress say that the old gentleman
had taken the Haunted Room.

"I wouldn't sleep there alone for all the world," she
observed to Carroty Dick, as they followed Mrs. Nettlebed up the great staircase; she with a candle, and he
carrying the stranger's portmanteau.

"Don't trouble yourself, Peggy," Dick said. "The
ghost won't meddle with him. He's too owd an' ugly."

And all three disappeared down the dark corridor.

IV.

HOW ABEL ROPER OBTAINED AN INSIGHT INTO THE OLD GENTLEMAN'S BREAST.

DOCTOR PLOT sat down by the fire.

As the steward entered, he glanced at the old gentleman, and the old gentleman glanced at him, but they took no further notice of each other.

Mr. Roper then took off his great-coat and gloves, and deposited them with his three-cornered hat on a chair. He was a respectable-looking middle-aged man, in an iron-grey wig, snuff coloured coat and waist-coat, striped worsted stockings, square-toed shoes and buckles.

"Has Frank Woodbine been here?" he inquired of the landlord.

"Yes, sir, he has; about half an hour ago, and he bade me say, if you chanced to arrive before his return, he would not keep you long waiting."

"That's well," Mr. Roper cried. "Just take out a pot of ale to my two friends outside."

"Won't they step in?" the landlord said. But receiving a reply in the negative, he delegated the commission to Tom Tapster, by whom it was executed, while Mr. Roper proceeded:

"And now, Mr. Nettlebed, I make no doubt you are all anxiety to know whether I have given notice of your intention to claim the flitch. I have. It is registered. But I have done still more. I have selected the Jury; six of the best looking young bachelors of the village, and six of the prettiest maidens; and I have told them to pay you their first visit of inquiry this evening."

"By the marry maskins! this is news," Nettlebed exclaimed, joyfully. "Here, Tom Tapster. Go and brew a strong bowl of punch, and bid the cook cut the plum-cake, and get the minced pies hot. I must give them fitting welcome. What a pity it is we've no music, or we might have a dance."

"I've taken care of that," Roper replied; "I told Simon Appleyard to bring the fiddles with him. I don't want to damp your satisfaction, Mr. Nettlebed, but I am bound to tell you there is another claimant, whose chances appear quite equal, some think superior to your own."

The landlord looked quite chapfallen.

"Oddsbodikins! who is it?" he asked.

"No other than the young man who is to meet me here."

"Frank Woodbine! I thought so. I protest against his claim. He can't take the oath."

"Why not? He bears an excellent character, and is supposed to be fondly attached to his wife; and she to him."

"He doesn't deserve her love—a rake, a libertine, a deceiver."

"Poh—poh: my good friend, you are wholly mis-informed."

"I can't be misinformed. I've seen it with my own eyes."

"Seen what?"

"Seen him make love to another woman."

"To Mrs. Nettlebed?"

"Zookers! no; not to her; I should like to see him do that; but to one who gave him a very different reception from what he'd meet with from my Nelly—one who kissed him and squeezed him."

"Pshaw! your eyes must have deceived you."

"No, they didn't. I can see plain enough when I desire it. I'll prove what I say, at the right time."

"But you must bring forward other evidence than your own. You will be supposed to be an interested witness—and will on that account be discredited."

"I'll bring 'damning proofs,' as the play-actors say," Jonas cried.

"What's that you say about 'damning proofs,' land-lord?" Plot said, getting up, and limping towards them. "So you have found the young man out, eh? Didn't I tell you man's constancy was all gammon? Take care he don't retaliate, and find *you* out."

"I defy him," the landlord replied.

"Humph!" Plot muttered. "Your servant, sir," he added, bowing to the steward. "Don't recollect me, I perceive? Physician to the unfortunate family who once resided here—Doctor Plot."

"The name is familiar to me, sir," the steward said, returning the salutation; but I confess I do not re-collect your features, though I must have seen you."

"Dare say not. Most people think me changed—sadly changed—broken down, in fact. I'm come here to spend a few days, and moralise upon the vanities of the world. Plenty of food for it here, sir. An old house gone to ruin: an old family gone to the dogs. And why? All the fault of a woman. And yet this credulous fool—this easy dupe, would try and persuade us that a miracle has been wrought in his behalf."

"I am neither a fool, nor a dupe, sir," Jonas re-joined. "And I'd have you to know that Mrs. Nettle-bed is not an ordinary woman. I don't wonder you have not met with such a one. Squire Monkbury, of Monkbury Place, says she hasn't her equal, and that he loves her like a daughter. And Doctor Sidebottom, the Vicar, calls her a *rara avis*. Perhaps, you know what that means, sir?"

"Pshaw!" cried the old gentleman.

"I hope we shall give you, before you leave, a better opinion of the sex, and of human nature in general, than you appear to entertain, sir," the steward said. "I know the sad circumstances of the case to which you allude, and greatly regret them. But I cannot think the unfortunate lady so much to blame as is supposed."

"Sir, you know nothing about it," Plot rejoined, sharply. "*I* know that Lady Juga was guilty. But no more of this. Let the dead rest in their graves."

"I wish they did—Lady Juga especially," the landlord groaned, aside.

"I would not disturb them; nor would I rake up any memories that may be painful to you, sir, as a friend of Sir Walter, for such I am aware you were. But I cannot but think the Lady Juga wrongfully judged; and at more fitting time and season I will endeavour to prove the truth of what I assert."

"If you can do so, you will remove a barbed arrow that has rankled in my breast for years, and soured all the sweetness of my nature, if it ever had any sweetness, which I doubt. And I care not if you kill me in the doing of it; since it was from my representations, and by my advice, that Sir Walter left his wife."

"Then I had better not disclose what I have to tell, sir."

"Yes, speak out, and spare not. Cut as deep as you will; or pluck out the shaft forcibly. I am too good a physician not to know that you must probe the wound, if you would cure it. But mine never can be healed," he added, in a tone of deep pathos.

"I hope otherwise, sir. I will find a convenient time to lay my relation before you. I have business just now with Frank Woodbine, and expect him here anon. Ah! sir; if you could but see his wife, she would change the ill opinion you entertain of women. An angel, sir."

"I have heard much of her, and should like to see her. Perhaps you can contrive it?"

"Easily," the steward replied. "Her husband will make you heartily welcome to his cottage."

"I would rather see her without him."

"Well, sir, perhaps it may be managed. I'll see."

"Here comes Frank Woodbine," Nettlebed cried, as the door opened to admit the young man.

At the same moment, Nelly came quickly down stairs.

V.

SHOWING THAT FRANK WOODBINE SHOULD HAVE LOOKED BEFORE HE LEAPED.

FRANK WOODBINE was a very handsome young fellow, certainly. No mistake about it.

He looked much better now than when the old gentleman saw him first, having doffed his shooting clothes, and put on others, which though plain enough, and perfectly suitable to his station, fitted him well, and set off his light, agile limbs to advantage.

Mrs. Nettlebed smiled upon him very graciously as they met; thanked him for his polite attention in bringing her the woodcock; inquired after his wife; and chattered so fast that she quite forgot where she was going until she found herself near one of the bay-windows. Frank Woodbine thought the evergreens very nicely arranged and told her so.

"It's my husband's taste," she replied, entering the recess—"but they are very pretty, I must say. Do come and look at them. My goodness gracious!—if I am not under the Mistletoe Bough."

Frank must have been a stupid fellow after all. It never occurred to him to take advantage of the situation. He looked up quite innocently at the branch, and then marched out of the recess. Nelly bit her ruddy lips with vexation.

"That doesn't look like the conduct of a rake,

Mr. Nettlebed," Roper observed, nudging the land-lord.

"He's on his guard now," Jonas replied; "he's cautious enough before people. D'ye think he'd have acted so, if we hadn't been by?"

"I hope he would. But you don't suppose your wife would allow him to salute her?"

"I'd ha' boxed his ears soundly if he'd attempted any such thing," Nelly said, overhearing the remark.

"And now, Master Woodbine," the steward said, "we've a little business to settle together."

"We have, sir," the young man replied. "I'm quite prepared for you."

"Glad to hear it. Suppose we begin with a glass of ale. It will help us through our work. Landlord, a jug of your old October."

"With all my heart, sir," Frank replied, taking a chair at the table with the steward.

The ale was speedily brought, and quite sustained Jonas's well-earned reputation as a brewer.

"And now oblige me with pen and ink," the steward said—"and a candle, too, if you please, Mrs. Nettlebed—for its getting dark, and we might make mistakes, and they don't do in money matters."

"Money matters! Oh! it's about money they've met—is it? I wonder whose going to receive, and who to pay?" Nelly muttered, as she placed the inkstand on the table and lighted the candle.

Meanwhile, Mr. Roper took a memorandum-book out of his pocket, referred to it, and laid it down. He next brought out a parchment, and laying that down too, looked at Frank.

"You have a letter for me, landlord?" the young man said.

"Beg pardon, Master Woodbine," Jonas cried. "It

quite slipped my memory. It's quite safe. Here it is, sir," he added, unlocking the drawer and producing the letter.

While this was going on, the old gentleman had resumed his seat at the fire, but he watched the proceedings of the party at the table with much curiosity.

"Two hundred pounds, Master Woodbine—that's the amount," the steward said. "I'll write out a receipt for you in behalf of Squire Monkbury, and deliver up the bond on payment of the money."

"Two hundred pounds!" Jonas muttered to himself —"I didn't think he could be worth half as much."

"Two hundred pounds!" Nelly thought. "Why, he must be as well off as Jonas himself."

"You shall have it in a moment, Mr. Roper," Frank said. And he tore open the letter.

"How's this?" he cried, with a sudden change of countenance, and springing to his feet. "No inclosure. It must have been abstracted from the letter."

"Abstracted!" Jonas exclaimed. "I'll answer for it nothing has been abstracted in this house."

"No—no—I was wrong," Frank cried, running his eye distractedly over the missive—"the money has not been sent."

"Am I to understand then that you cannot pay me, young man?" the steward said, in a severe tone.

"You see I am disappointed in my expectations, sir. The money ought to have been sent, but it has been refused;—I know not why. Grant me a week's delay, and I will engage to pay it you in full."

"I cannot consent to be thus trifled with, Frank Woodbine," the steward rejoined; "and though I am sorry to deal harshly with you, I must exact the full penalties of this bond."

"I need not remind you that the money was not

advanced to myself, Mr. Roper," Frank urged; "that I am only surety for another."

"But the principal being utterly unable to pay the debt, I must come upon you. It was on this understanding alone that I accepted your security."

"I can pay the debt, sir, if I have a little time."

"Time cannot be granted. I regret to be driven to these extremities, but as I am acting for Squire Monkbury, and not for myself, I have only one course to pursue, however repugnant it may be to my feelings. Unless you can find the money, I shall be compelled to place you under arrest."

"Arrest me!" Frank exclaimed.

"Ay, and send you to Chelmsford Jail."

"Mr. Roper, you are not a hard man. I know you are not, sir. You cannot mean this."

The steward shook his head.

"And you can have the heart to imprison me because I rescued a poor widow from impending ruin?"

"Do not put a false gloss on your conduct, young man," the steward rejoined; "you meant to do well, no doubt; but you have merely performed a good action at another's expense. If you signed this bond, without the certainty of fulfilling its conditions, you were highly to blame; and you will now experience the result of your incaution. But the squire must not be allowed to suffer from your folly; and since you are not prepared to meet your engagements, the law must take its course."

"My wife!—my poor wife!" Frank exclaimed, clasping his hands to his brow.

"You should have thought of this before," the steward said. "You will be imprisoned; will lose your situation; and bring your wife to beggary, it may be. from your want of prudence."

As the steward spoke, Frank's whole demeanour changed, and he looked as if he would make some fierce reply; but he checked himself, and said, with forced calmness:

"You are not the man I took you for, Mr. Roper. You speak with unnecessary harshness. I have shown no wish to break my engagements. I *can* perform them and I *will*. All I require is a little time."

"Young man, I have more than once told you, that I am merely Squire Monkbury's agent, and have therefore no option in the matter. But if you prefer it, I can select Mrs. Leslie instead of you."

"Arrest the poor old lady! Carry her off to prison —to die there of distress and shame. No, sir, that shall never be while I can prevent it."

"Then it was poor Mrs. Leslie for whom he was bound," sobbed Nelly to her husband. "My heart quite bleeds for him. Do pay the money. Do, Jonas. There's a duck."

"Pay two hundred pounds, my dear! Quite out of the question. A pretty fool folks would think me."

"Never mind them. Pay it, Jonas,—do."

"Mr. Nettlebed," said the steward, "have the goodness to tell those two persons outside to step in."

"You shan't go, Jonas—it's to do something horrid —I know it is," Nelly screamed.

"Don't alarm yourself, ma'am," the steward said, tapping against the window.

At the signal, two stout, ill-favoured men, with staves in their hands, rushed into the room, and on a gesture from the steward laid hands upon Frank Woodbine.

"Bumbailiffs!" Nelly exclaimed. "Catch me, Jonas —I shall faint—I'm sure I shall."

"'Udsdeath! I wish he hadn't arrested him here,"

the landlord said. "It 'll bring discredit on the house."

"Pay the money directly," Nelly cried, "or I shall go into hysterics—oh!"

"My life!—my angel!" the landlord exclaimed, endeavouring to pacify her.

"Take charge of your prisoner, gentlemen," the steward said to the bailiffs, "and convey him as speedily as you can to Chelmsford, and there lodge him in the jail. You understand, Isaacson."

"Ay, ay," the bailiff replied.

"Will you not allow me to take leave of my wife, Mr. Roper?"

"Better not," the steward rejoined.

"Much better not, young man," Isaacson added.

"Oh dear!—oh dear! It would melt a heart of stone," Nelly sobbed.

At this moment, Doctor Plot beckoned to the steward. Hitherto, the old gentleman had taken no part in the scene, except that of a deeply interested spectator.

On this, Mr. Roper motioned the bailiffs to stop. They did so, but still kept fast hold of the prisoner.

"I am interested about this young man," Plot said. "Feel half inclined to assist him."

"Very glad to hear it, sir. I assure you it gives me much concern to resort to extreme measures with him. But I am merely an instrument in the hands of another."

"I know that," Plot rejoined, impatiently. "But I want to know if Mrs. Leslie, for whom the young man became security, is a deserving person?"

"None more so, sir. The widow of a poor curate. You must recollect Mr. Leslie, sir. Pastor of Little Dunmow Church for fifty years and better. till at last they laid him in its churchyard. A sad day that for

us all, sir.   Never more were we to see his venerable
face nor listen to his earnest exhortations again—though
I trust some of his wise precepts have abided with us.
Oftentimes," pursued the steward, with marked emphasis, "he would preach Forgiveness for wrongs done us
—real or imaginary—Charity towards our fellows. And
many a man's wrath has been turned away by his
words—many friendships restored—peace brought back
to many an unhappy family.   He showed us the Black
Spot on our own hearts, and bade us purge it out by
penitence, not add to its dye, by quarrelling with our
neighbour, our offspring, or the wife of our bosom."

A strange agitation seized the old gentleman, as
these words were addressed to him.   The twitching
movements about his mouth became almost convulsive.
His hand wandered in his breast as if he would tear it
open, and lay bare its secrets to the steward.

At last he cried, regarding Roper fiercely :

"Why all this to me ?   What do I care for Mr.
Leslie, or his discourses ?   How do they apply to me ?
What have I to forgive ?"

"We have all much to forgive; or think we have,"
Mr. Roper replied.   "Pardon me, if I have touched
any chord in your heart that vibrates too keenly.   I
meant not to offend.   My aim was to show that our
Pastor was a good man, and spoke Truth without
fear."

"So far I respect his memory," Plot replied, more
calmly.

"But though he did his duty well, he was scantily
paid; and he died poor, so that his widow had a hard
time of it, and must have starved but for assistance.
A cottage was bought her, money lent, and she is now
easy and free from want."

"And this she owes to Frank Woodbine ?"

THE BACHELORS AND MAIDENS.

P. 39.

"Entirely to him. His wife, you know, is Mrs. Leslie's niece—at least, 'tis so reported. At all events she was brought up by her. Soon after Frank's marriage, the widow's main difficulties began, for Rose had been her chief support; the poor old body had been sorely put to it before—but now absolute want stared her in the face. Frank came forward. He consulted me. The widow wanted two hundred pounds to make all comfortable for her for life.; I got her the money from Squire Monkbury. I took Frank's bond for the sum. Only one stipulation was made by the young man : that Mrs. Leslie should not know to whom she was indebted; and that the matter should not be mentioned to his wife. You will acknowledge he has acted with considerable delicacy."

"I acknowledge nothing. What reason had you for thinking he would be able to pay you? What are his resources?"

"Not much, I grant," the steward replied, with a half-smile, "but I believed his representations; and I still believe," he added, with a certain significance, "that he has been disappointed by some person from whom he expected money. I don't think you could do wrong in assisting him, sir."

"I must first see his wife," the old gentleman replied; "and Mrs. Leslie, too."

"You will find Rose Woodbine all I have described her. I will go with you to her, sir, if you please."

"Thankee. Leave the young man here. I have told you I would rather see his wife when he is not by."

"Your humour shall be indulged, as good may come of it, sir. Will you go at once?"

The old gentleman nodded, and hobbled off in search of his roquelaure and muff.

While the foregoing conversation took place, the bailiffs, thinking it a little tedious, no doubt, had seated themselves near a table at the back of the room, with the prisoner between them. Here the young man was kindly visited by Mrs. Nettlebed, who by this time had recovered from her hysterics, and brought him the bottle of the old brandy by way of consolation. But Frank declined the offer.

"We shouldn't object to a glass, ma'am," Isaacson said. " Should we, Latcham ?"

"By no manner of means, ma'am," his partner replied. " We're 'nation fond of old brandy. And we knows it's the right sort here."

"It's not the right sort for you," Nelly replied, in supreme disgust. " Don't take on so, Master Woodbine. I dare say it 'll be all right."

"I'm thinking of poor Rose," he rejoined. " I've never been absent from her during one evening since we've been married. To-night she will be alone."

"A werry hard case," the senior bailiff observed, with a sneer. " Mrs. Isaacson's often alone of an evening. And she niver complains—niver."

"Rather likes it, Isaac, I should say," Latcham rejoined.

" Unfeeling monsters !" Nelly muttered.

Just then the steward advanced towards the group, and the two minions of the law rose to their feet.

"Don't disturb yourselves, gentlemen," Roper said. "You will remain here, for an hour probably, with your prisoner. I have some business to transact with Doctor Plot, and when it is done, I will return and give you further directions."

" Werry good, sir," Isaacson replied.

"An hour would suffice for me to take leave of my wife, sir," Frank cried. " Will you grant it me—will

you, sir ?   On my word I will be back within the time.
You may trust me.   Indeed, you may."

"Your vord von't do, young man," Isaacson said.
"Verivir you goes, the bailiffs goes vith you."

"And Mrs. W. mightn't like the sight on us," Latcham added.

"Barbarians!" Nelly ejaculated.   "I'll free him
from their clutches—come what may."

"It cannot be," the steward replied, shaking off
Frank, who grasped his arm.   "Make these gentlemen
comfortable, Mrs. Nettlebed.   Give them what they
want."

With this he turned away abruptly, as if to escape
from further importunity, and hastily putting on his
great coat and hat, followed the old gentleman, who,
attended by the landlord, had already gained the
door.

Frank sank upon a chair, and hid his face in his
hands.

"You heer'd, ma'am, vot the guv'nor said," Isaacson
observed to Nelly.   "Ve're to make ourselves comfer-
able, an' call for vot ve likes.   An' that I should say
vud be pipes an' baccy, an' summut 'ot, ey, Latcham?"

"Summut 'ot, by all manner o' means," the other
worthy replied.   "That ale sits woundy cowld on my
stomach."

"Then you shall each have a glass of brandy," Nelly
replied, helping them.

The pair smacked their lips with satisfaction.

"Halloa, my dear, what are you about?"   Jonas
cried, hurrying towards her, and trying to snatch away
the bottle.   "That's the old brandy.   I don't give that
to every-day customers."

"You don't call these gentlemen 'every-day customers,' I hope, my dear."

"No, and the less we see of 'em the better," Jonas replied.

"Help yourselves, gentlemen," Nelly said, giving Isaacson the bottle; "don't spare it."

"Never fear, ma'am," he replied, winking at his partner, and receiving a significant glance in return. "Here's your werry good health, ma'am; an' yours too, Muster Nettlebed, an' a-vishin' you may vin the Flitch."

"Come, they're not so bad as I thought. The brandy's not quite thrown away upon them," Jonas muttered.

"It's but a poor compliment, though, to Mrs. Nettlebed," Isaacson pursued, endeavouring to put on a gallant air—"to offer her the Flitch—it's a throwin' svine to pearls, as you may say—ho! ho!"

"Really the man's not such a monster as I thought him," Nelly reflected, rather pleased with this clumsy attempt at wit. "Get the pipes and tobacco, Jonas. Won't you take anything?" she said to Frank; adding, in a whisper, "Do as I tell you, and I'll set you free."

The young man signified by a slight gesture that he understood her.

As Jonas brought the materials for smoking, the dulcet notes of a fiddle were heard outside.

"Here they come! here they come!" the landlord cried, clapping his hands.

"Who come?" Frank inquired, raising his head.

"The Jury of Bachelors and Maidens to decide upon our claim to the Flitch," Nettlebed replied. "Come along Nelly."

And they both flew to the door, while all the household, attracted by the music, made their appearance— some from one place, some from another, Pretty Peggy, Tom Tapster, Carroty Dick, and even the fat cook from the kitchen.

VI.

THE JURY OF BACHELORS AND MAIDENS.

Six Bachelors and Six Maidens!

Hand in hand they enter the house, and as each pair crosses the threshold they salute the host and hostess, who welcome them with extraordinary heartiness. Jonas almost overacts his part; he is so much excited. The Youths do credit to the steward's selection. All are tolerably good-looking; all dressed alike in green square cut coats, white stockings, Spanish leather shoes, and buckles. The Maidens are the flower of the village. Not a plain face; not a bad figure among them. Pretty girls all. Very prettily dressed, too. And all alike, as in the case of the Bachelors. Fly caps with pink ribands; hair in little curls round the brow, and clubbed behind; velvet bands encircling the throat; pink tucked-up gowns, open in front, so as to display through the crossed ribands the white stomachers beneath; scarlet petticoats; blue stockings, and high-heeled shoes; ankles generally very neat; waists for the most part very trim.

The fiddlers come in, too, playing a lively air, followed by a little piper, and a fat man with a bassoon, as accompaniments.

A crowd of neighbours, of both sexes, attracted by the music and the sight, flock in after them. All are cordially welcomed by the host and hostess; and some confusion ensues for a few moments, during which the bailiffs, though alive to what is going on, look sharply after their prisoner. When it becomes known that Frank Woodbine has been arrested, great sympathy is manifested for him by the whole assemblage; the men accusing the steward of harshness; and the women patting Frank on the back, bidding him not mind; shaking their hands at the bailiffs, and threatening to clapper-claw their faces.

But Frank does seem to mind it a great deal. The merriment around him, in which he has no share, makes him still more sad and gloomy.

As to the bailiffs, they express their contempt of the opprobrious epithets applied to them, and the menaces of the ladies, by smoking their pipes very tranquilly, and sipping their brandy-and-water, occasionally proffering the glass to the more infuriated of their assailants, which, of course, is indignantly rejected.

Hats off! The Bachelors draw up in a line. So do the Maidens. The music ceases. The host and hostess take hands, and advance towards them as if inviting them to a dance; but it is not for that purpose. They are about to answer the interrogations of the Jury.

The questions are very precise, corresponding with the formula of the Oath. They are glibly answered both by Jonas and Nelly. Never were couple so united and happy. The endearments, in which they indulge, would prove it to the satisfaction of any Jury whatever; however sceptical they might be to begin with.

The Council of Twelve consult together; and the Bachelors put their heads so close to the Maidens, that their wigs brush their cheeks, and tickle their ears. The Twelve appear quite convinced by what they have heard; and seen.

"But this is only a preliminary inquiry, Simon Appleyard, the foreman, says. "Three days have yet to run before the full term; a Twelvemonth and a Day; required by the Charter, will have expired. And you may yet forfeit your claim."

"Not the least chance of it," Jonas replies, embracing nis wife anew.

"Not the least," she adds, ardently returning his caress.

"Master don't say a word about the Mistletoe Bough," Carroty Dick whispers to Peggy.

"Hold your tongue, dunderhead," the discreet chambermaid replies.

"On the fourth day from this, we shall renew our inquiries," the foreman pursues; "and if we find all satisfactory, as we trust it may be, we will give you our certificate to Mr. Roper; who will lay it before Squire Monkbury; and the next time a Court Baron is held, you can make your claim."

"Huzza!" Jonas exclaims. And the crowd echo the shout, till the old rafters echo with their joyous vociferations.

Then comes Tom Tapster bearing a large punchbowl, and places it on the table in the midst of them. Nelly and Peggy bring glasses; and the fat cook brings the minced pies and the plum cake. Jonas seizes the ladle, and begins to dispense the fragrant beverage. The Maidens are first served, and the Bachelors wait upon them. The punch is so hot, that it scalds their mouths; but they drink it nevertheless. The Bachelors are helped next, and as they pledge their partners, they make tender speeches about the probability of obtaining the Flitch in their turn.

Then comes everybody's turn; and Jonas for some minutes is actively engaged in supplying the wants of the thirsty crowd who besiege the table. Peggy and the others hand about the cake and the minced pies, and the pretty chambermaid comes in for her share of admiration from the young fellows; so much so that Carroty Dick waxes jealous. Everybody, at length, is helped; even the musicians.

Nelly has taken care of the bailiff, and given each

of them a full tumbler. Isaacson makes her a polite speech, and Latcham says ditto to it. While pretending to listen to them, Nelly hazards a whisper to Frank.

The punch speedily does its work, and everybody begins to laugh and talk loudly. There is a wonderful clatter of voices. The musicians strike up the prelude to a jig; and in a twinkling the large table is carried off, and the room cleared for a dance. No difficulty in finding partners. The Bachelors have got theirs already, and lead off. There is a contest for pretty Peggy's hand; and Carroty Dick is furious at losing her, and wants to fight his rival. But he is only laughed at. Jonas takes a turn with his wife, but the speed is too great for him, and he soon loses wind, and gives in, being fairly blown.

There is a great shout. Simon Appleyard discovers the Mistletoe Bough, and as he whisks round in the dance, draws his partner under it The damsel is coy, but she cannot escape. Another couple follows—another, and another, and another! Fine fun it seems, for there is nothing but giggling and laughter. Peggy finds herself there again, and Dick tears his red locks. Even the fat cook is kissed; and is so overcome she can scarcely get out of the recess.

While the merriment is at its height, Nelly comes up to Frank and proposes to him to take part in the dance. At first he declines, but Nelly won't take "No." The bailiffs are grown quite bland under the mellowing influence of the punch, and throw no obstacle in the way. Isaacson wants to dance with her himself; but to this Latcham objects; though Nelly, we fancy, would scarcely have consented.

Frank yields to her entreaties, and they stand up together; the bailiffs, with their pipes, moving towards the door as a precautionary measure.

This arrangement takes Jonas by surprise; and he does not altogether approve of it; but he won't interfere. So he finishes the glass of punch with which he has been recruiting himself after his fatigues, and looks on.

The couples go round merrily. Jonas is pleased to observe that Frank avoids the Mistletoe, though he passes close by it. The music plays faster and faster—so fast, the dancers can hardly keep pace with it.

Eh day! What's all this? Jonas can scarcely believe his eyes. Are his wife and Frank going upstairs? Yes, and very quickly too.

They are laughing loudly all the time. And everybody else laughs too; except Jonas—and the bailiffs. The latter laugh on the wrong side of their mouths, for they perceive they are tricked.

Jonas rushes forward: so do the bailiffs. But the staircase is invested by a compact crowd. All the couples have stopped there; and the minions of the law cannot force a passage. Simon Appleyard and the Bachelors drive them back.

Frank and his companion watch the futile efforts of their pursuers from the gallery above, and, after laughing heartily at them for a moment or two—the crowd beneath joining their merriment—they disappear down the dark corridor.

Jonas is lost in bewilderment, and thinks he must be in a disagreeable dream. But the bailiffs rouse him up by clapping him on the shoulder, and telling him they hold him responsible for the prisoner's evasion. The act of his wife is his own act. He must pay the debt himself. He must come down with Two Hundred Pounds.

Jonas looks distracted. But an idea suddenly strikes him.

"Come with me, gem'men, and you shall have him yet," he cries. "She means to let him out by a private door in the garden. You may catch him before he gets off."

And he is hurrying out of the house, when Simon Appleyard's outstretched leg trips him up, and the bailiffs, who are following close after, tumble over him.

The trio regain their feet as soon as they can, and set off towards the garden, attended by the majority of the assemblage, many of whom feel disposed to attempt a rescue, in case the fugitive should be captured.

VII.

HOW DOCTOR PLOT VISITED THE OLD PRIORY CHURCH OF DUNMOW.

DOCTOR PLOT found it bitterly cold.

The wind seemed to penetrate to his very marrow. Besides, he could scarcely keep his feet, owing to the slippery state of the road, which in some places was covered with ice. The steward, however, had a strong arm, and to this the old gentleman clung for support, and so kept himself from falling. Thus he toiled on, slipping and swearing, and grumbling incessantly at the severity of the weather, but exhibiting no inclination to turn back.

Mr. Roper found it very cold too, but he was well buttoned up, and had it not been for the gusts, which caught him at corners, and threatened to blow off his hat and wig, he would have cared nothing about the weather. To secure himself against mishap he tied his handkerchief over his head, and then bade lusty defiance to the hyperborean blast.

THE VISITANT TO THE TOMBS OF THE FITZWALTERS.

P. 49.

They had quitted the main town, and crossing the bridge over the frozen Chelmer, were slowly mounting the ascent leading to Little Dunmow—a work of some labour and difficulty to the old gentleman.

Before they got half-way up the hill, night came on; but the moon had arisen, and there was a brilliant array of stars in the firmament. The frosty particles on the hedges glittered like diamond spray. Very lovely was the scene around them in spite of the rigour of the season; and indeed, the sharp frost rather contributed to the beauty of the landscape than diminished it. The wind had dispersed the mists usually hanging over the marshy grounds in the valley, and an uninterrupted view was obtained of the course of the Chelmer for miles through the lowlands, its frozen surface sparkling in the moonlight. In other respects the country was beautifully undulating and diversified: in parts well wooded, and though the trees were robbed of their foliage, they formed fine dark masses on the hill sides. At some distance on the left, crowning the heights, might be discerned Stansted House, a noble mansion, belonging to Sir Gilbert de Montfichet. It was surrounded by a park, and an enchanting effect was produced by some clumps of timber on the slopes, and a few large single trees in the hollows. On the right, in the midst of another well-wooded park, was Monkbury-place, the residence of Mark Monkbury, Esquire, Lord of the Manor of Little Dunmow. Cottages and granges were scattered about at intervals; and nearer to Great Dunmow, and by the river side, were grounds and works showing where the woollen manufactures were carried on, for which the place had long been noted. Great Dunmow itself looked unusually picturesque in the magical light of the moon, which gave a kind of spiritual beauty to every object it fell upon; and a cheerful hum arose from the town, as if the inhabitants were all making merry.

A ruddy gleam burst from the windows of most of the cottages they passed, giving the little tenements an air of such comfort, that Doctor Plot was more than once tempted to stop and warm himself at their fires. Mirthful voices and laughter generally resounded from within. But this was not the case with a forlorn-looking and solitary hovel, that stood by the road-side. No smoke issued from its chimney ; no sound of cheerfulness arose from it; only a faint light struggled through its frosty panes. Its appearance was so miserable, that Doctor Plot's compassion was aroused, and he peeped in.

He beheld a wretched-looking object in female attire crouching before a few decaying embers. A farthing candle burnt on the table beside her, and revealed the forlorn condition of the place. A sad picture altogether.

Doctor Plot felt terribly cold just then. The wind was keener than ever. It cut him like a knife.

He was raising his hand to tap against the door, when the steward stopped him.

"What are you about to do, sir?" Mr. Roper said. "That woman does not deserve your charity. A bad, mischievous person, sir."

"Mischievous or not," Doctor Plot rejoined, "I cannot see her sit there and starve on such a night as this."

So he knocked. With slow and tottering steps the woman answered the summons. A ghastly-looking creature, prematurely old, with haggard features, and grizzled hair. Doctor Plot appeared to recognise her ; he uttered an exclamation of surprise, and bethought him of the steward's caution. But he had gone too far to retreat now, so hastily thrusting a piece of money into the woman's hand, he departed.

Not unseen nor unnoted, though. The woman had recognised him, also. She staggered back and sank into a chair; and it was long ere she regained her senses. On recovering, she fancied she had beheld a phantom. But a piece of gold was in her hand; so it must have been a living person she had seen. She looked at the gold long and steadily, and then laid it down upon the table, muttering:

"He is come back to judge me—he is come back. Reparation must be made before I join her in the grave."

Meantime, Doctor Plot and his companion toiled on. Thoughts of other days and other scenes, with which that haggard-looking woman had possibly been connected, passed through his mind, and he became perfectly silent and self-engrossed. The wind might blow as keenly as it listed now. He felt it not. An icier breath than that from the north chilled him.

The summit of the hill was at length attained, and before them stood the old Priory Church of Dunmow. All that remained of it at least, for the little structure, with its grey walls bathed in the moonbeams, its three round-arched windows, its solitary buttress, its tiny belfry surmounted by a quaint extinguisher-like roof, was the mere fragment of a vast and stately pile, which in its time had formed part of a range of monastic buildings, covering many a rood around. The ragged state of the masonry at either end of the church showed the devastation that had been committed, and the rude and imperfect character of the repairs.

Within, one aisle and part of the choir were all that remained of the original fabric. Of the long rows of columns once supporting the high-arched roof, how few

E

continued standing! The hand of the Destroyer had fallen heavily on the fane; hurling down solid walls and buttresses built in defiance of time; toppling the tower from its base; desecrating the shrines; stripping off the ornaments; tearing up the tombs; and shaking the pile to its foundations. Yet some little had been spared. Underneath a low-browed arch, encased like saintly relics in a coffer, lay the hallowed bones of the Lady Juga, by whom, early in the Twelfth Century, the Convent was founded, and dedicated to Our Lady. Of the various monastic edifices reared and endowed by the pious Juga, all were gone, save this fragment of the church. Not a stone to mark their site. And the holy men whom she appointed to abide there, were gone likewise: their very graves unhonoured and unknown. But her ashes had not been disturbed. A good spell guarded them.

Would that the same benignant power had preserved from mutilation the tombs of the Fitzwalters! Eleven generations of the house were buried here. An antique sculptured monument, bearing date 1198, covered the founder of the line, Sir Walter Fitzwalter, and his dame. Base hands and barbarous were those that shattered the fine recumbent figure of the old warrior, and 'twas pity he could not have burst his cerements and arisen to strike down the sacrilegious wretch!

Between two pillars, near him, lay his granddaughter; erstwhile, as fair a piece of clay, and as free from dross, as ever death, before its time, gave back to native dust. The alabaster figure on the tomb strove to shape forth the fatal charms of the hapless Matilda Fitzwalter; fatal to herself, inasmuch as they roused the passions of the ruthless John, by whom she was poisoned for her resistance to his lawless love.

Other graves were there belonging to the same ancient family, though not so noticeable as these. Most of them were reft of their memorials; the inscriptions defaced; the brasses torn from the stones. Little else was left, unless it might be the Old Oak Chair devoted to the winners of the Flitch, wherein, as we have seen, it was Jonas Nettlebed's ardent desire to be enthroned. This was kept here, though seldom called into use. The venerable monastic fane had dwindled into a little parish church, with whitewashed walls, and a few pews enclosing its pillars.

Walking up to the churchyard gate, Doctor Plot, whose feelings had evidently undergone some change since he had seen the haggard tenant of the hovel, expressed a strong wish to enter the little structure. The request might seem strange and ill-timed; but the steward, who by this time had apparently become acquainted with some of the old gentleman's peculiarities of character, raised no objection, but at once proceeded to a cottage hard by, and obtained the key from the sexton.

Armed with this, Doctor Plot left his companion beneath a row of limes in the churchyard, and hobbling up to the porch where he nearly stumbled over the sharp stones on which the fortunate couples were required to kneel while reciting their vow of conjugal felicity, he unlocked the door, and closed it after him carefully as he went in.

Why does he go there alone, and at such an hour? We may not disclose the dark secrets of his breast; but we can follow him, and see what he does.

After a step or two he pauses, overcome by emotion. A chill as of death falls upon his heart. The moonbeams are streaming upon the tomb of the first Fitzwalter and his dame, and very ghostly the statues look. The old man advances towards them slowly, as if invited by their stony regards. He is talking to himself aloud, but in hollow, broken tones. What words are those he utters? We dare not repeat them. They are such alone as the dead should hear.

No human eye he fancies can behold him; no human ear listen to him. His gestures become more frantic; his language more wild and incoherent. No one who had lately seen him, would recognise him now. His features have assumed a wholly different expression; very fearful to behold. Notwithstanding the death-like chill of the place, thick damps gather, like heat-drops, on his brow.

The fit passes off, and he grows calm; but so pale, he might pass for one of the marble group before him.

Then he staggers towards the arched recess, beneath which the saintly Juga is deposited, and kneeling before the sepulchral cist, strives to pray.

Why does he start back so suddenly? What sounds are those he hears? Can they be echoes of his own sighs and groans? They seem to issue from the very depths of the shell before him. He would fain speak, but his tongue is stayed with wonder and terror. He listens intently for a recurrence of the sounds. In vain. All is silent as the grave. He can see nothing; for the moon having momentarily withdrawn her lustre, the place is buried in darkness.

He puts forth his hand, and encounters only the lid of the sepulchral chest. He touches it reverently. Beyond this, he meets nothing but the stone wall forming the back of the recess.

He shakes off the terror that has numbed him, and asks, in a voice that seems to break harshly upon the stillness of the spot, " Who is there?" No answer. He repeats the question, more loudly and peremptorily. Still, the same result. At last he quits the church, in fear and perplexity.

He finds the steward pacing up and down beneath the little avenue of leafless lime-trees leading to the porch, and questions him.   Some one must have followed him into the church—or have been hidden there when he entered it ?

Mr. Roper declares this to be impossible.   He has never quitted his post for a moment.   No one could have passed through the door without being perceived; and as to any one hiding in the church at such an hour without special reason, it is idle to think of it.   What can have happened to occasion these inquiries ?

But Doctor Plot does not think it necessary to explain,—and the steward, who, before this, has begun to suspect that the old gentleman is not quite right in his upper story, is now confirmed in the impression.

So, though his curiosity is considerably excited, he relinquishes all idea of gratifying it for the present, and takes back the key, without further remark.

This done, they set off in the direction of the young gamekeeper's cottage, and speedily arrive at it.

VIII.

ROSE WOODBINE.

A PRETTY village.   Just the spot for humble love to dwell in.   No turtle doves could choose a nicer nest.

Roses and honeysuckles adorned its whitened walls in summer, and crept round its little windows to meet the thatched roof above.   The garden, too, though small, was tastefully laid out, and full of fragrant shrubs and flowers.   Odour or bloom, they had none now; but

they were there still, and ready to put forth new beauties
and blossoms with returning spring. The holly hedge
and the ivy on the wall alone showed any symptoms of
verdure or vitality.

A light was shining through the little diamond panes
of the window, and as the curtains were not drawn
across it, one might easily look in. The temptation
was too strong for Doctor Plot. He laid his hand on
his companion's arm to impose silence, opened the gate
with care, and walked noiselessly along the frozen
walk.

He did not require to be told whom he beheld. It
could be no other than Rose Woodbine.

Her back was towards him, but the perfect symmetry of her figure was distinguishable : the slender
waist, the spreading shoulders, the slim neck, and finely-
shaped head, with the fair abundant tresses gathered
behind it.

Nor had he to wait long before her features were
fully revealed. The clock struck seven ; and laying
down the needlework on which she was engaged,
Rose got up to prepare her husband's evening meal.
She was taller than Doctor Plot expected. But what
a lovely countenance ! Features cast in the softest
mould of beauty. Sweetness their characteristic
expression : sweetness that hung upon the lips,
fashioned like Cupid's bow ; that shone from the dove-
like blue eyes ; that sat upon the dimpled cheek,
tinted like the China rose ; that reigned throughout
the whole demeanour. Sweetness in every look ;
gentleness in every movement. Fair she was : very
fair : locks light as a summer cloud, skin of snowy
whiteness.

Apparently, there were no drawbacks in manner and
deportment. Her movements were full of natural grace

and modesty. Her dress, though simple, was the most becoming possible. No court dame, masking her charms in rustic guise, could have chosen her attire better; not half so well, probably. If Rose only proved as amiable as she looked, Doctor Plot could have nothing to say against her.

So far satisfied, he took a survey of the room. Though plain and unpretending, and consistent with the young gamekeeper's station, it was remarkably clean and tidy, and there was an air of great comfort about it. The furniture was substantial and well arranged, and there was a total absence of vulgar ornament, either in the way of tawdry pictures, or otherwise. Indeed there was evidence of some little mental cultivation on the part of the inmates, afforded by three or four book-shelves laden with goodly tomes. But the walls were chiefly occupied with the implements belonging to Frank Woodbine's calling; guns of various sizes and make, nets, landing-nets, fishing-rods, and tackle: all the apparatus, in short, of the angler and the sportsman. There were the gamekeeper's mud-boots, oilskin hat, and waterproof jacket for fowling in the marshes. Stretched before the fire, which was blazing cheerfully, was the large retriever, Dragon, who had accompanied his master on his first visit to the Dunmow Flitch.

The snowy napkin was spread upon the table, and the pigeon pie and cold ham set on it, with the white loaf and the brown jug ready to be filled with frothing ale on Frank's arrival. Rose glanced at the clock. Five minutes more were gone. He couldn't be long now. She smiled while thinking how she would welcome him.

Pity to dash that smile with tears!

Rose sat down again, and as she plied her needle, she

sang some snatches of a simple ballad, in a voice sc
sweet that its tones thrilled through the old gentleman's heart. It was like listening to a nightingale.

Doctor Plot was so transported that he quite forgot
himself, clapped his hands, and called out in applause.
Both the singer and the retriever were disturbed by
the exclamation, and the latter sprang to his feet, and
advanced, growling, towards the door. At first, Rose
thought it was her husband, but the anger of the
hound instantly convinced her of her error. Dragon
would not bark at his master.

The steward now thought it necessary to advance,
and secure their peaceable admission. Accordingly,
he tapped at the door, and announced himself, and
Dragon being silenced and sent back to his place on
the hearth, Mr. Roper stepped in, followed by Doctor
Plot, whom he introduced to the fair mistress of the
house.

IX.

DOCTOR PLOT GIVES REASONS FOR HIS DISBELIEF IN
CONJUGAL FELICITY; AND RELATES THE PARTICU-
LARS OF AN UNFORTUNATE MARRIAGE.

IF Rose Woodbine's voice was sweet and musical, her
manner was no less charming.

She received them very kindly, handed them chairs,
and addressing the steward, presumed that he came to
see her husband, with whom she knew he had some
business, though she was not aware of its nature;
adding, that she expected Frank home every moment.
Mr. Roper bowed, as if in assent to the remark. Refreshments were then offered them but declined. As,
in introducing Doctor Plot, the steward had mentioned
his professional connexion with the late family who

dwelt at the Old Hall at Dunmow, Rose regarded the
stranger with interest. Something in his features
struck her as familiar, either in look or expression.
She inquired whether he had been in the neighbourhood recently?

"Not for upwards of twenty years," he replied.

"Then I cannot have seen you before, since I was not
born at that time," she rejoined with a smile. "And
yet I seem to know your face."

Doctor Plot exchanged an almost imperceptible glance
with the steward.

"I see what it is now," Rose continued more quickly.
"With that smile playing upon your face, you remind
me of—whom do you think?"

"I can't guess, ma'am. Mr. Roper, perhaps?"

"My husband."

The old gentleman's smile immediately vanished.

"A compliment, I presume, is intended," he said,
gravely; "and I accept it. But I have no desire to be
thought like a gamekeeper."

"Nay, now I look again, you don't resemble him at
all. Frank always looks good-natured!"

"And I am not always so, you think. Well, there
you are right, my dear. I am generally considered a
cantankerous old fellow, and people don't care much
about my society, in consequence. I don't blame them.
I am dissatisfied with the world, and the world is naturally dissatisfied with me. So we are quits. If people
abuse me, I can rail at them in return. And, best of all, I
can shun them. I am what they call a misanthrope, my
dear."

"Perhaps you have had good reason for your quarrel
with mankind, sir."

"I have, or think I have. I have to complain of
violated friendship; of perfidy; of wrong—deep, irre-

mediable wrong; of dishonour. Some men can bear
these things without wincing; or, if they writhe under
the infliction for a time, wholly recover. I am not one
of the class. But I do not want to trouble you with my
griefs or my resentments."

"You do not trouble me, sir. On the contrary, you
interest me deeply, and I sincerely wish I could be of
any service in softening the asperity of your feelings,
and restoring you to a good opinion of the world."

"I fear it is impossible. I have been too harshly
dealt with. When I have found in the softest words
—falsehood—and in the sweetest smiles—betrayal:
when the hand, that grasped mine, plunged a dagger
into my breast, I am not likely to forget, or to forgive.
From that hour I abjured the world. I have no part
in it. I have forsworn my own kin. I have no ties,
no affections, no sympathies. I am alone—yes, utterly
alone."

"I pity you from the bottom of my heart, sir. I
can easily understand that your faith in the goodness
of human nature should be severely shaken by what
you have endured; but I cannot—will not believe it
has been utterly destroyed."

"Well, not utterly, perhaps—nearly so."

A slight pause ensued. It was broken at length,
by Rose. With a look of sympathy, she observed to
the old gentleman, "Your unhappy case puts me in
mind of what I have heard related of Sir Walter Fitzwalter and his ill-starred lady."

The steward would have diverted the conversation
from the turn it had now taken, but Doctor Plot
checked him.

"All such cases are alike, madam," the old gentleman said, "except in their consequences. Wrong on
one side; wretchedness on the other: nay, wretched-

ness on both sides. Woman will be false, and man will be her dupe to the end of the chapter. My history is not Sir Walter's only; but the history of a hundred families besides. I could give you a long catalogue if I chose, for I have them at my finger's ends; but I will spare you the recital. Most men are patient under injury, or feel it not: some few avenge themselves. Sir Walter was among the latter. He wiped out the stain upon his house in blood—in the blood of the villain who wronged him; and his wife—his guilty wife—expiated her offence by poison, self-administered. I know Mr. Roper entertains an opinion different from mine upon this tragic affair; but so it occurred."

"I know the unfortunate Lady Juga to have been innocent," the steward remarked.

"That makes it doubly distressing," Rose said. "Alas! poor lady."

"Alas! indeed, if what Mr. Roper says be true," Doctor Plot exclaimed, with something like a groan. "And alas! for Sir Walter, if he yet be living, and should have his lady's innocence proved to him. It would be his death."

"I hope not, sir," Mr. Roper said.

"It would, I tell you. And what is more, he would deserve to die; and I should not care if he were hanged like a dog. No, not like a dog, for I would *not* hang a dog; but like the blood-stained murderer he must be."

"You look very ill, sir," said Rose, rising in alarm; "let me bring you a glass of water."

"No, my dear—no, thank'ee," Doctor Plot rejoined, faintly. "I am subject to spasms of the heart. They will kill me, I dare say, some day; but the pang is past now. We have talked too much about this inhuman Sir Walter."

"I do not think him inhuman, sir," Rose rejoined.

"I gladly believe in the lady's innocence, as asserted by Mr. Roper, and should wish to see it established, even after this long lapse of time, and when it can only clear her name from reproach; yet still Sir Walter must have been deluded by false statements of her criminality; and therefore the real guilt cannot rest with him, but with the author of the direful charges."

"On that head be it, then," Doctor Plot rejoined with another groan. "But, supposing Mr. Roper to be right, nothing can be said in excuse for Sir Walter, except that he was of a suspicious nature, and easily aroused to jealousy. An irritable man, moreover; odd in speech; odd in his ways; difficult to please. Humorsome, exacting, imperious. You knew not where to have him. He slipped through your fingers like an eel; and when you thought to please him best, you were most likely to give him offence."

"You describe him skilfully, sir," Rose said; "but you give only the dark side of the picture. Let us look on the bright side. Sir Walter must have had some good qualities to redeem the bad."

"Perhaps he had, my dear. I could never find them out. Some people said he did good, but it was in an odd way, and to please himself; so there was little or no merit in it. Some few thought him generous. Most people called him close-fisted, and they were nearer the mark. Originally, I believe, he had kindly qualities, but they were early soured; just as his personal appearance was destroyed by bodily infirmity. He was lame, my dear—lame like myself—lame on the same leg—and it was this circumstance that made him take a liking to me. It would have been well if I had never seen him. He inoculated me with some of his peculiarities and prejudices, and I should have been better without them."

"You disparage him, somewhat, I think, sir," Rose remarked. "To my eyes, his character appears full of interest—deep, painful interest."

"If what I have said has produced that effect, so far from disparaging him, I must have spoken more favourably of him than he deserves. There was little interest about him, I assure you. A very common-place personage, who might have passed through life without attracting observation, if he had been differently circumstanced."

"There I cannot agree with you, sir," the steward observed. "Sir Walter was no common-place person."

"You knew little of him, Mr. Roper. His faults were more numerous than his virtues—that I maintain. He was a sceptic—not on religious matters; on those he was a bigot: but, having no faith in himself, or in his own goodness, he distrusted his fellows. He thought them like him. He had little belief in man's honesty, less in woman's: valued professions of friendship lightly, and even sneered at them: fancied bad motives where none such, perhaps, existed; and often took offence when no offence was intended. His manner alienated his acquaintance, and resentment at their conduct prevented him from seeking fresh society. Thus he had no friends. Yes, I forgot; he had one— one, who remained with him."

"Yourself, I suppose, sir!" Rose hazarded.

"No. I was his worst enemy. He had one friend whom he believed deserved the title truly: who stood by him when others fell off; who seemed blind to his defects. For this friendship Sir Walter was not ungrateful. His friend became as a brother to him; nay, his second self. He had no secrets from him. Better he had cut out his tongue than have so betrayed him-

self!" Doctor Plot cried with an expression of rage.
"He was nourishing a viper. But to go on. Unlikely as it would seem that a breast like Sir Walter's
should entertain a tender passion, love found entrance
to it—not only found entrance, but lighted up a flame
that threatened to consume him. He was driven to
despair, for he dreaded refusal worse than death, and
had no hope of success. His friend soon became acquainted with this state, and bade him take courage.
He furthered the suit, with a dark design, as afterwards
appeared; and in the end Juga Baynard became Lady
Fitzwalter. For awhile, Sir Walter thought himself
the happiest of men. His doubts disappeared. He
had found a true friend and a loving wife. Fool! fool!
to be thus deluded," the old man exclaimed, gnashing
his teeth. "His happiness was brief. Well it might
be, for it had no real foundation. Lady Juga was very
handsome, and somewhat wilful. She claimed admiration as her right, and loved society as much as Sir
Walter disliked it. On this point they first disagreed.
The friend espoused the lady's part, and she gained the
day. The Old Hall was crowded with guests, and
the unwilling host was driven to his own chamber for
quiet. His lady did not like his odd ways, his eccen-
tricities of manner and speech, and rallied him upon
them. Quarrel the second. Again his friend took part
against him, and joined the lady in her ridicule. This
was hard to bear; but Sir Walter bore it as he could.
Trifles, I have said, irritated him; trifles at which other
men would laugh, but which he magnified into importance. Their next quarrel was about a trifle—so mere a
trifle that what it was—a frown—a gesture—an inad-
vertent word—has escaped my recollection. But on this
occasion his friend sided with him. The change of tactics
did not escape Sir Walter, and his suspicions were

awakened. He began to watch his friend narrowly. Blind dupe that he had hitherto been, he now detected a hundred grounds for jealousy! His breast was a prey to anguish inexpressible. He saw, or thought he saw, that all were laughing at him—that his very household mocked him. But he did not put an end to this state of things. He could have easily closed his doors upon his friend; but this did not suit him. He meditated revenge. Whatever his plans might have been, they were delayed by a circumstance, which would have calmed his fury, had he not seen in it addition to his supposed wrongs. Lady Fitzwalter gave birth to a child, and her husband traced its parentage to his false-hearted friend. If he wronged her by the suspicion—and he had no proofs beyond the doubts engendered in his own mind—then Heaven forgive him!"

"He *did* wrong her—most cruelly wrong her," the steward said, in a severe and emphatic tone.

Doctor Plot made no reply. He did not even raise his eyes to meet the other's gaze; but was visibly a prey to great emotion. After awhile, he proceeded:

"I now approach the darkest part of my story, and would willingly leave it untold; but I must end it, since I have begun. Sir Walter's manner, by this time, was wholly changed. He was no longer odd. He had become moody, morose, savage. Bitter in his taunts to his lady; fierce when contradicted. His friend was still his frequent guest, but he saw little of him. The lady was left to his society, and they could dispense with that of the husband. Sir Walter could not be prevailed to look upon the child which he did not believe to be his own; and on this score his lady felt, or feigned, great distress, shedding many tears to move him; but he continued inexorable. One day she suddenly invaded the sanctuary he had

chosen, and before he could prevent her, placed the
infant in his arms, bidding him look upon its innocent
face. Sir Walter did no such thing. A sudden transport of fury seized him. With a dreadful oath, he
dashed the infant on the ground, and amid his lady's
shrieks, rushed out of the room."

"Was the child killed?" Rose inquired, with a cheek
blanched with emotion.

"By miracle, not even injured."

"Heaven be praised!" Rose fervently ejaculated.
"I feared Sir Walter might have that crime on his
conscience; and if so, he were indeed lost to man's
pity, and to mercy hereafter."

"Providence for its own wise purposes, turned aside
his deadly hand," Doctor Plot responded, "and he was
spared that guilt. But let me hasten to the conclusion.
Enough had been done to separate Sir Walter entirely
from his wife. She could never forgive him this last
act of barbarity. In fact her health suffered severely
from the shock she had sustained by the frightful incident. Sir Walter reproached himself bitterly, as well
he might; he pitied his lady's sufferings, and was
more disposed to listen to reason. A reconciliation
was attempted to be brought about between them by
his insidious friend, whose purpose it was, not to leave
them disunited; and it might have succeeded, if Sir
Walter had not surprised a letter, addressed to his lady,
and written by the traitor himself, which confirmed his
worst suspicions. It referred to events that showed
the wretched husband had been long their dupe, while
it urged the necessity of keeping up appearances with
him, and ended by appointing a secret meeting for that
very evening. Sir Walter thought it a pity to balk
them of the appointment. But he resolved to be there,
too. The letter was resealed; delivered to the lady;

THE CUSTOM OF DUNMOW.

P. 67

and an answer sent by her. Night came, and with it came the gallant. He was privily admitted by a confidential woman. Fiends take her! but the women are all alike. This wretch was doubly treacherous; and now betrayed her mistress, as she had before betrayed her master. Scarcely was the villain housed, when Sir Walter burst into the room: fury and vengeance in his looks. He found his wife and her lover seated together; the lady in tears. At sight of him she had injured, she uttered a cry. Her lover started to his feet, and laid his hand upon his sword. Protestations of innocence were passionately uttered by the one; explanations more calmly attempted by the other. Sir Walter would listen to neither. All that wrath could supply of injury and scorn he heaped upon their heads. The affrighted lady clung to his arm—to his knees: but he cast her off. He struck his detested rival a blow upon the cheek with his clenched hand; and but for her, who held back their hands, the apartment would have been dyed with the blood of one or both of them. They parted to meet at earliest dawn; and Sir Walter's sword passed through his adversary's heart."

"A terrible history, indeed!" Rose said, heaving a deep sigh. "And oh! if Sir Walter were wrong, I pity him more than his victim."

"Say rather victims, since two perished by his instrumentality. Have I not hinted at Lady Fitzwalter's fate? Her husband never saw her more. He did not even return to his own house after the fatal duel. He became a wanderer, and he has been one ever since— if he yet exists. He made no inquiries after his lady; nor was it till some time afterwards, that he learnt how her death had occurred. She took poison."

There was profound silence for a few moments. Mr Roper then spoke.

"The worst part of the tale yet remains to be told," he said. "Sir Walter was throughout the dupe of his own suspicions. His friend was true to him, and so was his wife. Before she died, the Lady Juga drew up a statement of her innocence, which is still preserved, and which can be confirmed in all its circumstances. The letter, intercepted by Sir Walter, had no criminal significance whatever; and the object of the meeting it appointed was to bring about a good understanding— or at least an appearance of good understanding—between the unfortunate pair. Alice Aggs, the wretched woman who belied her mistress, bitterly repented of her share in the sad transactions, and yet lives to confess her culpability, and exonerate Lady Fitzwalter."

"I saw her to-night—a wretched creature indeed!" Doctor Plot remarked, with a shudder.

"Her offence has not gone unpunished," the steward continued. "Ever since that day misfortune has tracked her, and she rightly attributes her misery and sufferings to her ill conduct."

Doctor Plot seemed lost in deep and painful reflection. His head fell upon his breast.

Rousing himself as if by a great effort, he said: "We must see to this, Mr. Roper. Justice must be done."

"It must, sir," the steward rejoined, with stern gravity.

"You have not mentioned what became of the child of the ill-fated lady?" Rose inquired.

"I know nothing about it," Doctor Plot replied, evasively.

The steward also shook his head, to intimate that he was in equal ignorance of its fate.

"In speaking of Sir Walter's friend, you gave no name," Rose remarked to the old gentleman. "If you desire to keep it secret, let it be so. Otherwise, I would venture to inquire if allusion was made to Sir Gilbert de Montfichet?"

"How came you to guess it?" Doctor Plot demanded, sharply.

"Because I have heard that he fell in a duel," Rose replied. "I know something of his son—the present Sir Gilbert."

"True, Sir Walter's friend—his enemy I should say —left a son. He was a widower when he visited at the Hall—when the events I have mentioned occurred. But what do you know of young Sir Gilbert?"

"Not much," she replied, blushing.

"I must explain," Mr. Roper interposed. "Rose knew him as a suitor for her hand. It was talked about in Dunmow of course, because Sir Gilbert made no secret of his attachment or of his refusal."

"Strange indeed!" the old gentleman muttered. "But how came you to refuse so good a match, my dear? Is not Sir Gilbert handsome? His father was considered particularly good-looking! Moreover, the young baronet is rich,—or supposed to be so."

"Sir Gilbert is all you have described, sir," Rose answered with a smile; "young, rich, titled, handsome. But I had the best of all reasons for refusing him. I loved another."

"Pity the other could not offer you as much. You made too great a sacrifice, methinks."

"I made no sacrifice at all," Rose returned, earnestly. "Happiness, as you know, is not to be purchased by rank or money, and I have gained that priceless blessing with my husband."

"I am glad you have spoken out so heartily, Rose," the steward observed. "Amongst his other heresies, Doctor Plot is an entire disbeliever in conjugal felicity.

Unfortunately, he has some reason for his incredulity, as he has shown. Now, I hold the contrary doctrine. I believe there is no perfect happiness except in the married state. My opinion is grounded on my own experience, and I uphold it. "I do not consider," he added, with a slight laugh, "that Mrs. Roper and myself are quite qualified to claim the flitch ; still, in spite of some little differences, we have for many, many years entertained a warm attachment for each other, which time has strengthened rather than impaired. Mine is a mere example of every-day life ; but yours I consider a peculiar case, Rose. And I have taken the liberty of bringing Doctor Plot with me, that he might receive from your own lips confirmation of my assertion ; that here at least, a loving couple may be found."

"On all accounts I am glad you have brought him with you, Mr. Roper," Rose replied ; " and if I am able to give him a better impression of human nature than he has hitherto entertained, I do not think he will regret his visit. That I am happy is no merit of mine, since I am blest with the best and kindest of husbands ; but I, at least, know how to appreciate Frank's goodness, and strive in every way to deserve his affection. It may seem strange, and perhaps bold in me to affirm so much ; but I do not think we *could* quarrel. No cloud has ever darkened our union since we were first joined together. Having entire confidence in each other, doubts and misgivings are impossible. When the heart is full of love it can admit no meaner passion ; and I believe there is a sanctity about Wedded Affection, when it is perfect and unalloyed, that will repel all unworthy feelings. Love's brightness cannot be sullied by a speck. You, sir, have mentioned," she continued, addressing Doctor Plot, "that Sir Walter Fitzwalter's earliest disagreements with his lady were occasioned by trifles, and I can easily understand that such might have been the case, because graver matters would naturally be viewed with corresponding seriousness. But trifles do not disturb our harmony. Love's music is so well attuned with us that not a note is out of order. My husband, no doubt, has made great allowances for my imperfections : but he has never told me so. Nay, if I am to believe him (which I always do), he cannot discern any faults in me. And I am sure I can find none in him."

"You make out your case fairly enough, I must say," Doctor Plot remarked ; "and, in fact, your speech carries conviction with it. I am sorry to throw cold water on such honest, heartfelt warmth, or to express doubt as to the lasting nature of your affection. But I have imbibed some of Sir Walter's opinions. I am a sceptic like him. As yet your love has been subjected to no trial. Do you think it would stand the hard test of reverse of fortune—of poverty—of distress? Or the still harder test of sudden elevation? In the one case it might be benumbed, or totally extinguished : in the other, it might turn giddy, and losing its proper balance, fall to the ground, and break in pieces."

"The latter case is more improbable than the former," Rose replied ; "but I trust, and believe, our affection would be proof against the severest ordeal it could be put to ; and that neither prosperity nor adversity could crush it."

"Well, I hope it may be tested in neither way," Doctor Plot observed. "The best wish I could desire for you is, that you should remain contented, as you are."

"Contented I shall always be, whatever betide," Rose rejoined. "With my husband near me, I am

sure to be reconciled to my lot.   But how time flies !
I thought he would have been home half an hour ago."

"There, you are uneasy?" Doctor Plot, remarked,
rather maliciously—" I saw him at the Flitch. Mrs.
Nettlebed, I dare say, has detained him.   A pretty
woman that landlady—with an eye for a handsome
young fellow."

The shaft fell harmless.

" I am not in the least uneasy," Rose replied, with a
smile. " My husband is often kept out beyond the
time I expect him ; so there is nothing unusual in the
circumstance.   As to Mrs. Nettlebed, I think you do
her an injustice.   She is very fond of her husband ;
and Jonas is very fond of her."

" Humph !" Doctor Plot exclaimed.   " They would
have us believe them to be a couple of turtles, always
billing and cooing.   I have my doubts about the sin-
cerity of their attachment."

"Doctor Plot is a heretic, you know, Mrs. Woodbine," the steward observed, laughing heartily.

"May I ask you one question, my dear?" the old
gentleman said.   "A straightforward one—but pardon
it.   I'm an eccentric person you know.   Does your
husband always trust you with his affairs ?"

" As much as he chooses, sir. I desire to know
nothing that he does not care to confide to me."

" Want of interest—hum ?"

" Want of curiosity, rather."

" Well, I abominate a prying woman.   So you don't
know his business with Mr. Roper ?"

" How should I, sir, since he has not mentioned it
to me !"

" A matter of money, Mr. Roper—eh ?" Doctor Plot
said.

" A trifling debt, sir."

" How much—may I inquire?"

" Why, sir, two hundred pounds."

" Two hundred pounds!" Rose exclaimed, in astonishment.

" That's not such a trifle,—to a man in Frank Woodbine's situation," Doctor Plot said.

" Oh! he can pay it," the steward observed, in an
off-hand way.

" Of course he can," Rose exclaimed, with a look of
entire confidence in the assertion; " or he never would
have incurred the debt."

" Odd! he shouldn't have mentioned it, though," the
old gentleman said. " Does he never condescend to
explain his ways and means to you?"

" Frank earns his money honestly. Further explanation I do not require; nor should I give it, if I possessed it," Rose answered, in a tone calculated to check
further remark.

" I crave your pardon, my dear, if I have offended
you," Doctor Plot said. " I am shockingly inquisitive
—that's the truth. But let us change the subject As
I came hither just now, you were singing, and a few
words of your song reached me. They interested me.
Would it be asking too much, if I were to beg for a
repetition of the ballad?"

" I will sing it to you with pleasure," she replied,
with the utmost good nature. " It is a mere simple
ballad, descriptive of our old Dunmow custom; and
as it is somewhat long, you must check me, if I weary
you. At all events, it may serve to beguile the time
till Frank's return."

And in those tones of delicious sweetness, which had
previously charmed the old gentleman, and which
imparted magic to words, in themselves of little moment, she sang as follows:

The Custom of Dunmow.

SHOWING HOW IT AROSE.

Fytte the First.

A Fond Couple make a Vow before the Good Prior of the Convent of our Lady of Dunmow, that they have loved each other well and truly for a Twelvemonth and a Day; and crave his Blessing.

I.

"What seek ye here, my children dear?
  Why kneel ye down thus lowly
Upon the stones, beneath the porch
  Of this our Convent holy?"
The Prior old the pair bespoke
  In faltering speech, and slowly.

II.

Their modest garb would seem proclaim
  The pair of low degree,
But though in cloth of frieze arrayed,
  A stately youth was he:
While she who knelt down by his side,
  Was beautiful to see.

III.

"A Twelvemonth and a Day have fled
  Since first we were united;
And from that hour," the young man said,
  "No change our hopes has blighted.
Fond faith with fonder faith we've paid,
  And love with love requited.

IV.

"True to each other have we been;
  No dearer object seeing,
Than each has in the other found;
  In everything agreeing.
And every look, and word, and deed
  That breed dissension fleeing.

V.

"All this we swear, and take in proof
  Our Lady of Dunmow!
For She, who sits with saints above,
  Well knows that it is so.
Attest our Vow, thou reverend man,
  And bless us, ere we go!"

VI.

The Prior old stretch'd forth his hands;
  "Heaven prosper ye!" quoth he;
"O'er such as ye, right gladly we
  Say ' *Benedicite!* '"
On this, the kneeling pair uprose—
  Uprose full joyfully.

Fytte the Second.

*Good Prior merrily bestoweth a Boon upon the Loving Couple;
and getteth a noble Recompense.*

I.

JUST then, pass'd by the Convent cook—
  And moved the young man's glee;
On his broad back a mighty Flitch
  Of Bacon brown bore he.
So heavy was the load, I wis,
  It scarce mote carried be.

II.

" Take ye that Flitch," the Prior cried,
  " Take it, fond pair, and go :
Fidelity, like yours, deserves
  The boon I now bestow.
Go, feast your friends, and think upon
  The Convent of Dunmow."

III.

" Good Prior," then the youth replied,
  " Thy gift to us is dear,
Not for its worth, but that it shows
  Thou deem'st our love sincere.
And in return broad lands I give—
  Broad lands thy Convent near ;
Which shall to thee and thine produce
  A Thousand Marks a Year !

IV.

" But this Condition I annex,
  Or else the Grant's forsaken,
That whensoe'er a pair shall come,
  And take the Oath we've taken,
They shall from thee and thine receive
  A goodly Flitch of Bacon.

V.

" And thus from out a simple chance
  A usage good shall grow ;
And our example of true love
  Be held up evermo :
While all who win the prize shall bless
  The Custom of Dunmow."

VI.

" Who art thou, son ?" the Prior cried,
  His tones with wonder falter—
" Thou should'st not jest with reverend men,
  Nor with their feelings palter."
" I jest not, Prior, for know in me
  Sir Reginald Fitzwalter.

VII.

"I now throw off my humble garb,
    As I what I am, confest ;
The wealthiest I of wealthy men,
    Since with this treasure blest."
And as he spoke, Fitzwalter clasp'd
    His lady to his breast.

VIII.

"In peasant guise my love I won,
    Nor knew she whom she wedded ;
In peasant cot our truth we tried,
    And no disunion dreaded.
Twelve months' assurance proves our faith
    On firmest base is steadied."

IX.

Joy reigned within those Convent walls
    When the glad news was known ;
Joy reigned within Fitzwalter's halls
    When there his bride was shown.
No lady in the land such sweet
    Simplicity could own ;
A natural grace had she, that all
    Art's graces far outshone :
Beauty and worth for want of birth
    Abundantly atone.

L'Envoi.

Hence the Custom.

WHAT need of more?   That Loving Pair
    Lived long and truly so ;
Nor ever disunited were,—
     For one death laid them low !
And hence arose that Custom old—
    The Custom of Dunmow.

Something in the story, thus related, seemed to surprise Doctor Plot ; and he, more than once, consulted his companion by a glance, but the other did not, or would not understand him. Both, however, appeared equally enchanted, and the old gentleman frequently gave utterance to his applause.

"Strange I never heard that legend before," he exclaimed, when the ballad was concluded. "Were you acquainted with it, Mr. Roper ?"

MY OLD COMPLAINT.

P. 77.

"I have heard something like it, sir," the steward replied.

"It was related to me by my husband," Rose said; "and I shaped it into the simple ballad you have just heard."

"Sir Reginald Fitzwalter must have been the best, as he was the happiest of his family, if we are to believe this tale," Doctor Plot remarked.

"Let us hope there may yet be others of the family equally good, and equally happy," the steward rejoined.

"Heaven grant it may be so!" Rose ejaculated; "and if Sir Walter's offspring survives, may the good wish alight upon him!"

"On *him!* How know you it was a son?" Doctor Plot replied, regarding her sharply.

"Nay, I know it not," she answered with a smile. "I merely supposed it might be so, and seconded Mr. Roper's kindly aspiration. May happiness be the portion of son or daughter, be it as it may!"

"Amen!" the steward exclaimed, fervently.

Doctor Plot might have chimed in, but his voice was choked, and he could only give utterance to a sob.

"It really does get late," Rose exclaimed, again regarding the clock; and now, with some anxiety. "I wonder what can have detained Frank?"

"Shall I tell you?" Doctor Plot said, regarding her fixedly.

The look somewhat alarmed her. And she was about to inquire, eagerly, as to the nature of the intelligence he had to communicate, when, at the moment, her uneasiness was dispelled by the sound of footsteps in the garden.

"He comes!" she cried, joyfully, springing to her feet, and flying to the door.

But Dragon was quicker than she, and ¹he hound's
instinct told him the footsteps were not his master's.
He looked at her as if in warning, and began to bar
furiously.

"Who is it?" Rose demanded, as some one stopped
at the door, and knocked against it loudly.

"'Tis I," a voice replied—"Sir Gilbert de Montfichet."

"Sir Gilbert de Montfichet?" Rose echoed in surprise, looking round at her companions, both of whom
appeared as much astonished as herself.

X.

THE PIGEON AND THE ROOK.

THE door opened, and the young baronet stepped in.

Another person came after him, and the latter was
so tall that he had to stoop considerably on passing the
threshold, and so bulky, that he had to squeeze through
the door. However, he got in at last, though not
without difficulty.

Sir Gilbert de Montfichet was extremely handsome.
Fine features, fine eyes, and a slight elegant figure—
too slight, perhaps, for a perfect Adonis. There was a
marked air of foppery in his attire, and no doubt it
would have been equally conspicuous in his manner, had
he been entirely master of himself. He was wrapped
in a foreign pelisse, lined with the finest sable, but
this he threw off as he entered the room, showing that
he was habited in a scarlet riding-dress, trimmed with
gold. His flaxen peruke was rather dishevelled, either
from accident or design, his fine lace ruffles were sullied, and his long neckcloth, edged with mechlin, had

MONTFICHET COMPELLING CAPTAIN JUDDOCK TO
APOLOGISE TO ROSE.

P. 79.

FLITCH OF BACON.

got awry. His gait was somewhat unsteady, and his
speech had a thickness in it, not usual with him. He
wore jack boots, and had a silver-hilted sword by his
side ; and in his hand he carried a heavy hunting-whip,
a crack of which sent Dragon growling into a corner.

The young baronet, on entering, took off his richly-
laced and feathered hat, and bowing as ceremoniously
as the unsteadiness of his gait permitted, to Rose, apologised for the intrusion. He seemed somewhat surprised
and disconcerted by the appearance of Doctor Plot and
the steward, who had risen on his appearance, and
looked as if he wished them at the deuce; but Rose,
who was evidently much annoyed by the unexpected
visit, implored them, by a gesture, to stay. And they
complied.

Doctor Plot, in fact, had no desire to go. He appeared profoundly interested by Sir Gilbert de Montfichet, and kept his eye steadily fixed on him.

The young baronet now thought it necessary to introduce his friend; and the large gentleman in question, who had stood a little aloof, with his head almost
touching the ceiling, now came forward, kicking out
a pair of enormous funnel-topped boots in which his
huge legs were encased, jerking himself to and fro,
sticking out his elbows, twirling his hat with the points
of his fingers, and making many absurd grimaces,
until he finally delivered himself of an obsequious bow
to Rose.

Captain Juddock really was a giant, and might have
been exhibited with effect at Bartlemy Fair. Indeed
he had appeared there, for aught we know to the contrary. Though he occasionally put on a ferocious air,
and endeavoured to heighten its effect by a black horse-
hair wig pulled down over his brows, Juddock was a
good-natured fellow, and little disposed to be quarrel-

some. Giants are generally good-tempered. However,
it suited the captain's purpose to give himself a belli-
cose look, and adopt a braggadocio manner; so he wore
a long blade by his side, with a brass handle, and a
long black sheath, tipped with brass; a great brass
buckle on his belt; brass buttons on his blue military
coat; brass spurs on his heels; brass chains and brass
epaulettes; so that he might well say of himself, as
he not unfrequently did say, that " he looked as bold as
brass." His countenance had rather a bloated, bran-
dified look; and his red gills hung over his collar like
a turkey's wattles. Very likely he had been drinking,
as well as the young baronet. But he was a seasoned
cask, and did not show it.

After bringing himself as nearly as he could to the
ground, but which only reduced his head to the level
of those of other people, Juddock drew up again, and
regarding Rose with an impudent leer, said, in a stentorian voice, to Montfichet :

" Gadzookers! Sir G., this cannot be the gamekeeper's wife. You told me she was a beauty—but
this is an angel—a seraphic creature. If she should
belong to the gamekeeper, he must look well to his
own preserves. Hang me, if we sha'n't all turn
poachers—ha! ha!"

" Prithee, hold thy confounded tongue, Jack," Sir
Gilbert replied, laughing, " or thou wilt get us both
turned out of the house at once."

" Hang me if I go," Captain Juddock rejoined,
bringing himself to anchor upon a chair that cracked
beneath his ponderous weight. " You may evaporate
if you think proper, Sir G.; but split me if I stir a
step."

" Pray pardon him, Rose," Sir Gilbert said. " My
friend Jack is a droll dog. But there's no harm in him."

"I should think not," replied the gigantic individual, with a wink—"any more than there is in this pigeon-pie, to which I mean to address myself. My ride from Stansted House has given me an appetite."

"'Sdeath! captain, you're not going to begin again?" Montfichet cried. "You ate enough to satisfy a trooper two hours ago — to say nothing of the punch after dinner."

"A mere trifle—a mere trifle, Sir G. Nothing to what I get through generally. Don't mind me, Mrs. W. I'm accustomed to make myself at home."

"So it appears, sir," the steward observed, rather amused by the giant's familiarity.

"Always do, sir," the captain responded. "At home wherever I go. Quite unceremonious, as you see. Happy to make your acquaintance—and your's too, sir," he added, nodding to Mr. Roper and Doctor Plot, the latter of whom regarded him with disgust.

As he spoke, Juddock applied himself industriously to the viands set out for poor Frank's supper. It was wonderful to see how rapidly he disposed of them, and what huge mouthfuls he swallowed.

"Your friend is a very strange person, Sir Gilbert," Rose said, with a look of reproach at the young baronet. "Why did you bring him here? Why did you come at all?"

"I'll tell you why I came, presently, Rose," replied Montfichet. "I cannot speak before these people. Would to the devil they were gone! What are they doing here. Old Roper I know, but who's the other?"

"Doctor Plot."

"And who the deuce is Doctor Plot? I'm no wiser, Rose."

"He was physician, I believe, to the Fitzwalter family," she replied, with some hesitation.

"Ah! indeed!" he cried; a sudden flush dying his handsome countenance.

"He came in with Mr. Roper, who has business with my husband. Frank will be home presently."

"I don't think he will," Montfichet replied, with a significant smile.

"Why not?" she demanded, uneasily.

At this moment Captain Juddock, having cleared out the pie-dish, applied to the brown jug, and finding it empty, elevated his voice as follows:

"My dear Mrs. W., I make no doubt you've a prime tap here. The pie was excellent, and the ale can't be otherwise. Might I trouble you to fill the jug, ma'am?"

"You have not answered my inquiry about the cause of my husband's absence, Sir Gilbert," Rose said. "You appear to know something."

"I *do* know something. But pray get that noisy fellow some ale, or there will be no peace."

And as she unwillingly complied, he went towards the table, and slapping the captain on his stalwart shoulder, said: "Recollect, Jack, that you are not in a tavern. 'Sdeath! man, behave properly. Be agreeable, if you can."

"Behave properly, Sir G.! I should like to see the man with better manners than J. J. Let me offer you a pinch of snuff. Help yourselves, gentlemen," he added, handing the box to the others. "I believe that's making myself agreeable. Zounds, sir! is that the way to return a civility?" he roared, as Doctor Plot threw the snuff-box impatiently on the table.

A look, however, from Montfichet restrained him, and the appearance of a foaming jug of ale at the same moment completely restored him to good-humour. He endeavoured to kiss the tips of Rose's fingers as she gave him the jug, but she hastily withdrew her hand.

"Trying to make myself agreeable," he said, with a wink at the young baronet. No go. Try again presently."

Having poured out a glass of ale, and smacked his lips over it, he addressed himself to Rose.

" Perhaps, you'd like a song, ma'am. I'm considered a good voice by the bloods at the Cocoa Tree; and Sir G. himself gives me the preference to Signor Tramontano Falsetto, of the Italian Opera House—don't you, Sir G.? You shall judge for yourself, Mrs. W. My song will explain the alarming state in which I found myself a short time ago. I'll just wet my whistle, and begin."

And without waiting for further encouragement, in a voice richer and mellower than might have been expected, he struck up the following ditty :

My Old Complaint.

ITS CAUSE AND CURE.

I.

I'm sadly afraid of my Old Complaint—
  Dying of thirst.—Not a drop I've drunk
For more than an hour: 'Tis too long to wait.
  Wonderful how my spirits have sunk !
      Provocation enough it is for a saint,
      To suffer so much from my Old Complaint !

II.

What is it like, my Old Complaint?
  I'll tell you anon, since you wish to know.
It troubles me now, but it troubled me first,
  When I was a youngster, years ago !
      Bubble-and-squeak is the image quaint ;—
      Of what it is like, my Old Complaint !

III.

The Herring, in very few minutes, we're told,
  Loses his life, ta'en out o' the sea ;
Rob me of Wine, and you will behold
  Just the same thing happen to me.
      Thirst makes the poor little Herring so faint ;—
      Thirst is the Cause of my Old Complaint !

G

IV.

The bibulous Salmon is ill content,
  Unless he batheth his jowl in brine:
And so, my spirits are quickly spent,
  Unless I dip *my* muzzle in Wine!
      Myself in the jolly old Salmon I paint:—
      WINE is the Cure of my Old Complaint.
      Give me full bottles and no restraint,
      And little you'll hear of my Old Complain

V.

I never indulge in fanciful stuff,
  Or idly prate, if my flagon be full ;
Give me good Claret, and give me enough,
  And then my spirits are never dull.
      Give me good Claret and no constraint ;
      And I soon get rid of my Old Complaint!
      Herring and Salmon my friends will acquaint
      With the Cause and the Cure of my Old Complaint!

Whatever effect the captain's ditty might have produced elsewhere, it had little success now : the only
person who laughed heartily being Sir Gilbert, though
a smile was wrung from Mr. Roper.

"I must entreat you to take this man away, Sir
Gilbert," Rose said. "I am sure his presence—and
indeed yours—will be an annoyance to Frank ; and if
you really desire to oblige me, and render me a service,
you will go."

"Put Frank out of the question for a moment, Rose,"
Montfichet rejoined. "Is my presence really irksome
to *you ?*"

"Since you ask me the question, I must reply plainly
that it is. Nor could I have permitted you to stay
so long, if those two gentleman had not been present."

"Deuce take 'em for being in the way!" Montfichet
muttered. "Well, you shan't dismiss me till I've said
what I came to say. It is this. My dear Rose—for
my dear Rose you must always be—if you happen to
want a friend—you may count upon me."

"I do not understand you, Sir Gilbert."

"Yet, I've spoken distinctly enough, methinks. I

beg to offer my services as a friend—a friend whose purse is at your disposal—and that's the kind of friend you don't meet with every day, eh, Jack?"

"Very true, Sir G." the captain rejoined. He was still busy with the jug of ale. "An excellent remark, and particularly applicable to the present circumstances. Your health, Mrs. W., and may you never want two friends like Sir G. de M. or your humble servant, J. J."

This piece of impertinence roused Rose's spirit. With a look of offended dignity, and flashing eyes, she said to the young baronet :

"I will not comment upon your choice of acquaintance, Sir Gilbert, though it does little credit to your taste or discernment. But I will not have such a person as this intruded on me; and I call upon you as a gentleman, to rid my house of him at once."

The young baronet seemed seized with sudden fury. He rushed up to the giant, and laying his puny hand on the latter's brawny shoulder, he succeeded at last in getting hold of his collar, and dragging him by it to where Rose was standing, compelled the unwieldly monster to go down on his knees before her. In this posture, with the jug in one hand and the glass in the other, the leviathan's appearance was so ludicrous, that even Rose could scarcely refrain from laughter.

"Apologise instantly, dog," Montfichet cried, with mock fury, holding the point of his drawn sword towards him—"or, by all that's terrible, I'll cut your throat."

"You may cut it with pleasure, if you're so minded, Sir G.," Captain Juddock rejoined, "but as long as it remains unslit, I must continue to express the wish that our lovely acquaintance may ever find a friend like you."

"Up with you, incorrigible buffoon," Montfichet

cried, hitting him with the flat of his weapon. "And do you pardon him too, Rose," he added, as the giant retreated to the table—"for the fellow means no offence. Pardon me, also," he continued, in an altered tone, and with as much feeling as he could assume, "for my intrusion, and do not reproach me too severely for my choice of wild companions. I have been reckless ever since you refused me, Rose. I have sought relief in riot—in excess—but I have not found it. You know not how I have loved you, Rose—how much I love you still."

"I do not wish to know it," she replied, coldly.

"Yes, you must—you *shall*," the young baronet passionately exclaimed.

"And he would have thrown himself at her feet, but for the interposition of Doctor Plot, who now confronted him.

"No more of this, Sir Gilbert de Montfichet," the old gentleman said, sternly "You forget what is due to Mrs. Woodbine and to yourself."

"I shall not forget to chastise your insolence, sir," the young baronet cried, in a transport of real rage.

"Look at me well, Sir Gilbert, before you attempt to put your threat into execution. Look at me well. Have you never seen me before?"

The tone in which these words were uttered, startled every hearer, but especially him to whom they were addressed. He *did* look at the old gentleman, but he speedily averted his gaze, as if appalled by the glances darted against him, and the firm and even majestic demeanour of the speaker. He made no answer to the question.

"You now know, I perceive, with whom you have to deal, and will not repeat your threats," Doctor Plot pursued. "Away! young man—away!—and take your low-bred and reprobate associate with you."

"Ho! ho! What's this?" Captain Juddock roared, starting to his feet. "'Low-bred' and 'reprobate!'—those be pretty terms to apply to a gentleman like myself, holding his Majesty's commission, and who has served under the Duke of C. Zounds and fury! I will crop the base old curmudgeon's ears close to his pate, as the hangman shears the rogues' heads at the pillory."

"Which same pillory you are likely to grace yourself, sirrah, if you be not careful, for I know you as well as your master," Doctor Plot rejoined, drily, and without betraying a particle of apprehension. "Take hence your man, Sir Gilbert."

"'Sblood! sir—'master and man!' Do you take me for Sir G.'s lacquey?" the giant roared.

"'Tis the fittest post he could appoint you to," Doctor Plot retorted.

Juddock's rejoinder was cut short by Montfichet, who bade him, authoritatively, hold his peace; adding, "I have no desire to quarrel with this gentleman."

"Oh! that entirely alters the case," the easily mollified captain observed; "if you do not quarrel with him, Sir G., neither do I. Though I could crack him in pieces, joint by joint, and think no more of eating him afterwards, than I would a boiled lobster."

With this rhodomontade speech, he clapped on his hat, and swaggered towards the door, planting himself before it.

"Before I leave, Rose," Montfichet said—(he was quite sobered by the recent occurrence, and adopted a different tone and demeanour)—"before I leave, let me explain the real object of my visit. I do not desire to distress you; but I accidentally heard—only half an hour ago—that your husband had been arrested for a debt of two hundred pounds; and I hurried hither at once, to offer you the money to release him. Will you permit me to place this pocket-book in your hands?"

"And so put her under a painful obligation to you," Doctor Plot rejoined, with severity. "No, Sir Gilbert, Mrs. Woodbine will not accept it. She can dispense with your assistance. She has friends to whom she need not scruple to apply, and whose motives are perfectly disinterested."

"You do me wrong, sir," Montfichet cried. "I have no such design as you appear to attribute to me."

"You may thank yourself for incurring the imputation, Sir Gilbert. Your own conduct has given rise to it," the old gentleman rejoined.

"I seem as if I were in a dream," Rose cried. "Things pass around me which I imperfectly comprehend, though I listen to them with wonder and uneasiness. Is it really true, sir, that my husband has been arrested?" she added, appealing to Plot.

"Perfectly true," the old gentleman replied; "but since I engage my word for the payment of the money, I imagine it will be sufficient for the creditor, who is no other than Mr. Roper."

"Mr. Roper—I still dream," Rose cried, bewildered.

"I am only the agent for Squire Monkbury," the steward cried, advancing. "However," your husband is free. Here is the bond which he signed. Give it him on his return. I will now go back to the Flitch, where he has been temporarily detained, and send him to you. Gracious goodness! what can all this disturbance be about?"

The last exclamation was occasioned by a great noise

in the garden, occasioned by the loud clatter of many voices in various tones and keys. Dragon, too, who had been tolerably quiet of late, now joined in the uproar. On the application of some knocks against it, the door was opened by Captain Juddock, who retreated before the tumultuous assemblage that flowed in, almost filling the cottage.

The crowd consisted of the whole of the Bachelors and Maidens, with several of the Dunmow townsfolk, headed by Jonas Nettlebed and his wife, and including the two bailiffs.

"Oh! Mr. Roper!—oh, sir!" Jonas cried, as soon as he could find breath for utterance. "We've lost him, sir. He has escaped. And the bailiffs declare I must pay the money."

"His better 'alf aided and abetted the escape, so in course he must," Isaacson said.

"Yes, that stands to law," Latcham added. "Husbands is always liable for their wives—eh, Isaac?"

"Either you must pay, or he," the steward rejoined, scarcely able to refrain from laughing outright at the ludicrous distress of Jonas.

"You see how it is, ducky," Nelly said. "There's no getting out of the scrape. Pay the money without more ado."

"It's all very well to say 'pay'—but where is it to come from, I should like to know! How could you be so foolish as to help him to get off?"

"Recollect, my dear," Nelly replied, in an undertone. "We're *before people*. The Jury of Bachelors and Maidens is present."

"By the marry maskins! so it is," he rejoined. "I quite forgot the Jury. Well, if I must do it, I must. Ahem! Mr. Roper—I declare the words stick in my throat—about this debt—this two hundred pounds—

couldn't you come down a little in the amount—say half——"

"Impossible, Mr. Nettlebed."

"A hundred and fifty ?"

"Quite out of the question."

"Oh! dear! it's a large sum of money.   It was all Mrs. Nettlebed's doing—not mine—as the bailiffs can bear witness."

"No matter, sir.   You are liable, unless you repudiate your wife's acts—and then good-by to your chance of the Flitch."

"Sooner than that, I'll do it," Jonas cried, with a desperate effort, and plunging his hand into his pocket. "You see what a sacrifice I'm obliged to make, Mrs. Woodbine ?"

"The sacrifice is unneeded, Mr. Nettlebed," Rose answered with a smile.   "I won't keep you a moment longer in suspense.   The debt is already discharged.   I hold the bond in my hand, as you perceive."

"Huzza! Sing 'Oh be joyful!' " Jonas exclaimed, capering round his wife, with delight.   "You see how ready I was to comply with your wishes, my dear— even to my own personal inconvenience."

"Your compliance was very reluctant," she rejoined. "You don't deserve the least credit for it."

The announcement that the debt was settled seemed to give general satisfaction to everybody except the bailiffs, and they had little opportunity of expressing any opinion at all; for they were both forcibly ejected from the door by Captain Juddock, who applied the points of his big boots to them as they disappeared. After performing this feat, he strutted up to Mrs. Nettlebed, whose charms had attracted his attention from the moment of her appearance.

"Mercy on us! what a fine man!" she mentally ejaculated, eyeing Juddock as he advanced. "Why he'd make half a dozen of Jonas, I declare. He's just like Tregonna, the Cornish giant I saw in the booth at Chelmsford fair, last May."

"Monstrous pretty woman that, Sir G.," the captain observed, intending the remark to be overheard. "Who is she?"

"The very voice of Tregonna," Nelly thought.

"Oh, that's Mrs. Nettlebed—hostess of the Dunmow Flitch," the young baronet replied. "A deuced pretty woman, as you say, Jack. That's her husband," pointing to Jonas. "Folks say they mean to claim the Flitch."

"That's all gammon," Jack replied in a lower tone. "Nobody claims the Flitch now-a-days. If they do win it, I must come in for a rasher. I've heard the old inn is the best in Essex, and have half a mind to take up my quarters there for a few days."

"Not a bad idea. We'll sleep there to-night instead of riding back to Stansted. In spite of what has occurred, I've not given up all designs here."

"You're not the mettlesome spark I take you for, if you have," Jack replied.

Having been ogling her tenderly all the time, the amorous captain now thought it time to address Mrs. Nettlebed, and met with little discouragement. As to Jonas, he vainly attempted to call her to order, by reminding her that she was "before people." The giant soon sidled him out of the way, and managed to get her little hand under his huge elbow, preparatory to setting out. This important point achieved, he bestowed a prodigious wink on the young baronet.

Simon Appleyard, meanwhile, had taken the opportunity of conferring with Rose, telling her, on the part of the Jury and himself, that they should pay her a visit on some early occasion, when they might be sure of finding her husband as well as herself at home, and when they might be able to put the necessary inquiries to them both relative to the qualifications for the honourable prize, for which they were understood to be claimants. To this Rose returned a suitable answer, and in Frank's name and her own, expressed the pleasure it would give them to receive them.

Congratulations then followed on all sides on Frank's good luck, and everybody regretted that he was not there to be made acquainted with it. But he would be home soon, of that they were quite sure. If not, somebody was sure to meet him, and could tell him what had happened.

Nelly was the only person who really did know what had become of him ; but she kept her own counsel. When her husband and the bailiffs rushed into the garden, by the back door, they found her alone. The young gamekeeper, she declared, had leapt the wall and got off. But this was not the case. She had locked him in the cellar, putting the key in her pocket, and to the best of her belief he was there still.

Doctor Plot and Mr. Roper now took leave. The old gentleman received Rose's warmest thanks, and promised to call upon her on the morrow. Simon Appleyard took the arm of Lucy Flowerdew, the maiden appertaining to him ; made his bow and exit ; and the rest of the Bachelors followed his example. Captain Juddock, of course, continued to keep Mrs. Nettlebed's arm under his own, greatly to the perturbation of Jonas ; but neither looks, nudges, nor any other remonstrances availed to disturb the arrangement. So Jonas was obliged to walk behind them, looking like a dwarf in the wake of a giant.

Sir Gilbert de Montfichet was the last to depart. He

lingered for a moment in the hope of exchanging one look, one word, with Rose. He obtained neither. She did not raise her head till he had closed the door. And when he turned to gaze at her from the garden, he found the curtain drawn across the window.

What passed through Sir Gilbert's mind then, as he followed the laughing party before him, we shall not pause to inquire.

He found his servant with the horses waiting for him where he left him; mounted his steed, and rode to the Flitch. For reasons of his own, Captain Juddock went on foot. The groom led his horse to the Old Inn.

Everybody, except poor Jonas, enjoyed the walk home. Though it was excessively cold, nobody found it out. How they looked at the moon! how they tried to count the stars! what nice astronomical observations they made! and how pretty they all thought the old Priory Church. Just the place to be married at with the chance of the Flitch hereafter, Simon Appleyard remarked to Lucy Flowerdew. On which all the other bachelors laughed, as if a good thing had been said; and the whole of the six maidens simpered in reply.

As to Juddock and Nelly, they sometimes walked quick, sometimes slow—but there was no getting rid of Jonas. He regulated his pace by theirs; and was for ever beside them. Even if he stumbled in a slippery place, he managed to get up so quickly, as not to lose ground. Little notice of him was taken by his wife, who seemed vastly entertained by her companion, and laughed immensely at his jokes.

At last they reached the Old Inn. Sir Gilbert they found had preceded them; and Jonas, thinking all safe now, hurried forward to attend to the important guest. Ill-judging man! When Carroty Dick appeared at the door with a lantern, he thought he saw the gigantic gentleman bringing down his head very close to that of his mistress; but when the ostler related this incident afterwards to Peggy, she delared it was all a mistake, and that his eyes must have deceived him. He was always seeing things he oughtn't to see.

Nelly's first business was to go to the cellar. She unlocked the door, and called to Frank to come out. No answer. She went in.

The cellar was of considerable size, forming part of some old, disused vaults. Could he have got into these, and have tumbled into some dreadful hole, of which she was unaware? She went on, as far as she dared, looking around in fear and trembling.

No traces of him whatever : all she could see being her own shadow on the walls incrusted and shining with nitre ; all she could hear the echo of her own voice, hollowly returned from the arched roof. A terrible fright she was in.

But we must leave her, and return to the cottage.

Rose was left alone ; pondering over the strange things that had taken place ; and anxiously expecting her husband.

She had to wait for him long. Midnight came, and he had not returned.

She could bear it no longer. So wrapping herself in her cloak, and attended by Dragon, she went forth, and directed her steps towards the Old Inn.

Part the Second.

THE LORD OF THE MANOR OF LITTLE DUNMOW.

I.

AN ESSEX FOXHUNTER OF THE OLD SCHOOL.

MARK MONKBURY, Esquire, of Monkbury Place, commonly known as " the Squire " in that part of the country, where most of the resident gentry could boast of some title or other, being either baronets or peers ; Squire Monkbury, we say, was the owner of an ancient house, which he kept up at a bountiful rate, and the lord of many acres which had been in the possession of his family for centuries. There was not in the whole county of Essex, nor in any other county, a gentleman's house where hospitality was more profusely or more constantly exercised than at Monkbury Place. It was almost always full of visitors, and some of them stayed a long time, though scarcely ever longer than was agreeable to the host. The Squire was a true lover of country life, and abominated town, though he knew little about it, except by report, and could never be induced to go up to London. Indeed, he only went to the county town when compelled to do so by a summons to the Quarter Sessions, or by the desire to witness a horse race on Gallywood Common. His own estate, which was of considerable size, and came within a few miles of Dunmow, closely adjoining that of Sir Gilbert de Montfichet, afforded him admirable hunting, coursing, shooting, and fishing ; and in all these sports he delighted, pursuing them with nearly the same ardour, now that sixty years had flown over his head, that

he did in the season of his hottest youth.   He kept
a capital pack of hounds ; was constantly in exercise ;
and could not live without it, he said, though he never
made any trial how staying in-doors would agree with
him, except when he broke his arm or his collar-bone
from falls received while hunting ; and even these accidents did not keep him quiet long.   As to minor ail-
ments, he was never troubled with them, and enjoyed a
redundancy of health and animal spirits.   Indeed, he
had never known a day's real illness.   His countenance
was fresh and ruddy, beaming with health and good
humour ; and though he indulged rather too freely in
the pleasures of the table, and was, perhaps, somewhat
too convivial in his habits (it must be recollected it was
rather a hard-drinking age), these practices did not
appear to have impaired his vigorous constitution ;
though he did not ride so light, by some stones, as he
did at thirty, in spite of all his exercise.

Squire Monkbury was a confirmed old bachelor,
though by no means indifferent to the sex, and indeed
he was rather gallant than otherwise ; but he could
never be induced to commit matrimony, nor to listen
to any suggestions of the sort made to him by friends.
Country gossips pretended to assign as a reason for
this, that he had sustained a great disappointment
many years ago, and had never been able to get over it ;
but sentiment had so little share in the squire's composition, that it is scarcely probable this could have been
the real cause.   One thing is quite certain ; namely,
that he resisted all overtures made to him of a matrimonial nature.   People talked to him of the necessity
of having an heir to his ancient name and his large
property ; but even this argument, though sufficiently
cogent, one would think, failed in effect.   He shrugged
his shoulders, laughed, and said he had not yet arrived

at years of discretion. When he did, he might think of marrying—not before. If the truth must be confessed, the squire was almost as rank an unbeliever as Doctor Plot himself in conjugal felicity; and though he had no such experience as had fallen to the other's share, on which to found his opinions, he maintained them as stoutly as if he had. The freedom and happiness of a bachelor's life was ever the burden of his song; and his married acquaintance, of all degrees, were his constant butts. Not that he hit them very hard. He was too good-natured for that. But he liked a joke at their expense; and rarely omitted it.

Of late some change had been wrought in the squire's establishment by the introduction of a niece, confided to him by his only near relative—a sister who had died in a distant part of England. About a year ago, Bab Bassingbourne came to live with him. She was then a lovely girl of seventeen, and had now ripened into a perfect beauty. The squire had become uncommonly fond of her, and she did just what she liked with him. He who would never submit to the control of a wife, was now ruled by his niece. Sooth to say, the yoke was so easy, that he never felt it. Bab suited him exactly. She loved a Country Life quite as well as he, and never talked of Town, unless to decry it. She shared in almost all his sports and exercises, and regularly hunted with him. She managed his house; and managed it remarkably well too, as he soon found, by the improvement that took place in it. She did not interfere with his general arrangements, but kept him a little more select in his acquaintances; and he speedily perceived the benefit of the change. In short, the arrival of Bab Bassingbourne at Monkbury Place formed an important epoch in the history of its owner. In one particular, Bab especially resembled her uncle;

and this was in a decided aversion to matrimony. She rejected all offers, and plenty were made her, when it became known she was to be the squire's heiress. What was more, she could not tolerate the society of young men, and if any one approached her in the character of a suitor, he was sure (if she suspected it) to meet with a disagreeable reception. Such was the niece, whom hereafter we may have the pleasure of introducing in person to the reader. Our immediate business is with the uncle.

One important item in the description of Squire Monkbury must not be omitted. In addition to his other signorial rights, he was Lord of the Manor of Little Dunmow : a circumstance which, if he had possessed no other title to his respect, would have given him paramount importance in the eyes of Jonas Nettlebed. As Donor of the Flitch, Jonas regarded him with an awe little short of veneration. The Lordship of Little Dunmow was originally granted by Henry the Eighth on the suppression of the Priory to Robert, Earl of Sussex, but afterwards passed into the possession of other families, until it was eventually purchased some fifty years back by General Monkbury, and now formed part of the territorial property of his son.

A popular man was the squire ; popular with his neighbours ; popular with his tenantry ; popular with everybody, except the poacher, whom he dealt with pretty strictly. The only kind of vagrant he tolerated was the gipsy, and he confessed to a sneaking liking to this licensed vagabond, and seldom disturbed him, when his tent was pitched in his lanes, or on his commons. The squire had a kind word with all, and made little distinction as to classes in his style of address, though on the other hand, he would permit no undue familiarity, and indeed such was never attempted with him. With the wives of his tenantry, and their daughters, he was especially affable and condescending, and was an immense favourite with them in consequence. He liked to attend their marriages and christenings ; standing godfather now and then ; sometimes giving a pretty girl away, when there was no one else to do so ; and in such cases he never failed to bestow a little marriage-portion adequate to the circumstances. As Justice of the Peace, his functions were satisfactorily enough discharged, and his decisions rarely called in question ; though they were often given according to his own particular view of the case, rather than in entire accordance with strict rules of law. He was a staunch upholder of Church and State, and though he took no very active part in the Rebellion of '45, he had raised a troop at his own expense in '15. His sympathies were not on the side of the Stuarts, whom he looked upon as inimical to the Protestant Faith, and the true interests of the realm. A regular attendant at his little church in the park, he would once upon a time constantly slumber through the sermon, and keep up a tolerably loud bass accompaniment to the discourse of the chaplain, the Reverend Jeremy Bush ; but of late this habit had been corrected in him, in a great degree, by his niece, and though even she failed sometimes in making him keep his eyes open, she managed to check his snoring.

Very bountiful was the squire, and very charitable. His house was full of ancient servitors and retainers, many of them as old as himself, and some few older. Paul Flitwick, the first whipper-in who was with him, was full fifteen years his senior, though still a hale old fellow. The squire's entertainments were not confined to his wealthy friends. Humbler guests often sat at his board ; and those whom he did not care to admit to his own table were sent to the servant's hall, where he himself would see them regaled. None entered Monk-

H

bury Place without partaking, in some way or other, of
its lord's hospitality.

The squire's habiliments were of an antiquated cut.
Abhorring modern fashions, he stuck to the style of
dress in vogue in William the Third's time—whose
glorious memory he held in especial reverence, and
daily toasted.   And as the costume of that period was
far handsomer than any that had succeeded it, he could
not be blamed for his predilection.   He wore the broad-
leaved Spanish-looking hat, the flowing peruke, the long
graceful riding-dress (altogether different in make,
though similar in colour, being scarlet, to that of Sir
Gilbert de Montfichet), and flexible boots which could
either be drawn down or pulled high up on the thigh.

The squire's personal appearance was highly pre-
possessing. His broad, handsome, and thoroughly
Saxon physiognomy, was radiant with health and good
humour.   In height he was somewhat under six feet,
broad in the shoulders, stout in the leg, and portly in
person. His manner was hearty, yet not wanting in a
certain sort of dignity. His bright blue eye sparkled
with fun and enjoyment.

Doctor Sidebottom, Vicar of Dunmow, was a boon
companion of the squire ; and many a haunch of veni-
son had they consumed together, many a bottle of old
wine discussed in concert. The squire had been dining
at the Vicarage now, and as it was not unusual in those
days of good fellowship for gentlemen to adjourn to a
tavern after dinner, he expressed a wish to have a bowl
of punch at the Flitch, where he knew it was admirably
brewed, and the jovial vicar, nothing loth, agreed to
accompany him and partake of it.

Broad in the beam, and heavily laden with flesh
generally, was Doctor Sidebottom, and rather unwieldy
in his movements in consequence.   His long loose

waistcoat, with immense pockets flapping down to his knees, very imperfectly concealed his excessive obesity, and his enormous calves, protected by an under covering of lamb's-wool, bulged out his silken hose. He always appeared in his cassock and bands, well-powdered bushy wig, and clerical hat, looped up at the sides, with a huge rose in front. The doctor's face was large and dull, with great pasty cheeks, and a broad flat nose. With his equals or superiors he was friendly and familiar enough, but pompous and patronising to his inferiors. The highest of high churchmen was the doctor; rigorously orthodox; regarding any species of dissent as infinitely worse than infidelity.

A thin, frosty, but tough, wiry, hatchet-faced old fellow was Paul Flitwick. He had lost all his teeth, and his nose and chin rattled like a pair of nutcrackers, but though he mumbled in his talk, and over his food, old Paul could blow a horn, vociferate in the field, or utter any sort of huntsman's cry with the loudest or shrillest of them. His seat was still firm in the saddle; his judgment perfect; his knowledge of the country unequalled by that of any younger hand; and his whip was not a bit lighter than it used to be, as any faulty hound was sure to discover. Paul's costume would not have found favour with a modern huntsman; the only article bearing any resemblance to existing equipments being the jockey-cap. Boots, leathers, and jacket were all of a bygone day and bygone mode: but, like himself, they had known more wear and tear, than was ever perhaps experienced by the habiliments of his smartest successors, and were made for work, not show. In spite of his attire, and his years, old Paul was a very keen blade, and had a thoroughly sporting air.

Such were the three personages who now approached the Dunmow Flitch.

II.

THE WAGER.

To be sure, the disturbance Captain Juddock's arrival had occasioned at the Old Inn.

He threatened to turn it topsy-turvy. For some time, nothing was heard, but the clatter of his enormous boots, and the roar of his stentorian voice: singing, swearing, shouting—all in a breath. The old chairs were not safe for him—he broke the back of one in sitting down; and the solid oak table shook beneath the unaccustomed weight as he flung himself upon it. But he was never quiet for three minutes together. He must be doing something. And as Nelly had gone to the cellar (for a purpose we wot of), and had not returned, he began to make love to pretty Peggy, chucking her under the chin, and whisking her towards the mistletoe bough, which his quick eye detected in the recess; but his purpose was interrupted by Carroty Dick, who, planting himself in front of the window, forbade all approach to the sacred branch. During the scuffle that ensued, Peggy managed to make her escape, and Dick followed her in double quick time, his movements being accelerated by an application of one of the baffled giant's large boots.

All this had been witnessed, with many internal qualms, by Jonas, who bitterly bewailed the hour that had brought such an overgrown and unruly monster, to disturb the peace and comfort of his dwelling. He feared there would be no getting rid of him, since the impudent and intrusive rascal had once obtained a lodgment. Something dreadful was sure to happen: the long-coveted Flitch, itself, was in feaful jeopardy.

The circumstances seemed critical. He tried to sum-

ARRIVAL OF THE SQUIRE, THE VICAR, AND THE OLD
WHIPPER-IN AT THE FLITCH.

P. 102.

mon up his courage: to feel like a man. But the blustering deportment of the giant unnerved him; and his chicken heart quailed. However, he expostulated with himself; and got to the sticking-point, just as Peggy and Dick had taken to their heels A fitting occasion for a respectable landlord's interference, who piqued himself on maintaining decorum in his house.

Jonas coughed rather loudly to attract the giant's attention and clear his own throat. Juddock echoed back the sound from his mighty lungs in an infinitely louder key, and advancing towards the discomfited landlord, clapped him on the back, with such force, that poor Nettlebed's wig was nearly shaken from his head —water started to his eyes, and his red face grew redder than ever.

"Well, mine host—what now?" the captain exclaimed, in a voice of thunder.

"Really, Captain Juddock," Jonas replied, arranging his wig, and rubbing his shoulders, "I must be permitted to observe that I cannot allow such proceedings in my house. The Flitch is a particularly well-conducted inn, sir—the best in Essex, and it's my pride to keep it so. The servants know their places, the landlord knows his place, and he expects his guests to know theirs. If not, he can dispense with their company. By the marry maskins! I think I've hit him as hard as he hit me. I hope he'll take the hint," he added to himself.

Juddock burst into a great roar of laughter.

"Why, what a punctilious little fellow you must be, landlord!" he cried. "If you dismiss every guest who casts a sheep's eye at your pretty chambermaid, I'll warrant me you'll soon have a clear house. But you regard her as your own property, I conclude, and allow no interference with your rights, eh?—Zounds! man,

never look so sheep-faced.   Mrs. N.'s not by, now.
Where's Sir G. ?   Still in his own room, upstairs, I
suppose.   By-the-by, I must look after my bedchamber.
Tell your wife to show it me."

"I'll show it you, myself," Jonas rejoined, hastily;
"that is, if you're determined to stay all night.   Stop !
let me see.   How unfortunate !—but it can't be helped.
Sorry I can't accommodate you, sir."

"Not accommodate me !" Juddock roared.   "You
MUST.   I shall stay here a week—a month—a year—a
century, perhaps !   I shall NEVER leave !"

"Oh, dear! I thought he wouldn't," Jonas muttered.
"But what's to be done ?   There isn't a spare bed.
Sir Gilbert has taken the last."

"Then I'll sleep on that bench by the fireside," the
captain rejoined.   "Here I remain—that's flat.   You
won't easily get rid of me, landlord.   But I don't believe a word you say.   Mrs. N. told me there was a very
comfortable bed—quite at my service."

"Mrs. N., as you rather too familiarly call her, was
quite mistaken—I assure you she was.   Oh! the Flitch !
the Flitch !   It is written I am never to win it !" he
exclaimed aside.

"Well, we shall see when she makes her appearance,"
Juddock replied.   "Meantime, I'll keep up the fire in
case of accidents."

So saying, he lifted the huge Yule log from the
hearth as easily as if it had been a common fagot, and
tossed it upon the blazing coals, where it presently
began to spit and crackle in emulation.   Jonas could
not repress a groan ; but he was afraid to interfere, lest,
peradventure, he might follow the log.

"And now, landlord, what can we have for supper ?"
the giant demanded.   "The best inn in Essex must have
an excellent larder, especially at Christmas time : cold

chine, cold turkey, cold ham, cold pie, cold plum-pud-
ding,—cold everything, no doubt. But I want something hot — a carbanado—a grill — a devil. You
understand ?"

"Yes, I understand well enough," Jonas rejoined—
"but I'm extremely sorry——"

"More excuses!" Juddock interrupted, knitting his
brows. "Landlord, I will have none of them. Supper
I must have. A hot supper, mark me. The best must
be forthcoming. No paltry makeshifts—no miserable
kickshaws. A couple of wild ducks—nicely roasted
—I know they're in the larder, and who gave them—
Mrs. N. has let me into the secret."

"The devil she has!" Jonas muttered. "Oh! the
Flitch! the Flitch! What *will* become of it ?"

"Then, in the way of tipple, you've some prime
October, I'm given to understand—bright and pale as
sherris—I mean to give my opinion upon it. And
you've also got some wonderful old brandy I'm informed. I shall pronounce upon that, too."

Jonas lifted up his hands in absolute despair.

"The traitress! to tell such a swillbowl as this of
the old brandy."

"You see I've not lost my time, landlord," Juddock
continued, in a self-complacent tone. "Mrs. N. was
very confidential during our walk. I shall know all
your secrets before long. There's one more I've learnt ;
but that's no secret. You expect to carry off the great
matrimonial prize of Dunmow—the Flitch of Bacon.
Don't you wish you may get it? Ho! ho!"

"Most decidedly I do, sir," Jonas rejoined, bristling
up, and picking up a few crumbs of courage, for his
tenderest point had been touched by this sting. "Most
decidedly I do, sir," he repeated, looking up, and
staring the insolent giant in the face; "I not only *do*

wish I may get it, but by the marry maskins! I am certain I *shall* get it; and that's more. Have you any-thing to say to the contrary?"

"Oh, no! nothing at all," Juddock said, still in-dulging in his boisterous merriment. "If you and Mrs. N. choose to take the Oath, that's your concern, not mine."

"To be sure it is; and I don't think it at all likely you will be consulted on the occasion, sir."

"Hum! that remains to be seen," the giant muttered. "Well, I admire your confidence. Now what will you bet, that you don't win this prize after all?"

"What will I bet?" Jonas echoed, rather staggered. "I never do lay wagers."

"But if you're certain to win there can be no harm," the giant rejoined. "I'll lay you Ten Thousand to Fifty, you lose the Flitch."

"By the marry maskins! those are long odds," Jonas exclaimed, opening his eyes to their fullest extent. "Ten Thousand Pounds would be better than the Flitch itself," he muttered. "I'll take him. But he won't pay. These empty boasters never do. How-ever, I'll risk it. Done! captain,—done," he exclaimed, aloud—"I accept your bet. You are to pay me ten thousand pounds if I win the Flitch; but, if I lose it, I must hand you over fifty."

"That's it exactly, landlord," the giant rejoined. "But I shan't give you such a chance as this without a slight reservation."

"I thought not," Jonas observed drily.

"You must pay me a guinea a week till you're enabled to claim it. Not that I want the money—oh! no. I will hand it over to the High Bailiff of Dunmow to be applied to some charitable purpose. But this will bring the bet to an issue. Are you agreed?"

"I think I may safely do it," Jonas reflected. "Four days have only to run before I can legally make the claim—that's under the week. Yes, captain, I *am* agreed," he added, aloud.

"Your hand upon it then," Juddock cried, giving him a terrible squeeze that again drew water to his eyes. "And now, the caution-money?"

"The what?" Jonas cried.

"The guinea. You must pay one week in advance."

"Adzooks! I didn't count upon that," the landlord exclaimed, with a blank look. "Well, here it is," he added, producing a well-filled leather-bag, which seemed to attract the greedy giant's attention, and taking a piece of gold from it. "And now, sir, what security am I to have that you will pay me the ten thousand pounds?"

"What security?" the giant roared, putting on an offended look. "My word, sir. Is not that sufficient?"

"It must be, I suppose. But I would rather have your bond."

"Bond me no bonds—I will sign none of them. My word is my bond, as it is with every man of honour. Captain J. J. never said the thing he didn't maintain. Ten thousand pounds is yours, if fairly won. If not, the fifty pound's mine. That's settled. Book the bet, while I pay a visit to the kitchen, and ascertain, from personal inspection, the state of the larder. I'm an old campaigner, and accustomed to foraging expeditions."

So saying, he put his great clattering boots once more in motion, and marched off towards the back part of the premises.

"Well, I think I have him any way," Jonas soliloquised, looking after him "If he don't pay the bet he'll be obliged to decamp—that's one comfort. But I sadly begrudge my guinea."

The fat cook was in the kitchen, frying eggs and
bacon for the household supper, when the giant made
his appearance, and on perceiving what she was about,
his appetite, which was perfectly Gargantuan, was so
tickled by the inviting dish that he was fain to make
an immediate onslaught upon it, and with that view
endeavoured to snatch the frying-pan from her. But
though taken by surprise, mistress cook would not submit to such an indignity, but threatened to knock the
pan about his ears if he meddled with her; and the
menace had the desired effect, for Juddock turned
away and began to prosecute his examination of the
larder. This soon resulted in a discovery of the wild
ducks, and many other good things which Jonas would
have desired to keep in the background; and tossing
the birds towards the cook, together with a string of
black puddings, the captain bade her prepare them, as
soon as she could, for supper; telling her he would
begin with a dish of eggs and bacon, and conclude
with toasted cheese. These orders being authoritatively delivered, he returned towards the hall, and
meeting Peggy by the way, after again chucking her
under the chin, enjoined her to see them executed.

The pretty chambermaid found the cook quite flus-
tered by what had occurred, and uncertain how to act;
but Peggy told her she had better do as the tall
gentleman had bidden her, for missis was sure to be
content, whatever master might be; and, made easy
by this assurance, the cook finished off the eggs and
bacon, and sat down cheerfully, with Peggy, to pluck
the wild fowl.

On re-entering the hall, Captain Juddock found the
host and hostess and all the principal guests assembled
within it. Sir Gilbert de Montfichet had come down
stairs, and was pacing the chamber, to and fro, by him-

self. Doctor Plot and Mr. Roper were seated near the fire, and a screen being placed round their table afforded them a certain sort of privacy. Doctor Plot's presence was evidently a considerable restraint to the young baronet, and he hailed Juddock's return as a relief, since it gave him some one to talk to, as well as something to laugh at. Thinking Nelly looked uneasy, and attributing her anxiety to a private lecture she might have received from Jonas on his account, Juddock exerted all his powers of pleasantry for her diversion, and speedily succeeded in raising a smile upon her good-natured countenance. Nelly, it must be confessed, was not difficult to amuse. Very little did it. She felt every disposition to be entertained now, but her tendency to merriment was somewhat checked by thoughts of Frank, and speculations as to what had become of him. However, she made no allusion to the cause of her uneasiness, and by-and-by it disappeared altogether: Juddock's merriment was contagious. As to Jonas, though he could not shake off his dislike of the captain, nor feel less distrust in him, he could not help secretly confessing that he was a very droll and diverting fellow, nor avoid laughing at some of his jests. The wager was not without its effect in reconciling him to his troublesome guest.

In anticipation of supper, and to give a whet to his appetite, Juddock called for a jug of ale, and rose still higher in the landlord's opinion by the hearty praise he bestowed on the beverage.

Thus a better understanding prevailed among the party, when a loud rattling was heard at the window, and a " Yoicks ! tally ho !" given by a loud cheery voice, as if at a fox-chase, accompanied by the blowing of a huntsman's horn.

" By the marry maskins ! there's Squire Monkbury,"

Jonas exclaimed. "I should know his holloa wherever I heard it. Wife!—Nelly, get ready to receive him directly!—Coming, your honour, coming!"

"Bless us!" Nelly cried, looking rather annoyed, "what can have brought the squire here at this time of night, I wonder?"

"Can't say," Jonas replied; "but our business is to see what he wants. To the door, wife! to the door! What the deuce is the matter with the woman?"

Nelly, however, paid no attention to his injunctions, but ran off. Before she got half-way up the great staircase her purpose was arrested by the appearance of Squire Monkbury, who opened the door for himself, and stepped in. He was accompanied by Doctor Side-bottom, and followed by Paul Flitwick.

III.

IN WHICH THE TABLES ARE SLIGHTLY TURNED UPON CAPTAIN JUDDOCK; AND JONAS BEGINS TO LOOK UP A LITTLE.

"So HO! little Nelly—so ho!" the squire shouted in his cheery tones, as he caught sight of the landlady on the staircase. "Wearing off, eh? Nay, that won't do. We shall be after you, and in full cry, too, if you attempt to give us the slip. Hark, back! lass, hark, back! Why, you look as blooming and buxom as ever! —prettier, i'faith! Nelly Nettlebed is an improvement upon little Nelly Nodder. Egad! marriage seems to agree with you."

"It agrees with me tolerably well, thank your honour," Mrs. Nettlebed replied, demurely, and without raising her eyes. "Hope your honour is quite well, and the young lady, too?"

"Both hearty, thank ye, Nelly. Well, when you're tired of inn-keeping, you must come and take up your quarters with me. My women are all so abominably old and ugly I can't abide the sight of 'em. Besides, I want a housekeeper."

"Greatly obliged to your honour, I'm sure," Nelly replied, still in the same demure tone, and maintaining the same downcast looks; "but I fancy you are very well provided for in that respect. Miss Bassingbourne is said to be an excellent manager; and I'm sure you cannot complain of want of youth or beauty while she is with you."

"Fairly enough answered, Nelly," the squire rejoined; "but then my niece may not stay with me for ever, you know. One must provide against a rainy day, doctor."

"But not by carrying off Mrs. Nettlebed, I hope, squire," Doctor Sidebottom rejoined, with a fat chuckle. "Her worthy husband, I fancy," pointing to the host, who stood bowing and scraping before them most obsequiously, "would object to such a proceeding."

"Indeed I should, your reverence," Jonas replied. "Nelly is the apple of my eye; and I would not part with her for a king's ransom. I am mainly, if not entirely, indebted for the treasure I possess to his honour himself, since he was instrumental in obtaining Nelly for me."

"Poh-poh! say no more about it, man," the squire rejoined. "No obligation at all."

"Begging your honour's pardon," Jonas said, "I feel it to be a very great obligation, and one I shall never be able adequately to discharge. If your honour will recollect, you were good enough to mention Nelly Nodder to me—to paint her beauties in irresistible language, and to tell me——"

"'Sdeath! never mind what I told you," the squire interrupted.

"Your honour won't deprive me of the satisfaction of repeating it, I'm sure," Jonas pursued. "You told me you took an almost paternal interest in her, and would like to see her well married ; adding, in the most obliging and condescending manner, that she couldn't have a better or more suitable husband than myself. Her mother, your honour said, was a most respectable woman, and had lived with you, as—as—dairy-maid —till——"

"Well—well, we know all this," the squire said, looking rather disconcerted.

"Till she married Tom Nodder your cowherd, who didn't treat her as well as he ought, but went away, and left her with her sweet little babby—my own darling little Nelly that was to be. So your honour had naturally to look after the neglected mother, and became a sort of father to the infant, and a much better father you were than Tom Nodder : and took care of her, until Nelly coming of age, you wanted to see her comfortably settled, and thought I should make her a fitting spouse—and so if I was agreeable (which of course I was) you would engage to bring the matter about."

"Do stop his mouth, Nelly," the squire said.

"And while I was debating it in my mind," Jonas continued, holding his wife, who endeavoured to obey the squire's commands, at arm's length, "you decided me by declaring you would give her a good wedding portion—no, there I'm wrong, that didn't decide me ; but what did, was the assurance given me by your honour, that Nelly was such a sweet, amiable creature, that we couldn't fail to live happily together, and I was certain, through her means, to win the Flitch at last. That clinched it."

"How fond your husband must be of hearing himself talk, Nelly! Have you done now, Jonas?" the squire asked.

"Very nearly," the landlord replied. "To your honour's praise be it spoken, you made good your words in every particular. You brought Nelly and me together. Got us married. Gave the wedding portion. And now you mean to give us the Flitch."

"Halt there, friend Jonas," the squire cried. "That last donation is beyond my control. You must prove your title to it at the Court Baron, and take the Oath before I can confer it upon you. But these conditions I've no doubt you'll be able to fulfil—so I look upon your possession of the prize as a matter of certainty. In recommending Nelly to you, I knew she would do us both credit; and it's quite true, as you asserted, that I took, and always shall take, a paternal interest in her. Nelly was always a good girl—though a bit of a coquette —weren't you, child?—always one of my favourites."

"Your honour has only one favourite now," Nelly observed, somewhat reproachfully, and looking up for the first time. "All others have given place to Miss Bassingbourne."

"And very properly so too," the vicar remarked. "Very properly."

"Well, I confess my niece *is* my chief favourite," the squire rejoined, smiling. "Bab is a girl in a thousand, and suits my tastes exactly. You should see her with the hounds, Nelly. 'Tis a treat. Seat perfect, hand light as a fairy's. No fence can stop her. Clears everything. Always in at the death; and I don't know how many brushes she has got, though she has only

been at it for the last twelvemonth.   Never had a fall.
She knows every hound in the pack—Charon and Ringwood, Towler and Jowler,—just as well as old Paul
himself knows 'em."

"Ay, that a daas, yar han'r, and th' haands knaws
her, too, reet well, blass her pratty fece!" the old
whipper-in remarked.

"'Tis a picture to see her, when animated in the
chase," the squire continued, waxing enthusiastic; "her
countenance lighted up with pleasure and excitement.
Talk about damask roses, and that sort of thing; her
cheeks would put all the roses in my garden to the
blush.   And as to her eyes, they shine, like—I don't
know what—I'm a bad hand at a simile—but diamonds
may do; though they don't come up to the lustre of
Bab's sparklers."

"Udsbores ! a rare lass that, if all old Nimrod says
be true of her.   Have you seen her, Sir G. ?" Captain Juddock inquired of the young baronet, with whom
he had moved a little aside, on the appearance of the
new-comers.

"No; she had not come to Monkbury, when I was
last in Essex—some fifteen months ago," Montfichet rejoined.   "I never heard of her until t'other day, when
I was surprised to learn the squire had a niece residing
with him.   At the same time, I was told of her wonderful achievements in the field.   A perfect Diana, by
all accounts."

"But Miss Bassingbourne does not devote herself
merely to the pleasures of the chase, and out-door
amusements," Doctor Sidebottom remarked.   "Her
great merit in my eyes consists in her being so companionable and amusing in-doors."

"Companionable ! to be sure she is," the squire rejoined.   "She'll rattle away to me by the hour; and

when I'm tired of talking, will sing, or play the harp-sichord, or take a hand at dominoes or backgammon with me."

"Dominoes and backgammon!" Juddock echoed, con-temptuously—"poor sport that! Udsbores! give me doublets or gleek. Hazard is *our* game, Sir G. We like to hear the dice rattle—ha!"

"But as to housekeeping—your honour said the young lady looked after everything?" Nelly inquired.

"So she does," the squire replied; "so she does.— Bab looks after everything and everybody, and me into the bargain. She takes care of house, garden, farm, stables, horses, cattle, sheep, pigs, poultry. Baking, brewing, pickling, preserving, cooking, she's mistress of it all. Nothing comes amiss to her, from the curing of a ham to the making of a marrow-pudding. Her hand is so light at pastry that you might blow her puffs away."

"And no great loss either," Juddock observed. "I prefer something substantial. Crust an inch thick, at the very least. Puffs—pshaw!"

"All trouble is taken off my hands now," the squire pursued. "No more rating of servants. Under Bab's management, they never require scolding. How she does it, is the wonder. 'Miss Bassingbourne likes to have this,' old Mosscrop, the butler says—or 'Miss Bassingbourne prefers that.' Everything is right Miss Bassingbourne does. Her will is law at Monkbury. Nobody grumbles, now, and there was plenty of grum-bling, because the sloths had nothing to do, and at present there is not an idle person about the place. I'm a confirmed old bachelor, as you know, doctor. Feeling quite sure I should never be able to offer any legitimate title to the Flitch, about the possession of which our worthy Jonas is so anxious, I never would marry. But if I had chosen a wife, it should have been one on the model of my niece, Bab Bassingbourne."

"She wouldn't suit us at all, Sir G.," Juddock remarked. "Udsbores! such a girl would govern us, as well as the servants. It's clear she manages *him*."

"It's a wonder Miss Bassingbourne don't marry, since she's so clever, and so beautiful," Nelly observed, in a tone of slight pique; "but I dare say she will, one of these days."

"No, she won't," the squire said. "I've ascertained her opinion on the subject ; and she is quite decided on remaining single. To be sure, it's rather early to come to such a conclusion—seeing she is only just eighteen— but I think she'll adhere to it. At all events, I've had no hand in persuading her. I would never influence her, one way or the other. She will have my fortune, married or not. But she can't bear young men."

"Law! that *is* strange," Nelly exclaimed. "I shouldn't have been surprised if she couldn't bear old ones ; but not to like young men, passes my comprehension. As to changing her condition, I don't know but she may be right in remaining as she is."

"Oh, fie! Nelly—I didn't expect such a sentiment from you," the squire said. "I hope it was uttered inadvertently."

"It was—it was," Jonas interposed hastily. "Your honour mustn't attach the least importance to it. Do be careful," he added, aside, plucking her elbow.

"So it seems this matchless creature, who manages everything and everybody, dislikes us young fellows, and will have nothing to say to us," Juddock observed to Sir Gilbert. "Bodikins! I should like to try her."

"If I could only get Rose out of my head, I would soon satisfy the squire whether his niece's objection to an enterprising coxcomb, like myself, was firmly rooted or not," Montfichet exclaimed. "But hang it! Rose has got possession of my breast, and there's no dislodging her."

"No necessity whatever to do so at present," quoth his mentor. "But zounds! there's a vast deal of exaggeration in what we've just heard about the young lady. Old Nimrod has been sounding the trumpet, because he knew a rich young baronet was close at hand to listen to it. Only a lure, depend on't."

"You know nothing of the squire, Jack, or you wouldn't say so," Sir Gilbert replied. "He's the honestest, most straightforward fellow breathing; incapable of doing anything unbecoming a gentleman. He is not aware of my presence, I'll be sworn!"

And so it proved. For at that moment, the young baronet, who had hitherto been obscured by his towering companion, placed himself within the squire's ken, and was instantly hailed with a view holloa from the latter.

"Whoop! tallyho! why, who'd ha' thought it? Oddslife! if it be not Montfichet! Welcome, Sir Gilbert—welcome back to Essex," the squire exclaimed, advancing to the young baronet, and shaking hands with him cordially. "You've been a long time away from us—leading a gay life in Lunnun, I dare say? That is, you'd call it a gay life; but 'twouldn't suit me. You won't catch the old squire in town, I can promise you. I should be stifled—I know I should. So many houses—such crowded streets—no air, fit to breathe— no horses worth looking at—no hunting, except the Epping Hunt—and that a mere cockney affair, fit only for your fat and greasy citizens. No, no; I'm content with quiet Essex, its fresh air, open country, and healthful amusements. No town-life for me"

"I'm well aware of your taste, squire," Montfichet rejoined ; and so far agree with you, that I'm heartily sick of town, myself."

"Overdone it, eh, Sir Gilbert ?" the squire rejoined, with a laugh. "Pace too fast to keep up—ah !—You left us all on a sudden—I did hear the reason—something about a pretty girl, I think, but I forget what— and now you're come back on a sudden. Not in consequence of another love-affair, I hope ! Glad to see you again, at any rate. You must come over to Monkbury. Can't offer you any hunting just now, as you must be aware, owing to this confoundedly severe weather. Beg pardon, doctor—I ought not to complain of the weather, since it's doing the country so much good, and benefiting my tenantry as well as myself ; but a hard frost always makes a fox-hunter swear. But as I was saying, Sir Gilbert, you must ride over to see me. Come to-morrow morning to breakfast—to breakfast, mind,—and dinner afterwards, of course. I want to make you acquainted with my niece."

"There it comes, Sir G.," the giant whispered the young baronet. "Didn't I say so ?"

"It will charm me to be presented to Miss Bassingbourne," Montfichet said, bowing his acknowledgments. "I hear delightful accounts of her."

"I must prepare you for a strange madcap, Sir Gilbert," the squire rejoined. "Bab's as wilful as a filly that has never known the bridle. You musn't be surprised at any reception you may meet with from her. I let her have her own way completely."

"You pique my curiosity, squire," Montfichet said. "I'm all impatience to behold this charming, untamable creature ; being vain enough to think I may form an exception to the country bumpkins she has hitherto seen, and may be honoured with a smile "

"Well, we shall see, Sir Gilbert,—we shall see. I can't answer for her. But who's your tall friend, eh?"

"Your pardon, squire,—I ought to have introduced him before. Give me leave to present Captain Juddock to you. A town friend, who is staying with me at Stansted."

"Happy to make his acquaintance," the squire said returning the giant's exaggerated *congée;* "and of course as he is your guest, I shall be happy to see Captain Juddock with you at Monkbury."

"'Twill afford me the greatest pleasure, squire, to accompany Sir G.," the captain replied, toning down his usually loud notes to a dulcet sweetness, and assuming, as well as he could, the air of a *petit maître—* "Foregad! I shall be enchanted to behold that sylvan beauty, that lovely wood-nymph, your adorable niece."

"More than she will be with you—or I'm much mistaken," the squire observed, aside. "What a strange animal! If those are town manners we have the best of it, even in point of behaviour, in the country. And now, my worthy host," he added to Jonas, " let us have a bowl of punch, of your best brewing. Will you help us to discuss it, gentlemen?"

Sir Gilbert readily assented, and Juddock very reluctantly declined, alleging that having ordered supper, he must of necessity eat it, before he should be ready for the punch. That duty performed, he would be delighted to join them.

"What, a second supper, Jack?" Montfichet cried. "On my faith, your appetite passes belief."

The captain, however, was not to be laughed out of his supper, and as it was soon afterwards served, he sat down to it, alone—Sir Gilbert declining to eat anything —and speedily demonstrated, that however largely they might have been called on before, his powers as a

trencherman were still unexhausted. The wild-ducks
were done to a turn, and even the squire, as he sat at
an adjoining table with Doctor Sidebottom and Montfichet over a smoking bowl of punch, could not help
expressing approbation at the perfect manner in which
they were dressed.

"Those ducks were a present to me from Frank
Woodbine, your honour," Nelly said.

"Then you ought to have kept them for your own,
or your husband's eating—for I fancy there won't be
much left for hashing to-morrow," the squire rejoined,
with a laugh.

"There, do you hear that?" Jonas observed to her
in a reproachful whisper.

"And now a thimble-full of brandy, landlord," Juddock cried. "Mind it must be the good old stuff Mrs.
N. recommended—just to keep all quiet. And then,
as soon as I've discussed the toasted cheese, and another
glass of your excellent October, I shall be ready for the
punch. By-the-by, your fat cook is a famous hand at
black-puddings. I never tasted better. Take it as a
general order that I have some regularly at supper.
D'ye hear, landlord?"

"Oh! yes, sir, I hear," Jonas replied, pouring him
out a glass of brandy, and wishing, internally, it might
choke him. Instead of which, it appeared so satisfactory to the giant, that he immediately demanded a
further supply, and Jonas having replenished the glass,
was fain to make off with the bottle to prevent further
claims upon it.

"A perfect cormorant!" he muttered. "There'll be
a famine in the house, if he stays here a week."

"You were speaking of Frank Woodbine, Nelly,"
the squire remarked, as he helped himself to a glass of
punch. "An uncommonly fine young fellow he is ; and

I should be glad to have him as one of my own keepers if he were not otherwise engaged. His wife I'm told is a beauty. Odd! though they're tenants of mine, I don't happen to have seen her. But my steward, Roper, declares he doesn't know her equal."

"Mr. Roper is in the house now, your honour," Nelly remarked. "There, by the fire—with that old gentleman."

"Ah! is he so?" the squire exclaimed. "Inquire if if he will take a glass of punch with us, Nelly."

"I fancy he's engaged on some particular business with Doctor Plot," she replied.

"Oh, don't disturb him, if that's the case. I'll see him before he goes. Doctor Plot, you say, is with him. I never heard of such a person. A stranger, I suppose?"

"Family physician to Sir Walter Fitzwalter, I believe, your honour," Nelly said.

"Ah! was he?—I don't remember the name—but it's so long ago, it may have slipped from my memory."

"That old gentleman, whom you call Doctor Plot, must have more names than one," Montfichet remarked. "I have met him before—under particular circumstances which fix him upon my memory, and, indeed, he himself has reminded me of them to-night—and he was then known as plain John Johnson."

"Udsbores! he seems to have as many aliases as Bully Dawson or Jack Ogle," Juddock shouted from the supper table.

"A suspicious character," the squire observed. "I must make some inquiries about him of Roper. I wonder what has become of my poor old friend Sir Walter?"

"Oblige me by no further allusion to him, squire," Montfichet said, colouring angrily.

"I crave your pardon, Sir Gilbert, for my inadvertence. But I seem to forget everything. Let me see ; what were we talking about, before this question was started ? Oh ! Rose Woodbine. Frank, they say, makes her an excellent husband. Next to our model pair here, I'm told they're the happiest couple in Dunmow. Do you chance to have seen this pretty Rose, Sir Gilbert ?"

" Why, yes—I have seen her," Montfichet replied, with some hesitation. " But you must excuse my giving any opinion about her."

Nelly here leaned towards the squire, and whispered something in his ear, which caused the latter to whistle and feign to pull up one of his boots.

" Whew !—put my foot in it again ! Take a glass of punch with me, Sir Gilbert—and let's thank our stars we're still bachelors. There's just as good fish in the sea as any ta'en out of it. In spite of all these married folks may say, there's no life like a bachelor's life !"

" Exactly my maxim, squire," Juddock cried, drawing towards the table, and filling a tumbler with punch— " and I'll drink it in a bumper. Shake a loose leg as long as you can. I've seldom felt any disposition to matrimony, or if I have, there has always been this obstacle in the way, that the charmers by whom I've been smitten were married already."

While uttering this speech, he cast a tender glance at Nelly, and kissed the rim of the glass to her before he drained it ; but she took no notice of his gallantry. Ever since the squire's appearance, the landlady's deportment had totally changed. Pretending not to observe any of her admirer's leers and innuendoes, and turning a deaf ear to all his soft whispers, though he kept ogling during supper, now and then beckoning her to come near him, she kept entirely aloof, placing herself behind the squire's chair, and leaving Juddock

to the care of Tom Tapster and Jonas. The amorous
swain did not know what to make of it. Having gone
on so swimmingly before, this sudden coldness quite
took him aback. Not being easily discouraged, however, even after the failure of his last address, he made
an attempt to seize her hand as she passed near him,
but she snatched it away hastily—with a look of real,
or feigned displeasure.

This was a great rebuff, and not unobserved of Jonas,
who had already remarked his wife's change of manner,
and with infinite satisfaction, for although he attributed it to its true cause, the presence of the squire, he
was not the less pleased by it, as it gave him a momentary triumph over the impudent disturber of his
peace, and he determined to improve his position as far
as he could. Juddock's last piece of familiarity gave
him the desired opportunity.

"I think you must observe, captain," he said, with
sarcastic politeness, "that your attentions are not so
agreeable to Mrs. Nettlebed as to make their repetition necessary or desirable. I shall take it as a particular favour if you will desist from them—as a very
particular favour, sir."

"You are not perhaps aware, captain, that our host
is a candidate for the Dunmow Flitch?" the squire observed, with a laugh.

"Oh, yes, I am," Juddock rejoined—"I've a trifling
bet upon it."

"He calls ten thousand pounds a trifling bet," Jonas
thought. "His ideas are as lofty as himself."

"If you have betted against Jonas's chance, I think
you are likely to lose," the squire said. "At all events,
I will venture to back him."

"Oh! your honour is too good," the little landlord
cried, in a transport of delight. "My prospects begin

to brighten again," he added to himself, "and the Flitch once more appears fully in view."

"Well to confess the truth, squire," Juddock said, with apparently good-natured indifference, "I would rather lose than win. But having always doubted the possibility of any couple in these days venturing upon making such a claim, I offered the bet."

"I wonder whether he's in earnest," Jonas thought. "A man who can afford to throw away ten thousand pounds, and not care about it, must be a great man, indeed."

"Well, if no unfair advantage be taken, I think the claim will be successfully preferred in this instance," the squire said. "I've every reliance on Nelly."

"I trust I shall do nothing to forfeit your honour's good opinion," the little hypocrite replied. "Jonas knows how devoted I am to him."

An affectionate embrace was the landlord's reply.

"How easily some folks are bamboozled!" the giant muttered.

"You've heard, I suppose, there is another claimant besides yourself, Jonas?" the squire said.

"Frank Woodbine your honour means," the landlord replied. "But I don't think he's likely to get it. I know him to be an unfaithful husband; and I've evidence to prove it."

"You surprise me greatly," the squire said.

"Put me in possession of that evidence, landlord," Sir Gilbert cried, quickly. "I'll make it worth your while. Rose ought not to be left in ignorance of the worthless character of the man she has chosen."

"Step forward, then, Paul Flitwick, and declare what you have seen," Jonas exclaimed. "This is my evidence against Frank, Sir Gilbert, and his honour knows whether it may be relied upon."

" Maun a do't, yar han'r?" Paul inquired, scratching his frosty poll, and looking at his master.

" Do it—no!" the latter cried, with a sudden explosion of wrath. " What the devil business have you to meddle with other people's affairs, sirrah! Do you set yourself up for a saint, you hoary old sinner? Were you always true to your own wife, eh? And how would you have liked a d—d babbling old cur to bewray you? Keep a quiet tongue in your head in future, or I'll strip your red coat from your back, I will, you talkative hound. You want the whip, sirrah—and you shall have it, too, if you're in fault again." Then turning from the crestfallen whipper-in, who looked the very picture of despair, he addressed the landlord. " I won't allow mischief to be made between man and wife. There may be truth in what you have asserted, or there may not. Whatever it be, the seeds of unhappiness must not be wantonly sown. I therefore lay my strict injunctions upon you, Jonas, that you say nothing more relative to this matter, whatever inducement may be held out to you to speak, until you have laid the full particulars before me. I will then decide on what is best to be done."

Having thus delivered himself, the squire became somewhat mollified by old Paul's penitent looks, and thinking, perhaps, he had been rather too angry with him, he offered him a glass of punch.

" Never mind what old Nimrod says, Sir G.," Juddock whispered the young baronet, as he rose from his chair. " I'll worm out the secret for you. You can use it as you think fit. Frank Woodbine ought to be very much obliged to you, squire," he added. " I'm sure I should, under the circumstances."

And walking past the old huntsman, who was still sipping his glass of punch, he whispered:

" A guinea for what you know about Frank Wood-bine."

" Gie me twanty—fafty—a wadn't," Old Paul replied, with a grin. " Nawt wad mey me disobee mester. Na—na."

Juddock then moved towards Jonas, and plucking his sleeve, said in a low tone :

" Landlord, a guinea for your proofs against the gamekeeper. It's your interest to tell, you know."

" The guinea first ?" Jonas replied, in a whisper.

Juddock slipped the money into his hand. " Now !" he said.

" Well, then," Jonas replied, " my proofs rest with Paul Flitwick. Take him to Mrs. Woodbine and force him to disclose all he has witnessed."

The giant perceived he was sold. He made no complaint, however, but resumed his seat. The movement had not passed unnoticed by the squire, who guessed its import, but as he felt sure his caution would be attended to by both parties, he did not think it worth while to interfere.

" Egad ! landlord," Juddock exclaimed, " you deserve to be ranked among the benefactors of your species, since you brew such punch as this. It has quite put my voice in tune, and if not disagreeable to the company, I'll sing 'em a song. Sorry, my dear Mrs. N.," he added, turning to Nelly, " that I don't happen to recollect anything of an amatory or sentimental nature. My ditties are chiefly Bacchanalian. I'll give you a few words of caution which I'm in the habit of addressing to a landlord, when I suspect him of a design of putting me off with a bad bottle. They'll be quite out of place here—where all is superlatively good. No matter."

Whereupon, he broke into the following melody :

The Wine=Drinker's Declaration.

TO ALL AND SUNDRY WHOM IT MAY CONCERN,

I.

THE Toper who knows how to empty his can,
Is not half so afraid of a highwayman,
   As he is of indifferent tipple :
With the last a stout fellow may fight for his purse;
Of the other the consequence certain is worse,
   Down the throat if permitted to ripple.

II.

If acetose claret I happen to sip,
'Tis my wish, as the beaker I dash from my lip,
   That my throat to a short span would dwindle
But when I get hold of the vintage I prize,
I care not, although it should shoot out in size,
   Until like a crane's neck it spindle.

III.

All wat'ry potations I let them alone,
And never will use such, until I am grown
   A Hermit, and dwell in a cavern ;
But then the good Anchorite brandy must got
(An anker, right often,) his whistle to wet,
   Or else he will sigh for the tavern.

IV.

My maxim is ever to drink of the best,
And in that I resemble sound soakers at rest,
Our Fathers we always should follow :
Old customs, old manners, we never should quit,
Or the world will judge us, as some folks judge of it,
   And declare our professions are hollow.

The laughter occasioned by this song awakened Doctor Sidebottom, who, overcome by the coldness of the weather, or the potency of the punch, had fallen comfortably asleep in his chair, and now, after indulging in a most portentous yawn, exclaimed :

" Was I dreaming, or did I hear allusion made to Sir Walter Fitzwalter ?"

" You were dreaming, doctor," the squire rejoined, with a slight cough to call his attention to Sir Gilbert de Montfichet, who again began to frown.

The hint was disregarded.

" Well, it's very strange," the vicar pursued—"I thought I heard you speak of him, and directly after I fancied he was come back again to dwell in his old mansion."

" What, here !" Jonas exclaimed. " I'm very glad it was nothing more than a dream, your reverence."

" Dreams sometimes foreshadow coming events," Doctor Sidebottom remarked, gravely ; " and I have known some remarkable instances of their verification. I thought Sir Walter had returned to the hall of his ancestors. I saw him as plainly as I see——"

The rest of the sentence expired upon his lips.

" As you see what, doctor ?" the squire asked.

" Look there !—look there ! Do you see nothing, sir ?"

" Gracious Heavens ! can it be possible ?" the squire ejaculated, following the direction of the vicar's gaze, and becoming, like him, transfixed with astonishment, not wholly free from a superstitious dread, which presently diffused itself throughout the assemblage, though they scarcely knew why.

The screen had been removed, disclosing the figure of Doctor Plot, who, having risen to his feet, continued for a few minutes to regard the group fixedly.

" Why, that's the impostor you were inquiring about," Montfichet said. " That's John Johnson, who now styles himself Doctor Plot."

" John Johnson or not, he's no impostor," the squire rejoined, in a low, earnest tone.

" But I'll have it out of him—I'll know who he is," Montfichet exclaimed. " He bullied me just now ; but, by Heavens ! he shall not do so again with impunity."

" Sit down, Sir Gilbert," the squire said, with a certain look of authority not to be resisted. " Let him preserve his incognito if he will."

" You know him, then ?"

The squire nodded.

" Why not address him ?"

Monkbury shook his head.

" You, also, appear to recognise him, doctor ?" Sir Gilbert said, turning to the vicar. " Speak to him."

" Not I—unless he addresses me first," Doctor Side-bottom replied, in a low, solemn tone.

" I believe it's the old gentleman in person, Sir G.," Captain Juddock whispered. " Don't you notice his club-foot ? No doubt he has managed to conceal his tail."

" It certainly is very mysterious," Montfichet rejoined, staring at the singular personage on whom all eyes were fixed, and beginning to be infected with the general feeling of dread.

This feeling rather increased as Doctor Plot advanced towards them, slowly, and with as much stateliness as his deformed limb would permit. There was a melancholy kindliness in the regards which he addressed exclusively to the squire and the vicar—but chiefly to the former. As he drew near, Monkbury, who had looked hard at him all the while, stretched out his hand, but said nothing.

Doctor Plot shook his head mournfully, murmuring, rather than giving distinct utterance to the words— " Not yet!—not yet!" though what he meant to say seemed to reach the squire's ear. He then raised his thin finger to his lips; bowed gravely to the vicar, who respectfully returned the salutation; and imposing silence on him by a gesture similar to that addressed to the squire, moved silently on like a ghost.

On—on towards the staircase.

So impressive, so singularly awe-inspiring was his manner, that no one ventured to address him. Though

half-disposed to disobey the squire's injunctions, Montfichet felt his courage forsake him, and he sat still and
speechless. Juddock held his breath, as the singular
being passed him, and drew in his huge outstretched
shanks to make way. Jonas and his wife looked on in
mute wonder, and Paul Flitwick rubbed his eyes, as if
doubting whether they served him truly.

Arrived at the foot of the staircase, Doctor Plot encountered Peggy, who had just descended with Carroty
Dick, and taking a candle from her, slowly mounted
them, and passed along the gallery: all eyes following
him, and the same hushing silence prevailing, till he
disappeared down the dark corridor.

Everybody then breathed more freely.

The first to break the silence was Jonas.

"Why, I declare he knows his way about the house
as if he were used to it," he said. "He has gone
straight to his room, though no one has shown it to
him."

The next to find utterance was Paul Flitwick, who,
rushing up to his master, with his rough white locks
standing on end, ejaculated:

"Yar han'r seed un? Ya knaw'd un?"

"Saw him, and knew him, too, Paul," his master
rejoined. "But, as I intimated just now, a discreet
man will see everything, and say nothing. You understand."

The old whipper-in nodded his head, and retreated.

"I didn't perceive any caudal appendage; nevertheless, I believe it to be his Satanic Majesty in person,
or one of his principal envoys," Juddock said. "I shall
be afraid to remain in the house."

"A man of your thewes and sinews confess himself
afraid?" the squire exclaimed, in contempt. "You
ought to fear nothing of mortal mould, and he you

have just seen is fashioned like yourself — though of somewhat better clay," he thought. "Ah! Roper, I'm glad to see you," he added, as the steward, who remained near the fire till Doctor Plot had disappeared, now advanced. "Sit down! sit down!" he said, with a significant look at him. "We must raise our spirits again, which this unexpected incident has somewhat damped. Jonas, another bowl of punch!"

IV.

THE GHOST'S ROOM.

Down the dark corridor, at the very end, lies the Room. The fourth door, and the last.

Tread carefully. The boards are rotten in places, and you may perchance fall through them, and break your neck upon the pavement beneath. Shame to leave them in such a dangerous condition. Yet this wing of the Old House is so little frequented, it seems scarcely worth while to keep it in repair, Jonas thinks. A few years more, he says, and it will be altogether in ruins; if, indeed, it will last so long.

Peep into those disused chambers as you pass by; preserving amid woful dilapidation an air of former splendour. Many a lovely dame has rested there in days gone by. Conjure up, if you can, those phantoms of delight. Re-people the deserted chambers, and furnish forth again their crumbling walls with the glories of the looms of Flanders.

Strange noises the rats make! They swarm in this part of the house; and squeak and gibber, like the sheeted dead, behind the hollow wainscots; scampering after each other, and detaching fragments of wood and bits of mortar in their play. The clatter increases.

K

Are the noxious creatures bursting forth in legions to devour us, as they did Bishop Hatto, in his tower on the Rhine? No. 'Tis only the cat that has jumped down the chimney, and brought two or three loose bricks along with her. Shut the door, and leave grimalkin there, to keep those pestilent rats quiet.

How the casements rattle! The wind finds its way through the broken panes. Shield the light, or it will be extinguished. Those windows look upon the garden; and the tall trees in front of them cast a shade over the passage, making it gloomy, even at noontide, when the sun shines brightest.

Well! we have arrived without accident. Here is the Room.

But stop! before entering it let us note the glass-door at the end of the corridor, communicating with a flight of wooden steps outside, that descend into the garden. Through that glass-door, and down those steps, Nelly and Frank Woodbine hurried, when the latter escaped from the bailiffs. Hastily traversing an arcade below, running parallel with the upper corridor, and formed of open transom-windows of oak, supported by a wall, breast-high, they made their way by tortuous passages to the cellars where Frank was locked up, as already narrated.

But it is not merely in reference to this circumstance that we desire to call attention to the glass-door. Things less substantial, it is asserted, than the inn-keeper's buxom wife, and the young gamekeeper, have glided through it, without stopping to draw back the bolt. A female figure, enveloped in a shroud, has issued, at dead of night, from the adjoining chamber, and passing, with noiseless footsteps, along the corridor, has disappeared by that outlet. This phantom Carroty Dick, and others of the household, have witnessed with

their own eyes; and they will swear to the truth of the
story. Nay, more, pretty Peggy happening to be alone
on one occasion in the passage, was frightened almost
out of her wits, by seeing a ghastly face, with hollow
eyes, glimmering like fen-fires, stare at her through the
door-panes.

No one believes in ghosts now-a-days. Superstition
has not a leg left to stand upon; or rather modern phi-
losophy and scepticism have striven to cut the ground
from under it. Yet, in spite of our incredulity, very few
of us like to sleep in a haunted room; and if put into
one by chance, in an old country-house having fearful
traditions connected with it, our slumbers are apt to be
disturbed, though we care not to acknowledge our nocturnal alarms next morning at breakfast.

But a veritable Ghost's Room now awaits us. Let us
enter it boldly.

A cheerful fire at any rate, and ample provision in
that basket of wood for keeping up the blaze. Merrily
crackle the logs upon the hearth; the flaming pile being
supported by andirons, with heads like brazen shields.
The chimney-piece is immense; advancing far into the
room, and springing to the very ceiling. In the centre
of the upper compartment, once fairly painted and
gilded, may be discerned the proud blazonry of the
Fitzwalters. On either side of the many-quartered
'scutcheon, and placed in a little niche, is a saintly
image; the outer pilasters are crowned with busts. The
floors are of black polished oak; the wainscots of the
same wood, and partly hung with faded tapestry; one
piece of which, bearing date 1450, is worked with the
following legend:

> I pray God blesse the life
> Of Sir Walter Fitzwalter, his Wife,
> And all the children that with him wonnes,
> His five Daughters and seven Sonnes.

Another piece of taspestry, yet older, represents the good Samaritan, engaged in his office of charity. Here and there are portraits of the family painted upon panels. The ceiling is enriched with elaborate tracery, and there is a deep bay-window with stained glass in it, across which, if need be, a heavy curtain can be drawn. The moon shines through the window now. Not much furniture, but what there is, ancient, and in keeping with the room; consisting of a carved oak livery-cupboard, a high-backed chair or two with deep cushions, a tabouret, covered with faded velvet, and a small dressing-table, on which a fringed cloth is spread, near the window, with an antiquated and almost useless mirror, leaning over it from the wall. On the opposite side of the recess is an old embroidered prie-dieu, with a crucifix placed above it. Neither have been disturbed, out of respect to the memory of the last ill-fated Lady Fitzwalter, who was wont to offer up her prayers there. There are two deep roomy closets, screened with arras; one opposite the fireplace; the other near the prie-dieu.

Facing the window, to the left of the door, there is a great gloomy bedstead. Its lofty tester of black walnut-tree touches the ceiling; its twisted pillars and carved back are of the same dusky material; and the thick curtains, once of purple stuff woven with gold thread, have acquired by age a sombre, funereal look.

The fire burns cheerily; the moon shines brightly; yet neither firelight nor moonlight can dispel that chamber's gloom: a gloom, perceptible to the feelings rather than to the sight, and communicating an undefined sense of awe and mystery. Within that room, you feel, as it were, on the confines of the spiritual world, and, in spite of all efforts to the contrary, begin to yield to the influence breathed from that dread un-

known region. Thoughts to make the flesh creep, and
the blood run cold, irresistibly assail you, and will not
be chased away. Imagination peoples the brain with
phantoms; and these distempered creations seem to
have a strange and inexplicable connexion with visionary
beings of a different order, which await but the fitting
moment, when the intruder on their domain shall be
duly impressed by their shuddering influence, to appear
and hold communion with him. No one, who has slept
within that chamber of late years, but has experienced
sensations like to these, however resolutely he may have
battled with them. If he has escaped an actual supernatural visitation as well, he may esteem himself singularly fortunate. Those who have beheld the ghost do
not desire a repetition of the sight.

With this chamber the tragic history of the hapless
Lady Fitzwalter, whose spirit still haunts the scene of
her earthly sorrows, is intimately connected. Within
it occurred most of the events that brought her life to
an untimely close. Here she came as a bride, when her
surpassing beauty held captive Sir Walter's affections,
until jealous doubts and fancies estranged them. In it
was born their son; whom his father, perplexed by the
tormenting fiend, would not look upon; and whom his
mother, deeming the babe's innocent face would melt
the moody man's self-hardened heart, carried to him,
well-nigh causing the poor child's destruction.

Here her tears were plentifully shed after that sad
occurrence; and feelings of resentment at first en-
kindled by the wrongful suspicion entertained of her,
and the harsh treatment she experienced, were gradually
softened by returning love. Here took place the mis-
construed and fatal interview between the afflicted
lady, anxious to regain the place she had lost in her
husband's heart, and their mutual friend; interrupted

so terribly by Sir Walter himself, guided by the faithless confidante.

Sir Walter came through the closet opposite the fireplace, which communicates by a secret door with the next chamber, and as he drew aside the arras, and gazed upon her with flashing eyes and infuriated countenance, the unfortunate lady felt she was doomed, and that no time would be allowed her for justification. Yet she prevented instant bloodshed. The blow that was to pierce the bosom of a friend was not struck then.

O, the agony of that night! when husband and friend were gone; pledged to meet at daybreak in mortal conflict. In vain did she seek out Sir Walter, and protest her innocence: in vain supplicate for mercy. He was deaf to all she said. And Heaven seemed equally deaf to her prayers, for though she passed the whole night on her bended knees in earnest entreaties for its interference, the catastrophe was not to be averted.

A note from her lord, written in pencil at the place of meeting, informed her that Montfichet was killed. On receipt of it she shed no more tears, and prayed no longer. Rising up as if to utter imprecations upon his slayer, she became suddenly dumb. The torpor of despair had seized her.

She was indeed alone. Her child had been sent away by Sir Walter's command, and no one knew what had become of him. Thus the only link that might have bound her to the world was snapped asunder. What nad she to live for now?

O! if this chamber could but echo back the groans and heart-piercing ejaculations she uttered! And such woful sounds *have* been heard within it, as if the poor lady were weeping and lamenting still. Death would seem to have brought her neither rest, nor respite from earthly woe. Perhaps, because her end was sinful.

She was found, one morning, lifeless and cold within her bed, with an empty phial of laudanum in her grasp —thus proclaiming the manner of her death. She could not have lasted long, for she was wasted almost to a skeleton. But that did not make her crime the less.

In this very bed they say she died.

And so the Room came to be haunted.

V.

TOUCHING A MYSTERIOUS BOX FOUND IN THE CLOSET; AND ITS CONTENTS.

Two persons are in the Room just now.

One, seated on the edge of a large black portmanteau set on end, and inscribed with the name of DOCTOR PLOT, is whistling in a low key the air of the lovelorn ditty—"*I am a poor Shepherd undone*,"—and gazing sentimentally at the crackling logs, fancying they typify his own scorched condition. The other, having put the place in order as well as she can, is vainly trying to polish the surface of the dim old mirror, in which she beholds no flattering reflection of a very pretty countenance.

"A plague on the glass! how wrinkly and ugly it makes a body look," Peggy cried, abandoning her task in despair;—"I can't abide a mirror like this, and if I'd my own way, I'd break it into fifty shivers, that I would."

"Jist becos it tells truth, and shows you as you be, Peggy," Carroty Dick replied. "Now that's the sort o' plain-spoken glass I likes."

"But you don't think me old and ugly, I'm sure,
Dick?" the little syren rejoined, laying her hand affec-
tionately on his shoulder.

And as the enamoured ostler looked up and met her
tender eyes, he couldn't, for the life of him, say he did.
Still he felt very jealous; the recollection of several
circumstances that had recently taken place galling
him sorely.

"No great matter what I thinks, Peggy," he said.
"My love's o' no mich consequence, it seems ; an' I'm
no worth havin' when any one better is by."

"How can you tell such stories, Dick?" Peggy rejoined, coaxingly. "You've been in a shocking bad
humour all night, and deserve scolding, that you do,
you cross thing."

"And what's put me in a bad humour?" Dick asked,
reproachfully. "Haven't I had cause? Didn't I
see——"

"Stuff and nonsense! you've seen nothing," she interrupted, stopping his mouth. "It's all fancy. Well,
now, I've quite done here, so we may go down stairs.
Just heap a few more logs on the fire. The room looks
tolerably comfortable ; but I wouldn't sleep in it for all
Essex. Do you know, Dick, they say *she* died in that
bed?"

"No ; do they? What, the poor lady?"

"Yes. But don't let's talk of her. I feel a sort of
shivering and all-overishness, whenever I think of the
face I saw at the glass-door. Oh! good gracious!
what's that?"

"Only the portmantle a-tumbled down," Dick rejoined. "I hope there be nothin' wrong in it. It be
a smartish size, but mich too sma' to hold a man."

"Oh! Gimini! You don't think there's a man in
it, Dick?"

THE CUSTOM OF DUNMOW. 139

"If I did, I'd make short wi' him. I'd stick the red-hot poker down his throat. But the portmantle's woundy heavy, anyhow. My back aches consumedly wi' carryin' on it up-stairs."

"Shouldn't you like to see it opened, Dick?"

"No—I can't say I've any sich curiosity. But my stars, Peggy! look there!"

"Wh—where?—wh—what is it you see?" she inquired in great trepidation.

"The old gentleman," Dick rejoined.

"The old gentleman—below?"

"Yes—yes—no—no—not him—the old gentleman down stairs. Look at that picter," pointing to one of the painted panels. "It's as like him as two peas."

"So it is, I declare," Peggy replied, examining the portrait—"only younger, and a great deal better looking."

"O, Peggy, you're like missis—always set on good looks."

"Not a word against missis, Dick. I won't allow it. My aim is to resemble her, and if ever you and I come to be married, I trust we shall get the Flitch."

"I'm afeard we stand but a poor chance of it, Peggy," Dick replied, scratching his red poll.

"That may be your opinion, but it's not mine, sir," she rejoined, sharply. "Talking of likenesses, whom do you think this picture resembles?" pointing to another panel, on which was represented the kneeling figure of a knight in complete armour, with his helmet lying near him.

"Whom do I think? why, Frank Woodbine, to be sure. It's jist his nose an' chin—and his brown curly locks."

"Right, Dick. 'Tis Frank to the very life. I wonder I never noticed the likeness before. But I've always been too much frightened to look about me carefully.

Do you know, Dick, I'm dying to see the inside of those two closets."

"Dear ! dear! how full of curiosity you be, Peggy !"

"It's the priv'lege of my sex, Dick. I'll just take a peep now. Keep close behind me, in case anything should appear."

As she spoke, she went to the nearest closet (Dick following her), and cautiously, and not without misgiving, lifted the arras. Nothing met her view except a box, which her quick eye detected in an out-of-the-way corner.

"Bring it out, Dick," the inquisitive damsel cried. "I must have it opened."

The ostler obeyed. The box. on examination, proved to be locked.

"Plague on't ! how provoking !" Peggy exclaimed. "I wonder whether we can find the key. I dare say it's in the closet."

After some search, the object of their search was found on the floor, where no doubt it had dropped, and Peggy's curiosity seemed in a fair way of gratification. On being opened, however, the box was found to contain only an old white handkerchief, with several dark brown stains upon it. One of these, deeper, darker, and larger than the rest, attracted Peggy's particular attention. She guessed at once the cause of the spots.

Holding up the handkerchief to the astonished ostler, whose red locks bristled with terror, she exclaimed, in thrilling accents—"Blood, Dick—blood ! Murder has been done here—murder !"

"Lor' bless us ! I hope not," the ostler replied.

"It has," she rejoined. "Stay! there's something inside this handkerchief, that may lead to the detection of the murderer."

And she unfolded it with trembling hands.

Two letters, and a small phial.

The first note she touched was a mere scrap of paper; the writing on it traced in pencil. It was addressed to Lady Fitzwalter. With prying eyes she devoured it. Brief and terrible, it ran thus :

" This handkerchief is dyed in the life-blood of your lover. With it I have wiped the blade that has pierced his heart. Never again will you behold the husband you have dishonoured, but who is now avenged. Never again will you behold your child, who shall neither bear my name, to which he has no title, nor hold my estates, to which he has no rightful claim. Live in peace if you can. W. F'W."

Peggy read this savage missive twice over, without fully comprehending its import, and then turned to examine the other letter. It was addressed to Sir Walter Fitzwalter, and the seal, which was of black wax, was still unbroken. The chambermaid had few scruples, and if she had, her curiosity was so highly excited, that it would have overcome them now. Accordingly, she was just on the point of opening it, when her purpose was arrested by a startling sound from the closet.

Some one appeared to be stirring within it, though she knew it to be quite empty.

Consulting Dick with a look, she read in his white cheeks that he had heard the strange sound too.

" See who it is," she whispered.

Dick shook his head. " Hist !" he cried.

A profound sigh—such as only could proceed from a heavily-laden breast. At the same time, a singular vibration was felt throughout the chamber. And the candle seemed in their eyes to burn blue.

As they looked at each other in affright, the arras

was wafted forward. It might be by the wind—though
how came the wind to blow there? More likely, as it
seemed to them, the spectre was coming forth.

They saw nothing more. Leaving the box where it
was, and the letters and bloodstained handkerchief on
the floor, they made their way out of the room.

Flying along the corridor, and thinking the ghost
was at their heels, they never stopped till they reached
the great gallery overlooking the hall. They then considered what was to be done. After awhile, Peggy,
regaining a little confidence, and calling to mind the
state of disorder in which she had left the room, was
for going back to remove the damning proofs of her
curiosity, and put the mysterious box into the closet;
but no persuasions could induce Dick to accompany
her, and she dared not return alone. So, since there
was no remedy, she was obliged to submit; her only
chance being to attend the old gentleman to his chamber, when she might be able to remove the evidences
against her while he was by. This she resolved to do;
but when Doctor Plot took the candle from her at the
foot of the staircase, where she had held herself in
readiness for his departure for the night, his looks so
alarmed her, that quite forgetting what she was about,
she did not even recover her presence of mind till he
had disappeared. It was then too late, and discovery
was inevitable. But now seized by a new curiosity to
ascertain what the old gentleman did on finding the
things, she coaxed Dick to bear her company as far as
the gallery; but it took full half an hour's persuasion
of the most wheedling kind to induce him to move
another step. However, she accomplished her purpose
at last—as a woman generally contrives to do, when
resolved to carry a point—and the end of their mut-

tered conference was overheard by Frank Woodbine, while concealed in the secret recess.

Treading on tiptoe, they gained the door.

They listened, and thought they heard a deep groan. Another, deeper still—then all was silent. No key-hole through which they could see what was going on inside—no crevice in the boards to answer the same purpose. Resolved not to be balked, however, Peggy had just made up her mind to knock, on some pretence or other, when her arm was grasped by Dick, who exclaimed, in accents of wildest terror.

"There it be!—there it be!"

At once comprehending his meaning, and only ven-turing to cast a side-look at the glass-door, behind which she fancied something white could be distin-guished, she instantly took to her heels with her com-panion. On reaching the gallery, their terror was brought to a climax by the unmistakable appearance of a mail-clad phantom.

Though Peggy was well-nigh thrown into fits at the sight of this appalling spectre, so much more dreadful than anything she could have imagined, she did not fail to mark its resemblance to the knightly figure painted on the panel in the Haunted Chamber. The features were the same, though stained with blood, and more ghastly. It must be the old knight come from his tomb in the Priory Church to punish her indiscretion.

Scream after scream,—enough to bring the Old House about her ears! Poor Dick could scarcely sustain her.

VI.

IN WHICH IT IS SHOWN THAT THERE MAY BE MORE WAYS
THAN ONE OUT OF A CELLAR ; AND MORE ROOMS THAN
ARE GENERALLY SUSPECTED IN AN OLD HOUSE.

To explain the cause of Peggy's fright, we must now
see what has happened to Frank Woodbine.

Not expecting his confinement in the cellar to be of
very long duration, since Nelly had promised to liberate
him as soon as the coast was clear, Frank took it quietly
enough at first, amusing himself by thinking how
cleverly the bailiffs had been tricked ; but when a long
interval of time had elapsed—and it seemed much
longer to him than it really was—he began to find the
detention exceedingly irksome, and made several futile
attempts to force open the door.

Another hour of restraint increased his impatience to
such a degree, that, unable to rest inactive, he began to
grope about the place in every direction to ascertain if
by possibility, any other mode of egress existed. Though
he moved as carefully as he could in the dark, he managed to upset a good many bottles, and more than
once came in contact with a mouldy old beer-cask ; but
at length, he contrived to hit upon the entrance to the
inner vaults, and passing through it, went on, with even
greater caution than before ; becoming sensible from
the increased dampness of the atmosphere, and the
broken condition of the floor, together with the litter
scattered about, that he had got into some neglected
depository of rubbish, where there might be danger of
a serious fall.

A second doorway ensued, and a second vault, full of
rubbish like the first. Here he found a ladder lying on
the ground, and placed—as he luckily discovered in
time—across the mouth of a deep, circular hole: an

old well it might be, to judge from the dampness of the brickwork : into which he had a narrow escape of being precipitated, headlong.

Passing by this dangerous abyss, with a shudder at the risk he had run, he entered a third vault, terminated by a short flight of stone steps, down which he descended, wondering where they would land him. When at the bottom, his further progress was impeded by a door. It was locked; but being in no mood to be stopped, and the lock chancing to be on the side next him, he took up a brick from the loose pavement, and knocked off the rusty fastening with a blow.

No further hindrance then. A narrow passage presented itself; circuitous, and gradually rising as he advanced along it. He was delighted to find the air become fresher, and the obscurity decrease with each step he took, until at last, the full light of the moon burst upon him, shining down from a grated aperture in the walls. Unluckily, the aperture was out of reach ; but even if accessible, the closeness and strength of the bars rendered escape by it wholly impracticable.

Further on, a blank wall opposed him. The passage had evidently communicated with some chamber beyond, but the doorway had been blocked up, as was shown by the comparative freshness of the brickwork.

To all appearance, he had reached the end of his course. All this trouble had been taken, all this risk run, for nothing.

But he would not go back till he had looked carefully round. Trap-doors and secret passages he knew were to be found in many old houses. Might not similar contrivances exist here ? Thereupon, he examined the walls, and sounded the brickwork; but with no satisfactory result.

At last, when just giving up the search, he chanced

upon a small stone let into the wall, with the figure **V.** carved upon it.

What could it mean ? There was no corresponding mark near it that he could detect; and yet the figure must have some significance.

He counted five yards, and that brought him exactly to the blocked-up doorway. Returning to the starting-point, he took the like number of steps in the opposite direction, and being still within the scope of the moon's rays, clearly perceived the figure IV. cut on the wall. Four steps more brought him to III.; three to II.; and though the next movement almost involved him in gloom, he could trace with his finger, upon a piece of stone, the number I.

Here he halted.

The walls, on examination, proved to be of hard brickwork. The floor sounded firm beneath his tread, and returned no hollow reverberation. Looking upwards, he could just distinguish, in the partial obscurity, a chain dangling from the roof.

The chain seemed within reach, and springing aloft, he succeeded in grasping it, and in maintaining his hold.

But the attempt had nearly proved fatal to him. His weight brought down a heavy board to which the iron links were attached, and the edge of the wood striking him in its fall, and slightly grazing his temple, laid him prostrate and bleeding.

A wonder he had not been killed.

Serious, however, as might have been the accident, it rendered him an important service. The fall of the board had left a square opening in the roof, through which he could distinguish some portion of a chamber illumined by the moon. From the bolts and rings as well as the rusty chain attached to it, it was evident the board had been used as a trap-door.

How to attain the room above was now the question? He was not long in solving it. Bethinking him of the ladder he had met with in the vaults, he resolved to fetch it. The plan was no sooner conceived than executed; and on application, the ladder being found to reach the square hole above, it was soon securely planted, and mounting the steps with eagerness, he effected an entrance near the fireplace of a large deserted-looking chamber.

Deserted, indeed.

No human footstep, it would seem, had invaded that chamber for many and many a year. Whether it was equally avoided by members of the Invisible World was not so clear. A ghostly atmosphere seemed to pervade the place. The room had once been magnificently decorated; but time and neglect had despoiled it of its splendour. The lofty windows were boarded up, but some of the planks having given way from the effects of weather, the moonlight streamed in through the interstices. The walls were panelled, and the wainscots had been covered with rich tapestry, but the arras was mildewed, stained, and rotten, as were the window-curtains, and hung down in strips and tatters. The mirrors in their richly-gilt and curiously-carved frames were dull and tarnished. The moulded ceiling was cracked and blistered, and festooned with cobwebs. The furniture was of an antique and cumbrous form, but its gilt leather and silken coverings were sullied and motheaten. The portraits had nearly all perished, and the canvas on which several had been painted, had dropped from their frames.

Two only, from some unaccountable reason, remained in a tolerable state of preservation. Both of these were full-length portraits, admirably painted, and almost lifelike in character and expression. One was

the likeness of a man, between forty and fifty, habited
in a rich court dress of George the First's time; the
other that of an exquisitely beautiful woman, some
twenty years younger, and equally richly attired in
robes of the same period. Yet in spite of the lady's
beauty, there were traces of sadness in her looks. Her
splendid garb seemed to hide an anxious heart, and the
smile upon her sundered lips had a touch of melancholy
in it. She was of a noble presence, stately figure, and
majestic carriage, with a full person, rounded arms, and
fine shoulders. Her eyes were black and large, but
though their brilliancy was softened by the sadness
pervading the mouth, they were full of latent fire and
spirit. The brows were dark and well-defined; the hair
jetty, raised from the beautiful forehead, and crowning
the head as with a natural tiara. The features were
classical in shape; the complexion of a rich brown.

This portrait rivetted Frank Woodbine's attention.
He continued to gaze at it until tears rushed to his
eyes, and as a relief, he turned to the other picture.

To deny that the person here represented was handsome would be impossible. Yet his good looks were
almost entirely marred by a peculiar and forbidding expression. It was not easy to say in what the expression
consisted, or whence it arose. It might be pride, or
suspicion, or excessive irritability. All these feelings
seemed to lurk in parts of the singular physiognomy—
singular, because there was as much good in it as evil;
the former qualities being in such strength, that they
might have preponderated, if allowed fair play. Irritability, scorn, and sarcasm hovered about the mouth;
but they were held in check, or corrected by highly
nervous sensibility. Pride was the dominant expression of the face; and yet the haughty brow and imperious eye were tempered and restrained by a look

suggestive of benevolence, and even humility. So many opposite qualities were blended and confounded together, that the face seemed a mere bundle of contradictions, enough to puzzle any one who made it a study. The features were sharp, well-defined, and full of intelligence. In stature, this oddly-compounded personage was rather above the ordinary standard; but he lost something of height from lameness; a defect, which, instead of being concealed, was rather obtrusively displayed by the artist; probably at the suggestion of the original of the picture. Apart from this drawback, the figure was finely-formed, though, perhaps, too spare. The eyes looked out of the picture, steadily confronting the beholder, and seemed to follow him with their keen glances about the room.

The contemplation of this picture produced no such effects on Frank Woodbine as had been excited by the first portrait. On the contrary, his aspect assumed unwonted sternness, and he frowned angrily as he met the penetrating gaze it seemed to fix upon him. This sentiment of displeasure, however, soon gave way to pity; and, as if fearing his indignation might be re-awakened, he placed himself once more under the gentler though saddening influence of the lady's melancholy eyes.

While thus occupied, Frank completely forgot the situation in which he was placed. Thoughts of the past—painful thoughts—swept over his mind, to the exclusion, for the moment, of all other considerations. But at length, the necessity of exertion rousing him from his sombre reverie, he went towards the windows for the purpose of ascertaining on what they opened; ever and anon looking back at the two portraits, and thinking one of them was watching him with its keen glances.

Clouded with long accumulated dust, and further obscured by the action of the frost, the windows were so dimmed, that no view could be obtained from them, except through a broken pane ; and hence he discovered that immediately beneath him was a small secluded court, screened from outer observation by a thick belt of trees. This court, moreover, having been excavated to a considerable depth below the rest of the habitation, in all probability faced the walled-up chamber, once communicating with the passage he had recently traversed ; making it evident that every precaution had been taken to secure privacy and seclusion to this part of the building, when in occupation.   It became evident also, on further investigation, that the apartments had been very suddenly as well as very carefully closed, and had continued wholly undisturbed until his intrusion upon them.

Abandoning all idea of descent from the windows, Frank looked about for some other outlet, and was then astonished by a peculiarity in the chamber, which had hitherto escaped his notice.

There was no door to it.

Here, then, was a fresh dilemma, out of which he saw no means of extricating himself. He must go back after all, and had unwillingly come to this conclusion, when chancing to cast a glance at the portrait, the eyes of which seemed constantly tracking him, he fancied he could read so much mockery and malice in its looks, that he resolved not to give up his search for the secret entrance ; feeling convinced, from the peculiar arrangements of the room, that such an entrance must exist.

While shaking the panels, and pressing against them to see if one would slide back, he came upon a table on which an escritoire was placed, with writing materials near it; affording ample evidence of the suddenness with which the chamber had been forsaken and shut up. Nothing had been removed from the room; and probably no one had been allowed to enter it after its abandonment. The escritoire was open, and an unfinished letter was lying near it—the paper discoloured by time, and the ink faded. Incited by curiosity, Frank took it to the window to read it. Its perusal roused new emotions, and of a wholly different character, in his breast. He again glanced at the portrait, and fancy now changed the look he encountered to one of sadness and sympathy. Carefully folding the letter, he placed it within his breast.

Within the escritoire were several documents and papers, with none of which Frank thought it right to meddle, until he came to a packet sealed with black wax, and inscribed—" FOR LADY FITZWALTER. TO BE DELIVERED AFTER MY DEATH.—W. F'W."

With trembling hands, Frank took up this packet; his first thought being to secure it. But the portrait seemed to admonish him to desist, and he laid it down again, though not without reluctance.

He had scarcely done so, when he was greatly startled by an occurrence which, for the moment, seemed to partake of the supernatural; though it was presently explained. Appearing to detach itself from its frame the portrait advanced towards him. He hastily retreated; and it was well he did so, for he was scarcely out of reach when the picture fell to the ground with a tremendous clatter that shook the whole room, and filled it with a cloud of dust. The explanation of the occurrence was obvious. His own hasty movements had no doubt shaken the picture, and dislodged it from its supports, which it appeared, on examination, were rusty and decayed. With some difficulty he managed to rear it up again, though not to its former position, and in doing so, he perceived what he had been searching for so anxiously—a sliding panel.

On the fall of the picture, the panel had flown open; the spring being in some way connected with the frame, which had moved upon hinges like a door. His course was now uninterrupted.

The passage into which the sliding panel admitted him, was very narrow and intricate, and its close, mouldy smell showed how long it had been disused. After traversing it for some time, and speculating where and when it would terminate, for it evidently led to the other end of the building, he mounted a short flight of wooden steps, and came to a small closet.

It was now quite clear that he had gained the habitable part of the house. He could not only see a light through the chinks in the oak boards forming the front of the closet, but could hear voices, some of which he recognised. Jonas Nettlebed and his wife were making merry, it appeared, with company in the hall below.

Frank now knew where he was. The little closet was partitioned from the gallery, near the head of the staircase, and was no doubt quite unknown to the present inmates of the house. Nor did he desire they should be made acquainted with its existence, or with that of the chamber he had discovered. So he hesitated to go forth, though he easily detected a secret door amid the boards, and had only to press a knob of iron to become free. He was compelled to act thus cautiously from hearing a whispering sound in the gallery, as if two persons were standing there, engaged in muttered discourse. These persons he found were Carroty Dick and Peggy, and it was the light of the candle held by the pretty chambermaid that reached nim through the cracks in the boards.

While thus detained, Frank examined the place into which he had got. It was little more than a large cupboard, and constituted a receptacle for strange lumber. Amongst other things, he found a suit of old armour placed upon a stand. Most likely it had been put there out of the way, and forgotten. This knightly equipment, which might have belonged to the first Fitzwalter, as it had some of the peculiarities of the mailed statue on the tomb in the old Priory Church, was complete from top to toe—plate armour with a chain shirt beneath it. If the panoply could stalk forth, how it would terrify the loiterers in the gallery, and rout all the laughing company below. What so easy as to carry this notion into effect? Thinking so, Frank instantly set to work and arrayed himself in the old warrior's harness, putting on the chain shirt, the breastplate and greaves, the vantbraces and gaunt-lets; and binding his handkerchief round his head, finally clapped on the casque. The armour fitted as if fashioned for him.

When fully equipped, he moved towards the secret door, slowly and with difficulty, for the weight of iron considerably impeded his movements. Having reached the point of exit, he listened for a moment. All seemed quiet in the gallery, and the light was gone, but loud laughter and revelry continued to resound from below. He then drew down the visor, and touched the spring of the secret door. It flew open, and he stalked forth into the gallery.

It was at this moment, as already related, that Peggy issued from the dark corridor, followed by Carroty Dick. Her shrieks, as we have said, on beholding the mail-clad apparition, were loud enough to rouse the whole house, and dropping her candle, she fell back into the arms of the almost equally-terrified ostler.

Meanwhile, the spectre slowly advanced towards the great oak staircase.

Clank! clank! clank! The boards creaked awfully.

VII.

THE REGISTER OF THE COURT BARON OF LITTLE DUNMOW.

THE last bowl of punch ordered by the squire was capital, and highly approved by the company. By all, at least, except Sir Gilbert de Montfichet, who, ever since the departure of Doctor Plot, appeared pre-occupied. Taking no part in the conversation, he at last rose, and walked moodily towards the fireplace, where he sat down by himself. The squire looked after him, and shook his head; but Captain Juddock said there was nothing to be uneasy about; Sir G. was often down in the mouth, but soon came round, if left alone; truth being, he was desperately in love.

Nelly, still standing behind the squire's chair, could not help inquiring with whom? And when informed by the giant, who saw no reason for concealment, that it was with Rose Woodbine, she lifted up her hands in wonderment, exclaiming, "Dear! dear! only to think of it! And she a married woman!"

"Rose cannot help Sir Gilbert's being in love with her," remarked Mr. Roper, drily, "any more than you, Mrs. Nettlebed, can prevent Captain Juddock, or Captain Anybody-else, from admiring you. However, I myself can bear witness that his attentions are extremely disagreeable to her, and I sincerely trust they will cease. Indeed, after the scene that occurred this evening at the cottage—and the lesson the young baronet received from Doctor Plot—I do not think them likely to be repeated."

" Ah! what is it you allude to, Roper," the squire asked.

" Excuse my entering into particulars just now, sir," the steward replied. " It may be sufficient to state, that Doctor Plot interfered to protect Rose from annoyance, and I cannot but think that Sir Gilbert's present abstraction is attributable to some other circumstances connected with this mysterious gentleman, with which he has been—or supposes himself—mixed up, rather than to the disappointment occasioned by the unsuccessful issue of his frolic."

" Very likely," the squire rejoined, with a significant look at Roper.

" Fire and fury !" Juddock roared; " I can't pretend to say what may be Sir G.'s intentions in respect to this Doctor Plot, or Doctor Johnson, or whatever the fellow's vulgar name may be ; but if my honourable friend does not call him to account for his impertinence, I will. That's flat."

" I advise you not to meddle with him, captain," the squire observed. " He may be dangerous."

" Dangerous ! why so am I, sir,—the more dangerous of the two, I rather opine. Dangerous—ha !" And Juddock swallowed a glass of punch to allay his indignation.

The squire laughed ; the vicar chuckled ; indeed, everybody was amused, and no one more so than Jonas. The giant swore several tremendous oaths, but finding they only served to increase the general merriment, he held out his glass to be replenished, and grew calmer.

" I believe, Mr. Roper, you are steward of the manor

of Little Dunmow?" he said. "May I inquire, as
matter of curiosity, how many successful applications
have been made for the Flitch, in your time?"

"Not one, I'm sorry to say, captain," the steward
replied, with a smile. "But our conditions are so
hard, that few can subscribe to them. Besides, the
witnesses are very strictly examined."

"Udsbores! witnesses are necessary — are they?"
Juddock ejaculated.

"Certainly. Corroborative testimony is required by
the Court Baron in support of the application; and
witnesses are heard *per contra;* both sides being cross-
examined. Then the verdict of the Jury of Bachelors
and Maidens must be unanimous. One dissentient
voice would be fatal to the demandants. A severe
ordeal, I assure you, captain, for married folk. Few
are able to brook it."

"You hear all this, landlord?" Juddock remarked.
"Oddsfish! man; have you no misgivings?"

"None whatever, captain," Jonas replied. "Have
we, ducky?"

"Oh! none at all!" Nelly said, quite confidently.

"Numerous demands have been made," the steward
pursued; "but they have all been rejected on some
plea or other. I happen to have the Register of the
Court Baron in my pocket, containing a list of the
claimants, and the objections made to them, and with
the squire's consent, I can read you a few extracts
from it."

"You will oblige me eternally, sir, by doing so,"
Juddock rejoined. "I shall be glad of any information
I can obtain on the subject."

"What makes him so curious, I wonder?" Jonas
muttered. "The rascal must have some dark design
against me."

"I am sure your honour won't refuse us!" Nelly cried, looking entreatingly at the squire. "It will be so entertaining to hear how many deluded creatures there are—fancying themselves happy and devoted to each other—won't it, Jonas?"

"Very entertaining, indeed—very!" he replied, trying to force a laugh, but with indifferent success. "That won't be our case—oh! no."

"Read what you please from the Register, Roper," the squire said. "All claims being publicly made, there can be no reason for secrecy."

Permission being thus accorded, the steward took from his pocket a clasped volume, bound in white calf-skin, and, opening it, observed:

"The Register of the Court Baron commences with the year 1702, in the same month, and pretty nearly on the same day that Queen Anne ascended the throne. The first entry is as follows: 'Roger Appleton, of South Bemfleet, in this county, tailor, and Tabitha, his wife. Not allowed, because it was proved by a credible witness that the said Tabitha, on one occasion, had styled her husband 'the ninth part of a man.'"

"Served Snip right," Juddock cried, laughing. "Uds-bores! if Dame Tabitha had had nine tailors for husbands, she would only have been as well off as any ordinary married woman; eh, Mrs. N.?"

Mr. Roper read on.

"John Trott, of Thaxted, baker, and Prudence, his wife. Approved: recited the Oath; and received the Flitch; but words ensuing between them as they got into the chair, the prize was held to be forfeited, and they were deprived of it accordingly!"

"How very foolish!" Nelly exclaimed.

"Why foolish?" Juddock asked.

"To quarrel at all, to be sure," Nelly quickly rejoined.

"No more demands were made in this year," Mr. Roper continued, turning over a leaf,—"but in the next there were several, amongst which was one on the part of Sir Conyers de Gaunt, of Waltham, and Dame Arabella, his spouse; and owing to the importance of the parties, and the peculiarity of the circumstances, this application excited much attention. Considerable disparity it appears existed between the pair in point of age—Sir Conyers being nigh seventy, and described as a battered old beau, while Lady de Gaunt was a very beautiful young woman, of three-and-twenty, who had been an actress, and was well known by her maiden name of Bell Fairbank, but not a whisper had been breathed against her fair fame. Twenty witnesses examined. All proved the entire happiness of the parties; and some declared they had never seen such a couple before. This phrase, appearing ambiguous, was explained by the witnesses to mean, that they had never known two wedded persons so much attached to each other. Twenty-first witness (a female) declared that she had once heard her ladyship say, 'Better be an old man's darling, than a young man's warling.' Held an objection; but might be overruled, if nothing stronger appeared. Next witness (a discharged housemaid) swore she had given her ladyship a note, which had been hastily concealed as Sir Conyers was heard approaching. Mr. Humdrum, the head valet-de-chambre, had given witness the letter. Mr. Humdrum recalled, reluctantly admitted the truth of the statement, and being further interrogated, confessed that the note was from Charles Clipsby, her ladyship's cousin, who had been forbidden the house by Sir Conyers. Why was Charles Clipsby forbidden the house? To this demand from the Court, Mr. Humdrum professed utter inability to reply. The next and last witness, Juliana

Clipsby, wife of the before-mentioned Charles, declared
that her husband was neither cousin, nor relation in
any degree to Lady de Gaunt, but had been passed off
as such as a blind, for purposes which would be apparent to the Court when she read a letter from her ladyship, which she had taken from her husband's pockets,
wherein Sir Conyers was described as an old dupe and
dotard, with sundry other epithets by no means com-
plimentary to him, or expressive of affection on the
part of his lady. The Court declined to hear the letter
read in full, and at once rejected the application. Me-
morandum to this case. Sir Conyers not only lost the
Flitch, but his wife into the bargain; for separating
from her in consequence of the disclosures made in the
course of the investigation, he subsequently obtained a
divorce."

"But he got another wife, for he married Mrs.
Clipsby, who was likewise divorced from her husband,
as I perfectly recollect," said the squire. "Proceed,
Roper."

"The next demandants are Nehemiah Wagstaff and
Margery his wife, of Chipping Ongar," the steward
said, "and in this case the lady was thirty years older
than her husband; a fine strapping young fellow, six
feet four in height, and two and a half broad from
shoulder to shoulder."

"'Slife! a proper young fellow—eh, Mrs. N.?"
Juddock cried, slapping his leviathan thigh.

"In addition to this, Mrs. Wagstaff had only one
eye," pursued the steward.

"Then Wag got on her blind side it is to be presumed," the giant remarked, with a loud roar

"But she was very well off," Roper continued—
"very well off, indeed. And so folks generally supposed Nehemiah had married Margery Gimcrack for

her money; but to all appearances, no couple could be happier than they were. Mrs. Wagstaff doted on her spouse, and her spouse seemed to requite her affection. When the Oath was recited, Wagstaff was observed to hesitate a little at the second line, where the jurants declare that

'They ne'er made nuptial transgression,'

while his wife fixed her single eye rather sharply upon him. Being required to repeat the line, he hurried quickly over it, upon which Mrs. Wagstaff insisted on its being pronounced for the third time, and more deliberately; adding loud enough to be heard by the Jury, that she began to think her suspicions in regard to her housemaid, Susan, must be correct. Claim hereupon refused."

"That Oath has proved a sad stumbling-block, it must be owned," the vicar observed, "but I hope the guilt of false-swearing has not been incurred by any of the parties."

"Your reverence cannot be too impressive on that point," Juddock said, glancing at Jonas.

"Peter Proby and his wife, of Coggeshall, who stand next on the list," the steward pursued, "shared the fate of the Wagstaffs, for they could not affirm they had never offended each other

—'Since they were married man and wife
By household brawls or contentious strife.'

But Humphrey Chickweed of Romford, brewer, and Lettice, did very well till they came to the couplet:

'Or since the parish clerk said Amen
Wished yourselves unmarried again,'

Here upon Lettice remarked that people could not help their thoughts. Being questioned as to the meaning of the expression, she replied that she might sometimes have *thought* she had better have remained single ; but she had never given *utterance* to the wish. Rejected. Mrs. Trinket of Billericay said she could not positively swear that she loved her husband Timothy as fervently as she did on the day of her marriage, and therefore desired to omit the lines :

> ' But continued true and in desire
> As when they joined hands in holy quire.

Claim disallowed.   But the hardest case of all appears to be that of Dick Honeymoon of Braintree, and Theriaca his wife, who lived in perfect love and amity for a whole twelvemonth, and then, as appeared on inquiry, had words on the day over."

"Mind that, landlord," Juddock remarked. "Mind that !"

"In short," the steward said, closing the Register, and putting it into his pocket, "insuperable objections have been raised to every demand.   Unless the applicants can take the required Oath fully and unreservedly ; unless their own declaration can be supported by unquestionable evidence ; they are certain of refusal. Ours being a time-honoured custom, we are determined to maintain it in its integrity, and to carry it out in the spirit in which it was ordained.   And as the reward we give is intended as a testimonial of the highest domestic merit, so nothing but decisive proofs of the existence of such merit will satisfy us.   Accordingly, we are obliged to adopt unusual means of arriving at the truth.   Every circumstance connected with the parties is inquired into, and we pierce, somewhat inquisitorially it may be, into private affairs.   But this is unavoidable.   Every thought, word, and deed must be laid open to us.   A cross look would be sufficient to nullify a claim."

"And all this gives you no uneasiness, landlord?" Juddock inquired. "You are prepared for these searching inquiries—eh?"

"Fully prepared, captain," Jonas answered, with something of a quaver in his tones.

"Well, you're a bold man, that's all I can say," the giant rejoined.

"Sir, I have good reason to be bold," Jonas returned, plucking up his courage as he took his wife's hand, and looked tenderly into her face. "And so would you be if you were in my shoes."

"I wouldn't stand in your shoes for a trifle," muttered Juddock; adding aloud, "Well, Mr. Roper, I thank my stars I'm not married, and am not, therefore, likely to trouble you with any application on behalf of self and spouse; but I must say your conditions are too hard. 'Sblood! sir, they act as a prohibition."

"The greater the difficulty the greater the honour," the steward replied. "Our ordeal is strict, and very properly so, since we do not profess to reward common cases of domestic happiness, but such as are exceptional, and worthy of honour. Without referring to the loving couple here, who I trust are in a fair way of success, I may express my belief that Frank Woodbine and his wife will have no difficulty in substantiating their claim. I am quite aware that Jonas is of a different opinion, and means to produce evidence reflecting upon Frank's perfect fidelity to his wife; but I am pretty sure it will be explained away."

"I am glad to hear you say so, Roper," the squire observed. "Here Paul," he added to the old huntsman, "take another glass of punch, man. I'm not angry with you now. My curiosity is quite stimulated about this Rose Woodbine and her perfections. Where can she have hidden herself that I have never caught

FRANK WOODBINE APPLYING THE HORSEWHIP TO JUDDOCK.

P. 162.

a glimpse of her? I thought I knew every pretty girl in the neighbourhood, but, by all accounts, I have missed the prettiest."

"Just as well for Frank your honour has missed seeing her, in my opinion," Nelly said roguishly in his ear.

The squire laughed, and remarked, " She was Mrs. Leslie's niece, I believe, Roper?"

"It is so given out, sir. But I rather think she is her grand-daughter."

" Her grand-daughter?" the squire exclaimed, starting, and looking hard at Roper.

" Some other time I will explain myself," the steward said; " but I always thought it strange your honour never chanced to behold her."

" Why, it is strange—exceedingly strange!" the squire cried, after a moment's reflection. " Often as I have been at Mrs. Leslie's during the good old curate's lifetime, and since, I never once came across the grand-daughter. It would almost seem as if she had been kept out of the way purposely."

" It looks very like it, indeed," Nelly remarked, in an undertone.

" What was Rose's maiden name?" the squire asked.

" Mildmay," the steward answered. " She came from Cumberland."

" From what part of the county?" the squire said.

" From Penrith, I have heard," was Mr. Roper's reply.

" Penrith!" the squire exclaimed, in surprise. " Why, my niece comes from Penrith."

"Yes, sir—I know it," the steward answered evasively. " Mrs. Leslie, if you remember, had a daughter who died in that part of England."

" Oh! yes, I recollect," the squire interrupted some-

M

what hastily; "but Grace Leslie died unmarried, Roper."

"Then, of course, she can't be Rose Woodbine's mother," Nelly observed. The little hussy had been listening attentively to what was said.

"I can't pretend to say whether Grace Leslie was married or not," the steward rejoined—"but I believe Rose to be her daughter."

"You do!" the squire exclaimed. "Zounds! we must talk this over to-morrow. Why was the circumstance never mentioned to me before? You neglected your duty in not acquainting me with it."

"I hope not, sir," the steward rejoined, in an apologetic tone. "At all events I acted for the best."

Squire Monkbury got very red in the face, and seemed to have some difficulty in controlling his passion.

Mr. Roper, too, looked uneasy, and fidgeted in his chair.

"I wonder what all this means," Nelly muttered. "It quite passes my comprehension. But I'll try and find it out."

There was a brief silence, which was broken at length by the squire.

"Well, I must see her, and without delay," he said. "It's too late to go to the cottage to-night."

"Mercy on us! I should think so," Nelly exclaimed; "why it's getting on for midnight. Rose has been a-bed, and fast asleep these two hours, I'll be bound. That is, if nothing has happened to Frank," she added to herself.

"Well, well—then it must be to-morrow," the squire said, once more lapsing into deep thought.

"Yes, to-morrow," the steward rejoined. "Sleep upon it, sir."

"Landlord," quoth Juddock, finding it rather dull, since no one seemed inclined to talk to him, "I understand your house is haunted. It looks like a receptacle for ghosts. There must be some marvellous story connected with it. Let us have it, I pray of you?"

"I can sing you a ballad about a ghost, captain," Jonas replied, "but it does not relate to this house."

"No matter for that—so the stave be good. Enliven us with it. Attention, gentlemen."

And Jonas sang as follows:

Old Grindrod's Ghost.

A BALLAD.*

I.

OLD GRINDROD was hanged on a gibbet high,
  On the spot where the deed was done;
'Twas a desolate place, on the edge of a moor,—
  A place for the timid to shun.

II.

Chains round his middle, and chains round his neck,
  And chains round his ankles were hung:
And there in all weathers, in sunshine and rain,
  Old Grindrod, the murderer, swung.

III.

Old Grindrod had long been the banquet of crows,
  Who flocked on his carcase to batten;
And the unctuous morsels that fell from their feast
  Served the rank weeds beneath him to fatten!

IV.

All that's now left of him is a skeleton grim,
  The stoutest to strike with dismay;
So ghastly the sight, that no urchin, at night,
  Who can help it, will pass by that way

V.

All such as had dared, had sadly been scared,
  And soon 'twas the general talk,
That the wretch in his chains, each night took the pains,
  To come down from the gibbet—*and walk!*

* Founded on an incident, related to me, with admirable humour, by my old and much-valued friend, GILBERT WINTER, ESQ., late of Stocks, near Manchester

VI.

The story was told to a Traveller bold,
   At an inn, near the moor, by the Host;
He appeals to each guest, and its truth they attest,
   But the Traveller laughs at the Ghost.

VII.

" Now, to show you," quoth he, "how afraid I must be,
   A rump and a dozen I'll lay;
That before it strikes One, I will go forth alone,
   Old Grindrod a visit to pay.

VIII.

" To the gibbet I'll go, and this I will do,
   As sure as I stand in my shoes:
Some address I'll devise, and if Grinny replies,
   My wager, of course I shall lose."

IX.

" Accepted the bet; but the night it is wet,"
   Quoth the Host. " Never mind!" says the Guest;
" From darkness and rain, the adventure will gain,
   To my mind, an additional zest."

X.

Now midnight had toll'd and the Traveller bold
   Set out from the inn, all alone;
'Twas a night black as ink, and our friend 'gan to think.
   That uncommonly cold it had grown.

XI.

But of nothing afraid, and by nothing delayed;
   Plunging onward through bog and through wood ;
Wind and rain in his face, he ne'er slackened his pace,
   Till under the gibbet he stood.

XII.

Though dark as could be, yet he thought he could see
   The skeleton hanging on high ;
The gibbet it creaked ; and the rusty chains squeaked ;
   And a screech-owl flew solemnly by.

XIII.

The heavy rain pattered, the hollow bones clattered,
   The Traveller's teeth chattered—with cold—not with fright.
The wind it blew lustily, piercingly, gustily ;—
   Certainly not an agreeable night !

XIV.

" Ho! Grindrod, old fellow !" thus loudly did bellow,
   The Traveller mellow,—"How are ye, my blade ?"—
" I'm cold and I'm dreary ; I'm wet and I'm weary ;
   But soon I'll be near ye!" the Skeleton said

xv.

The grisly bones rattled, and with the chains battled,
    The gibbet appallingly shook ;
On the ground something stirr'd, but no more the man heard,—
    To his heels, on the instant, he took.

xvi.

Over moorland he dashed, and through quagmire he plashed,
    His pace never daring to slack ;
Till the hostel he neared, for greatly he feared
    Old Grindrod would leap on his back.

xvii.

His wager he lost, and a trifle it cost ;
    But that which annoyed him the most,
Was to find out too late, that certain as fate,
    The Landlord had acted the Ghost.

Juddock laughed very heartily at the landlord's ditty,
as indeed did the rest of the company, including the
squire, who was roused by it from his reverie, and at
its conclusion proceeded to replenish the glasses.

"I suspect, Mr. Jonas, you youself are the cunning
landlord who enacted old Grinny's ghost," the giant
observed, after taking off his punch.

"No—no, captain, I've as much courage as any man
of my inches," Jonas responded, drawing himself up ;
" but I'm not quite equal to that.   Howsomdever,
you're not so far out.   The landlord in question was a
relative of mine, and kept an inn on Pendleton Moor,
near Manchester, close to which old Grindrod was
hanged in chains.   I had the tale from the landlord's
own lips—so I know it to be true.   But talking of
ghosts—our lady in white is sometimes very troublesome.   I wish your reverence," he added to the vicar,
" would lay her in the Red Sea,"

" Spirits, I fear, are not as easily exorcised as they
used to be in Popish times, landlord," Doctor Sidebottom replied, " when the priests compelled them to
depart according to the forms prescribed by Saint Gre-
gory and Saint Anthony, as mentioned in the life of

the latter by Saint Athanasius. One adjuration, I remember, runs in this way, and I will pronounce it, that we may see whether it will prove efficacious." And extending his pipe like a wand, he pronounced these words in a solemn, emphatic voice : " *Adjuro te, Spectrum horribile ! per Judicem vivorum et mortuorum, per Factorem mundi, qui habet potestatem mittere te in Gehennâ, ut ab hac domo festinus discedas. Audi Spectrum ! et time, et victum et prostratum recede ir Sinû Arabico !*"

" That sounds very dreadful," Jonas exclaimed, in a quaking voice ; " the exorcism quite makes one's flesh creep. Lady Juga I hope will hear it, and rest quiet in future."

" Can anybody give us another ghost-story ?" the squire asked. " You look as if you had one ready, captain."

" Egad, squire, I can sing you a ballad which may match the landlord's, if that will serve your turn ?"

" Nothing better.—Let us have it, by all means."

And wetting his whistle, according to custom, Juddock commenced the following legendary strains, which he sang right merrily.

The Barber of Ripon and the Ghostly Basin.

A TALE OF THE CHARNEL HOUSE.

I.

Since Ghost-Stories you want, there is one I can tell
Of a wonderful thing that Bat Pigeon befel :
A Barber, at Ripon, in Yorkshire was he,
And as keen in his craft as his best blade could be.

II.

Now Bat had a fancy,—a strange one, you'll own,—
Instead of a brass bowl to have one of bone :
To the Charnel-house 'neath the old Minster he'd been,
And there, 'mongst the relics, a treasure had seen.

III.

'Mid the pile of dry bones that encumber'd the ground,
One pumpkin-like skull with a mazard he found ;
If home that enormous old sconce he could take,
What a capital basin for shaving 'twould make !

IV.

Well ! he got it, at last, from the Sexton, his friend,
Little dreaming how queerly the business would end :
Next, he saw'd off the cranium close to the eyes ;
And behold then ! a basin capacious in size.

V.

As the big bowl is balanced 'twixt finger and thumb,
Bat's customers all with amazement are dumb ;
At the strange yellow object they blink and they stare,
But what it can be not a soul is aware !

VI.

Bat Pigeon, as usual, to rest went that night:
But he soon started up in a terrible fright :
Lo ! giving the curtains and bedclothes a pull,
A Ghost he beheld—*wanting half of its skull!*

VII.

" Unmannerly barber " the Spectre exclaimed ;
" To desecrate bonehouses art not ashamed ?
Thy crown into shivers, base varlet, I'll crack,
Unless, on the instant, my own I get back !"

VIII.

" There it lies on the table !" Bat quakingly said,
" Sure a skull cannot matter when once one is dead."—
" Such a skull as thine may not, thou addlepate fool !
But a shaver of clowns for a Knight is no rule !"

IX.

With this the wroth Spectre its brainpan clapp'd on,
And holding it fast in a twinkling was gone;
But ere through the keyhole the phantom could rush,
Bat perceived it had taken the soap and the brush.

X.

When the Sexton next morn went the Charnel-house round,
The great Yellow Skull* in its old place he found :
And 'twixt its lank jaws, while they grinningly ope,
As in mockery stuck, are the Brush and the Soap !

Again the laughter and plaudits were loud and long.
Again the glasses were replenished.

* This ghostly relic may still be seen in the curious Charnel-
house of Ripon Minster.   And the legend connected with it is
devoutly believed by the Sexton, its narrator.

" Well, it's easy to make a jest of supernatural appearances when we're all comfortably seated round a
table, well provided with appliances for good cheer, as
we are now," the squire remarked; " but, let me tell
you, it's very different when you're alone in a large, dark,
solitary room; reported to be haunted. I don't think
it any reproach to my manhood to confess that I have
felt uneasy under such circumstances."

" I guess what your honour alludes to," Nelly observed. " You refer to the night you once passed
here when you occupied the Haunted Chamber. You
may remember I tried to dissuade you from using it,
but you laughed at me, and told me you weren't afraid
of ghosts or hobgoblins. Doctor Plot sleeps in the
room to-night, and he said much the same thing to
me. We shall hear whether he changes his note to-
morrow."

" I hope he will be spared the sight I beheld—or
fancied I beheld," the squire rejoined, with a slight
shudder.

" Adzooks ! what was it you did see, squire ?" Juddock asked.

" On my soul, I don't like to talk of it, captain."

" Ah ! gentlemen, this is a very mysterious house,
and strange things have happened in it," quoth Jonas,
shaking his head; " and no wonder some of the old
family can't rest in their graves. Lady Juga is not the
only one that walks."

" Why, who else does, in the name of wonder, Jonas ?"
Nelly cried. " I never saw any other spirit."

" But I have," her husband replied, shaking his
head solemnly. " I once beheld a dreadful apparition ;
in the likeness of a man with a great, gaping wound
in his breast, and his shirt all dabbled over with blood.
The ghost came out of a closet in the Haunted Room."

Nelly uttered a faint scream.

" Whose ghost could it be Jonas ?" Roper inquired.

" *His* father's, sir," the landlord replied, in a low, mysterious tone, pointing over his shoulder to Sir Gilbert, who was still seated by the fire. " The late baronet, who was killed in a duel, as you know, by Sir Walter Fitzwalter. I'm quite sure it was he."

" This is strange, indeed, landlord," the squire observed.

" Very strange !" Roper cried.

" Still stranger you never mentioned it to me before," Nelly cried, rather piqued.

" I didn't like to alarm you, ducky," Jonas rejoined. " A proof of my great consideration for your feelings."

" By all accounts the house seems to swarm with spectres," Juddock exclaimed. " I hope my room is free from them."

" Can't answer for it," Jonas replied. " Spirits have a great deal of malice, and play strange tricks—especially she-spirits."

At this moment, a singular noise at the head of the staircase attracted general attention.

VIII.

THE MAIL-CLAD APPARITION.

ALL eyes were turned in the direction of the sound, and to the astonishment and horror of the beholders, they saw a tall, mail-clad, apparition issue from the sliding panel The visor of the helmet was raised, disclosing a pale, blood-stained countenance. Nelly screamed, and fell into the arms of her husband, who had enough to do to sustain her, being terribly frightened himself. The rest of the company stared aghast.

There could be no illusion in this case. The spectre was palpable enough to sight and hearing too. Its heavy tread sounded on the boards of the gallery, like blows from a paviour's rammer.

Meanwhile, Peggy and Dick having come forth from the corridor, the screams of the pretty chambermaid were added to those of her mistress. Utterly disregarding them, and heedless of the fright it occasioned to the party below, the spectre began to descend the great oak staircase.

Slowly! step after step. Clank! clank! clank! Thump! thump! thump!

Some centuries had elapsed since those knightly trappings had been worn. Some centuries had elapsed since such a figure had stalked down those stairs.

The ghost came on, but no one appeared inclined to address it. No one stirred from his place.

Nelly alone spoke. She had now left off screaming, finding it of no use, and whispered to her husband— "Look, Jonas, look! It's one of the old Fitzwalters. Don't you recollect his picture painted on one of the panels in the Haunted Chamber?"

"Yes, I recollect it," Jonas rejoined, his teeth chattering with fright, and his lips trembling; "but the ghost's very like Frank Woodbine."

"Why, so it is, I declare," Nelly said, recovering her courage a little.

Still the spectre continued to thump the stairs in its slow descent. Clank! clank! clank!

Suddenly, Sir Gilbert de Montfichet starting to his feet, drew his sword, and hastened to confront the apparition. The encounter took place at the foot of the staircase. Nothing daunted, the ghost, with its gauntleted hand, snatched the sword, pointed at its breast, from the young baronet's grasp, and shivered it in twain upon the floor. It then took Sir Gilbert by the shoulder, and thrust him forcibly backwards several paces. Exclamations of surprise were uttered by all the spectators, and Jonas would have taken to his heels if he had not been withheld by his wife, who began to have some glimmering of the truth.

But as it had now become quite evident to all, that the supposed ghost, which had occasioned them so much terror, was a creature of flesh and blood like themselves, there was no limit to their expressions of indignation at the unjustifiable trick played upon them. Jonas declared he had seen through it at once, and had only waited to ascertain how far it would be carried before he resented it. Great oaths were discharged by Juddock, like shells from a monster mortar; and even the squire swore lustily. But the first to aid Sir Gilbert—perhaps because he chanced to be nearest him—was old Paul Flitwick.

"Tak that, warmint," the ancient huntsman cried, aiming a blow at the ghost's head with the butt-end of his heavy hunting-whip. "Tak that."

Well was it for Frank that a stout casque protected him; or his tale had then been told. The blow sounded like the stroke of a hammer on the anvil; and for a moment it staggered the young man, but recovering himself, he snatched the whip from Paul, and laid it across his shoulders.

"Haud hard, mon—haud yar hond, a say! What the Dule be'st at?" vociferated the old huntsman, yelping like a beaten hound.

"Paying off a little score I owe you for mischief-making, Paul," Frank replied, giving him another cut or so. "Don't you know me, you old fool?"

"Whay, zaunds! af at ben't Fraank Woodbane—the gaam-keeper," Paul cried—"haud hard, Frank—tells ee."

"Frank Woodbine!" exclaimed Juddock, in stentorian tones, and with a terrific imprecation. "Is this he? I'll be the death of him."

"Oh! don't let 'em harm him, your honour," Nelly cried, with great earnestness, to the squire. "Frank's such a nice young man. I don't know how he got that armour on; but I'm sure it was with no ill intention. I can explain how he happens to be here."

"Explain it, then, to me?" whispered Jonas. "Oh! you wicked hussy!"

Meanwhile, some half-dozen immense strides brought the giant within reach of the young gamekeeper, who, mistaking his purpose, ordered him to stand off.

"You are a big man and a strong, and are armed with a warrant, I make no doubt," Frank cried; "but I advise you not to lay hands upon me, or you may get the worst of it, Mr. Bumbailiff."

"Bumbailiff! I a base bumbailiff!" the giant roared, transported with fury. "'Sdeath! fellow, I am an officer."

"So I conclude," Frank said; "an officer of the meanest kind, employed by Mr. Roper to arrest me."

"I am employed by his Majesty King George the Second, sirrah; and I will carve you in minced-meat for your impertinence," the giant roared, making a pass at him with his lengthy blade, which did him no injury whatever, being turned aside by the steel breastplate. Frank seemed invulnerable.

Not so Captain Juddock. The lash of the heavy hunting-whip was again called vigorously into action, and seemed to find out the tenderest parts of his person. Stamping and roaring like a mad bull under the severity ɔf the application, he at last fairly took to his heels, ɩnd fled, howling with rage and pain.

Frank was left by himself; master of the field; and flourishing the conquering hunting-whip.

The squire, and indeed everybody else, except Sir Gilbert, laughed at the boastful giant's discomfiture. As to Jonas, his fat sides shook with merriment; and tears of exquisite delight rushed to his eyes. "I can forgive Frank anything for this good service," he thought.

"How comes Frank Woodbine to be here at this time of night, and tricked out in that knightly gear?" the steward inquired.

"I locked him up in the cellar, please you, Mr. Roper," Nelly said.

"And why did you so lock him up, mistress?"

"Ay, answer that, mistress," Jonas whispered.

"To keep him out of the way of your bailiffs, Mr. Roper," Nelly replied. "But he manged to get out somehow: for when I went to look for him, the bird was flown."

"How I contrived it, would puzzle me to explain," Frank cried, overhearing what was said; "but I found my way with a deal of difficulty, and in a very round-about manner, to a closet where I discovered this old suit of armour; so I clapped it on, as you see, and came forth, thinking I should be able to escape, undetected."

"But you're bleeding!—You've hurt yourself?" Nelly exclaimed.

"A mere scratch," Frank replied, taking off the helmet.

"Here, Peggy!—a napkin and a basin of water—quick!" Nelly said to the chambermaid, who with Carroty Dick had now ventured to come down stairs. "And bring the balsam from the cupboard."

"Have a moment's patience with the young man, sir," Mr. Roper said to the squire, "and keep Sir Gilbert and his friend quiet, if possible," pointing to the young baronet and Juddock; both of whom were evidently breathing vengeance against Frank.

"Gad's life, Roper, you're a strange fellow," cried the squire—"you pretend to know nothing, and you are in everybody's secrets. I warrant me you know more about that young man than you choose to admit."

"Well, sir, perhaps I do," the steward rejoined, with a smile.

"I was quite sure of it," the squire said. "Zounds! now his face is cleansed from blood, the youth is very handsome."

While Frank, occupied with the napkin and ewer which Peggy had brought him, was effacing from his features so far as he could the marks of the accident, Sir Gilbert and Juddock seemed not ill-disposed to draw fresh blood from him, and it required all the squire's authority, backed by that of the vicar, to restrain them from an attack. Very assiduous was Nelly, meanwhile, in her attentions to the young man; making him sit down; carefully removing his clotted hair, and bathing his brow. She had just applied a sovereign remedy to the hurt, when the outer door was opened, giving admittance to Rose Woodbine, and Dragon.

As she entered, Rose hastily and anxiously inquired of Jonas if anything had been seen of her husband. The landlord replied by pointing to the young man.

At first, Rose scarcely recognised him in his strange disguise; but then with a cry of mingled delight and uneasiness, she rushed towards him, and threw her arms round his neck. Dragon was considerably puzzled too; and examined his master's greaves before he could be quite satisfied it was him, after which, he expressed his delight by barking loudly and leaping upon him.

"I cannot take you to my heart as I desire, Rose," the young man said, with a smile. "I do not know how in times of chivalry, knights, when fully equipped for fight, contrived to embrace the ladies of their love; but I should be afraid of injuring you, sweetheart, if I clasped you in my arms now."

Certes, in the days to which Frank referred, it would have been difficult to find, search where you might, among press of knights, a goodlier person, or comelier features than fell to the young man's share. His was one of those noble faces the mould of which seems to be lost, since we never meet with it in these days; picturesque, beautiful, manly, chivalrous in expression. Frank bore him in his steely apparel as if constantly accustomed to it, and not as if he had donned it for the first time. His deportment seemed to have undergone a complete change, and there was a stateliness in his manner, and a certain haughtiness of carriage— altogether unusual—that impressed every beholder with surprise. Not that there was any haughtiness—but, on the contrary, deepest love,—in the look he fixed on Rose, as with fond arms twined around his neck, and earnest eyes turned upwards, she gazed admiringly and tenderly upon his face. And if he appeared like proud knight of old, was she not worthy to match with him? Was she not fair and graceful as he was hardy and well-favoured? Was she not worthy of his devotion? Ay, marry was she. Lovelier dame than she never nerved arm at tilt or tourney. Brighter eyes than hers never stirred knightly bosom. Sweeter lips never rewarded knightly prowess. And Frank thought so, and felt so too, as he bent his stately neck to kiss them.

A comely pair indeed ! Kindly as comely ! Loving as kindly !

"Well, I declare it's quite a picture !" Nelly exclaimed, unable to refuse her meed of admiration at the sight. "I never saw anything prettier. And the dog too—how well he comes in !"

Dragon, in fact, formed no bad addition to the group.

But Nelly had other causes of admiration presently. Finding her husband was hurt—a circumstance she had not remarked in the first joy of their meeting—Rose displayed the greatest anxiety, till it was relieved by the light manner in which he treated the accident, coupled with assurances, on his part, that Nelly had quite cured him with the balsam she had applied; on which his wife could not thank the hostess sufficiently.

"No jealousy, I perceive," thought Nelly. "*I* couldn't have thanked *her* "

Then again, when Rose inquired how he came by the armour in which he was clad—telling him at the same time how well it became him—and wondered what had detained him so late?—she was quite content when informed that all would be explained by-and-by. Nay, she was more than content, for was he not safe and happy ?—that being all she desired to know. Neither did she heed his expressions of regret at the uneasiness his unavoidable absence had occasioned her. Sufficient, it was unavoidable. Could better understanding subsist between two people ? Nelly thought not. Still she could not help commenting to herself on such singular conduct.

"She has no more curiosity than jealousy," Nelly thought. "Now, if I had a handsome husband and he were to stay out late, I should go distracted, and would make him account for every minute of his absence. And if Jonas were to get into a suit of armour—though

I don't think any would fit him—I'd never let him rest till I knew why he put it on. But Rose takes everything quietly. How differently people are constituted, to be sure!"

Not knowing what had happened, Rose thought it better to acquaint her husband in a whisper that the debt to the steward had been settled, and that she had the bond at home. Frank saw she had some further explanations to give, but he forebore to make inquiries now.

"You have greatly relieved my mind, Rose," he said—" and there can now be no obstacle to my immediate return home. But as I can scarcely go forth in this garb, you, love, shall perform the part of a faithful squire, and help your loyal knight to take off his harness—that, I believe, is the proper term."

And as both Nelly and Rose helped to disarm him, the task was quickly performed, and the young gamekeeper was left in his customary attire.

"Now you're like yourself, Frank," Rose cried, embracing him.

"I know who he was like when he had the armour on," Nelly said. "Somebody he might be very proud to resemble."

Frank looked hard at her, but made no remark.

Rose's unexpected appearance produced different effects upon different persons among the company. On seeing her, Sir Gilbert ordered Captain Juddock to follow him, and ran hastily up the great staircase ; so she was not aware of his presence, though he and the giant continued to watch what was passing from the gallery.

But no one was so much interested as the squire, and his countenance expressed the variety of emotions that agitated his breast on sight of Rose. Astonishment,

delight, affection—were all painted upon it by turns,
—and he had some difficulty in restraining himself.
Indeed, he would have rushed towards her, if he had
not been withheld by the steward.

"I must speak to her, Roper—I *must*," he cried.

"Not to-night, sir—not to-night, I beseech you," the
steward rejoined. "I will engage to bring her and her
husband—or Rose, at all events—to Monkbury Place
to-morrow morning. Defer the interview till then.
Something has to be done in the interim—with Doctor
Plot—you understand."

"No—I don't understand it at all," the squire cried,
very impatiently, "but I know that you torment me
worse than the devil. However, be it as you will. On
the understanding that you *will* brink her to Monkbury
to-morrow morning, I am content to wait till then.
But I shan't sleep a wink to-night for thinking of her.
Bless her pretty face! how like she is to her mother!
But I must be off! If I stay here a minute longer I
shall break out in spite of you. To-morrow morning,
without fail, Roper!"

"Without fail," the steward emphatically replied.

And without waiting to say good-night to the vicar,
or to any one else, the squire rushed out of the house,
followed by Paul Flitwick, and more leisurely by the
reverend gentleman himself, upon whom the punch
had made considerable impression.

A few words then passed between Roper and the
young gamekeeper and his wife. On learning that the
squire desired to see them at Monkbury Place next
morning, Frank readily agreed to go; but though Rose
offered no remonstrance, a deep flush overspread her
features, quickly succeeded by perfect paleness. Her
emotion did not escape the notice of the steward, who
endeavoured to reassure her by a look; though it passed

unobserved by her husband, as he turned at the moment to take leave of Nelly. This point achieved, Mr. Roper went his way.

Soon afterwards, the pair took their departure; Jonas and Nelly attending them to the door, with many professions of regard. As may be supposed, they had much to talk of on the way home, and scarcely noticed the gambols of Dragon by their side.

Ere half an hour more had elapsed, the inmates of the Old Inn were buried in repose.

All except One.

Part the Third.
THE HAUNTED CHAMBER.

I.

A VOICE FROM THE TOMB.

HE went down the dark corridor, slowly and silently. He hesitated at the door of a room he knew well—alas! too well—and sighed as he opened it.

Profound emotions were awakened in his bosom as he set foot within that chamber. Scenes of other days arose before him with the vividness of reality. He beheld himself in the full vigour of manhood, ardent, impassioned, blessed with the hand of her he loved, and anticipating a cloudless future. He beheld her, as she was when he first called her his own; young, fresh, superbly beautiful. Her accents were those of endearment; her looks, tenderness and love. They smote him now like a poignard's point driven to his very

heart. He did not think he could have borne a pang
so keen, and live.

His torture was not yet ended. He saw her standing before the mirror, tiring her jetty hair; her stately
figure and marble neck ravishing him with admiration.
A picture of beauty never to he effaced from his memory. But it was maddening now. Why, he asked in
despair, could not the past be recalled—or for ever
cancelled? Why could not men live their loves over
again, to repair the wrongs they had done, and regain
lost happiness?

Pressing his hands before his eyes, he tried to shut
out the beautiful, but agonising vision. Not being
presented to the visual ray, but to the mind, it could
not be excluded. Staggering towards a chair, he sank
upon it: a prey to intolerable anguish. Avenging
furies beset him, and lashed him with whips of steel.
His groans and frantic ejaculations might have awakened
pity even in those who had suffered from his severity
and injustice.

He could not rest. He strode about the room. He
even thought of quitting the house; denouncing himself as a madman for having come within it at all.
But where was he to go? He must endure the torture.
Perhaps it would subside. Little hope of it.

He walked to the fire. Ay, there he stood where he
had stood years ago. O, how unlike his former self!
how different in feeling. Then he had some youth
left—and at least, had hope. Now, he was an old,
broken man, crushed by the weight of despair; self-
widowed; self-exiled; a stranger to his kinsmen. No
fond accents had ever termed him—"Father."

The latter wrong, at least, could be repaired. Pride
might oppose the step as humiliating. Go to. It must
be taken. Abase thyself to the dust, proud man.

Expiate, so far as thou canst, the wrongs thou hast committed. Bow the stiff neck, and bend the stubborn knee. Make ample reparation; and then have done with a world, that has long since done with thee.

Arriving at this determination, he grew somewhat more composed, but his trouble was awakened anew, by the discovery of the handkerchief, which he had not as yet remarked.

Picking it up, he started as if a serpent had stung him. He knew whose it was, and in whose blood it was imbrued. He recognised his own cypher worked in the corner—by *her!*

Another vision arose—very different from the first, and far more terrible.

Grey dawn, with scarce light enough to see an object distinctly, revealed two men in a secluded spot, with swords crossed in conflict. Their secconds stood by, anxiously watching each pass they made, and glad when a thrust was successfully parried. A slight wound might, they hoped, end the fight. Such was not the intention of one of the combatants, a stern man, the peculiarity of whose posture showed him to be lame, and who breathed nothing but vengeance. Suddenly he made a feint, his adversary replied, laid himself open, and the vengeful sword passed through his breast to the hilt. The blade was drawn forth, and he fell. He essayed to speak, but could not—and fixed an imploring and forgiving look upon his slayer. The other was unmoved. Regarding his expiring foe with a look of gratified vengeance, he calmly wiped his dripping sword. Then tearing a leaf from his tablets, he traced a few lines upon it with a pencil, and folding the missive in the blood-stained handkerchief, bade his friend deliver it to his wife. While this took place, the wounded man died; and the others quitted the field. He who was charged with the ruthless commission, hastened to obey it.

Who talks of Retribution? Can Retribution be made for a deed like this? Yet men acquit him. Faugh! how foul blood smells! Throw away that handkerchief.

What more? Another letter and a phial. Are these, too, evidences of his guilt? The phial has held laudanum. She died by such a draught. Can this have contained the poison? The letter! It is addressed to himself—by *her!* The seal is unbroken. He tears it open. After reading a few lines, his brain reels; his eyes swim; the paper drops from his hand.

His first emotion, on recovering, was one of regret to find himself yet living; but he checked the thought as it rose, murmuring, "No, I must not die yet. My task is not ended. I have much to do before I quit this Vale of Tears."

He then trimmed the light, and summoning all his fortitude, resumed the perusal of the letter. These were the words that had shaken him:

"Farewell! for ever, Sir Walter! This is my last leave-taking. Trouble yourself no more about me. When these lines meet your gaze I shall be past all earthly consideration. I have drained the fatal phial, and already feel its numbing influence. Insupportable grief has driven me to the desperate step, but an All Wise Power, knowing the extent of my sorrows, and my utter inability to bear them, will, I trust, pardon me. I have prayed fervently for your forgiveness, and my own. May those prayers be heard at the throne of Infinite Mercy! In this my latest hour, I utter no reproaches against you; and I take the whole guilt of the rash act I have committed in thus rushing, unsummoned to Eternity, upon my own head. Nor, in asserting with my latest breath my entire freedom from criminality, such as you have imputed to me, do I design to reproach you. But it is needful you should know the truth, and not continue to labour under a delusion, which if not dispelled, may work mischief to our child, as it has brought misery and destruction on me. As I hope for pity hereafter, I have been a true wife to you, Sir Walter—in thought and deed."

While reading this, he could not repress a groan.

" Nay more, I have loved you with unwavering affection, even when unjustly doubted, and harshly treated. From such error as might bring dishonour upon your name—nay, from the slightest shade of it, my conscience is free; but I must own to lesser faults, which, I cannot now, on the brink of the grave, attempt to palliate, feeling they have produced these sad consequences. At the time, they seemed light and venial to me, and to others; but now I view them differently, and regret from the bottom of my heart that I have acquired the knowledge too late. The faults I impute to myself are wilfulness, and caprice : too great confidence in the power over you of my own personal attractions, coupledwith the desire to exhibit it. Assuming an air of levity, foreign to my natural disposition, I appeared to listen to flattery which I despised. Affecting a passion for society because you preferred seclusion, though our tastes in this respect, as in most others, were alike, I chose to be surrounded by company, when you desired to be alone ; thus contradicting you when our sentiments were secretly in accordance. A spoiled, pretty woman, accustomed to indulge my whims and fancies, and imbued with the notion that men were created to be my vassals, I thought my husband ought to submit to me in all things, and live but to please me. I cannot excuse myself on the plea of ignorance of your peculiarities. I was perfectly aware of them, and rather played upon them, than avoided, as I ought to have done, any chance of provocation. Feeling secure in your devotion to me, and confident in the power of my own charms, I thought little of the risk I ran. Nor when I first found out my mistake, did I care to repair it. Though aware of the fault I had committed, I would not own myself in the wrong—least of all to you. So the breach was widened—widened irreparably as it proved—which at first might have been easily closed. Thus considered, light offences become crimes, and for these I suffer. Those wedded persons who trifle with their happiness would do well to weigh this in time; and my unfortunate case might serve as warning, if there were any to profit by it. In my own justification, I may allege that I did not believe matters to be so bad as they eventually proved. Thinking you were merely piqued, and would love me all the better when our reconciliation occurred, I looked anxiously forward to it. Alas! it never came. On the contrary, my imprudence had engendered suspicions in your breast, which could not be removed."

Here he laid down the letter, and some minutes elapsed before he was able to go on with it.

"In exculpating myself, I must needs exculpate another, and though I would not add one pang to those you must already feel, justice requires that I should clear from aspersion the memory of one who was a true friend to both of us—but chiefly to you, Sir Walter; who ever painted your good qualities in the brightest colours; and shielded your defects, if you have any; who hesitated not to tell me of my faults, and to point out the mischief they would probably occasion: who ever strove to mediate between us ; and who even, when he found he had incurred your suspicion and displeasure, persevered in his good offices.

"I will not recapitulate the afflicting circumstances that led to our complete rupture. I know you were transported by passion and jealousy, and am sure you must have bitterly repented your blind fury. Reflection convinced me of this, though I understood it not at first: and having sharply experienced the unhappiness occasioned by my own folly, I determined to make a last great effort to retrieve myself in your opinion by fully confessing my faults, and throwing myself upon your compassion. With this view I sent for Sir Gilbert de Montfichet to aid me with his council as to the best means of effecting my purpose. Here again I acted indiscreetly : but I was so agitated that my better judgment deserted me, or I should not have appointed a secret interview with him. I have since learnt that my woman, Alice Aggs, betrayed me to you. May Heaven forgive her ! Scarcely had Sir Gilbert heard my plan, and expressed approval of it, and willingness to undertake it, than you appeared. O, the terror of that scene ! Frenzy seemed to possess you. I tried to tell you all I have here written. You would not listen to me. I clung to you, and you shook me off. Blood only would satisfy you—*his* blood. O, death ! O, despair !

"Left alone, I could not believe what had occurred. It must have been a horrid vision—too horrid for reality. The terrible truth soon forced itself upon me. After futile messages, I sought you out in your private chamber, and tried to move you, and was again repulsed —savagely repulsed—but I heeded it not. I would have submitted to any indignity to avert the catastrophe I dreaded. It came ; and sooner than I expected. I have said I mean not to reproach you, Sir Walter—nor will I. Yet methinks, if you could have witnessed the effect of your message, you would not have sent it. O, that bloodstained handkerchief! I needed not your note to tell me what had happened."

He paused.

Cold damps bedewed his brow; and a severe spasm crossed his breast, the anguish of which extorted a cry. The paroxysm over, he arose, took up the handkerchief and the phial, and regarded them fixedly. He then sat down again to conclude the letter.

"A fearful change has taken place in me since I commenced; but while my senses remain, let me conjure you, Sir Walter, by all you hold sacred and just, not to disown our child! He is your son; let him be regarded as such. This is the dying request of a wife, who forgives you the wrongs you have done her. Since the poor child will never know a mother's care and love, let him have a father's. Do this, Sir Walter, and I will intercede for you above. May our son be a consolation to you, and a blessing! Teach him to think kindly of me. And in long after years—which I trust you may live to see!—may he find, in some fortunate union, a happiness denied to us. My blessings on you both!　　　　　　　"THE UNHAPPY JUGA."

He wept aloud.

"How have her wishes been fulfilled!" he exclaimed, at length. "My son neglected and disowned—a stranger to his father. Yet how could I act otherwise, since this letter has never reached me till now; being kept back, no doubt, designedly. But by whom?—Perhaps, by the same hand that placed it here—together with those other fearful mementos. It may be Roper who has done it—yet it seems scarce likely. Be it accident or design, I am equally thankful for the discovery I have effected. Reparation shall be made, and promptly."

II.

PHANTOMS.

HE did not attempt to court repose. Sleep was out of the question in his present state of excitement. Then wherefore seek his couch, till he was calmer?

Calmer! should he ever be calm again, till his brain had ceased to work, and his heart to beat? should he ever know profound repose, till he slept the sleep of death?

And what was to insure him rest even within the tomb? Had he not been told that her sad spirit wandered abroad at night to pour forth its lamentations? Had not he himself, not many hours ago, heard supernatural sounds within the Old Priory Church? And did he not involuntarily connect those sounds with *her?*

But he rejected these evidences. Reason derided them. Idle tales were those of ghosts, invented by poltroons and dotards. In his own case, mere delusion—fancy's coinage—products of an overwrought mind. No—no! Death was utter annihilation!

Then what was life?—Did he deny the soul's existence? As well one as the other. He knew not what he doubted—what he denied. He felt on the verge of madness.

Let him kneel down and pray. There was the little 'broidered cushion on which *she* was wont to offer up her addresses to Heaven. It invited him to approach. Yet he could not. It would be profanation. Besides, in his present agitated frame of mind prayer would be unavailing.

He pray!—ha! ha! Would Heaven listen to him, if he did?

The devil was busy with his heart, suggesting a dark

and desperate deed, perplexing him with wild and fearful fancies, tossing him to and fro as on a tempestuous
sea, and pointing to one only refuge from black despair.

He strove to resist the dread suggestion ; but it grew
upon him with fearful force, and soon bore down all
opposition.   How could he face the son after the
wrongs he had done the mother ?   He must ever shun
his sight.   Then why live ?   True, there was one
gentle being united to that son who had listened to
his sad history with tender interest, and seemed to
compassionate him.   But when she knew the whole
terrible truth, would she not hate and shun him ? Nay,
was she not so entirely devoted to her husband, that
whatever he did she would do likewise ?   No chance
then of sympathy from her.   He had broken all human
ties—forfeited all human love.   Such were the prompt-
ings of the Fiend.

Suicide had once already been committed in this
chamber.   Fit theatre—accursed, as it was !—for such
another deed. Ah ! the very phial that conveyed the
deadly draught to her lips. Would it were replenished !
But he was not unprovided with weapons by which the
same fatal end might be attained, and more expe-
ditiously.

No pang so great as those he now endured.   And if
there were—it would be over as soon as felt.

His resolution taken, a dreadful calmness succeeded.
Bolting the door for fear of interruption, he proceeded
deliberately to unfasten his portmanteau, and took from
it a case of pistols and a sword. A choice of death. He
smiled grimly at the notion.   He could afford to jest
now.   The pistols would be speediest in effect ; but the
sword would be the more appropriate instrument of
destruction, inasmuch as it was the very weapon with

which he slew his friend. This consideration decided him. He laid down the pistol-case, unsheathed the shining blade, and placed its point against his heart. An instant more, and all had been over. But a merciful interposition stayed his hand.

Ere the irrevocable step was taken, something had to be done. He was not yet quits with earth. He was bound to render explanation to his son; to remove every difficulty from his path; and, above all, he was bound to clear the memory of his ill-fated wife from dishonour. This might be accomplished in writing. However irksome the task, it must be performed. It was the last; ay, the last. And a ghastly smile again played upon his white lips.

Laying down the sword with reluctance, he took out his watch. It wanted a quarter of midnight. Before one o'clock all should be ended.

Again having recourse to the portmanteau, and taking from it an escritoire and a bundle of papers, he placed them upon the table, and drew a chair towards it. Amongst other documents, the bundle contained his will, and having glanced at it, he re-inclosed it with the other papers, sealed the packet carefully, and directed it to Abel Roper.

This done, he began the letter to his son, which occupied him for some time, as he wished to make it full and explanatory. After entering into such details as he deemed necessary, he concluded by expressing entire approbation of the marriage the young man had made, and a firm conviction that the partner he had chosen, however inferior she might be to him in point of birth, was in all respects calculated to make him happy; and he earnestly implored him to persevere in the course he had commenced, and to cultivate wedded love and calm domestic happiness as the first of human blessings;

solemnly enjoining him to consider how the neglect of these duties (though trifling in the first instance) had led to disastrous consequences in his own case. Thus, while enjoying perfect felicity of the best and purest kind, his son might, in the fulness of time, be remembered as an example worthy of imitation ; while he himself, if rescued from deserved oblivion, could be only held up as a warning !

Though his purpose of ridding himself by violence of the load of care that oppressed him still continued inflexible, his thoughts during the composition of this letter, took a gentler turn, and some clinging feelings to things of earth betrayed themselves, especially as he dwelt upon his son's wedded happiness and the affectionate nature of his wife.

Oh, if that gentle being had been near him then, she might have diverted him from his direful purpose. Her image almost sufficed to do it.   But he remained firm ; finished and sealed the letter, having first enclosed Lady Fitzwalter's sad communication within it ; and was about to address it, when a slight and singular vibration shook the chamber, and a deep sigh, apparently uttered near him, broke upon his ear.

He raised his eyes.   Heavens ! the sight he beheld. Between him and the window, through which the moonlight was streaming, stood a figure wrapped in a winding sheet of white linen.   The grave-clothes were folded round the head, so that the face alone could be discerned, and that indistinctly ; but as much of it as could be seen was deathlike and cadaverous in hue. The eyes were deep sunken, with no speculation in them. Changed as those features were from what they had been in life, he knew them.   He essayed to address the phantom, but his tongue clove to the roof of his mouth, and refused its office.

BAB BASSINGBOURNE AND GIPSY.

P. 192.

The figure came nearer, without noise, without perceptible motion. Nearer—still nearer!

As it advanced, an atmosphere, chilling as death, by which it appeared to be surrounded, fell upon him. Shudderingly, he watched the spectre approach the table, point to the weapons upon it, solemnly shake its head as if forbidding their use, and then retire.

Slowly, noiselessly, without apparent movement, on it came, still facing him: still regarding him, with fixed and mournful gaze.

Into the closet it passed. The arras seemed wafted aside as it neared them, closing upon it, as it glided in.

Then, and not till then, did he recover power of speech and movement. Arising, and wildly ejaculating her name, he made his way to the point of disappearance.

He raised the arras, but did not enter the closet, remaining as if transfixed.

The spirit of his wife was gone, and in its place stood another apparition infinitely more appalling. A shadowy figure, thin as air, luminous with pale phosphorescent flame diffused around it, yet having the semblance of a man, stripped to the shirt as if for conflict, with a wound in the breast, from which blood had flowed. The phantom appeared to regard him sorrowfully rather than vengefully, and motioned him backwards. He let fall the tapestry.

"Pardon!—pardon, injured shades!" he exclaimed, dropping on his knees. "I abandon the wicked purpose I had formed, and will devote such life as may be spared me to the reparation of the wrongs I have done you!"

Another sigh reached his ear, but less profound than the first. And the same vibration as before was felt throughout the room, though in a slighter degree.

He looked up, hoping the spirits might re-appear, but nothing was visible.

Part the Fourth.

MONKBURY PLACE.

***

I.

BAB BASSINGBOURNE.

To see Bab at her best you should have seen her in the fox-chase.

Heavens! how beautiful she looked then. Her whole soul was in the sport. Fire flashed from her liquid hazel eye, a bloom richer than roses dyed her downy cheek, and a triumphant smile played upon her proud ruby lip, as, mounted upon her favourite bay mare, Gipsy, she rattled along;—the hounds in full cry, and making the woodlands ring with their music, Reynard in view, and she herself leading the whole field, clearing everything before her—hedge, brook, bullfinch, hurdles, gate of many bars, no matter what—and sure to be the first in at the death.

What a perfect horsewoman she is! With what incomparable ease she sits her bounding steed! how lightly she holds the rein! She and Gipsy seem as one. No effort in that leap, though those who follow her hesitate to take it. Gipsy seems scarcely to feel her rider's weight, and careers along joyously, as if proud of the lovely burden. And well she may be. Fairer huntress than Bab never joined in the chase since the days of peerless Dian.

The squire may well be envied the possession of such a treasure, and many an effort is made to carry her off from him. The attempts are unavailing. Sir John Grubham, who longs to make her mistress of Grubham

Park, gets a decided refusal; so does young Chipchase, of Clayberry; and so does Colonel Clotworthy, who threatens to blow out his brains if he is not accepted. However, neither Grub, Chip, nor Clot, as the squire styles them, will take a "nay," but still persevere in their attentions. Frequent contests occur among Bab's admirers for a place by her side as she rides to cover, and fortunate is he who can out-manœuvre a rival. On one occasion, poor Grub gets horsewhipped by the fiery Clot for pushing rudely past him, and a duel must have ensued but for the squire's interference. Of late, whenever these quarrels begin, Bab cuts the matter short by riding off, and leaving the wranglers behind.

Bab is the pride of her uncle's heart, and the delight of his eyes. What is still more to the purpose, she is understood to be his heiress. Naturally, she is the toast of every fox-hunter throughout Essex. We know not how many bumpers of claret poor Grub daily drains to her honour—but with each glass he sighs and groans more deeply, till at last he sinks under the table, and for a time forgets his woes.

Clot sings about her at his club at the Axe and Bottle at Braintree, and overcome by punch and sensibility pulls out a pistol and threatens to terminate a wretched existence. Nobody interferes to check his deadly purpose, for the scene is of nightly occurrence. Young Chip takes the matter more easily, and flatters himself he is a little in advance of his rivals. We can tell him he is mistaken.

Not alone is Bab the admiration of huntsmen of high degree, but she is positively idolised by all those under her sway. Will Crane, the head huntsman, is never so happy as when he gets a smile from her, never so proud as when she commends him. Tom Deane

o

the second huntsman, is just the same. Nat Smith, the feeder, thinks the day has not fairly begun till her sunny face has shone upon him. Even crusty old Paul Flitwick is not insensible to her sovereign attractions, but bows before them like the rest. There is a witchery in her voice that exercises a spell over the meanest and sourest-tempered; and all are alike obedient to its silver sound.

Though Bab looked best in the chase, it is not so we intend to present her. Unluckily, a severe frost prevailed at the time of our story, and hunting was therefore out of the question. A pity this, but it cannot be helped.

The reader will be pleased to accompany us, on the morning after the events previously narrated, to the large hunting-kennel at Monkbury Place, where he will find a splendid pack of fox-hounds—the best in Essex—and something better worth viewing than the finest hound that ever ran.

The something better is a lovely girl.

Ay, a very lovely girl, with healthful bloom upon her cheek, and pure blood racing in her veins. Rosy lips sundered to show the pearls they conceal. Bright hazel eyes dancing with light-hearted mirth. Rich auburn locks, so inestimable in the eyes of the amorous Grub, that he offered a thousand pounds for one of them, and vowed he would place it in a locket, and wear it for ever next his heart. As to complexion, what matters it if sun and air have somewhat darkened the peach-down on her cheek, and scattered a few freckles on her snowy brow! Is she the worse for that? Not a bit, cries young Chip, and he's not a bad judge. Her features are not quite regular. No! But the best sculptor that ever handled chisel could turn out nothing more charmingly coquettish than that saucy little nose, more bewitching than that dimpling chin, or that Cupid's bow of a lip. Beauty, my good sir, has moulds beyond the reach of art.

A figure light, slight, and elastic, and possessing all the points that female symmetry requires, set off, as you see, by a graceful, sky-blue riding-habit, laced with silver. And how becoming is that broad-leaved white beaver, with the sportive feather in it!

There, sir, you have before you the reputed heiress of Monkbury, and the toast of the Essex fox-hunters. If you are not a stickler for classical features, you will own she is perfectly beautiful. No wonder Grub, Chip, and Clot, and so many other swains, are so much in love with her.

The inclosure in which Bab stands is the grass-court outside the principal kennel—for the squire has a couple of well-built receptacles for his hounds—and in summer it is pleasant enough, for it has three or four fine horse-chestnut trees to shade it—with a clear brook flowing through it—but now the trees are leafless, and the brook frozen. There is an inner-court, with brick floor and a well in the centre of it—and beyond this are the kennels. The whole space is surrounded by high pales, and skirted by more trees. In the middle of the grass-court is a little mound, and on this Bab has taken her station. She is talking to Will Crane, and just below them are Tom Deane, old Paul Flitwick, and Nat Smith. Will Crane is a handsome stout young fellow, with a ruddy complexion, clear blue eyes, and curly hair; not unlike what the squire himself may have been in his younger days. Will, by-the-by, is high in his master's good graces, and is much favoured by Bab herself, who is far more condescending to him than she is to some of his superiors. So marked is this, that it provokes the jealousy of poor Grub, who rails against his ill-luck, and wishes he could change places with the handsome huntsman.

Having said what she has to say to Will Crane, Bab orders Nat Smith to turn out the hounds, and forth they all presently come, lifting up their mellow voices as they enter the grass-court, and thronging eagerly towards the mound. Several of them struggle and quarrel for a foremost place, much in the manner of Bab's admirers in the field. Old Charon—a staunch hound, and considered the leader of the pack—seizes Ringwood by the throat for presuming to push past him ; and like quarrels ensue 'twixt Twanger and Trueboy, and Goblin and Griper. Rare uproar they make. But the strife is speedily settled by a touch of Bab's whip, and harmony restored. While the rougher dogs are fighting, two of the privileged of the opposite sex—Madcap and Saucebox—make their way to the top of the mound, and by their caresses engross Bab's chief attention. Yet she is not neglectful of the rest, but has a word of encouragement for all.

Anon, the clock in the old turreted and embattled gate-house near the stables strikes nine. It is the hour of breakfast, and Bab must obey the summons.

But where is her uncle all this while ? He generally meets her in a morning, either at the kennel or the stables. She has seen nothing of him as yet. Imposing silence upon the noisy crew, she listens for the cheering cries that usually announce his approach. She hears nothing but a cough, proceeding from Mr. Mosscrop, the fat butler, who is waddling towards the kennel, as fast as his gout will permit, evidently charged with a message for her.

What can have happened ? She knows her uncle was out late the night before, and perhaps may have drunk a little too much punch. She hopes all is well. Still, it is not without anxiety that she asks Will Crane whether he has seen his master, and receives from him a reply, which at once relieves and surprises her.

The squire has been astir unusually early. He was at the stables more than two hours ago, and has sent off three mounted grooms; one to summon Doctor Sidebottom; another to fetch Mr. Roper; and a third with a letter to Doctor Plot, an old gentleman staying at the Flitch at Dunmow.

At the mention of Doctor Plot's name a knowing smile crosses old Paul's crabbed countenance, and he looks as if he could tell something if he chose. But nobody puts a question to him.

By this time, Mr. Mosscrop has come up, and wheezes out his message somewhat as follows:

The squire sends his excuses to Miss Bassingbourne —is obliged to breakfast in the library—not ill in the least—only a slight headache, which will go off presently—has important papers to examine—wishes to be alone—mustn't be disturbed on any account.

If any guests should arrive—and the squire thinks it not improbable two gentlemen whom he invited last night may ride over to breakfast—Miss Bassingbourne will be pleased to do the honours for him.

Of course Miss Bassingbourne will be happy to do all her uncle desires—but who are the two gentlemen expected?

They are Sir Gilbert de Montfichet and Captain Juddock.

"They must be coming now. I hear the sound of horses' feet in the avenue," Will Crane cries out, leaping upon the mound to obtain a better view. "Ay, there they be, sure enough. The young man in scarlet is Sir Gilbert, and no doubt the great big chap behind him in the blue riding-coat is the captain."

"Bless me! what am I to do with them?" Bab exclaims in a tone of vexation. "How tiresome in my uncle to shut himself up in this ridiculous way, and leave me to entertain such people as these. However, I suppose I must do it. It won't do to send them away."

"No, that it won't, Miss," cries the butler. "The squire was very particular in his directions. 'Tell my niece, Mosscrop,' he said, 'she must show 'em every hospitality.'"

"You had better go to them, Will," Bab says to the huntsman, "and explain how matters stand. Get rid of them if you possibly can."

Will laughed, and set forth on his errand. As he passed the butler, he received a wink from the latter, which informed him what he ought to do.

Either he must have been very stupid, or the newcomers would not take a hint, for to Bab's mortification her envoy presently returned, with the strangers following him.

On nearing the kennel, Sir Gilbert sprang from his horse, and flinging the bridle to Tom Deane, entered the grass-court, and made a ceremonious bow to Miss Bassingbourne, while Mosscrop took upon himself the office of gentleman-usher, and duly presented them to each other. Bab's salutation was as distant as she could make it,—and her reception of the gay young baronet anything but flattering to his vanity; but Mr. Mosscrop played his part so well, was so uncommonly civil, and even cordial, saying everything his master would have said on the occasion—and perhaps a trifle more—that Sir Gilbert did not feel as much discouraged as he might otherwise have done—more especially as Bab—from common politeness—was obliged in some degree to acquiesce in the butler's expressions of welcome.

"Breakfast will be ready very shortly, Sir Gilbert," Mosscrop said, in conclusion. "The men will take your horses round to the stables. You will remember his honour was very particular in begging you and your friend would make yourselves quite at home."

"Oh! no fear of that," rejoined the young baronet, laughing. "A very civil fellow, that butler of yours, Miss Bassingbourne," he added, as Mosscrop waddled off towards the house.

"He presumes a good deal upon his favour with my uncle," Bab replied, coldly, and without raising her eyes from Saucebox, whose head she was patting.

Most men would have been daunted by her manner, but luckily Sir Gilbert's assurance stood him in good stead.

"I ought to apologise for coming at such an unseasonable hour," he remarked; "but my old friend the squire was so pressing in his invitation, and my impatience to behold one of whom I have heard such rapturous accounts was so great, that——"

"Peace, Coxcomb," Bab cried, to one of the hounds. "Peace, sirrah!"

"I had heard a great deal of Miss Bassingbourne's beauty," Sir Gilbert continued, not in the least abashed, "but I must say the description came very far short of the reality."

"Give Bouncer the whip, Paul," Bab cried, "and make him hold his tongue. Would you like to see the stables?" she added, abruptly, to Sir Gilbert.

"Of all things, if you will show them to me."

"I was going to bid Will Crane go with you; but if you would prefer my doing so——"

"Can you doubt it?" Sir Gilbert exclaimed, gallantly.

"Pshaw! I hate compliments," Bab cried, pettishlv.

"And I never pay them," the imperturbable baronet rejoined. "Indeed, I should think flattery impossible where Miss Bassingbourne was concerned."

"This is insufferable," Bab cried. "Do you take me
for a fool, Sir Gilbert?"

"I take you for a very charming person."

"I'm not at all charming, and I hate those who call
me so."

"Then you must hate every man who addresses you."

"Perhaps I do. At all events, I prefer hounds and
horses to men. The former have no nonsense about
them."

"You cannot complain of the involuntary homage
paid to your beauty."

"When homage ceases to be respect, and takes the
form of adulation, it becomes offensive, and as such I
resent it. I would rather not be admired at all, than
admired in such a way. I have no idea of any coxcomb who pleases amusing himself at my expense."

"No fear of that, Miss Bassingbourne, with the
weapons of wit you have at command. But here comes
my friend Captain Juddock. Permit me to present
him to you."

"What a strange-looking object!" thought Bab, as
the giant approached her, kicking out his great booted
legs to the infinite disturbance of the hounds in his
path, arranging his long, dangling cravat, pulling down
his black horse-hair wig, and giving himself what he
conceived to be an excessively killing air.

If Juddock expected to achieve a conquest of the
beauty, he was a little out in his calculations While
making her a flourishing congé, what did he do but

bring down his heavy three-cornered, gold-laced hat plump upon Charon's head, so provoking the choleric old hound, whose temper had been previously rather ruffled by Ringwood, that he instantly flew at him; while Twanger and Trueboy, and some half-dozen others who had suffered from the giant's careless feet, joined in the attack. Old Paul could have called them off in a moment, but there was a glint in the corner of Bab's bright eye which did not escape him, and he let them alone. Will Crane and the others were outside the court with the horses, but very probably they would have acted in the same manner as the old whipper-in. Even Sir Gilbert could not help laughing at his friend's position. Juddock, however, thought it no laughing matter; and finding the number of his foes momently increasing, he kicked his boots about more vigorously than ever, bellowing all the time like a baited bull. At last he took to his heels and fled, with the whole pack after him, dashing through the gate of the inclosure, and making for the park. So excessively diverted were Will Crane and his companions with the scene, that they had to hold their sides for laughter, and could render the fugitive no assistance whatever. Besides, he was gone in a moment; and he might have been in possession of the seven-leagued boots, so tremendous were the strides he took. But though he kept a-head of his pursuers for awhile, he would not have come off with a whole skin, if it had not been for a young man, who suddenly started up, and quickly succeeded, by his voice and gestures, in stopping the yelling pack.

In a minute or two more, Will Crane and Tom Deane came up, their merriment still breaking out at intervals, in spite of all efforts to repress it. The giant was helped from out a tree up which he had clambered for safety, and the hounds were driven back to the kennel. Juddock looked about for his preserver, but the young man had disappeared.

Bab, we must admit, had been amused by the occurrence—at least, by the first part of it; but when the chase began in earnest, she ordered Will Crane and the others to follow instantly, and prevent mischief. They would have been too late, however, if it had not been for the opportune help which Juddock received.

Not a little crestfallen, as may be supposed, the giant returned to the neighbourhood of the kennel; but he declined to enter it again. Bab now came out to him, and expressed her regrets at the disaster; but her looks rather contradicted the wicked little creature's assertions, and Juddock smiled incredulously.

" Don't distress yourself, Miss B.," he cried. " It's all right now. Udsbores ! those rascally huntsmen of yours ought to be hanged, especially the old whipper-in. I heard him set the hounds upon me. Egad, I felt very much like the fox, and I should have shared the fate of a fox, too, if it hadn't been for an acquaintance of yours, Sir G., who started out of the ground as if by magic, and saved me from becoming dog's meat."

" When you say ' an acquaintance of mine,' Jack, you don't refer to a certain old gentleman who generally makes his appearance from below ?" Sir Gilbert remarked, suiting the action to the word.

" No, faith ! this is a young gentleman. But he must have dealings with the old one, to account for his sudden disappearance. He was gone before I could turn round in the tree in which I sought refuge ; and both of those scoundrelly huntsmen declare they saw nothing of him. I believe the rascals were lying, though."

"Relieve my impatience, and tell us who he was," Sir Gilbert said.

"Prepare yourself for a start, as the actors do, Sir G. On my life, it was no other than Frank Woodbine."

"He here! are you sure it was Frank?" Bab exclaimed, quickly. And then feeling she had displayed too much interest in the question, her cheeks became the colour of carnation.

Her confusion did not escape Sir Gilbert.

"I couldn't be mistaken about him," Juddock said, in reply to Bab's remark; "though he was much better dressed than usual—in fact, quite like a gentleman. He must have put on a suit of his master's clothes."

"Strange he should be here. Do you know this young gamekeeper, Miss Bassingbourne?" Montfichet asked, looking hard at her, as he put the question.

But her momentary embarrassment had passed away, and she answered with apparent unconcern—"Oh yes, I know him. It is odd he should be in the park at this early hour."

"Quite unaccountable," the young baronet said.

"'Tis a wonder he can leave his pretty wife—ain't it, Sir G.?" Juddock cried, with a great laugh, and winking at his patron.

"Hush!" Montfichet said, checking him by a look.

"Oh! I'm mum," the giant replied.

"What can you have to say about her?" Bab exclaimed, regarding him scornfully.

"Oh! nothing whatever to her disadvantage," Juddock replied; "only she's a great deal too good for her husband—that's all."

"You are the very last person who ought to say so," Bab rejoined, sharply, "after the service that, by your own account, Frank has just rendered you."

" Whew! I've put my foot in it, somehow," Juddock whispered the young baronet.

" There's something behind the scenes that I don't clearly understand," Montfichet answered, in the same tone. " Keep your eyes open, Jack, and let me know if you see anything more of this ubiquitous young gamekeeper."

The giant replied by a cunning look and a rapid succession of winks, which seemed to imply—" Leave J. J. alone for finding it out. J. J.'s eyes are always wide open."

While they were conferring apart, Bab had grown impatient, and made a move towards the stables, whither they followed her. The stables were on an extensive scale, and would almost have served for a cavalry barracks, so great was the accommodation they offered. They were built at the same time as the Hall —that is, about the beginning of the seventeenth cen- tury — but had been enlarged and improved of late years. The squire, it appeared, had many capital hunters in his stalls, all of whom were duly admired, but Montfichet was most interested in Harold — an aged black horse whom the young baronet remembered as the wonder of his boyhood. The old steed had indeed enabled the squire to perform some of his greatest hunting exploits, and was treated with the consideration due to his long services. A paddock was usually allotted to him, but he was now turned into a loose box for the winter. The brave old steed, rather stiffer in his limbs than when Montfichet first beheld him, neighed a welcome to Bab, and moving forward as quickly as he could, pushed forth his grizzled nose to be patted by her tiny hand. Hereupon, the young baronet launched into a description of Harold's former feats, and spoke with so much enthusiasm, that he rose considerably in Bab's estimation. She deigned to promise him he should see Gipsy, whom she had not, up to this moment, intended to exhibit. Having taken leave of the old hunter, Bab repaired to the yard, and word being given to a groom, Gipsy, the beautiful, was brought out.

Montfichet was not a bad judge of a horse, but it did not require any extraordinary knowledge to discern Gipsy's merits. They were perceptible to an unpractised eye. In her way, she was as perfect a beauty as her mistress. Nearly thorough-bred, she had the finest limbs possible, and the sleekest skin. A bright bay with black mane. As she tossed her proud little head, and raised her veined neck, some dames might have envied her her luxuriant hair. In an instant she was beside Bab, receiving and returning caresses. Though full of fire in the field, Gipsy was gentle as a lamb now —and her eyes were as soft as those of an antelope.

"What do you think of her?" Bab demanded, proudly, as she rested her arm upon Gipsy's arching neck.

"That I never beheld her peer," Montfichet cried, with enthusiasm.

"Well, there you are right," Bab replied, well pleased. "She has not her equal. But you should see her in the chase."

"I hope I may have an opportunity of doing so," the young baronet said.

"You would never think, as we ride gently to cover," Bab continued, with increasing animation, her eye kindling with fresh fire as she spoke, "what courage and speed Gipsy possesses—but when the huntsman's halloo is given—when the squire cries 'Found! found!' —when the hounds begin to raise their voices—then you would see what she is made of. He would believe what you can do—wouldn't he, darling?" she added to the mare, who really looked, with her dilated eyeballs and expanded nostrils, as if she comprehended what was said.

""A glorious pastime, the chase!" Montfichet cried, rapturously. " No wonder you take so much delight in it. No wonder, with such a matchless horse, you perform such feats."

" All the credit is due to my sweet Gippy," Bab replied. " I could do nothing without her."

" Say, rather, she would do nothing without you," the young baronet observed, gallantly. " You have made her what she is."

" Haven't I told you I hate compliments—and they are now more undeserved than ever. Praise my horse as much as you please, but spare me.—After all we *do* suit each other, Gippy and I,—don't we, my pet?"

" Oh! would I were a horse!" sighed Juddock.

" But you had only just broken cover, when you described Gipsy's style of running," Montfichet said. " I should like best to see her when the hounds are off, and the whole field on the move. No one is near you, I'll be sworn—unless it be the squire."

" Right," Bab returned, answering at once to the lure thrown out to her by the young baronet; " and my uncle is not always with me either, for he doesn't ride so boldly as he once did. You *should* see a good run with Gippy. Hark forward! hark forward! tally ho! You would say she went along, if you beheld her when the fox takes to the open—over Felsted Common, or along the vale of the Blackwater. But she don't go as fast as she could for I never allow her to press upon the hounds. As to a jump, she refuses nothing. She will take any fence you can show her. I have cleared the Chelmer with her. A stiff country is my delight;

the hedges cannot be too high for me, nor the ditches too wide. The last time we were out we ran into Suffolk, and Sir John Grubham, who would follow me, was soused into the Stour, young Chipchase disappeared in a dyke, and Colonel Clotworthy was thrown head foremost into a quagmire—ha! ha! But Gippy bore me safely through all difficulties, and brought me in at the death. What is it you hear, my winsome lassie?" she said, as the mare suddenly raised her head, and pricked her delicate ears.

Presently, the clatter of horses' hoofs, which had caught Gipsy's attention, became audible to the others, and a few seconds afterwards, three gentlemen rode into the yard. All were well mounted; all in pink hunting - coats, black hunting - caps, buckskins, and boots.

"'Foreheaven! the three unfortunate individuals you have just mentioned, Miss Bassingbourne," Sir Gilbert exclaimed, recognising acquaintances of his own in the new-comers.

II.

GRUB, CHIP, AND CLOT.

THE three suitors set up a shout on sight of Bab, were off their horses in a trice, and stood before her, paying their respects, cap in hand.

Grub was not bad-looking—rather the reverse. But his features were vacant in expression—or, if they had any expression, it was that of a silly and sickly sentimentalism, which was borne out by his manner and discourse. As he bowed to Bab, he fixed a look upon her like an expiring cod-fish, which excited risibility rather than sympathy.   Grub might be about thirty, was getting rather fat and florid, as if the claret he swallowed began to tell upon him, and was tightly buttoned up in his scarlet coat, and tightly squeezed into his boots and buckskins.   Young Chip was a sporting-looking chap, tall, lathy, ginger-haired, and ginger-coloured ; he had light blue eyes, legs evidently without calves, and a head apparently without much brains in it. Clot was older than his companions, and stouter even than Grub.   Face almost crimson, with a shade of yellow about the mouth struggling with the blue tinge of the beard.   Lips coarse and large, as was the principal feature in the countenance—which may be described in a word, as a bottle-nose—eyes watery and bloodshot— hands uncommonly red and fat, and gloveless.   Such was the *personnel* of Colonel Clotworthy, and it may be matter of surprise that such an old buck should presume to fall in love with Bab Bassingbourne.   But which of us, boys, young or old, does the mischievous little urchin spare ?

"Pray do not remain uncovered, gentlemen," Bab said, curtseying to her suitors.   "You will take cold. To what am I indebted for this early visit ?   There is no likelihood of any hunting, as you must be well aware."

" Miss Bassingbourne asks what has procured her the pl asure of an early visit from us," Grub said to Chip. apparently embarrassed by the question.

"Well, tell her—can't you?"   the latter replied, curtly.

"No, let the colonel speak," Grub cried.

"Colonel, I look to you," Bab said.

"Me," Clot replied.   "Sir John can never find his tongue when it's wanted.   Well, we were all three at the Axe and Botttle, at Braintree, last night——"

"Supping with the club," Grub suggested.

"Don't interrupt me, sir—or tell it yourself," Clot cried, fiercely. "Well, we were supping, or drinking our punch—I don't recollect which——"

"Drinking punch, colonel," Chip said.

"Toasting Miss Bassingbourne," Grub added, with another cod-fish look at Bab.

" *Will* you let me finish what I've got to say, gentle-men?" the exasperated colonel roared, getting redder in the face than ever. "Well, we had drunk the toast, which I proposed——"

"I beg your pardon, colonel—*I* had the gratification of proposing Miss Bassingbourne's health," Grub said. " *You* drank it, colonel, but *I* proposed it."

"You, sir?" Clot exclaimed, stamping with rage, and puffing out his cheeks. " 'Sdeath! do you venture to assert in my hearing, and in the hearing of Miss Bassingbourne, that *you* originated that toast? Re-collect, sir, what happened on a certain occasion. I'll repeat the lesson—by the Lord Harry! I will." And he cracked his hunting - whip in a very menacing manner.

" Fie, colonel, you will drive me away, if you go on thus," Bab said. "Even darling Gippy is frightened at you."

Thus called to order, Clot apologised for his irrita-tion, which he trusted was excusable under the circum-stances, as he would yield to no man in devotion to Miss Bassingbourne—while Chip endeavoured to ex-plain to Bab by signs, that it was in reality *he* who had proposed the toast.

" The long and the short of the matter is, Miss Bas-singbourne," Clot said, " we passed a resolution, last night, to——" And he come to a full stop.

" Go on, colonel," Chip cried.

P

" 'Sblood! sir, I can't," the man of war replied. " If Sir John wants to speak, now's his time."

" A word of encouragement from Miss Bassing-bourne, and I will pour forth my soul," Grub cried, with a gush of tenderness.

" I'm at a loss to understand what all this means, gentlemen," Bab said, laughing. " But let me ask you a plain question. Have you breakfasted ?"

" Have *you* breakfasted, gentlemen ?" Grub asked, appealing sentimentally to the others. " For my own part, I subsist entirely on love, and am indifferent to grosser fare."

" I shouldn't like to dine with him," Juddock observed to his patron. But, udsbores! he looks, somehow, as if the low diet agreed with him."

" The colonel and myself have not breakfasted, Miss Bassingbourne," Chip said. " In fact, in pursuance of a resolution we came to last night at the club, we rode over for the purpose of partaking of that meal with the squire, and settling a little matter of business we have with him afterwards."

" My uncle, I fear, will not be able to see you at present," Bab replied, " as he has some urgent business to attend to; but a little later on in the day he may, perhaps, be less engaged, and then you can have an interview with him. Meanwhile, I shall be happy in your company at breakfast."

Enchanted by the proposition, all three eagerly accepted it, and expressed their delight in the various styles peculiar to them. There was so much more condescension than usual about Bab's manner, that each secretly drew an augury favourable to himself from it. This important affair being settled, they had thoughts for other matters, and eyes for other objects than Bab, and discovering Sir Gilbert, who was personally known to all three, shook hands with him heartily, and were introduced by him to Juddock. Meanwhile, their horses were taken to the stable, and Gipsy being bidden by her mistress to return to her stall, obeyed the injunction of her own accord. After which, the whole party repaired to the house, Bab leading the way.

III.

WHAT MONTFICHET BEHELD FROM THE BAY-WINDOW.

MONKBURY PLACE was a noble old mansion of the period of James the First, or a little earlier, and in excellent preservation.

Looking to the west, the principal front presented a very imposing appearance from the two lofty octangular towers that sprung on either side of the arched entrance. These towers had large bay-windows extending over the doorway on the first floor; and the parapets and stone-work were richly ornamented. The wings were terminated by gables. Situated on a gentle elevation, the mansion was surrounded by an extensive park—groves haunted by rooks, and glades traversed by deer. How beautiful are these old English halls, and how picturesque! What an air of comfort and hospitality there is about them! In what perfect keeping they are with the climate, and the immemorial woods in which they lie embosomed. Some quarter of a mile from the house, but in full view of the windows and terraces, was a large sheet of water, constantly maintained at a certain height by the Chelmer, which flowed through the park. At a short distance on the left, amidst the trees, might be seen the square tower of the little, sequestered, grey

old church, where the squire used to meet his tenants
on a Sunday, and sit in his large pew with his niece, to
listen to the discourses of the Reverend Jeremy Bush,
his chaplain. The comfortable naps in which the worthy
gentleman used to indulge during these discourses had
been checked by Bab, and he had become quite a pattern
of decorous attention.

Attached to Monkbury Place were large and enchanting gardens, laid out in the good old style, with terraces,
mazes, moats, bridges, mounts, knots, fountains, statues,
dials, bowling-greens, and many other delights. These
gardens were Bab's constant resort in summer, and she
found never-ending pleasures within them. But we
must now follow her and her guests into the house, and
enter as they did by the western porch. This brings
us at once to the great hall, from which rises a magnificent staircase of many turnings, leading to the upper
story. The uprights on each landing are decorated
with rampant nondescripts, with beaks and wings re-
sembling griffins, sculptured in oak, and supporting
armorial shields. There is a long gallery above, containing many full-length portraits of the family, but
we must tarry in the hall below. It is spacious and
lofty, with a magnificent, richly-carved oak screen at
the further end. The wainscots are partly panelled,
partly decorated with fanciful designs in plaster. The
furniture is all of oak, old as the house itself Buff
coats, head-pieces, thigh-pieces, bucklers, bandileers,
bugle-horns, gauntlets, and glaives, decorate the walls ;
and wherever a place can be found for it, hangs the
antlered skull of a great stag of the first head. A
wood-fire crackles on the dogs beneath the huge, yawning chimney-piece.

At one end of a long oak-table, placed at the side of
the room opposite the fireplace, a snowy cloth has been

laid, and on this are set the materials for a substantial morning repast. Having already been apprised of the addition to the number of guests, Mr. Mosscrop has prepared accordingly. The larder of Monkbury Place is generally well supplied—especially about Christmas time—and if there had been five-and-twenty unexpected and hungry visitors, instead of five, they would not have fared badly. Bab did the honours charmingly. She was assisted by the chaplain, the Reverend Jeremy Bush aforesaid, who being a widower, without incumbrances, not yet turned of fifty, and passably good-looking in his own opinion, secretly indulged a hope that his modest merit might not be overlooked by his patron's lovely niece. Poor, self-deluded Jeremy! Bab never bestowed a thought on thee—except as a decent middle-aged gentleman who said grace, liked a good dinner, and a bottle of claret after it—did not object to a pipe or a bowl of punch—could ride out with the hounds on occasion, and sing a jolly song if required—had plenty of racy jests for the men and a rogue's eye for the maidens. Bab was not very particular, but she did not quite like such a parson as this; and if she had had her own way, would have dismissed him the house. But Jeremy suited the squire; and when his niece remonstrated with him, the worthy fellow declared that Bush might have his faults, but he was no worse than his brethren—and so far he was right, as any one who cares to examine into the manners of the lower clergy at the time will discover.

Well, they all sat down to breakfast, and famous appetites some of them had. It would have done you good to see how they cleared the dishes—how piles of cutlets disappeared—how broiled kidneys and turkeys' legs were despatched—how slices of ham were devoured. There was a continual cracking of eggs. Amongst his

other accomplishments, Parson Bush was an admirable
carver, and his skill was repeatedly called into play on
this occasion.   There was a corned round of beef on
which he had to operate—a roll of Cambridge brawn,
the sauce for which he artistically compounded with
vinegar, mustard, sugar, and salt—and a pigeon pie,
into the bowels of which he dived.   Juddock had an
immense respect for him.   He had never met with a
parson he liked so much, and told him so, emphatically.
Jeremy seemed pleased by the compliment, and sent
him the wing of a pheasant.   And seeing the giant did
not get on well with coffee or chocolate, or tea in the
minute china cups then in vogue, he pushed a large
silver tankard towards him, filled with the primest
October.   Lifting it to his lips, Juddock did not set it
down till he had drained the last drop.   A pleasurable
smile irradiated Jeremy's jolly face, and he ordered
Mosscrop to replenish the tankard.   And Mosscrop
smiled too, as he obeyed the chaplain's injunction.

Bab sat at the upper end of the table, and dispensed
the fragrant and innocuous beverages to those who
applied for them.   On her right was placed Montfichet,
and on the left Sir John Grubham.   Poor Grub sipped
his chocolate, and trifled with the thin toast of a man-
chet—but to gaze at the idol of his heart was enough
for him.   Bab had something wondrously captivating
about her.   Lured by those bright eyes, the poor moths
flew towards them, and got their wings sadly scorched.
Still, they fluttered round as foolishly as ever.   Every
one tried such arts of pleasing as he fancied he possessed, and every one failed.   Sir Gilbert by this time
had caught the general infection.   Excited by the contest going on, he could not fail to take part in it, and
soon became as eager as the rest.   At first he only
dipped his foot in the stream of love; now, he was over

head-and-ears in it, and carried away by the current. Rose's image became fainter and fainter, until it was well-nigh effaced from his breast. Yet, he could not account for it, she was somehow mixed up in his thoughts with Bab, and though no two persons could be more unlike, he persuaded himself there was a re-semblance between them. Only Bab was infinitely prettier than Rose.

Bab laughed at all the compliments paid her, and would not be made to understand any tendernesses of look or speech. When breakfast was over, and she had quitted the room, there was not one of her suitors who could say he had made the slightest advance in her good graces. Montfichet felt piqued, and mentally resolved he would not be defeated. Grub sighed and groaned and railed against his constant ill-luck. Chip swore he couldn't understand it—Clot growled, and called to Mosscrop for a glass of brandy. Juddock and Parson Bush seemed the most unconcerned, and wished the single married, and the married happy, over a glass of hot mulled claret—a flagon filled with that delectable compound having just been set upon the table by the considerate butler.

"Well, gentlemen," Clot cried, getting up, "we must to business. Since we can't see the squire, we must write to him."

"What about, colonel?" Montfichet inquired.

"About his niece, to be sure," Clot replied. "We want to marry her."

"Not all three of you, I suppose?" the young baronet said, laughing.

"The squire must make his choice—take the best man among us—that's our business here," Clot cried. "Another glass of brandy, Moss crop, and bring us pens ink, and paper—d'ye hear?"

The butler bowed, and departed.

"'Sdeath! if I'm refused," Clot continued, "I'll blow my brains out on the spot—by the Lord Harry I will! I've brought a pistol with me for the purpose."

"Don't produce it, colonel, I beg of you," Grub remarked. "The sight of it always gives me the shivers. If I make away with myself, I shall choose drowning."

"I don't mean to die at all," Chip laughed. "I shall come in and win."

"You!" Clot ejaculated with a sneer. "Puppy!"

"Will you let me add my name to the list, colonel?" Sir Gilbert said.

"Humph!" Clot cried, doubtfully. "I don't know what to say to it."

"Oh! let him—he's no chance," Chip whispered.

"If Sir G.'s name goes in, mine must go too," Juddock cried.

"And mine also," Parson Bush subjoined.

"Pshaw! the squire 'll think it a jest. He'll laugh at us," Clot exclaimed.

"Let us each write separately," Grub remarked.

"No, I've a better plan than that," Juddock cried. "Let's throw for the chance. He who wins shall at once write to the squire and propose for his niece. The losers shall all support him. How say you, gentlemen?" he added, with a sly wink at his patron, as much as to say, "Leave it to J. J."

"Agreed! agreed!" everybody responded except Clot, who, however, was overruled.

Juddock produced a box and dice from his capacious pockets, and the bones speedily rattled upon the board. Clot threw first. Eight, by the Lord Harry! He stamped upon the ground, and felt for his pistol. Then came Chip. Ten! The young man capered about with delight.

"Wait a bit," Bush cried. Nine! No chance for him. Chip is still the best man.

Grub threw next. Five! His usual ill-luck! In his despair, he tore a couple of locks out of his flaxen periwig.

The giant was the next caster. Twelve! Bravo! bravissimo!

" Give me the box," Montfichet said. Twelve again! The matter is not yet decided.

The giant rattles the dice furiously, and prepares a decisive cast. At the moment he is about to throw he winks at his patron. Three!

"I think I can beat that," Montfichet cries—and throws twelve again. "Gentlemen, the chance is mine," he adds laughing, and clapping his hands.

He then sits down, and full of excitement writes a letter to the squire, offering his hand and fortune to his lovely niece; and while he is so occupied, another letter is indited by Clot, urging the squire to accept the young baronet's proposal. This recommendation is signed by all the party, with the exception of the individual mentioned in it. Both communications being completed, are put under one cover, sealed, and delivered to Mosscrop, to be by him conveyed to his master.

Poor Grub looks as if he would faint as the butler departs on his errand. Clot and Chip look blank, but Montfichet can scarcely contain himself for his delight. Having nothing else to do, Juddock walks to the great bay-window, and looks out from it upon the terrace. What is it he sees, that induces him to come back so quickly to Sir Gilbert, and drag him to the window?

" Look there!" he whispers triumphantly. " Trust

J. J. for keeping a sharp look-out. Look there, I say. Do you see him?"

"I see a young man standing before an open window on the ground floor, on the right," Montfichet replied —"but his back is towards us."

"It is Frank Woodbine. There, he turns his head. You are convinced it is he, now?"

"Whom is he talking to so earnestly?" Montfichet cried, growing pale with the thought that crossed him.

"You'll learn, presently," Juddock replied, with a suppressed laugh. "A lucky dog that gamekeeper!"

Perdition seize him! Montfichet can scarcely believe his eyes. A beautiful head and neck are popped out of the window. It *is* Bab, then, who has been talking to him. Presumptuous fellow! He can't mean it? He won't dare! By Heavens! he *does* put his arm round her neck, and kiss her. In his rage, Montfichet cannot help rapping upon the glass. The beautiful head is withdrawn in a moment, and Frank Woodbine walks away in some confusion.

"In a few minutes you'll know your fate, Sir Gilbert," Parson Bush observed, coming up. "But I cannot doubt you'll be made the happiest of men."

"Not in the way you expect, sir," Montfichet cried. "I've changed my mind, and shall write to the squire to tell him so."

"How is this?" Grub cried, springing forward.

But Clot pushed him aside.

"You've no right to change your mind so quickly, Sir Gilbert. Assign a reason for your extraordinary conduct," the colonel thundered.

"I shall give none," Montfichet replied. "I resign my pretensions to the young lady."

"But I insist upon an explanation, sir," Clot cried, fiercely.

"Insist, sir!" the young baronet exclaimed. "I do not recognise any authority on your part to catechise me. I refuse any explanation whatever."

"Then sir, let me tell you——"

"My good colonel," Parson Bush interposed—"permit me to say you are rather intemperate. Sir Gilbert is certainly acting rather strangely to make a proposal one minute, and withdraw it the next, but probably he has some motive which we do not clearly understand."

"'Sblood! sir—I beg your pardon for swearing—we have all supported him," Clot exclaimed. "We are all committed in the matter. He *shall* go through with it. He *shall* marry her if she accepts him—by the Lord Harry, he shall. He shall fight us all—if he declines—not you, sir, because you're a parson, but all the rest of us."

"Ay, all the rest," added Grub and Chip.

"Very well, gentlemen—as you please," Montfichet replied. "I won't marry Miss Bassingbourne, and that's flat."

"I don't think you will, sir, if she herself is consulted," Bab said, partly opening a door in the great oak screen.

At the same moment, another door opened, and who should enter from it but Rose Woodbine. She was in a bonnet and cloak, as if she had just arrived. On seeing Sir Gilbert and the others she would have retired at once, but the young baronet sprang forward, and detained her.

"Rose," he cried, "I must say a word to you. Your husband is utterly unworthy of your love. He has wronged you—cruelly wronged you."

"Let me go, Sir Gilbert. I will not listen to a word more," Rose replied.

"You think I am deceiving you," Montfichet continued, vehemently, "but I swear I speak the truth. Not many minutes since I beheld him with his arms round the neck of a lovely young woman—very superior in station to himself—superior to you too, Rose —though far—very far inferior in beauty."

"We saw him kiss her," Juddock cried, coming up— "kiss her, Mrs. W. Oh! shocking doings! shocking doings! Frank ought to be ashamed of himself. Such a charming wife, too! Udsbores! I'd be revenged upon the faithless fellow, if I were you."

"Revenge is in your power," Montfichet cried. "Fly at once with me."

"Yes, fly with us," Juddock added. "Leave the base deceiver behind."

"Release me, I command you, Sir Gilbert; or I will place myself under the protection of these gentlemen."

"Have you no jealousy, Rose?" the young baronet replied, regarding her with astonishment, as he let go her hand.

"Not the slightest," she replied. "I have perfect faith in my husband."

"But I swear to you I saw him embrace Miss Bassingbourne—tenderly embrace her," Sir Gilbert cried.

Rose's tranquillity did not seem in the least disturbed.

"What's that we heard about embracing Miss Bassingbourne, Sir Gilbert?" Clot demanded, coming up at this juncture with the others.

"A moment's patience, gentlemen. You shall have every explanation anon," Montfichet replied.

"We must have it now—without an instant's delay," Clot cried. "Miss Bassingbourne's name must not be used disrespectfully."

"Miss Bassingbourne is much obliged to you, gentle-

men, but she can take care of herself," Bab cried,
stepping forward. "Come this way, Rose, dear. Your
husband is in the next room. I have been looking for
you."

Rose instantly flew at the call, and the door closed
upon them.

"Amazement!" the young baronet cried. And the
exclamation was repeated by all the others.

IV.

CONTAINING EXPLANATIONS, RECONCILIATIONS, AND JUBILATIONS.

WE will now, if you please, proceed to the library.

It was in this room, that, in his capacity of Justice
of the Peace, our worthy squire transacted business;
signed warrants, summonses, recognisances, and orders;
heard complaints, settled disputes, and granted licenses.
Here, also, he gave audiences to such as were desirous
of consulting him, saw his tenants, and received his
rents. Here he relieved the poor, and dispensed his
charities with no stinting hand.

The room was plainly furnished, and possessed only a
few old-fashioned oak chairs, and a large oak table, on
which writing materials and certain books of reference
—the "Magistrate's Assistant" amongst others—were
placed. The squire was no great reader,—especially of
divinity, in which department of learning his library
was unusually rich, but his shelves were well furnished
with goodly tomes. Over the chimney-piece hung a
portrait of his father, General Monkbury—a very different person from his son, to judge from his morose
countenance. There were two doors to the library;
one, communicating with the hall, which, was masked

by a large Japan screen; the other opening upon a passage connected with a waiting-room, where those who had business with the squire tarried for admission to his presence.

The squire was now seated with his back towards the table, and his face to the fire, the light of which showed that his usually cheerful visage was somewhat troubled. Near him sat Doctor Sidebottom and Mr. Roper. Though dying to know why he had been sent for, the vicar had not yet obtained any information on the subject from his friend, and did not like to appear too curious. On his side, Monkbury was extremely desirous of imparting what he had got to tell, but he dreaded, above all things, being laughed at; and such, he did not doubt, would be one consequence of the disclosures he was about to make. So, contrary to his usual practice of going straight to the point, he avoided the matter uppermost in his thoughts, and kept chattering about things in which he felt comparatively little interest—the frost—Jonas's chance of the Flitch— Montfichet's return to Stansted House—the young baronet's extravagance and debts. Mr. Roper was better informed than the vicar. Having arrived half an hour before the reverend gentleman, during that time he had had a long and interesting conversation with the squire, and had made some arrangements for him.

But things could not go on in this way for ever, so at last, Monkbury screwed his courage to the sticking point, and began—" You'll be surprised to learn, doctor, —now don't laugh, I beg of you—don't even smile—or I shall never get on.—You'll be surprised, I say, to learn that I, whom you have always looked upon as an old bachelor, should have been——"

" Well, sir," Sidebottom said, preserving his gravity as well as he could, for there was something very comical in the squire's expression of countenance—"I am all attention."

"Tell him, Roper," Monkbury cried—"for, may a murrain seize me, if I can bring my lips to utter it."

"The squire wishes to acquaint you, Doctor Side-bottom." the steward said, "with a secret connected with himself, which, for reasons he will, no doubt, presently explain, has been hitherto carefully preserved. His hesitation in disclosing it arises probably from the fear that you might censure his conduct."

"You'll think me a great fool, and perhaps something worse—I know you will, doctor," Monkbury exclaimed, getting up and stirring the fire.

"Don't anticipate my verdict," Sidebottom said, in a bland and encouraging tone. "In some respects I am a latitudinarian, and can make large allowances for the indiscretions of youth."

"I know you can—but you would never suspect this of me—scarcely believe it, when told. It's contrary to my maxims of celibacy. It's a folly I've been laughing at, in others, all my life. Now, they'll laugh at me, and deservedly."

"Am I to understand, sir, that you have committed matrimony?" Sidebottom inquired.

"Yes, you are, doctor. Instead of an old bachelor you behold a widower. There, now it's out. Did you imagine I could make such an ass of myself? Ha! ha! Why don't you laugh, doctor?"

"I feel no inclination for merriment, sir. I fancy I can understand why you have kept this matter secret—and why you have given it out that you would live and die a bachelor."

"False pride, doctor—false pride. Contemptible weakness. I despise myself for it. Mine was a secret marriage—secret, because the proud old general (whose frowning face looks down upon me now), with the blood of the Mordaunts in his veins, would never consent to my union with a poor curate's daughter. It was never afterwards disclosed, from a weak, silly, and unworthy sense of shame on my part, coupled with a dread of ridicule. My wife, doctor, was Grace Leslie, the daughter of your old curate."

"Now you indeed surprise me, sir," Sidebottom rejoined. "I remember Grace well—a most beautiful young person. This, then, was the cause of her sudden withdrawal from her father's roof. I was far from thinking she had married, and am glad to have your assurance of the fact. I fear poor Leslie and his wife were no better informed than myself. Grace went into Cumberland, as I understood, but I never knew what became of her. I did not like to make inquiries."

"She died there during my father's lifetime," the squire said, with a saddened look, "and that was one reason why the marriage was never acknowledged."

"In justice to her memory the avowal *should* have been made," Doctor Sidebottom remarked more gravely than he had hitherto spoken. "And this was an imperative duty if there were children."

"You are quite right, doctor, and I have sadly neglected my duty. However, I will make amends."

"Then I am to understand there *are* children, sir ?"

"You have seen one. She is mistress of this house. My so-called niece is in reality my daughter — my youngest daughter."

"And your eldest daughter, sir !—where is she ?"

"Pardon me, doctor, if I do not satisfy your curiosity on this point at the present moment. Thus much I will tell you. Until last night I was scarcely aware of her existence, for she was removed from her mother's care almost in infancy, and owing to a betrayal of ᴊrust on the part of a person to whom she was confided, I could discover no traces of her. Now, thanks to Roper, all has been satisfactorily cleared up—and I am, or speedily shall be, in possession of my lost child."

"You will choose your own time for revealing the matter fully to me," Sidebottom said—"though I think I can guess the truth. But permit me to ask one question. Is your niece—that is to say, your daughter—aware of the exact relationship between you?"

"Why, yes," the squire replied, with some hesitation —"but she is not acquainted with the whole truth. Poor Grace had pledged herself never to reveal our marriage without my permission—and I never gave it her."

The vicar shook his head, and was about to reprove the squire for his unjustifiable conduct, when his censures were nipped in the bud by the entrance of Mosscrop, who announced Doctor Plot.

Glad of the reprieve, the squire instantly arose and advanced to welcome his friend, who walked slowly into the room. The old gentleman's countenance bore traces of the severe mental and bodily suffering he had undergone, and all present were struck with the great change which had taken place in him. Still, though very feeble, and moving with difficulty, owing to his lameness, he maintained his customary dignified deportment.

"My dear Sir Walter," the squire cried, as soon as Mosscrop had retired, "how glad I am to see you here! How kind in you to come to me. I will explain to you presently why I sent for you—but sit down—sit down."

"Thank ye, Monkbury, thank ye," Sir Walter replied, sinking into the chair offered him. "I did not think you and I should ever meet again—still less, that

I should ever more set foot in this house. But here I am—and Heaven be praised! I am spared strength for an interview with you, which I much desire. I am glad you are here too, Doctor Sidebottom—and you, Roper. You look hard at me I perceive, my good friends. You find me wofully altered. More than twenty years have flown by since I was last in this house. Those years have done their work upon me, but I have been more changed in the last few hours than by the half century preceding them. Oh! such a night as I have passed," he continued, shuddering; "such gony as I have endured—such terrors. But I am a better man, doctor—a much better man. I am no longer proud and unyielding—I am humble of heart, penitent, seeking forgiveness."

"I rejoice to hear you say so, Sir Walter," Doctor Sidebottom observed. "Those are signs of a wholesome change. You will do well to ease your bosom of its load. You are sure of our interest and sympathy, as well as our best counsel—if you need it."

"Bear up, Sir Walter—bear up, manfully," the squire said, squeezing his hand. "We have all our faults—all."

"But few have such faults as mine, Monkbury," Fitzwalter replied, shaking his head sadly. "I have committed great crimes in error—and though I repent them, it is not enough — I must make reparation. Listen to me, and believe—implicitly believe—what I am about to relate to you. Last night, as you know, I was guest in the house of which I once was master, and I occupied a room full of terrible reminiscences. Scarcely had I entered it, when I accidentally made a discovery that in a moment swept away a world of false suspicion that had gathered round my heart, and cankered it. A letter came into my hands—a letter

from my dead wife—completely establishing her innocence, and proving how foully I had wronged her by
my unjust suspicions."

Here his utterance was choked by sobs, and for a
few moments he was unable to proceed.

"Conceive my emotions on making this discovery.
But no! you cannot conceive them. You have not my
guilt upon your souls. Despair and madness stared me
in the face, and shrieked in my ears the crimes I had
committed—a friend murdered—a wife destroyed! I
resolved to put an end to my own existence."

"Heaven be thanked your rash hand was stayed!"
the vicar exclaimed.

"How I was saved you shall hear. I had a document to prepare, which even in that terrible moment
could not be avoided, and when all was completed, and
I had taken leave of the world, a messenger was sent
from the grave to arrest my fell purpose. My dead
wife stood before me—commanding me to desist. She
vanished—and another phantom rose up in her place."

"Another phantom?" Roper exclaimed.

"Ay, another—and far more terrible than the first
—that of my slaughtered friend."

A deep silence succeeded this narration, which had
painfully interested the listeners. At the mention of
the second phantom, Roper glanced at the squire.

"I will not say that the visions you beheld were
creations of o'erwrought fancy Sir Walter," Doctor
Sidebottom observed, at length; "though, under such
circumstances as you have described, the conclusion
would be natural. I am bound to say that the room
you occupied is supposed to be haunted by the spirit of
your late wife, and many persons affirm they have seen
the apparition."

"Amongst the number, I affirm so," the squire said.

" I saw her as plainly as I see Sir Walter himself. As
regards the second phantom, you will recollect, doctor,
that Jonas told us last night he had been scared by a
spectre with a gash in its breast, and that its lineaments
seemed to resemble those of the ill-fated Sir Gilbert de
Montfichet."

" Summon him not before me," Fitzwalter almost
shrieked, clasping his hands before his face, as to ex-
clude some dreadful object from his vision. " That
breast was pierced by my sword—that blood was shed
by my hand, and will rise up in judgment against
me."

" Be comforted, Sir Walter," Doctor Sidebottom said,
kindly. " To the truly penitent grace is never denied,
and you may yet, in some degree, atone for your
offences."

" Much, unhappily, is irreparable," the squire added;
" but not all. You have a son whom you have disowned. Be reconciled to him."

" It is my sole desire," Fitzwalter replied. " The
document I just now mentioned, which I supposed
would be delivered after my death, was intended for
him. It was to put him in possession of my property,
and clear his mother's memory from reproach. My
chief motive in coming hither, in compliance with your
summons, Monkbury, was to request you to act for
me as if I were no more. I shall place the paper in
your hands, and then hide myself for ever from the
world."

" You shall do nothing of the kind if I can prevent
you, Sir Walter," the squire replied bluntly, yet kindly.
" I hope you have many happy years in store for you,
to be passed in the society of your son. Whatever
your intentions may be towards him, you may make
them known to him, yourself, as soon as you please, for

I may as well at once inform you that he is here—in this house."

"I cannot face him," Sir Walter cried, rising, as if to depart. "Take this packet. Give it to him. It will explain all. I will write further."

"You shall not go till you have seen him," the squire said, detaining him. "You need not fear his reproaches."

"I do not fear reproaches. I could bear them. Kindness would kill me."

"Tut!—tut!—I know better. Bring Alured Fitzwalter to his father, Roper."

"A moment!" the old man cried, imploringly. But the steward heeded him not, and left the room.

Sir Walter pressed his hand to his side as if to still the beating of his heart, and looked towards the door eagerly, yet timorously.

At last, quick footsteps were heard approaching.

"He comes! he comes!" he cried. "Now for the trial! Help me to sustain it, Heaven!"

As the prayer was uttered, the door opened, and the young man we have known as Frank Woodbine, entered the room, followed by Roper.

Father and son gazed at each other for a moment, unable to give utterance to their deep emotions.

Then Alured started forward, and springing into Sir Walter's outstretched arms, was strained to the old man's bosom.

Truly, it was a moving sight. The squire had to dry his eyes, and both the vicar and Roper coughed and cleared their throats.

"I have not known such joy for years," Sir Walter cried at length, gently disengaging himself. "We must never part more, my son. I will make full atonement for the past. Have I your forgiveness?"

"You have it from the bottom of my heart, father," Alured replied.

"There, I told you how it would be, Sir Walter," the squire said. "I knew all would be right in a minute, as soon as you two came together. Atonement and forgiveness are the order of the day, and I must take my turn at them. I hope I may get off as well as you. We've been a couple of hard-hearted, unnatural parents, it must be owned, Sir Walter, and have stood very much in the way of our own happiness."

"*I* have done so, most undoubtedly, my good friend," Fitzwalter replied. "But as to you——"

"Nay, I've been just as bad," the squire cried. "I won't attempt to palliate my own misconduct. But Sir Walter looks faint. Lead him to a chair, Alured."

"Oh, my boy! my boy; that I could ever desert thee!" Sir Walter ejaculated.

"And oh, my daughter!—my daughter! that I should have done the like by thee!" the squire exclaimed.

"His daughter! What means he?" Fitzwalter inquired.

"He alludes to my wife," Alured replied.

"Yes—yes, it's quite true," the squire said. "Things have come about most strangely. If we had planned them, they would never have happened so. I hope you don't object to your son's marriage, Sir Walter?"

"Object!" Fitzwalter cried. "Alured indeed has got a treasure. Never was man more fortunate. May Heaven bless them both, and keep them as it has done hitherto!"

"I cry 'Amen' to that wish with all my soul!" the squire said fervently. "But I must prepare for my own ordeal. Where is Rose?"

"She is with Miss Bassingbourne," Alured replied.

" With her sister Bab Monkbury, you mean," the squire rejoined. " These disguises are at an end now. I have two daughters, you must know, Sir Walter. Rose is my eldest."

" A dozen like her were not too many," Fitzwalter replied.

" I don't know that," the squire rejoined. " Two are quite enow. I shall divide my lands between them."

" No necessity for that," Sir Walter said. " My son is rich enough. My estates are his. He shall not wait till I am gone for his inheritance."

Alured would have remonstrated, but a look from his father checked him.

" I cannot give you my title," Sir Walter added ; " but it will soon be yours."

" I shall lose Bab if I don't take care," the squire remarked with a laugh. " Scarcely a day passes but I get an offer for her hand, and this very morning I have received one from Sir Gilbert de Montfichet, backed up by an array of supporters. However, I can have nothing to say to him, even if Bab were inclined to listen to his suit, for Roper tells me he is a ruined man."

" Do not reject him on that score," Sir Walter said, quickly. " The young man has been a spendthrift and a gambler, and has fallen into bad hands, but he has been preserved from utter ruin. He has not a bad heart, and may reform—nay, I am persuaded, if he gets a good wife, he will reform. Recollect, we are not quite faultless ourselves, my good friend. I will tell you more about him at a fitting opportunity. And now, Alured," he continued, turning to his son, " answer me one question, ere we see your wife. Does she know you are my son ?"

" No, my father," he replied. " My true name she knows, but not whence it is derived—nor has she ever sought for an explanation which she felt I might desire to withhold. Aware I had good motives for the adoption of an assumed name, and being almost similarly circumstanced herself, she readily comprehended the necessity for concealment in my case. When we first met, she had no reason to believe me other than of humble birth ; and as, in addition to all other motives for disguise, I wished to win her heart for myself alone, I did not undeceive her. She thought me peasant born. As a peasant I wooed her. As a peasant I received her hand. And as a peasant I should have continued to her, had it not been for this reconciliation with you, my father !"

Sir Walter murmured a few words of self-reproach, and the young man went on.

" As Alured Fitzwalter I wedded her, while she came to me as Rose Monkbury. To all others she had been Rose Mildmay. With me she had no mysteries. Nay, almost on our first acquaintance, and before she gave me her whole heart, she warned me that a cloud hung upon her birth. She told me whose daughter she was —but she feared her mother had been wronged."

" There she was mistaken," the squire cried. " Grace Leslie was my true and lawful wife. The ceremony was performed by my present chaplain, Parson Bush. We were secretly married in the little church in the park. Roper knows all about it, for he stood father on the occasion, and gave the bride away. Besides, there are plenty of witnesses still living—old Paul Flitwick—Mosscrop—Tom Deane—and the certificate duly signed by Bush and Roger Bowes, the clerk."

" I am fully satisfied, sir," Alured said—" but it was only this morning, at a very early hour, that Rose became acquainted with the happy fact in a letter she received from worthy Mr. Roper, who detailed all the circumstances you have mentioned. You may conceive her joy at the intelligence—for it removed the only affliction of her life."

"How she must have hated me!" the squire exclaimed. "Zounds! I quite hate myself!"

"Rose can hate no one—much less one to whom she owed her birth—but she confessed she could not look upon you—and purposely avoided you. These prejudices arose, no doubt, from some motive not worth inquiring into now, which had been early instilled into her breast. But all that is past."

"And a good job it is," the squire said. "Would that the same disclosure had been made to Bab. It would have saved the necessity of explanation."

"Make yourself easy on that score," Alured replied. "Bab knows all. On my arrival here I instantly communicated to her the substance of Roper's letter, and her ebullition of delight at the news was, I think, not without a witness in the person of Sir Gilbert de Montfichet."

"Did Rose never meet her sister?" the squire asked. "She could not have the same antipathy to her, that she naturally had to me."

"I beseech you to believe, sir, that she had no antipathy to you. As you have asked the question, I must tell you that the sisters did occasionally meet —and I myself was once surprised in an interview with Bab, by Jonas Nettlebed and your old whipper-in, Paul Flitwick, which gave rise, I believe, to some misconstruction on their part."

"Soh—this was the story Jonas had to tell, which was to prove your inability to win the Flitch, to the little landlord's great contentment."

"If any married couple ever deserved to obtain that prize for perfect happiness, love and devotion to each other, we are justly entitled to it," Alured said.

"And by Heaven you shall have it!" the squire exclaimed.

"Hold! sir, hold!—make no rash promises," Roper interposed. "The claim must be preferred under the proper names of the parties, and decided upon at the Court Baron."

"I know what the decision will be," the squire said.

"And I know what it ought to be," Sir Walter added. "My son has the best of wives—that I will maintain"

"And if you will listen to Rose, Sir Walter, she will maintain she has the best of husbands," Roper said.

"And she is perfectly right, for they are admirably matched," the squire cried; "but do let her come in, and speak for herself. Since I find I have no more explanations to give, I am perfectly easy. Is she within call, I wonder," he added, going to the door, and raising his voice—"Rose! Rose!—where are you, my darling?"

"Who is it calls?" she exclaimed, quickly responding to the summons.

"Your father," he rejoined, catching her in his arms as she entered the room, and folding her to his breast. "Heaven bless you, my child! How like your dear mother you are, to be sure!" he added, gazing at her features, through eyes half blinded by tears. "Say you forgive me, Rose, and I shall be quite happy."

"I do indeed forgive you, father,—if I have anything to pardon," she replied, fondly returning his embrace.

Again, there were moist eyes among the lookers-on.

"Which am I to call you now, sir—uncle or papa?" Bab cried, archly. She had followed her sister into the room, but remained near the door.

"Papa, of course," the squire replied, holding out

an arm for her—"there is room here for you both.
Zounds! I don't deserve to be so happy. But I'll
make everybody else as happy as I can. This shall be
a day of rejoicing in the hall—a grand day—such a
merrymaking—such feasting—such carousing. A cask
of the strongest ale shall be broached—the best wine
in my cellar shall be brought out—and we'll drink a
health to my two daughters. I'll keep open house for
a week—ay, for a month. All my tenantry shall be
entertained—and even strangers shall be welcome. No
man shall be turned from my gate. Go, Roper, and
assemble the household in the hall—all the folk in-doors
and out-of-doors,—everybody—mind!—I'll present my
daughters to them. Stay! there are guests in the
house. Request their attendance here, and tell them
why I desire it. It will save time and trouble, and explanations which I abominate."

"Your commands shall be obeyed, sir," the steward
replied, departing.

"A word with you, Bab," the squire said, taking her
a little aside. "What do you think of Sir Gilbert de
Montfichet? A handsome, gay young fellow—eh?"

"La! papa, I've scarcely given him a thought. He's
a shade better than Sir John Grubham, perhaps."

"Well, he has sent me an offer. What answer shall
I give him?"

"A decided and positive 'No.' I'd rather die single
than have him."

"Poor fellow! I pity him," the squire exclaimed.

"You needn't give yourself any concern about him,
papa. I heard him declare just now that he had
changed his mind—and wouldn't have me, even if you
consented."

"I know why that was," the squire rejoined; "he
saw a young gentleman there," nodding at Alured.

"conversing with you—and he didn't quite understand why you should be so intimate with him. But that would be at once set to rights. The only question is what you——"

"I've given you my answer, papa."

"Recollect he is a baronet."

"Still, I say no."

"Large estates—fine house—capital stables."

"No—no—no."

As the last negative was pronounced Montfichet, the three suitors, Juddock and Bush, entered the room.

"Glad to see you, gentlemen," the squire cried, advancing to meet them. "You could not have visited me more fortunately. At all times you are welcome—now you are doubly so. Would I could have all my friends round me to rejoice with me on this happy occasion. Roper no doubt has explained to you what has occurred, so I have only to present you to my daughters."

Such congratulations followed this address—such shaking of hands—such a general manifestation of delight and good-will on all sides—that the like was never seen. Transported with joy, the squire slapped Bush on the shoulder, crying—"This is the parson who married me. He will tell you all about it."

"That I will, sir," the Reverend Jeremy replied. "I'm ready to answer all inquirers. Date, 1 May, 1729. Parties, Mark Monkbury, Esquire, of Little Dunmow, bachelor, and Rose Leslie, of Great Dunmow, spinster. Minister, Jeremy Bush. Clerk, Roger Bowes."

"I have bided my time with patience, Alured, but it is well-nigh exhausted," Sir Walter said to his son; "nor is it right that your wife—now that she has thus been publicly acknowledged—should remain a moment longer in ignorance as to the true station of her husband. Inform her of it quickly, and let those around us hear you."

"Rose," Alured said, taking her hand, "I have kept only one secret from you, and that is the secret of my birth. All necessity for further concealment is at an end. As the avowed daughter of the representative of one of the oldest and proudest families in the county, it is right you should know—and that all others should know—that you have married one of equal rank with yourself."

"Equal rank!" the squire exclaimed. "By Jove! you belong to the older family of the two. You go back to the twelfth century, and had a title then."

"A title! he, a title! Did you mark that, Sir G.?" Juddock whispered his patron. "I thought that young fellow was something out of the common order. Everybody seems to be somebody else in this house. There's our old friend Doctor Plot—or John Johnson—I'll be sworn he has got another name."

"Peace!" Montfichet cried. "I think I have already found him out. If so——" And he ground his teeth with rage.

"Behold my father," Alured continued, leading his wife up to him—"and know him as Sir Walter Fitzwalter."

"Know him as my oldest friend," the squire cried.

"And as my deadly enemy," Sir Gilbert muttered, putting his hand to his sword.

"Udsbores! is that Sir Walter?" Juddock exclaimed. "I must make myself scarce." And he managed to steal out of the room unobserved.

Meanwhile, the old gentleman having tenderly embraced his daughter-in-law, laid his benediction on her gentle head.

"You will pardon my intrusion upon you last night

Rose," he said, "but I wished to convince myself of the truth of the delightful description I had received of you—for, to my shame I confess it, I was at that time no believer in female perfection. I am a convert now. My son is truly fortunate."

"Not more fortunate than I am sir," Rose replied. "Our little cottage has been the abode of perfect happiness, derived from the love we bear each other—a love not dependent upon wealth or station—as I ventured to tell you last night—but wholly unbiassed by them. We love each other for each other's sake. The change that has just occurred, therefore, will make no change in us. It may extend the sphere of our affections, but cannot diminish their intensity. Rose Fitzwalter will not be less meek, faithful and affectionate, than Rose Woodbine."

"Nor will Alured Fitzwalter be less tender, and devoted in his love than Frank Woodbine," the young man said.

"How very pretty !" Bab cried. "It's well I'm not married. I should never be meek and submissive. I must have my own way."

"You shall have your own way in everything with me," Grub exclaimed, throwing himself at her feet.

"And with me," Chip cried, prostrating himself on the other side. "My greatest happiness would consist in serving you."

"You shall scold me as much as you please," Clot said, taking up a similar position in front. "But I don't believe you could scold."

"Don't try me," Bab rejoined. "You don't know what a tongue I have. Does he, papa ?"

"You'll never win the Flitch, Bab," the squire observed, laughing.

"No—nor any one else," she rejoined; "and till

some one does—I remain single. Poz. So you have your answer, gentlemen, and may get up as soon as you please."

The three suitors obeyed, and retired, looking dismally blank, and condoling with each other.

Sir Gilbert de Montfichet, who had taken no share in the foregoing conversation, but remained apart, now came up to the two Fitzwalters, and sternly regarding the elder, said :

"So, this then is Sir Walter Fitzwalter. At last we have met. And I proclaim him to his face as assassin."

"Recall that word—recall it, Sir Gilbert," Alured cried, fiercely—" or by Heaven! I will strike you to my feet."

"I am glad you have taken this quarrel upon yourself, sir," Montfichet rejoined. " I cannot fight an old man—but with you the case is different. I repeat the term I used. He is——"

Alured raised his hand, but Sir Walter threw himself between them.

"Touch him not, my son—touch him not—leave him to me," he cried. And seizing the young baronet's wrist with a grasp of iron, he dragged him to a little distance from the other. " You have indeed a father's death to avenge in me, Sir Gilbert," he pursued, "and if my blood alone will satisfy you, I will bare my breast, and you shall plunge your sword within it—but lift my hand against you I will not, nor shall my son. Yet ere you proceed to any act of violence, hear what I have to say. "You remember me," lowering his tone, "as John Johnson, and the occasion when I saved you from sharpers."

"I have not forgotten it," Montfichet replied. "You lent me money, and stood by me when I was assailed."

"We had odds against us," Sir Walter pursued, "and the assistance I rendered you must have convinced you I am no contemptible swordsman. It is therefore from no fear of the result that I refuse to fight you. But, as I have said, you shall have revenge — full revenge, if you require it."

"Have you done, sir?" Montfichet cried, trying to shake him off.

"Not yet," Sir Walter rejoined, still further lowering his voice. "You are a ruined man, Sir Gilbert. You have lost all at play. Stansted House and your large estates will be seized upon, and sold in less than a month."

"If I am ruined I am not dishonoured. Cease these taunts, or you *shall* fight me, Sir Walter."

"I do not desire to taunt you, but I must speak the truth. You have given bonds and deeds to Jews and usurers. You have parted with your whole substance like a prodigal. I know it all. I have watched your whole career."

"To what end have you done so?" Montfichet demanded, fiercely.

"To save you," Sir Walter replied. "I knew the miscreants by whom you were surrounded, and who were making you their prey. I also knew it would be in vain to warn you against them, or to check you in your mad career. I had only one course left. It was to counteract their schemes. I succeeded in my attempt. I will not say that it cost me nothing—or that you have lost nothing. But if you learn wisdom, and profit by your experience, you will be a gainer, while I shall be content if my expiation be deemed sufficient."

"How am I to understand you, Sir Walter?" Montfitchet demanded, looking at him with astonishment.

"You are to understand that all the bonds and

securities you have given are in my possession, and shall
be delivered over to you. That the money you have
borrowed was in great part lent by me, and therefore
you are indebted to no one but me, and I give you a
quittance in full. Now do you understand, Sir Gilbert? You may still call Stansted yours—you need
not sell an acre—nor cut down a tree. You are much
in the position you were when you started for town—
a few thousands minus, but they are of no account.
Are you satisfied? Do you still desire to take my
life?"

"I only desire your friendship. You are a noble-
hearted gentleman, Sir Walter; and I am profoundly
moved by your generosity."

"In the event of my death these deeds would have
been delivered to you," Sir Walter pursued; "together
with my release from all claims. Purblind fool that
I was! I imagined I was working out a scheme of re-
fined vengeance, when I was only making atonement.
No thanks—no thanks. I desire none—deserve none.
The sole condition I would willingly annex to the gift
is, that you reform—as I may not be able to watch over
you in future. As the best means of doing so, I recom-
mend you to marry."

"That I will, without delay Sir Walter,—if you will
find me a wife."

"Can you not induce the squire to give you his
youngest daughter?"

"Oh! if he could be persuaded—or she would
consent!"

"Monkbury," Sir Walter cried, turning round, "Sir
Gilbert and I have settled all our differences—and I
am happy in giving you my full assurance that our
young friend's fortune is in no respect impaired, and
his estates entirely free from encumbrance. He there-

R

fore considers himself in a fit position to renew the offer he made in writing this morning, and solicit from you the hand of your daughter."

" Sir Walter has but made himself the mouthpiece of my wishes," Montfichet subjoined.

" What says Bab ?" the squire demanded.

" How poor Bab is teased, to be sure," the little beauty rejoined. " No—no—no! No one shall have my hand till the Dunmow Flitch is won."

" Then we still may hope," the three suitors said. " Jonas Nettlebed is sure to gain it. We'll support him."

Montfichet looked greatly disconcerted, but Monkbury told him that point was sure to be settled, whatever Bab might think, when the next Court Baron was held, and encouraged him to persevere in his attentions.

Just then, Mr. Roper entered and informed the squire that, in pursuance of his instructions, he had collected together the whole of the household in the hall. On this, the worthy gentleman, begging his son-in-law and his friends to follow him, took a hand of each of his daughters, and led them forth.

Such a shout as arose when the three appeared.— The roof rang again.

How proud he felt at that moment, and how happy! —Before him were a host of honest countenances, glowing with delight, while his ears were filled with expressions of heartfelt satisfaction. For a moment there was a silence—to hear the squire speak—and he uttered a few words, introducing his daughters. Hereupon, the vociferations were more enthusiastic than ever, and emboldened by the kindly smiles of the two fair creatures they beheld, some of the foremost of the retainers rushed forward, and contended for a shake of the hand, which was in no instance refused. Blessings were showered upon their master's head, and upon the heads of his children, by the elder domestics—while the younger were louder and more demonstrative in their manifestations of regard. The ceremonial of presentation over, immediate and active steps were taken to prepare a feast—a feast such as never before had been seen at Monkbury, and which, when it once commenced, knew no cessation, from mid-day until midnight. For the joyous news spread about like wildfire, and the farmers and their wives and daughters flocked in by dozens to the Hall. Even Jonas and Nelly were brought from Dunmow, and the Bachelors and Maidens, composing the Jury, came with them. Nelly heard all particulars of the marriage from Parson Bush, and wondered whether the squire had had any more wives, and any other daughters; and the Reverend Jeremy chucked her under the chin, and told her that not unlikely she herself might be one of the latter. He had always thought so. And Nelly blushed, and looked delighted. With the party from Dunmow came the fiddlers — so there was no lack of music. Mosscrop was kept constantly employed — and had to pay repeated visits to the cellar, and fill basket after basket with wine. Every fresh arrival was a fresh bottle at least—and so vast was the consumption of ale, that instead of one cask being broached there were three— and all emptied. In the evening they danced in the hall, and the squire led off a country dance with Nelly —and both of his daughters joined in it—in fact, Bab was in such high glee, that she consented to dance with her three suitors, beginning with Grub and ending with Clot—and when she had done with them, she ran Sir Gilbert out of breath in a jig. Not seeing Sir Walter, who took no part in the festivities, and who in fact had quitted the Hall, Juddock ventured to show

himself again, eating, drinking, and singing as jollily
as ever, and arousing Jonas's jealousy once more by his
attentions to his pretty little wife.

Altogether, it was the merriest day merry Monkbury
Place had ever known, and was long remembered by
those who participated in its pleasures.

V.

THE LAST NIGHT IN THE HAUNTED ROOM.

Sir Walter, we have said, took no part in the festivities of Monkbury Place.

His spirits were not equal to so great a demand
upon them as participation in such rejoicings would
have occasioned; and feeling he should only check
the general hilarity by his presence, he announced his
intention, early in the day, of returning to Dunmow.
The squire would fain have detained him, but he was
not to be turned from his purpose. He had made up
his mind, he said, to re-visit the old Priory Church,
and to pass another night in the Haunted Room.

Finding opposition useless, the squire was obliged
to yield. "Well, if you must go, you must," he said ;
"but I rely on your coming back to-morrow. I shall
then have a communication of importance to make to
you—unless I am forestalled in the interim, as may
possibly be the case. I am not at liberty to mention
the matter now. I need not tell you to consider this
house as your own. Use it as you please. Rooms
shall be prepared for you, where you will be perfectly
undisturbed—quite left to yourself, if you prefer soli-
tude. Bring any one you choose with you—I mean,
supposing you should unexpectedly meet with a friend."

A YEAR AND A DAY.

(JONAS AND NELLY NETTLEBED.)

P. 247.

"Little likelihood of that," Sir Walter replied, with a faint smile. "My friends were never very numerous, and I am well-nigh forgotten by the few who remain."

"But it may so happen," the squire remarked. "We frequently meet with people we least expect—sometimes, with those we fancy wholly lost to us."

This was said with a certain significance, which did not escape Fitzwalter at the time, though he afterwards more fully comprehended his friend's meaning.

Equally deaf was the old baronet to the entreaties of Alured and Rose to stay with them; and while he was bidding them farewell, a hasty conversation respecting his movements took place in private between the squire and Roper; the result of which was the immediate departure of the indefatigable steward on some errand of importance.

Mounted on one of the best hunters in the stables, Roper was soon out of the park, and on the way to Dunmow, where he arrived before Sir Walter had quitted Monkbury Place. Owing to the delay of the postilion, who was making merry in the servants'-hall, and did not like to leave his comfortable quarters—and it may be, also, owing to a hint from the squire to Mosscrop, the old baronet's post-chaise was not brought round for an hour or more. So the steward got a good start, if he wished to be beforehand with him.

At last, Sir Walter drove off, and pursuing the same road as Roper, in due time reached Little Dunmow. Alighting at the sexton's dwelling, he obtained from him the keys of the Priory Church, and proceeded thither alone.

Once more he stood among the tombs of his ancestors.

His emotions were deep and solemn, but less painful

than those he had experienced on a former occasion.
Remorse had ceased to goad him. Calmness had succeeded agitation. He could meditate with composure
upon death, and life hereafter. His earthly pilgrimage
he thought drew towards an end, and he might hope,
ere long, to meet again his departed wife.

Some time was passed in such contemplations, and
he then entered the arched recess, and knelt before the
saintly relics enshrined in the cist within it.

As he concluded a prayer, and bowed his head upon
his breast, he heard a slight sound behind him. A
footstep! Yet how could that be? He had taken the
same precaution as on his former visit to the sacred
edifice, and locked the door. No one ought to be
within the church. A chill came over him, and he
hesitated to look round.

Why should he fear? The church was not illumined
by ghostly moonbeams now, but full of garish light;
and the sun shone upon the marble tombs and upon
the gravestones on the floor.

Were those gravestones yawning to give up their
dead? Did his eyes deceive him, or was yon ponderous
slab closing slowly like a trap-door? Delusion!—mere
delusion!

One thing was palpable enough—a letter. It was
lying on the ground, close to the monument of the
founder of his line. Not many minutes ago he stood
on that precise spot. It must have been placed there
since. But how?—by whom?

Hastening to pick it up, he glanced at the superscrip-
tion. It was addressed to himself. He could not be
mistaken as to those well-known characters. The hand-
writing was his wife's! The ink fresh as if just used.
Merciful Heaven! if such a thing could be!

His limbs almost failed him, and his senses seemed

fleeting from excess of motion. He had not strength to open the letter on which his hopes rested.

At last the effort was made, and doubt gave way to wildest exultation.

These were the words he read:

"*Be of good cheer, Sir Walter. The worst is past. Return to the Old Inn. Seek the Haunted Room. At midnight all shall be revealed.*"

"She lives!—she lives!" he cried. "The tale I heard of her death was an invention. I shall behold her again—shall clasp her to my heart once more. Kind Heaven support me!—or this flood of delight will overwhelm me, and I shall die before the appointed hour."

He leaned against the tomb, and strove to control his tumultuous feelings.

At first, some misgivings would intrude upon his joy; but, by-and-by, they wholly disappeared, and his confidence in a speedy meeting with his lost wife became firm.

He had entered that little church a sad man, with his thoughts upon the grave, anxious only to rejoin one gone thither before him. He quitted it, hopeful, joyful, clinging to the world, which he found she still tenanted.

On arriving at the Old Inn at Dunmow, he was received by pretty Peggy, the chambermaid, who told him her master and mistress were gone to Monkbury Place, in consequence of what they had heard from Mr. Roper of the great rejoicings occurring there; but she would do her best to make him comfortable in their absence. Sir Walter was surprised to find that Roper, whom he fancied he had left at the Hall, should have been at the Flitch, and he could not help connecting the steward's hurried visit with the mysterious circumstance which had just taken place at the Priory

Church. No matter. If Roper gave him back his wife, he should be for ever indebted to him.

The old baronet at once proceeded to the Haunted Room, where some refreshments were set before him by Peggy, who cared little for ghosts in the daytime, and could dispense with Carroty Dick's company. However, she was punished for her temerity. Something she saw, on quitting the room, at the end of the dark corridor, made her set up a shriek, and caused the destruction of a plate she held in her hand.

Sir Walter came forth to see what was the matter, and found that the chambermaid's terror had been occasioned by a woman in tattered apparel, and of haggard looks, who was now slowly advancing towards them. Sir Walter recognised her at once. It was Alice Aggs—the mischief-maker—the cause of such dire calamity to himself, and to his wife. He motioned the woman to keep aloof, but she would not be forbidden, and creeping on, threw herself at his feet, imploring his forgiveness. Peggy pretended to hurry away—though her curiosity prompted her to remain within earshot.

"I do forgive you, woman, for the injuries you have done me," Sir Walter said, "and may Heaven forgive you likewise."

"Then you know my lady was innocent," Alice Aggs replied. "I came to make a clear breast of it, and tell you so. I have been a sinful woman, Sir Walter, and Heaven has requited me for my wickedness. Since the time when all those dreadful things occurred—and especially since my poor injured lady's death—I have not known a day's happiness. Nothing has prospered with me. I should have prayed to be released—but I feared to die. Your forgiveness has made me feel somewhat easier. Oh! if I could obtain hers!"

" Do not despair of that," Sir Walter rejoined,
touched by her piteous accents. " Her heart was ever
open to compassion."

" I know it," Alice groaned—" but that heart is cold
now. Not even your words can move it. Hear me,
Sir Walter. A curse has been laid upon my head by
dying lips—and it clings to me, and will cling to the
last. Poverty and distress have come upon me, and
shame. But for a scanty pittance allowed me by Mr.
Roper, I should have died of want long ago. All
those I have known have cast me off—all others shun
me. I have no refuge—not even the grave. I am
ever brooding upon the past—ever lamenting it—and
when you entered my miserable abode last night, I
was trying to persuade myself that all would yet come
right, and that my dear mistress, whom I have often
seen in my dreams, not with a countenance of frowns,
but with a benignant smile like an angel's, would forgive me."

" And so she will," Sir Walter said. " Get up, Alice,
get up. You shall know the truth. Your mistress
yet lives."

" Lives !" Alice cried — " lives ! You would not
deceive me, sir, I am sure. Yet my heart almost
refuses to credit such glad tidings. Shall I see her
again ?"

" You shall. And let that assurance content you
for the present," Sir Walter rejoined. " Go below,
and remain within the house till you are summoned.
It may be past midnight before I send for you."

" I will await your pleasure, sir—if it be till dawn,"
Alice replied, departing ; while Sir Walter re-entered
the room.

" What a wicked woman !" Peggy mentally ejaculated, preceding her—" and what a very strange old

gentleman. Not summon her till past midnight, indeed! I wonder why. It's quite clear I shan't get much rest to-night—but it don't matter. Master and missis won't be home till late, I dare say, from Monk-bury Place, and Carroty Dick will sit up and keep me company."

Time past slowly with Sir Walter, whose impatience was so great, that he thought midnight would nevei arrive. He tried to read, but could not fix his attention upon the book he opened. A hundred times and more did he refer to his wife's letter to assure himself of its reality.

It grew dark, and Peggy, escorted as far as the door by Carroty Dick, brought in candles. As she threw fresh wood upon the fire, inquiring if the old gentleman wanted anything more, and receiving an answer in the negative, the inquisite chambermaid stole a glance round the room, but she saw nothing to reward her curiosity. She could not hear even the rustle of a petticoat.

"She's not come yet, Dick," Peggy remarked to her red-polled lover on her return. "I wonder whether he expects the ghost to come to life, or what? It's something very extraordinary. I can get nothing out of old Alice. We must wait till midnight—and then, if he calls her, I'll follow her up-stairs. You'll come with me?"

Dick gave a very reluctant assent, and they moved off.

The wished-for hour arrived. The clock struck— TWELVE !

Scarcely had the last vibrations ceased, than Sir Walter heard a slight noise in the mysterious closet. The tapestry hanging before it was drawn aside, and a female figure stood before him.

It was Lady Fitzwalter.

Pale—very pale—almost a shadow—robed in white, and looking so unearthly, that her husband, for a moment, doubted if she could be living.

Another instant, and his doubts were dispelled. She lived—she breathed. He had knelt to her—had heard her voice murmuring forgiveness—had clasped her hand, bathing it with his tears—had strained her to his heart.

Heaven grant he should not go mad with delight! Extreme joy was harder to bear than extreme woe. He thought he had nerved himself for this moment, but all gave way before the torrent, and he wept like a child.

He grew calmer. He examined her features through his blinded gaze. Still the same to him though so fearfully attenuated. Still the same to him, though the raven locks were blanched, and the dark eyes deeply sunken in their sockets. Enough for him she lived. His beloved—his deplored—his injured Juga lived. He held her in his arms. The troubled dream was over, and he had awakened to indescribable happiness. He seemed to have become younger by twenty years than he had been a few moments ago.

The first delicious transports of the meeting over, he was able to ask for some explanation; and amidst frequent interruptions on his own part—tenderness, self-reproaches, and new entreaties for forgiveness— received from her the following particulars.

An antidote to the fatal draught she had swallowed had been promptly procured by Roper, and other restorative measures being adopted, she was brought back to an existence, which at that time was hateful to her. At first, she was incensed against her preserver, but after a time, her heart being softened by the religious counsels of worthy Mr. Leslie, she became reconciled to life. But she desired it to be given out

that she was no more—and so earnest were her entreaties in this respect, that her wishes were complied
with, and due precautions being taken, all believed in
her decease. She lived in the greatest obscurity, and
was visited by no one except Roper and the curate. Her
little cottage adjoined the garden of the old Hall, and
communicated with it at the back. Hence, she could
easily visit her former abode at night, and constantly
did so. As long as the house remained untenanted,
these nocturnal visits were little observed, though,
even then, reports arose that a white figure had been
seen gliding along the corridor; but when the place
was converted into an inn, and she was more than once
encountered in her walks, it could not be doubted that
an apparition had been seen. Wishing to encourage
the notion, she aided her spectral appearance by shroud-
like attire, and managed to render her movements
almost noiseless. She had recourse to other contrivances to give effect to the character she assumed.
In this way she succeeded in scaring all the guests
from one wing of the house, and could weep and pray
as of old, and pass the long hours of the night in the
room which had once been her own. Thus years flew
by. She saw nothing of her son, who had been taken
from her when a child—or of her husband. Both
believed her dead. How indeed she continued to live
on was a marvel. But at the bottom of all her grief
there was Hope. Roper had always assured her that,
some day, her innocence would be established, and a
reconciliation take place between her and Sir Walter.
That day was long in coming—but it had come at last.

Her nocturnal visits were not entirely confined to
the old house. Sometimes she repaired to the little
Priory Church to pray. She had access to the vaults,
from which there was a secret entrance to the interior

of the sacred fabric, by means of a movable grave-stone. She was there when Sir Walter entered the sacred structure on the previous night. She had heard his self-accusations and bitter regrets—and had with difficulty refrained from declaring herself. But she had not then consulted with Roper, and waited for his advice. Not seeing the steward that night, she paid her customary visit to her old room—and it was need-less to repeat what had then occurred. When she was hastily apprised by Roper, on the morrow, of her husband's movements, she again sought the old Priory Church—found Sir Walter there—and placed the letter in his way.

Then came Sir Walter's turn. He acquainted her with all that had recently happened to him. He told her of his reconciliation with their son. He expressed his perfect satisfaction at Alured's marriage—and spoke in rapturous terms of their daughter-in-law. He de-tailed the strange discoveries that had been made at Monkbury Place—which, strange as they were, were not equal to the last and greatest discovery reserved for him—that of his lost wife. And then he recollected, from the hint thrown out by him, that the squire must be aware that Lady Fitzwalter was still alive,—having, no doubt, been made acquainted with the secret by Roper.

One circumstance only required explanation. Sir Walter approached it with a vague sense of dread—but all must now be made clear.

"On your disappearance last night," he said, "when I followed you to the verge of that closet, another phantom—as I then deemed it—rose before me. Was it of your contrivance?"

"No," she replied, looking hard at him.

"Then, indeed, it was a spirit I beheld," Fitzwalter

pursued. " It stood there—there, where I point—ha !"
And he became suddenly fixed in an attitude of terror.

" What do you behold?" Lady Fitzwalter demanded,
looking in the same direction, but perceiving nothing.

" It is he—my friend," he rejoined. " His aspect is
wholly changed. It wears a heavenly smile. I am
pardoned—pardoned. He accepts my atonement."

And he dropped upon his knees, stretching out his
hands.

" Is it gone?" Lady Fitzwalter asked, observing a
change in his countenance.

" Even so," he replied. " Pray with me, Juga,—
pray with me."

She complied, and they joined together in fervent
supplication.

When they arose with lightened hearts, Alice Agos
was summoned to receive her lady's forgiveness. It
seemed as if the wretched woman was but spared for
this, for next day she went to her account. But she
died in peace.

Part the Fifth.

THE PROCESSION OF THE FLITCH.

I.

AMURATH THE TURK.

NEARLY six months had elapsed, and June had
arrived in all its warmth and beauty.

A delightful evening. Beneath one of the great elm-
trees in front of the Old Inn a large and merry party

were assembled. They were enjoying the refreshing coolness of the twilight hour—and a bowl of capital punch at the same time.

A bench encircled the enormous trunk of the old tree —from one of the arms of which the famous sign of the Flitch was suspended—and this accommodated Jonas and his wife; but the rest of the party were gathered round the table, on which pipes, glasses, and a mighty punch-bowl were set. The company consisted for the most part of the Jury of Bachelors and Maidens; but besides these there were the Bailiff of Dunmow and two of the burgesses, Parson Bush, the squire's chaplain, and Will Crane, the squire's head huntsman. All were guests of the hospitable landlord, who had invited them to a little merry-making, preparatory to a very important event, in connexion with himself, which was to come off on the morrow.

At a smaller table, beneath the sister elm-tree, the Dunmow minstrels were placed—two fiddles, a flute, and a bassoon—ready for song or dance, as the company might require.

The evening, we repeat, was delightful—cool, calm, and bright. Laden with sweet scents from new-mown meadows on the banks of the Chelmer came the soft western breeze. Swifts and swallows were skimming past, twittering, or catching flies on the placid stream. Among the still-busy fields might be seen well-filled hay-carts wending their way towards lofty stacks. Pleasant sounds reached the ear—the warbling of the blackbird and thrush — the merry laughter of the jocund band of haymakers—the mower whetting his scythe—the cawing of rooks—the hum of the door-fly —and the distant jingling of tiny bells, announcing the approach of the Chelmsford waggon.

Viewed in that rosy twilight, how picturesque and

beautiful looked the Old Inn! And how well the merry party beneath the great elm-tree harmonised with it! It was the very hour on which to arrive there. And so thought a traveller who was slowly approaching it in the Chelmsford waggon, before mentioned.

But before this traveller reaches his destination, let us see what our worthy host was about. Full of confidence in the speedy realisation of his long-cherished wishes, the little fellow was in a state of positive beatitude. Next day, the Flitch would be his own. At noon, to-morrow, his claim was to be made at the Court Baron of Little Dunmow, and the decision was certain to be in his favour. Quite certain. Could he not answer—most satisfactorily—every question likely to be put to him? Could not Nelly do the same? Had they not plenty of witnesses to corroborate their assertions?—highly-respectable witnesses—the Bailiff of Dunmow, and the two burgesses—to say nothing of Peggy, Carroty Dick, and the rest of their household—all of whom were prepared to depose on oath to the excellent understanding (as far as they knew) between the landlord and his spouse, and to their perfect conjugal felicity. It was true that Alured Fitzwalter and his wife were candidates for the prize. But what of that? Jonas Nettlebed and Nelly stood first on the Register, and if they were successful (as they were sure to be), Alured and Rose must wait for another twelvemonth—the gift having been discovered, on careful examination of the Charter by Mr. Roper, to be limited to one couple during the year.

One person only had Jonas dreaded. Luckily, that detested individual was away; and not at all likely to appear against him as a witness. Nothing had been seen of the impudent rascal since the great rejoicings

at Monkbury Place, on the day after which he had disappeared—various reasons being assigned for his sudden
departure, but none particularly to his credit. No, no,
Captain Juddock was not likely to trouble him. He
was quite easy on that score.

Taking this cheerful view of things, Jonas surren-
dered himself to the full enjoyment of the moment;
and was laughing, jesting, and filling the glasses of his
friends, when the Chelmsford waggon came up.

Nelly had just remarked that she always associated
the jingling of its bells with the arrival of Doctor Plot
—Sir Walter she meant—and she wondered whether
anybody, as singular as that eccentric old gentleman,
was coming now. Scarcely were the words out of her
mouth, when Ben the Waggoner announced that he
had a guest for the Flitch.

"And a rum un he be," Ben said, grinning from ear
to ear. "Fro' foreign parts, I reckon. He ben't dressed
like a Christian."

A stranger from foreign parts! Nelly's curiosity was
instantly excited. So was Jonas's—but a feeling of
uneasiness (he knew not exactly wherefore) stole over
him. He disliked strangers—especially from foreign
parts—though their visits to the Flitch were few and
far between. However, Carroty Dick and Peggy were
called forth; and presently from the back of the waggon emerged a most extraordinary personage, whose
like had never before been seen at Dunmow. His appearance fully justified Ben's description.

Everybody rose from their seat to gaze at him.
Nelly was struck with admiration; and Jonas looked
quite dumb-founded.

A Turk of gigantic proportions—yes, a Turk! How
he came to be in the Chelmsford waggon Nelly could
not conceive—but there was no doubt as to the fact. A

s

Turk he was, if ever there was one, as was shown by his loose white trousers, his embroidered sandals, the sash round his waist, in which a silver-sheathed ataghan was stuck, the short crimson jacket edged with gold, the curled scimetar at his side, and the enormous many-folded turban on his head, with the crescent in front of it. A Turk beyond all question, and a prodigiously hand-some Turk, too, Nelly thought, with his long, shining black beard, and his flashing black eyes, full of Oriental roguery.

Carroty Dick ventured to inquire for the Turkish gentleman's luggage. A large, shabby-looking port-manteau was brought out, together with a long cherry-stick pipe, and a pouch filled with tobacco. The port-manteau was carried off by Dick, but the pipe and the pouch were delivered by Peggy to the Turk, who re-ceived them from her hands with something so like a wink, that it called a blush to the cheeks of the in-genuous chambermaid.

" Does the Turkish gentleman speak English ?" Jonas inquired of the waggoner.

" Ay, ay, sir," Ben replied, still grinning. " He can make hissel pratty well understood."

" Then I'll address him," Jonas said. And making a very low bow to the stranger, he respectfully begged to know his pleasure.

" Salam aleikoum !" the Turk said, returning the salutation in truly Eastern style. " Aleikoum salam ! My pleasure, worthy host, is to rest for the night within your caravanserai. Let the man who hath brought me hither be paid."

" The waggoner," Nelly interposed, curtseying—" oh yes, sir. How much, sir ?"

" Give the dog a sequin," the Turk said. " Ah ! by Allah ! I forget. The fair Frank knows not the coin.

Give him a piece of silver. Thy father shall be repaid."

"My father!" Nelly exclaimed. "If you mean Jonas, sir—he's my husband."

"Bismillah!—can it be?" the Turk cried. "The aged infidel is unworthy of such a treasure. You deserve a place in the Sultan's seraglio—by the beard of the Prophet, you ought to be a sultana!"

"By the marry-maskins! I must put a stop to this," Jonas thought; "I cannot permit him to call me an aged infidel, or to tell my wife she ought to be a sultana." The landlord's misgivings were almost confirmed, his perceptions being quickened by jealousy.

"Allow me to ask your name and title, sir?" he added.

"You may call me Amurath," the Turk replied. "I am Ex-Aga of the Janissaries, and recently of the Court of his Sublime Majesty the Sultan Mahomet the Fifth."

"Oh, gracious! did you hear that, Jonas? Amurath, Ex-Aga of the Janny — Janny — what-d'ye-call-ums. What a grand title!"

"Too grand by half. I'm not to be taken in by it," Jonas replied. "I've found him out. Why, you silly thing, don't you perceive it's Captain Juddock?"

"Well, I declare you're right, now I look at him again," Nelly said. "But the Turkish dress and the beard deceived me."

"I'm not to be so easily taken in," Jonas rejoined. "What the devil can have brought him back, I wonder?" he added to himself.

"Ho! ho! ho!—so you recognise me, eh! my worthy host?" the giant roared. "I didn't mean to discover myself to you, or your pretty wife, till I had enjoyed a hearty laugh at your joint expense. But by Allah! I swear I have told you the fact. I am no longer Juddock—but Amurath. I am a Mussulman—one of the faithful."

" Then you really are a Turk !" Nelly exclaimed.

" Really and truly, my dear Mrs. N.," the giant replied. " I had some slight scruples at first; but they were overcome, because considerable advantages were to be derived from a change of creed. Amongst these was the privilege of marrying six wives."

" Six wives !" Nelly ejaculated. " How shocking. But surely, you never availed yourself of that wicked privilege ?"

" Didn't I, though. I left six lawful spouses behind me, together with a dozen Georgian, Nubian, and Circassian slaves, composing my hareem, in my hasty flight from Constantinople."

" Oh ! the base renegade !" Jonas muttered. " Would that his wives had followed him ! They might have kept him quiet."

" But do tell us what took you there ?" Nelly said.

" Do me the favour to fill my pipe, my dear Mrs. N., and then I will," the giant replied, handing her the tobacco-pouch, and squeezing her fingers at the same time. " Come and sit beside me," he added, taking up a position on the circular bench, with his legs crossed under him, and inhaling a few whiffs from the pipe. " Sit nearer to me, I pray of you. An Osmanli is always respectful. To begin. After that agreeable and eventful night at Monkbury Place, when I had last the pleasure of seeing you, I repaired next day to Harwich and finding my friend Captain Culverin of the *Hurl thrumbo* about to sail for Constantinople, I embarked with him, and duly arrived at the Turkish capital. War, as you know, had just broken out between the Sultan and Elizabeth Petrowna, Empress of Russia. Detesting the latter aggressive and barbarous power, and sympathising with the respectable Ottoman, I entered the service of Mahomet the Fifth, and fought under the banner of the Crescent against the Russians. Need I say I served with distinction? The Czarina, in her thinned hordes, has reason to remember me. Returning to Constantinople, after a brief but brilliant campaign, I was received with great distinction by the Sultan, and speedily rose to high dignities. From a Bey I became a Pasha, and his Sublime Highness offered to make me Aga of the Janissaries. But to this end, it was needful I should embrace the Mahometan faith. I had objections,—but they were overcome, and I was appointed leader of the Sultan's body-guard. A beau. tiful villa was bestowed upon me on the banks of the Bosphorus, where I enjoyed the society of my six wives, and my numerous lovely slaves—and there I might be still—but for an unlooked-for and unfortunate event."

" What was it ?" Nelly inquired.

" I must take a few whiffs before I can proceed," Amurath replied. " I must cut this part of my story as short as I can. It affects me too deeply. In an evil hour, the Sultan's chief favourite, Budoor, cast eyes of affection upon me Her charms proving irresistible, a meeting took place between us. Had it ended there, all had been well. But no—we met again—and by treachery were surprised. Little mercy was shown us —or rather little mercy was shown poor Budoor. She sleeps beneath the waves of the Bosphorus—I escaped the bowstring by flight."

" If I had been the Sultan, you shouldn't have escaped me," Jonas said. " I'd have given you the sack, as well as Budoor. Poor thing, I pity _her_. And so you came back with your friend, Captain Culverin. I suppose ?"

" You've hit it exactly. I did," the giant answered.
" I got on board the *Hurlothrumbo* just as the captain
was weighing anchor, and after a quick passage to
England, was put ashore last night at Southend, whence
I found my way to Chelmsford—and here I am."

Whatever credit the party round the table might
attach to the giant's story, it served to amuse them very
much, and on its conclusion, Parson Bush proposed the
health of the Ex-Aga of the Janissaries, which was
drunk with cheers and laughter.

Amurath now called for a bottle of cider, and, while
the order was being complied with by Tom Tapster, he
volunteered a song in return for the compliment paid
him—addressing himself chiefly to Jonas.

Cider of Devonshire.

I.

CIDER good of Devonshire—
That just now is my desire.
Let the blockheads laugh, who will,
Quick, mine host, the flagon fill
With the admirable juice,
Which the apple-vats produce.
Better 'tis, I will maintain,
Than the stuff you call champagne.
Thirst I feel—and my desire
Is the drink of Devonshire.

II.

Cider fine! thou hast the merit,
With thy lightness and thy spirit,
Not to mystify the brain!
You may fill, and fill again.
Quaff as much as you require
Of the drink of Devonshire.

III.

'Tis the property of cider—
Ne'er to make a breach the wider.
With your friend you would not quarrel
Were you to consume a barrel.
Idle bickering and fooling
Dwell not in this liquor cooling.
Generous thoughts alone inspire
Draught of dulcet Devonshire.

IV.

Cider sparkling, cider placid.
False it is to call it acid.
To the light you hold the cup,
How the atoms bright leap up!
How the liquid foams and bubbles,
Ready to dispel your troubles!
How its fragrancy invites!
How its flavour fine delights,
As the lip and throat it bites!
Pour it down! you'll never tire
Of delicious Devonshire!

Just as the song was concluded, Tom Tapster appeared, and the cider being poured out, the foaming pot was emptied by the giant at a draught.

Meanwhile, Tom Tapster took the opportunity of saying to his master:

"Ben the Waggoner would like to have a word with you, sir, before he goes—about the Turkish gentleman, I believe, sir."

"Oh indeed!" Jonas exclaimed. "I'll come to him directly. Give him a jug of ale, Tom, and bid him sit down for a few minutes, and make himself comfortable. I wonder what he has got to tell me," he mused, as the drawer departed.

Though delivered in an undertone, this communication did not escape the ears of Parson Bush, between whom and the Ex-Aga some sort of understanding seemed to subsist, to judge from the glances they now and then exchanged.

"And now, my worthy host, that I have acquainted you with my adventures, it is but fair you should let me know what has befallen you during my absence," Amurath said. "I presume I may congratulate you upon having obtained the object of your desires. The Flitch has long since been won—and eaten—not a rasher left—eh?"

"Not exactly won, captain," Jonas stammered out.

"Not won!—Then your claim was refused by the Court Baron—ha! ha!—By Allah! I thought it would be so."

"Not so fast, captain. No Court Baron has been held since you were here. The Court sits to-morrow, and then my claim will be allowed. Is not that your opinion, my good friends?" Jonas said, appealing to his guests. "Don't you think the decision will be in my favour?"

"No doubt of it," several voices cried. "You're sure of the prize."

"Yes, I flatter myself I am," Jonas remarked. "But the captain looks incredulous."

"Captain not me," the Ex-Aga cried. "I'm a captain of captains. Bismillah! I rank with the Commander-General of the Forces. Now listen to me, Jonas. You're confident of winning. Good. I'll take ten to one you don't."

"I won't bet," Jonas replied. "Nor can I advise any one else to bet with you, because I question your capability of payment. All your money is in the Turkish loan, and that doesn't stand well in the market just now—ha! ha! Besides, there's an old-standing bet between us—ten thousand pounds to fifty—that must be settled first."

"By the beard of the Prophet! so there is," the Ex-Aga cried. "I now recollect the wager perfectly. Other matters had put it out of my head. You were to pay me a guinea a week till the claim was made. Let me see—that's twenty-five weeks. I'll trouble you for twenty-five guineas, Mr. Jonas."

"We'll talk about that to-morrow," the landlord replied, rather uneasily; "on my return from the Court Baron. Fill your glasses, gentlemen—bumpers, I beg of you. Ladies, permit me to assist you. Don't

stint it. More punch can be brewed when this is done.
Lend me your ears, and I'll give you a song which I
composed, when Nelly and I had completed the term of
probation required by our custom of Dunmow.

A Year and a Day.

I.

A YEAR and a Day is the period named
When, according to Custom, the FLITCH may be claimed;—
Provided the parties can swear and can prove,
They have lived the whole time in true conjugal love.

II.

'Tis a very old Custom of ours at Dunmow,—
Fitzwalter established it ages ago.
Its antiquity, sure, can be doubted by no man,
Since 'tis mentioned by Chaucer, and trusty Piers Plowman.

III.

That it is a good Custom, as well as an old,—
Our Custom of Dunmow—you needn't be told—
A prize matrimonial—claim it we may—
Nell and I have been married a Year and a Day.

IV.

With all the conditions we've duly complied—
And our love and fidelity well have been tried;
Kneeling down at the Church-door, we dare to confess
That not, e'en in thought, did we ever transgress.

V.

No woman, save Nell, has attractions for me:
And as I feel, I needn't assure you, feels she:
No man in the world, be he ever so big,
Can say Nelly cares for his nonsense a fig.

VI.

I'm a pattern to husbands, as she is to wives—
We teach all transgressors to alter their lives.
We show how much better it is to be true,
Than each other neglect, as some married folks do.

VII.

In short, we're as happy as couple can be,—
No long curtain lectures sweet Nell reads to me,
By no silly squabbles we're ever put out,
Nor do I ever scold, nor does she ever pout.

VIII.

As to wishing that we were unmarried again,—
A notion so stupid ne'er entered our brain:—
For rather,—we give you our honour,—we would
Be married twice over again, if we could!

IX.

Three times did I marry the FLITCH to obtain—
Three times unsuccessful—the fourth time I gain :
Blest with Nelly, sweet Nelly, they can't say me nay,—
We've not had a wrong word for a Year and a Day !

"Well sung, Jonas—excellent well!" the Ex-Aga.
cried, approvingly. "I caught your playful allusion to
me, you rogue—'The man be he ever so big'—ha !
ha ! Very fair—very fair ! You'll hear what the big
man has to say, if he should be called as a witness to-
morrow."

"He never must be called," Jonas muttered in a
sombre tone. "Would he were at the bottom of the
Black Sea !"

"My pipe's out," the Ex-Aga cried. "My dear
Mrs. N., you shall have the office of my favourite Circassian slave—fill, and light for me."

"By the marry-maskins ! she shall do nothing of
the kind," Jonas cried.

"Of course not without your permission, ducky,"
Nelly said. "But you wouldn't like me to appear un-
gracious."

"Of course he wouldn't," the Ex-Aga said.

"Oh, very well—very well—just as you please, my
dear," the landlord said, swallowing his displeasure.

So the pipe was re-filled by Nelly, and the match
applied to it by her.

"Now place the amber mouthpiece to your lips," the
Ex-Aga said to Nelly, "and draw a few whiffs. My
fair Circassian always did so."

Nelly was about to comply, but Jonas snatched the
pipe from her.

"Whatever your fair Circassian may have done, sir,"
he cried to Amurath, "and I dare say she did a great
many things she ought not to have done, my Nelly

shall never follow her pernicious example. She shall never smoke. I'm sure you'll say I'm right, ducky?"

"Quite right—as you always are, ducky," she replied, not looking over-pleased, though.

"I knew you'd say so. You see, my friends, what a treasure I've got. She yields in an instant. No exertion of authority is required. The simple expression of a wish on my part is sufficient for her."

"Landlord, I'll try a glass of your punch," Amurath said—"and at the same time I'll thank you to return my pipe."

"I thought you preferred cider," Jonas remarked, as he complied with the Ex-Aga's request.

"By the beard of the Prophet! I like all liquors," the other returned, smacking his lips over the punch. "In Turkey I used to drink Sherbet, Boza, and arrack—and in Russia, Bostandschi Oglu, and Kisslyschtxhy."

"Dear me! what a nice drink that must be!" Nelly exclaimed. "Kissylipsy—did you call it?"

"Kisslyschtxhy," the Ex-Aga repeated. "It is delicious, especially when drunk with a pretty Muscovite maiden. Shall I warble you the tender strain which I sang to the beautiful but hapless Budoor, as she accompanied me on her kitar?"

Nelly seemed disposed to say "yes;" but glancing at Jonas, and reading a decided negative in his looks, she was obliged to decline the offer.

"Give us a Bacchanalian ditty," Jonas cried. "That's more in your way than a love-song."

"Well—anything to oblige you," Amurath replied. "I'll give you a snatch, written by way of epitaph, upon old Temperance Closefist, the miser and water-drinker. His fate will never be yours, I'm sure, Mr. Jonas—nor mine. Make ready, musicians."

The Old Water-Drinker's Grave.

I.

A STINGY curmudgeon lies under the stone,
Who ne'er had the heart to get mellow ;—
A base water-drinker !—I'm glad he is gone,
We're well rid of the frowsy old fellow.

II.

You see how the nettles environ his grave!
Weeds only could spring from his body.
While his heirs spend the money he fasted to save,
In wine and in women—the noddy!

Politeness detained Jonas during this song, but at its
close he would have made off to Ben the Waggoner, if
the Ex-Aga had not laid his heavy hand upon him, and
compelled him to sit down.

"I want to hear something about my friends," the
giant said. "How are the Fitzwalters?—the young
couple—Frank Woodbine and Rose, as we used to call
them. How are they going on, eh?"

"Remarkably well, I believe," Jonas replied.

"They are living with the squire at Monkbury Place
for the present," Nelly added, "and will remain there
till Clavering Castle is finished. Sir Walter has bought
it for them, and fitted it up magnificently."

"Is Sir Walter at Monkbury Place?" Amurath inquired, glancing at Parson Bush.

"He has been there for the last five months," the
reverend gentleman answered—"and Lady Fitzwalter,
too—so much improved you'd scarcely know him—and
the old lady has got back some of her good looks. A
fine woman still, in spite of all she has gone through.
Old Mrs. Leslie has likewise come to live with the
squire—and is as happy as need be with her grand-
children. Her daughter, you may remember, was pri-
vately married to the squire. As to Sir Walter and
Lady Fitzwalter, they quite dote upon the young couple

—Mr. Alured and his wife, I mean—and are always
with them. Of course, they're to live at Clavering
Castle when the place is ready for them; but meanwhile they seem quite content at Monkbury."

"No wonder," Amurath replied. "Quarters no one
would object to. I thought young Fitzwalter and his
wife were candidates for the Flitch!"

"So they are," Parson Bush replied. "But Jonas
and Nelly stand first on the list, and the prize can only
be bestowed once in the year. Mr. Roper has carefully examined the Charter, and finds this is an express
condition."

"So you see they'll have to wait till to-morrow
twelvemonth, Mr. Amurath," Jonas observed.

"You think so?" the giant replied.

"Pray, is there any such custom as ours of Dunmow
in the East?" Nelly asked. "Do Turks ever claim the
Flitch?"

"We good Mussulmans abominate the unclean animal," Amurath said; "and consequently bacon is in-
terdicted. As to a prize for constancy, that would be
scarcely possible where polygamy prevails."

"All Turks, I suppose, wear beards like yours?"
Nelly said, innocently.

"All—without exception," the Ex-Aga replied. "I
should be glad to introduce the fashion in England.
A beard would be a great improvement to Jonas."

"Perhaps it would," she said. "But he looks very
nice as he is."

"Mark that, Mr. Amurath?" the little landlord
cried, delighted.

"Never mind her flummery, Jonas, but make a
movement in favour of the beard. Attend to me."
And the giant once more broke into song.

THE FLITCH OF BACON ; OR,

𝔗𝔥𝔢 𝔅𝔞𝔩𝔩𝔞𝔡 𝔬𝔣 𝔱𝔥𝔢 𝔅𝔢𝔞𝔯𝔡

I.

In masculine beauty, or else I am wrong,
Perfection consists in a beard that is long;
By man it is cherished, by woman revered,—
Hence every good fellow is known by his beard.

II.

Barbarossa, and Blackbeard, and Bluebeard, we know
Let the hair on their chins most abundantly grow:
So did Francis the First, and our Harry the bluff,
And the great Bajazet had beard more than enough.

III.

Now the faces of those bearded worthies compare
With the faces of others divested of hair;
And you'll very soon see—if you've got any eyes—
On which side the superiority lies.

IV.

Then take to the BEARD, and have done with the razor!
Don't disfigure yourself any longer, I pray, sir!
Wear a Beard.   You will find it becoming and pleasant,
And your wife will admire you much more than at present.

V.

Of cuts we've the Spanish, Italian, and Dutch,
The old and the new, and the common o'ermuch;
You may have your beard trimmed any way that you please,
Curled, twisted, or stuck out like chevaux-de-frise.

VI.

You may wear, if you choose, a beard pick-a-devant,
A beard like a hammer, or jagg'd like a saw,—
A beard called " cathedral," and shaped like a tile,
Which the widow in Hudibras served to beguile.

VII.

A beard like a dagger—nay, don't be afraid,—
A beard like a bodkin, a beard like a spade;
A beard like a sugar-loaf, beard like a fork,
A beard like a Hebrew, a beard like a Turk.

VIII.

Any one of these beards may be yours if you list—
According to fancy you trim it or twist,
As to colour, that matters, I ween, not a pin—
But a bushy black beard is the surest to win.

IX.

So take to the BEARD, and abandon the razor!
Have done with all soaping and shaving, I say, sir!
By a scrub of a barber be never more sheared, sir :
But adorn cheek and chin with a handsome long beard, sir!

Everybody laughed very heartily at this song, and Jonas among the rest. But his glee was checked, as he bethought him of Ben the Waggoner, who appeared to be on the move. He started up to fly to him, but was again forced down by the giant.

"Sit still, landlord, sit still, till you have answered one other question. How goes on my friend, Sir G. de M. ?"

"If you mean Sir Gilbert de Montfichet by those initials, Mr. Amurath, I beg to say he is going on extremely well. Quite a reformed character—no longer drinks—no longer games—no longer rakes—but keeps good company—and has entirely abandoned his worthless associates."

"Ho! ho! ho!" Amurath laughed. "Is he married ?"

"No, sir, he is not married; but the probability is that he very speedily will be so. The consummation of his wishes depends upon the realisation of mine."

"Landlord, you speak in riddles."

"My husband means, that Miss Monkbury, to whom Sir Gilbert has been paying his addresses, and with whom he is understood to be passionately in love," Nelly said, "has declared that she will never marry any man till the Flitch has been won. So to-morrow the young baronet may possibly gain her consent, if we are successful."

"She has three other suitors who are likewise awaiting the issue of the claim," Parson Bush remarked, with a laugh.

"Grub, Chip, and Clot—I remember them," Amurath replied. "Another glass of punch, and another song, landlord."

"Bless us! the bowl's empty—I didn't observe it. More shall be brewed directly," Jonas cried, breaking from the giant's grasp, and hastening to the waggoner, who was just about to start.

"Well, Ben, what have you to tell me about him?" he asked.

"Look at this, mester," Ben replied, putting a play-bill, adorned with a large woodcut, into his hands.

"Yes—yes—I see—but what has this got to do with him?"

"A vast deal," Ben replied. "You see the pictur a-top—the Turkish giant. Read the bill—read it aloud."

"I will—I will," Jonas replied. "SHEEPSHANKS AND SWINEY'S BOOTH — Near the Bridge, Chelmsford. Extraordinary and Unprecedented Attraction — THE FALL OF BAJAZET. The part of Bajazet by Amurath, the celebrated Turkish Giant. That's he! that's he."

"Ay, that be he, sure enough," Ben said. "I seed he were a-gammonin' of you—so I thought I'd let you know the truth. But he be absent without leave."

"What do you mean, Ben?"

"I mean what I says. He ought to act to-night at Chelmsford, according to that there playbill. He's under an engagement to Sheepshanks and Swiney, and has forfeited fifty pounds by taking hissel off in this way. Swiney told me so, hissel. Swiney said he'd arrest him at once, if he could find him—but he were stowed away in the waggon, and Swiney never thought of looking for him there."

"Why didn't you give him up?" Jonas cried.

"I didn't like," the waggoner replied. (The rogue didn't say anything about the guinea he had received for aiding the giant's escape.) "But if you want to get rid of him, only let Swiney know, and he'll take him off your hands pretty quickly."

"I'll do it—I'll do it," Jonas cried. "I'll send a man and horse over to Chelmsford. I'll give Isaacson and Latcham a hint. He shall be nabbed, Ben—nabbed before he knows what he's about. I don't think he will appear as a witness against me at the Court Baron —ha! ha! There'll be a feast here on the day after to-morrow, Ben, and I shall be glad of your company to eat a rasher from the Flitch—the Dunmow Flitch, Ben—d'ye understand?"

"Thankee, mester, I'll be one of the party wi' pleasure," the waggoner replied, cracking his whip, and making a start.

While this was passing, Parson Bush got up and took a place on the circular bench by the side of the Ex-Aga.

"Sir Gilbert depends upon your appearance at the Court Baron at noon to-morrow!" he said, in a low tone.

"You're sure I may do so with safety?" the other rejoined. "Nothing to apprehend from Sir Walter —eh?"

"Nothing whatever. Sir Gilbert will bear you harmless from all consequences. But take care Jonas doesn't manage to entrap you. The sly little fellow is talking, as you see, with Ben the Waggoner, and will learn from him how you are circumstanced. Sheepshanks and Swiney may receive information of your retreat, and pounce upon you. Once within the Court House, you are safe."

"Never fear. Leave J. J.—Amurath, I mean—to take care of himself. Count upon seeing me."

Satisfied with this assurance, Parson Bush returned to the table, and Jonas having given some private instructions to Carroty Dick, came back rubbing his hands, and looking quite happy and unconcerned.

T

Smiling upon his apparently unsuspecting victim, he proffered him a glass of punch from a fresh bowl brought by Tom Tapster, which the other graciously accepted.

Another song was now called for, but as no one responded, Jonas thought a dance might be agreeable to the Bachelors and Maidens; and as they were quite of his opinion, word was given to the musicians, who instantly struck up a rigadoon, and very soon all the younger part of the company were footing it merrily on the sward. For a while Amurath preserved his grave deportment, and continued to puff away solemnly at his pipe; it being unbecoming the dignity of a Turk to take part in such a boisterous pastime. But at length the fun and frolic rose to such a pitch, that, unable to resist the attraction, he sprang to his feet, and offering his hand to Nelly, before Jonas could interpose, whisked her off into the mazy ring. Wonderful was it to see the giant capering about in his flowing Turkish attire —wonderful was the agility he displayed—and at the end of the rigadoon, he had to take off his enormous turban and mop his close-shaven pate.

After the dance, more punch was consumed, and then the company dispersed,—the bailiff, the two burgesses, and Simon Appleyard, shaking hands with Jonas, and congratulating him beforehand on the anticipated event of the morrow. A word at parting was likewise exchanged between Parse Bush and the Ex-Aga—and then the latter withdrew to the house, and was shown by Peggy to the apartment wherein he was to pass the night. Arrived there, his first business was to throw open the window, as he said he could not sleep without plenty of air.

Jonas turned for a brief space outside, after the departure of his guests, and during that time a mounted messenger was despatched with secret instructions to Chelmsford—and information was given to Isaacson and Latcham to hold themselves in readiness for a summons. This done, the landlord retired to rest, and slept soundly till towards morning, when he had a strange dream, in which he fancied his three departed wives appeared to him, and told him he would never win the Flitch.

In his efforts to reply to them, he awoke, and found Nelly awake too, and laughing at him. She said he must have had a dreadful attack of nightmare, as he had roared out most lustily.

Jonas was rather troubled by his dream, and feared it boded him no good. However, he said nothing about it to Nelly, as he thought there was no use in making her uneasy. Besides, he didn't like talking to her about his former spouses.

So he went to sleep again, and lo! he had another dream. This time he thought he had gained the Flitch, but was robbed of it by the giant, who devoured it before his eyes.

II.

HOW JONAS AND NELLY SET OUT TO CLAIM THE FLITCH.

On rising, the landlord's first inquiries were as to the Turkish gentleman. He was not astir yet. So far good. Had the messenger returned from Chelmsford? No. That was provoking. Still, it was early, and the giant was safe in his room.

About nine o'clock, the two bailiffs came to see whether their services would be required, and Jonas, after some consideration, determined to take upon himself the responsibility of detaining Juddock a prisoner till the arrival of Messrs. Sheepshanks and Swiney—or at all events till the great business at the Court Baron was settled. Accordingly he sent the two functionaries of the law up-stairs, and Peggy attended them to the door of the giant's chamber, against which Isaacson rapped authoritatively with his truncheon. No answer being returned, the summons was repeated—and then the door was tried, and found to be locked. After a little debate, Jonas was sent for, and by his order the door was instantly burst open. The bird was flown, having escaped, it was evident, through the open window. Juddock had discarded his Turkish habiliments, which were scattered about the room, and had gone off in some other clothes taken from the portmanteau, as that was empty.

Nelly, of course, had come up-stairs with her husband, and her attention was called by Peggy to something very like a horse's tail lying on the dressing-table near the Ex-Aga's enormous turban. A suspicion of the truth instantly flashed upon the landlady, and rushing up to the table, she found her surmise correct. A false beard. How shocking! After all he had said and sung about beards too.

Jonas was greatly dismayed. His plans were baffled, and the worst was to be apprehended. He consulted with the two bailiffs, and wanted them to go in quest of the fugitive. It would be of no use, they said. They couldn't detain him. They must wait for Sheepshanks and Swiney and the writ. Then, and not till then, could they act. So Jonas was obliged to be content, and hope for the best.

He had a good deal to do, and that helped to dispel his anxiety. Besides a great many directions to give, he had to dress with unusual care; and by the time he had spent nearly an hour in decorating his person, his

breast once more beat high with confidence. The last
touches given, what a smart little fellow appeared in the
glass. How well his pea-green coat, made for the occasion, became him! The tailor had done him justice.
His flowered, white satin waistcoat was beautiful, and
everybody must admire his amber shorts and his salmon-
coloured silk hose, and the shapely limbs they defined
so perfectly. Not unadmiringly was he glancing at
himself over the shoulder, to see how well the pea-green
coat fitted behind,—and how nicely the double queue
of his well-powdered periwig dangled down,—when he
caught the reflexion of a very pretty face in the mirror,
and was delighted to find that his wife's toilette was as
satisfactorily completed as his own.

Nelly looked quite charming in her pretty fly-cap,
with her fair hair drawn back beneath it, arranged in
tight little curls at the sides, and gathered in a club at
the back; her cherry-coloured silk stomacher, laced
across; her hooped petticoat; and her tiny muslin
apron. Nor were her feet entirely concealed from
view — as why should they be? Had she not got
a pair of red morocco high-heeled shoes, of the last
fashion, from town? They must be seen,—if feet and
ankles, which had not their match in Dunmow, went
for nothing.

"Well my love, I declare I never saw you look
better!" Jonas exclaimed, rapturously.

"And I don't think I ever saw you look so well,
ducky," she rejoined. "That pea-green coat fits without a crease, and those amber shorts are perfection.
But you haven't tied your cravat quite tight enough.
I'll do it for you. There, that's better."

"Take care—you'll choke me," Jonas cried, getting
very red in the face.

"Now for the nosegay in your breast," Nelly con-

tinued, fixing a bouquet as large as a sunflower in his
second button-hole. And then making him turn about
so as to face the chambermaid, she cried—" What do
you think of your master, Peggy ?"

" I think he's the properest man in Dunmow, mem,—
as you are the prettiest lady," the chambermaid replied.

" By the marry-maskins, Peggy, you're a good judge,"
Jonas cried.   " I'll raise your wages.   You're very
nicely dressed yourself, Peggy—and look very well—
extremely well, Peggy."

" Don't praise me too much, sir," the chambermaid
whispered. " You'll make missis jealous—and that'll
spoil all."

" A discreet wench i' faith," Jonas rejoined. " Don't
forget what you've to say in Court, Peggy. And take
care of Dick."

" You needn't be afraid of me, sir," Peggy replied.
" And as to Dick, I've let him know that his chance of
my hand depends upon his conduct to-day.   So you're
quite safe with him."

" That's right, Peggy—that's right.   Oddsbodikins !
if it isn't eleven o'clock !—and the messenger not yet
returned from Chelmsford."

" Oh ! never mind the messenger," Nelly cried. " We
can't wait for him.   I want to show myself."

" And so do I," Jonas rejoined. " No, we won't wait
any longer."

" You'll have plenty of people to see you, I can promise you," Peggy remarked. " All Great Dunmow is
out ; and Little Dunmow, they tell me, is just like a
fair. Crowds have been flocking there from all parts of
the country since six o'clock in the morning."

" No, have they ?" Jonas cried, delighted. " They're
quite right to be in time.   Oh ! it'll be a grand sight
—a wonderful sight !"

And he began to caper about the room with delight.

"Will Crane told me last night," Peggy pursued, "that the squire has invited all his friends. Half the gentry in the county are expected."

"Half the gentry! By the marry-maskins! they do us too much honour—really, they do," Jonas said. "However, it's very flattering—very gratifying—and we're quite sensible of the distinction shown us—ain't we, Nelly?"

"All the squire's tenantry are of course invited," Peggy went on—"wives, daughters, and sons; sons' wives, and sons' daughters — everybody, in short. After the ceremony at Little Dunmow, there's to be the grandest merry-making ever known in Monkbury Place, to which all comers will be welcome. Nobody will be refused. Will Crane said there would be music, dancing, country-sports, and all sorts of pastimes. Preparations have been made for the feast for the last week; and Will says it'll surpass anything ever seen in these parts."

"How very kind in the squire to take all this trouble for us, and go to such an expense," Jonas remarked. "No doubt he meant this entertainment as an agreeable surprise to us, my love, and took care we should hear nothing about it. I always said the worthy gentleman was like a father to you, Nelly—and treated you exactly as if you were a daughter of his own."

"Don't talk nonsense, sir," Nelly cried. "Perhaps these preparations mayn't be for us, after all. The squire may expect young Fitzwalter and his wife to win. It looks very like it, I must say."

"They win! Pooh! pooh! I've no fear, unless that confounded giant should turn up."

"Oh! I'm not in the least afraid of him," Nelly cried.

"You're not! then I'm quite easy. Let's be off! Stay, we must take care nothing is forgotten. Tom Tapster and the cook are away to the Court House— eh, Peggy?"

"They started nearly an hour ago, sir, and must be there by this time."

"Good. And the bailiffs are below awaiting the arrival of Sheepshanks and Swiney?"

"They're outside the house, sir—smoking their pipes, and drinking the jug of ale you ordered 'em. They won't leave the spot, they say, till the man comes back from Chelmsford."

"Very good, Peggy.—What splendid weather, my dear. Was there ever such a glorious day seen?"

"It's much too warm, I think," Nelly rejoined. "We shall be broiled before we get there. Fetch me my large green fan, Peggy."

"Here 'tis, mem, and your smelling-bottle, and your handkerchief, and your nosegay."

"Are you quite ready, my love?"

"Quite ready, Mr. Nettlebed."

"Then we'll be off at once. Is the cart at the door, Peggy?"

"The cart, Jonas!" Nelly exclaimed, with a scream. "Haven't you ordered a postchaise?"

"N—no, my love, I thought a cart preferable."

"Then you thought wrong, sir. I've a good mind not to go. Get a chaise directly."

"Impossible, my love—there isn't time. We should be too late. If we were a minute after twelve o'clock, our claim would be set aside, and that of young Fitz-walter and his wife preferred. You'll find it a very nice cart—with a very easy seat—plenty of room for two—and Dick will drive you most carefully, won't he, Peggy?"

" And you'll be much better seen than in the po'chay, mem—think of that," the chambermaid insinuated.

The last argument prevailed, and Nelly yielded, though with rather a bad grace. But all her sullenness disappeared the instant she went forth, and nothing but smiles irradiated her countenance, as she saluted the two bailiffs, who were seated at a table under the great elm-tree, drinking and smoking. She also acknowledged very graciously the cheers of the lads and lasses collected to witness their departure. Jonas handed her into the cart, gave her her fan, handkerchief, and nosegay, and then, having placed Peggy in a back seat, got up himself with some difficulty. This done, Carroty Dick, who was seated in front, and who was as smart as Sunday clothes and a bunch of cabbage-roses in his breast could make him, touched his horse with the whip, and the vehicle was set in motion.

Then arose acclaims from the two bailiffs, who waved their hats, and wished them success. The vociferations of the myrmidons of the law were echoed by the youthful throng, as well as by some venturesome urchins who had clambered up the old elm-tree—and it was regarded by Isaacson as a bad omen, that one of them who had planted his feet upon the famous sign-board of the Flitch, contrived to knock it down Luckily, however, Jonas was not aware of the disaster.

The cart moved slowly along, for neither husband nor wife desired to proceed too quickly—and a large and constantly-increasing concourse accompanied it in its progress through the main street of the town—shouting and huzzaing the whole way.

The day was magnificent—a little too hot, perhaps, but the brilliant sunshine added to the general effect. Nelly could not have got on without the large green fan, and shielded her pretty face with it. All Dunmow

was astir. People were at the doors and windows,.
looking on, waving handkerchiefs, and swelling the
clamour with their cries. Jonas was almost beside himself with delight. Every now and then he stood up in
the cart, and bowed to an acquaintance at a window,
or in the street, and Nelly began to be so much employed in kissing hands right and left, that the fan
and nosegay had to be laid down.

The pretty landlady was greatly admired, and Jonas
was envied by most of the male beholders. We cannot
say that Nelly's lot was coveted in the same degree by
any of her own sex. Peggy came in for her share of
admiration ; and Carroty Dick's breast was torn with
jealous pangs as he heard his mistress chatting and
laughing rather familiarly with a pack of impudent
fellows who marched by her side. He longed to cut
at them with the whip, and would have driven off, if
he had dared.

In this way they reached the centre of the town,.
and when near the old cross, they were joined by
another long cart, covered over with green boughs.
instead of a canvas tilt, and drawn by four horses.
It contained the Bachelors and Maidens, who were
waiting to accompany them to the Court House.
Here, also, they were joined by the musicians—so.
that henceforward their progress took the character
of a procession.

Now the shouts were redoubled, and strains of music
were added to the din. The greater the uproar, the
better Jonas was pleased. Nor did it subside when
they got out of the town. The Court House was two
miles off, but the distance did not deter hundreds from.
marching thither. Thus they went on—the Bachelors.
and Maidens taking the lead, and Jonas and his wife
following after; the crowd huzzaing, and the band

playing until they came within a bow-shot of the Court House, when they were brought to a halt by a signal from Timothy Tipcat, the beadle, who, staff in hand, and in full official costume, was stationed at the door.

III.

HOW ANOTHER COUPLE WENT TO MAKE THE CLAIM.

THE stoppage gave Jonas and Nelly an opportunity of looking about them. This is what they beheld.

Drawn up at the side of the road, all the way to the old Priory Church, which was nearly a quarter of a mile off, were carts and other vehicles filled, for the most part, with fresh-looking country lasses, dressed in their best, and, generally speaking with ribands in their caps and upon their stomachers as blooming as their cheeks. Such a number of pretty girls had never been seen in Dunmow before—nor, up to this moment, had Jonas imagined that the whole county of Essex boasted so many. However, all the women were not young; some were middle-aged, respectable matrons, not entirely destitute of good looks, taking care of their daughters; and a few—the grandmothers of the damsels—were well stricken with years. But, old or young, they all appeared happy and merry; and as the rosy-cheeked Phillises had plenty of Corydons by the side of their carts, no wonder they enjoyed themselves —while mothers and grandmothers mindful of the days of their youth, smiled complacently at what was going on.

It was only among the oldest of the assemblage that any could be found who had been present on a similar occasion; and old dames with nodding heads told their young listeners how William Parsley, of Much Easton, and Jane his wife, had won the Flitch in 1701—long before they or their mothers even were thought of. "A pretty sight that," the ancient bodies declared; " but nothing—nothing whatever to the present."

But, besides the farmers' wives and farmers' daughters in carts, and young farmers on foot, bent upon becoming husbands and fathers themselves, there was a great collection of sturdy yeomen on horseback —many of them tenants of the squire—though the greater part were strangers; for the anticipated suc- cessful claim of the Flitch, coupled with Squire Monk- bury's promise of a feast, had attracted folks from all parts of Essex—and even from the adjoining counties. They had come in all sorts of vehicles—in postchaise, coach, or cart—on horseback or on foot—from far and near—from Thaxted, Braintree, Coggeshall, and Wit- ham—from Saffron Walden, Bishop Stortford, and Chipping Ongar—from Great Bardfield and Little Bardfield, from Great Saling, Panfield, and Rayne. How so many were to be entertained at Monkbury Place, Jonas could not conceive. The squire's hospi- tality would be severely taxed. Meantime, some re- freshments were afforded to the crowd by itinerant vendors of meat-pies and fruit-pies—and by others, with little carts or barrows, who sold bottled ale and cider, and draught beer from the barrel.

Throughout the large concourse, the utmost mirth and good-humour prevailed. Plenty of noise, but no disorder. On the contrary, all were remarkably well conducted ; and though, every twenty yards or so, there was stationed a well-dressed personage, with a long white wand in his hand, to keep the road clear, the active services of these individuals were scarcely needed. Altogether, it was a most lively and amusing scene, and was never forgotten by those fortunate enough to witness it.

Most propitious was the weather, as we have already remarked ; the sky cloudless—and the sun shining brilliantly. Nature was in her fullest beauty, and richest wealth of foliage and flower. The bells in the old Priory Church rang blithely—and the lads scattered about in groups—mounted on the hedge-banks—on the gates, or on the walls, or in the trees—shouted till they were hoarse.

Nearer the Court House the equipages were of a superior description. Jonas counted ten coaches, half a dozen of which he knew to belong to families of importance. Then there were a great many ladies and gentlemen on horseback, and their numbers were constantly being increased by fresh arrivals. Some few dismounted, and left their horses with the grooms, but the greater part remained outside ; otherwise, the Court, which possessed but limited accommodation, would have been inconveniently crowded.

The first coach, which was setting down just as Jonas came up, and barred his approach, contained Sir Walter Fitzwalter, his lady, and Mrs. Leslie. It was succeeded by another containing Doctor Sidebottom, Parson Bush, and Mr. Roper—and then a third drew up, from which Sir Ralph Gernon of Little Lees, Lady Gernon, and the three Misses Gernon, descended. Then came the Dennys—then the Lovels—then the Parkers —then the Houblons—after which, Jonas thought he should be able to move on. But no!—Timothy Tipcat again signalled to the driver of the Bachelors and Maidens and to Carroty Dick to keep quiet, and remain where they were—and of course they could not disobey the beadle.

The reason for the order was presently apparent. A

loud and continuous shouting, not confined as heretofore to the juvenile part of the assemblage, but proceeding from persons of all ages—proclaimed the approach
of a cavalcade. It was headed by the squire and his
daughter Bab, both of whom courteously acknowledged
the enthusiastic greeting with which they were welcomed. Always popular, the squire was now quite the
idol of his tenants, and of all who knew him. The
worthy gentleman looked remarkably well, and so full
of happiness that he seemed to diffuse some of it around
him at every step taken by his steed. All loved to look
upon his kindly countenance. Mounted as she was on
her favourite Gipsy, Bab was seen to the greatest possible advantage, and looked beautiful and bewitching
as ever. Behind her were her three suitors—Grub,
Chip, and Clot—and on the right, and almost alongside
her, rode Sir Gilbert de Montfichet. Wonderfully improved in personal appearance was the young baronet.
He had entirely lost the rakish air which had previously
operated as a drawback to his good looks, and was now
as fine a young gentleman, and as manly-looking, as
need be.

The cavalcade was closed by a couple, for whom if
the shouts were not so loud as for the squire and his
younger daughter, it was because they excited even
stronger and deeper interest than those popular personages. People were too much occupied in gazing at
them, and admiring them, to cheer.

The fond pair, upon whom all eyes were now fixed,
and in praise of whom all lips were loud, were Alured
Fitzwalter and his wife. One steed bore them ; she
sitting on a pillion behind him, with her arm round his
waist. The attitude was tender and affectionate And
every look and gesture bestowed on each other by the
pair were replete with love.

THE PROCESSION OF THE FLITCH.

P. 289.

Never was the recollection of the goodly couple effaced from the memory of those who beheld them as they rode together on that day. He so handsome, so frank, so courteous—she so fair, so sweet, so good. Her soul shone out in her speaking countenance. Her gentle nature could be read in her deportment.

Kindly were the looks, and cordial the words addressed by the pair to those nearest them. Grateful were they for the blessings showered upon their heads. Little children were lifted up to look at them, and the tiny things clapped their small hands, and lifted up their infantine voices with delight, at the beautiful pageant passing by—which haunted them ever afterwards like a bright and pleasant dream. Old trembling hands were stretched out to bless them; and many a mother prayed that her daughter might be like Rose—many a father trusted that his son might, in some respects, resemble Alured.

So the pair went on, shedding smiles around them, and reaping such a harvest of good wishes as seldom falls to the lot of mortals, until they reached the door of the Court House, where Rose sprang lightly to the ground, and being instantly followed by her husband, they entered the building together—he smiling, and fondly encircling her with his arm.

IV

SHOWING WHO WON THE FLITCH, AND WHO LOST IT.

THE Court was assembled.

On an elevated judicial bench, with a desk before him, sat the squire—as Lord of the Manor. Against the wall at the back of the bench was hung a large 'scutcheon, painted with the armorial coat of the Monk

burys.   Near it was an old scroll containing the Charter
of the Barony. On either side of the squire were Doctor
Sidebottom, Parson Bush, Sir Walter Fitzwalter, Sir
Ralph Gernon, Mr. Denny, Mr. Houblon, and other
gentlemen of the county. The ladies occupied places
behind—Lady Fitzwalter and Mrs. Leslie sitting together.   The old curate's wife bore her years bravely,
and though winter had sown its snows thickly upon her
head, her cheek was still fresh, her eye bright, and the
general expression of her countenance exceedingly
lively and pleasing. She was, indeed, a very charming
old lady ; and as grandmother of the fond pair whom
we have just conducted to the Court House, felt she
had good reason to be proud and happy. So also felt
her neighbour. Time's ravages and those of sorrow
could not, of course, be wholly repaired in Lady Fitzwalter ; but it was wonderful how much of her pristine
beauty had returned to her. Once more her figure had
acquired its fullness, her carriage its stateliness, and
her glances somewhat of their former fire : and as she
had all the advantages derivable from rich attire, she
produced a very striking effect. Those who had never
seen her before were much impressed by her ; and
those who remembered her in the meridian of her
beauty, thought her but little changed.

But the centre of attraction was Bab.   The little
beauty sat beside Mrs. Leslie, and talked a great deal
more to grandmamma than to Sir Gilbert de Montfichet, who was next her, on the other side.   Grandmamma, however, being very good-natured, and taking
compassion on the young baronet, who had become a
great favourite with her (reformed scapegraces always
are favourites with elderly ladies), contrived to mix him
up in their conversation. But she could not extend
equal indulgence to three suitors, who fluttered about

Miss Monkbury, and made so much noise that they were, at last, requested by the usher of the court to be silent, and sit down.

Immediately below the bench, at a table furnished with pens, ink, and paper, and having the register of the Court open before him, sat the steward of the manor, Mr. Roper, and his clerk Hopkinson. Around him, arranged in a semicircle, were the bailiff and the burgesses of Dunmow, with some of the squire's principal tenants, and several gentlemen who could not be better accommodated—for the Court was crowded to excess, and by this time not even standing-room could be obtained, and the doors were ordered to be closed. In a raised box on the right of the bench the Jury were placed—the six maidens in front, smiling and blushing at their novel position, and endeavouring to appear composed—and the six bachelors behind—with their foreman, Simon Appleyard, noticeable for his consequential air and manner.

A small platform, about two feet high, with rails in front, and covered with green baize, was reserved for the Claimants. Near it stood Will Cane, bearing a pole, on the top of which the flitch itself was set—the entire side of a huge hog, well cured, and well dried, as plump as my Lord Chancellor's woolsack, and as brown as a cake of chocolate. Tied to it by a riband was an ancient silver chain worn by Sir Reginald Fitz-walter, the founder of the Custom, supposed to be an amulet, and fashioned of the letters composing his name, linked with those of his wife.

Opposite the Jury was the witness-box.

Neither of the couples, who, it was understood, were about to demand the prize were present; but both were in waiting for a summons.

Silence being enjoined by Hopkinson, and peremp-

u

torily enforced by the usher, the proceedings were
opened by Mr. Roper.

"Know all present," the steward said, looking round,
"that in accordance with a time-honoured Custom, instituted in the early part of the Thirteenth Century
by an ancestor of the illustrious family of Fitzwalter
—the existing representative of which ancient house is
now amongst us—in accordance with this Custom, not
less to be venerated for its antiquity, than to be admired and lauded for its noble aim and purpose,
namely, that of furnishing a reward for the most perfect conjugal love and fidelity—has this court met to
decide upon the claims of any couple conceiving themselves entitled to the Flitch, and to award the prize to
such couple, provided they shall establish a title to it;
inasmuch as the bestowal of the donation in manner
aforesaid is imposed by the Charter under which the
lordship is held, upon the Lord of the Manor of Little
Dunmow—now represented by the very worshipful
gentleman sitting on the bench, Mark Monkbury,
Esquire; whose pride and pleasure it has always been,
and whose sedulous aim it will continue to be, to maintain this ancient Custom in its integrity. Thus much
premised, a word may be said in reference to the
donation itself. Such a prize must not be estimated
for its rarity and splendour, but for the distinction it
confers on those fortunate enough to obtain it.
Homely is the Flitch, because the virtues it represents
are of home—homeborn, homefelt. These domestic
virtues gild and grace it, and make it richer than a
crown of gold. Enviable are those on whom the prize
is conferred, for they have not only established a claim
to honour and respect, but have secured themselves
felicity but rarely enjoyed on earth. The fame of the
Dunmow Flitch has travelled beyond Essex. It has

spread throughout England. It has been sung by the poets,—by the Father of English poetry, Chaucer. It has become proverbial. To say that any couple deserve the Flitch is a high compliment. To say that they have actually won it is to proclaim them amongst the best and happiest of mankind. Such a couple must live in story and in song as an example to all coming after them. But in proportion to the value and importance of the prize is the difficulty of its attainment. The Court must be fully satisfied of the merits of the Claimants before an award can be made in their favour; and so hard are the conditions, that few, if any, have been found able to comply with them. Fifty years have flown since it was won last. May better fortune attend the candidates on the present occasion!"

Mr. Roper's address was very well received, and the squire having expressed his satisfaction at it, the steward went on: "There are two couples on the list —the first in order being Jonas Nettlebed, of Great Dunmow, innkeeper, and Nelly, his wife.—Let them be introduced to make their claim."

A loud buzz was now heard in the Court, above which sounded the voice of the usher, crying out, "Jonas and Nelly Nettlebed, come in and make your claim. And see ye prove your title to the Flitch to the satisfaction of the Jury, and the Most Worshipful the Lord of the Manor, or it will not be delivered to you."

A smile pervaded the assemblage as Jonas and Nelly presented themselves in answer to the summons of the usher. Way being made for them to the platform by the official, Jonas helped his wife to mount it, and then skipping after her with unwonted activity, bowed profoundly to the squire, and then to the assemblage generally. Nelly seemed a good deal abashed at first, and her cheek was suffused with blushes, but by degrees her timidity wore off, and she ventured a glance at the throng around her.

Jonas was not in the least discomposed. He never felt easier, or more at home in his life. The position in which he found himself was exactly to his taste ; and he only regretted that the ceremony must so soon be over. Casting a look at the Flitch, now overshadowing him, he regarded it as already his own.

After allowing a few minutes to elapse, Mr. Roper opened the business.

"Jonas Nettlebed," he said, "the Court has received notice that you and your wife demand that the Flitch be delivered to you, according to the Custom of Dunmow. Is it so ?"

"It is, sir," Jonas replied, bowing. "We do make the demand—respectfully, but emphatically make it."

"You are aware of the oath prescribed for the occasion, and are prepared to take it ?"

"We are, sir."

"I require an answer from your wife," the steward said

"Now, Nelly, why don't you speak ?" Jonas whispered, nudging her. "You hear the question."

"Have you any hesitation in taking the oath, Nelly ?" the squire remarked.

"Oh! none in the least, worshipful sir," she replied, curtesying—"only I thought that came at the church."

"The oath will be there solemnly recited," Roper said—"but your examination as to its substance takes place here. Well, then, you are both able to swear— mind, to swear—that you 'ne'er made nuptial transgression.' Look at me, Jonas, and lift up your eyes, Nelly. You can both swear that ?"

Both replied, "We can."

" You can affirm that no ' household brawls or con-tentions' have ever disturbed your peace ?"

"We can affirm a great deal more than that," Jonas cried.

" Confine yourself to my question.   You can solemnly declare you have never quarrelled ?"

" Oh, never quarrelled—never at all, sir," Nelly re-sponded.

" What a hurry you are in," Jonas whispered.   " We ought to answer together."

" It's you who are slow," she replied.

" What's that I hear ?" the squire cried, sharply.

" Nothing, worshipful sir—nothing," Jonas replied. " We're both ready to swear we've not had a wrong word since we were married."

" Quite ready to swear it," Nelly added.

" And have never offended each other ?" Roper de-manded.

" Have I ever offended you, love ?" Jonas said, turn-ing to her.

" Never," she replied.   " Have I ever offended *you*, ducky ?"

" Never since you were born," Jonas rejoined.   And here he thought of embracing her, but reflecting that such a demonstration might not be deemed respectful to the Court, he abstained.

" And you can conscientiously declare you never wished yourselves unmarried ?" was Roper's next in-terrogation.

" I can conscientiously declare it, sir," Jonas said, with emphasis.

" And you, Nelly ?" the steward asked, appealing to her.

" Yes, sir—con—con—con—what's the word, Jonas ?"

" No prompting," the steward interposed severely. " Attend to me, Nelly.   Have you ever wished your marriage dissolved ?"

"Ever wished to be single again?" Jonas subjoined.

"Oh! dear no," Nelly cried. "I can swear I never wished that."

"I must caution you, Jonas, that these interruptions cannot be permitted," the squire said. "So far the Court rests satisfied with your conjoint declarations. What witnesses do you produce in confirmation of your statements?"

"Here is a list of them, worshipful sir," Jonas replied, placing a paper in the cleft point of the usher's wand, by which means it was handed to the squire, who, after glancing at it, gave it to the steward.

The first person called was the bailiff of Dunmow, and his evidence was deemed perfectly satisfactory, as was the testimony offered by each of the burgesses who succeeded him.

Tom Tapster, the next witness, said his master and missis was a pleasure to live with, they was so fond of each other, and for ever billin' and cooin' just like two lovyers! an assertion that caused Jonas to simper, and Nelly to blush, and hang down her head.

The fat cook said she couldn't give 'em too good a character. They fulfilled their matterymoonial dooties in every pertikler; and havin' bin a married ooman herself, she parfitly understood what those dooties was.

Carroty Dick objected to be sworn, but a glance from Peggy, who was close at hand, quickly brought him to, and he gulped down his scruples. A very perplexing interrogatory was put to him by the Court. Had he ever known his master guilty of indiscretion? "What maun I say to that, Peggy?" Dick roared, amid the general laughter of the Court. "Speak the truth, of course," the steward rejoined, frowning. "What be indiscretion, then?" "Making love to a neighbour's wife," the squire intimated. "Oh, I never knowd master guilty o' that," the ostler answered, scratching his head. This being all that could be extracted from Dick, he was sent down.

Peggy came next, and she looked at Mr. Roper with a confident smile, as much as to say, catch me if you can. She extolled her master and missis to the skies, and only hoped, if ever she married, she might just find such another husband as Mr. Nettlebed.—Did her master ever exhibit jealousy of his wife?—Jealousy! —not he. There wasn't a patienter man breathing than Mr. Nettlebed.—Was his patience ever tried, then?—Oh yes, he put up with a great deal.—A great deal of what—scolding—ill-usage—bad temper—what? —Oh no, nothin' of that kind. Missis never scolded, and never was ill-tempered, and master submitted to everything. — Perhaps she considered submission a merit in a husband?—The greatest merit he could possess. Mr. Nettlebed never said "No" to his wife, and consequently was the best of husbands.—Did Mrs. Nettlebed ever make any unreasonable requests of her husband?—Unreasonable—no. Master never denied missis anythin' she asked. If he did grumble a bit, it was behind her back.—Then he did grumble occasionally?—Of course. It was human nature. Everybody grumbled. People couldn't live without it.— True. And therefore, perhaps, Mrs. Nettlebed sometimes grumbled!—A little, maybe, now and then. But, Lor' bless you, never before master. Missis never let him see a cross look, or hear a cross word, however much she might be put out.—Oh! then, she *was* put out sometimes. With her husband—eh?—Lor' bless you, no—with Dick—with cook—with Tom Tapster— with me—never with master!

Mr. Roper declined to ask any more questions, and Peggy went down, fully satisfied with what she had done.

The Jury now consulted together, after which Simon Appleyard stood up, and said he had an observation to make, but the steward begged him to defer it until after the examination of the next witness.

Jonas had thought all was over, and was congratulating himself upon the triumphant manner in which the affair had been brought to a conclusion, when a knell to his hopes almost sounded in his ears as he heard Captain Juddock evoked by the usher, and directly afterwards, beheld that gigantic individual towering above the assemblage, as he stood in the witness-box.

Juddock had no longer anything of the Turk about him, not even the beard, which, as we know, had been left at the Old Inn, but appeared in his customary attire—a blue military coat with brass epaulettes, and brass buttons, and with the old brass-handled sword by his side, and the old funnel-topped boots on his legs. Glancing triumphantly at Jonas, who regarded him with mingled feelings of dismay and disgust, the giant awaited Roper's interrogations.

" Last winter, you passed a night at the Old Inn at Dunmow, Captain Juddock," the steward said. " Have you any remark to make on Mrs. Nettlebed's conduct towards you ?"

" Her conduct was exactly what a landlady's should be. She was exceedingly attentive."

" Too attentive, perhaps ?"

" I do not think so. Possibly, her husband might. I didn't give myself much concern about him."

" Did they strike you as being a happy couple ?"

" Undoubtedly. They managed to keep up appearances extremely well."

" Keep up appearances !" Jonas cried, unable longer to contain himself. " How dare you make such an insinuation as that, sir? 'Appearances' in your teeth, sir."

" I must call you to order, Jonas" the steward said. " Any remarks you may have to make, must be addressed to me, and not to the witness."

" Then tell him his testimony is worthless," the landlord cried.

" It will be for the Jury to decide on its value," Mr. Roper replied. " Do you wish the examination to be pursued ?" addressing the Jury.

The foreman answered, they did.

" You are renowned for your gallantry, and for your conquests among the fair sex, I believe, Captain Juddock," Roper said, in continuation. " Pray, did Mrs. Nettlebed ever give you encouragement ?"

" I must beg respectfully to decline answering that question, sir," the giant replied.

" Your refusal to reply will be considered tantamount to an admission of the fact," Roper remarked.

" I cannot help that, sir," Juddock said.

" I scorn the imputation," Nelly cried. " I never did give him encouragement, and when he wanted to kiss me, I slapped his great, fat, ugly face."

"Oh! he wanted to kiss you—did he?" Jonas exclaimed, surprised out of his caution. " You never told me so."

" So you keep secrets from your husband, Nelly, do you ?" the squire remarked.

" Nothing of any consequence, worshipful sir. I didn't think it worth while to trouble him about such a trifle as this."

" Oh, you call this a trifle ?" Roper cried. . " Perhaps, it's a matter of every-day occurrence ?"

" Oh no, it ain't, sir. It's very rarely anybody attempts to kiss me.—Mr. Alured Fitzwalter, when he was Frank Woodbine, never did."

Amidst the laughter occasioned by this reply, Jonas whispered to his wife—"You'll ruin our chance, if you don't mind."

"Well I can't help it. I won't allow a pack of stories to be told of me," she rejoined.

"Concealment is not all on one side," Juddock observed. "Jonas has secrets to keep as well as his wife."

"I thought so," Nelly whispered. "Now it's all coming out."

"Be quiet, my love, I implore of you," Jonas rejoined. "Prove your words, Captain Juddock—prove them, sir."

"So I will," the giant replied. "I saw you myself, very tender with pretty Peggy, your chambermaid."

"I deny the charge—indignantly deny it," Jonas cried.

"Let Peggy be recalled," the squire said. And as the chambermaid once more appeared in the witness-box, he continued—"You have heard what Captain Juddock has declared. Is there any truth in the assertion ?"

"Master was always what a good master should be." Peggy replied. "I've no reason to complain of him."

"Very likely not," the squire said, laughing. "But has your mistress ?"

"I should be sorry to think so, sir."

"Recall Carroty Dick," the squire cried. And as the red-polled ostler reappeared, with a cloud upon his brow, he said to him—"Captain Juddock has affirmed that he saw some familiarities between your master and Peggy. What is your opinion as to the correctness of the statement ?"

"My opinion be that it's true," Dick replied, with gloomy rage. "I saw him kiss her, mysel'."

"Oh, indeed—when ?"

" Last Christmas, under the mistletoe-bough — but I've often seen him kiss her since."

" You have !" Nelly screamed. " Oh ! the faithless little wretch."

" There, now you have done it, Dick," Peggy cried; " and you've done for yourself, too—for you shall never have me."

" I dunna care," the ostler replied, sullenly—" I've had my revenge."

Seeing the Jury consult together, and fearing an unfavourable verdict, Jonas endeavoured to sustain his tottering cause by a vehement protest against Juddock's evidence.

" He is not a credible witness," he said—" he is an impudent and audacious vagabond. I have heard say —and I appeal to two gentlemen here present—to Sir Walter Fitzwalter and Sir Gilbert de Montfichet, to corroborate the assertion—that he has been a common gaming-house bully and sharper. I know him to be an impostor and stroller, who has absconded from his employers, Messrs. Sheepshanks and Swiney, owners of a booth now at Chelmsford."

" That's quite true, worshipful sir," the usher said, addressing the squire. " Tim Tipcat, the beadle, has just been in to inform me that Mr. Swiney is now out-side, with Isaacson and Latcham, the bailiffs of Dun-mow, waiting to seize the individual styling himself Captain Juddock, when he comes out."

" Show them in," the squire rejoined. " Do not leave the witness-box, sir," he added, authoritatively, to Juddock.

The next moment the trio were introduced. A little sharp-featured, high-shouldered man was Swiney, and clad in a light-brown square-cut coat. He had a hooked nose like a vulture, and looked altogether like a bird of prey.   Fixing his keen eyes upon Juddock, he cried out in a shrill, and rather cracked voice—"There he is—that's my giant."

"Your giant?" the squire said.   "Do you claim a property in him, my good man?"

"An absolute property, worshipful sir," Swiney replied.   "He is bound to me—bound hand and foot. I've exhibited him for many years at all the country fairs—and at Southwark and Bartlemy Fairs in town. One year he was Plinlimmon, the Welsh giant — the next, Pennigant, the Yorkshire giant—the year after that, Tregonna, the Cornish giant."

"Yes, I recollect seeing him as Tregonna, at Chelmsford Fair," Nelly remarked.

"Another piece of concealment," Jonas whispered "You never told me that."

"Dare say you do recollect him, ma'am," Swiney pursued.   "He was there last May twelvemonth—but he deserted soon after that, and took to bad ways—frequenting low gaming-houses and coffee-houses, and picking up a livelihood how he could, instead of living respectably with me and Sheepshanks.   But he came back last winter, and has been with us ever since, until he bolted yesterday, and spoiled our performance of the 'Fall of Bajazet.'   We lost ten pound, if we lost a shilling by his sudden disappearance, worshipful sir."

"May I put a question, sir?" Montfichet observed, rising and addressing the squire.   And receiving a nod in reply, he went on—"Do you desire to go back again to Mr. Swiney, Juddock?"

"I shouldn't mind, Sir G., if I weren't bound," the giant replied.

"You shall have a release, then," Montfichet rejoined.   "What is your claim against him, Mr. Swiney?"

"Why, it should be a hundred pounds, Sir Gilbert —but we'll say seventy."

"Seventy be it—and henceforth the giant is a free agent. You may now withdraw, Mr. Swiney. All shall be settled with you presently."

Hereupon the keeper of the booth and the bailiffs bowed and retired.

After the merriment which this interlude occasioned had somewhat subsided, Simon Appleyard stood up, and said that from the evidence offered them, the Jury were unanimously of opinion that the demand of Jonas Nettlebed and his wife had not been sustained, and must therefore be rejected.

"Rejected!" Jonas exclaimed, in despair. "Reconsider your verdict, I implore of you, Simon. It is founded on the evidence of a person utterly unworthy of credit—a convicted impostor—a giant with three names instead of three heads—Plinlimmon, Pennigant, and Tregonna."

"You are mistaken, Jonas," Simon Appleyard replied. "We had agreed upon our verdict before Captain Juddock's examination took place. I repeat, that in the opinion of the Jury your claim to the Flitch cannot be sustained."

"The demand is rejected," the squire said. "Such is the decison of the Court."

"Then farewell for ever to my chance of the Flitch," Jonas said, pathetically regarding it. "What a magnificent side of bacon it is!—the finest and fattest I ever beheld! And there's a silver chain fastened to it, which would have just suited you. Alack! and well-a-day!"

"Come down directly, sir," Nelly said, "and don't make yourself foolish by these idle lamentations. Bear the loss like a man."

" So I will," Jonas blubbered ; " but to think of being within an ace of winning it—and then to be balked in this way. Alack ! alack !"

" Keep up your spirits, Jonas," the squire said. " You are not worse off than ninety-nine married men out of a hundred, so you needn't repine, I shall hope to see you and Nelly, by-and-by, at Monkbury Place."

" Thank your honour," Jonas replied. " Farewell ! thou beautiful Flitch !" he added, casting a wistful eye at it as he stepped down.

" Proceed to the next claimants, Roper," the squire said.

" With pleasure, sir," the steward replied. " They are Alured Fitzwalter, Esquire, of Little Dunmow, and Rose, his wife. Let them be called," he added to the usher.

Amid a hush of expectation, the loving couple came in, and ascended the platform, where they stood hand in hand, answering promptly and cheerfully to the interrogations put to them by the steward.

This done, Roper turning to the squire, said—" I must now request you, sir, to conduct the inquiry, as I myself am a principal witness."

So saying, he ascended to the box, and being questioned, declared, that from his own knowledge and observation, he could confirm all that had been stated by the demandants in respect to their perfect domestic harmony and devotion to each other. He had never known a couple so happy.

Twenty other witnesses eagerly pressed forward as the steward concluded, and the testimony of all such as were examined was to the like effect.

" Can any one contradict the evidence offered to the Court ?" the squire asked.

"I have a remark to make, if you will please hear me, worshipful sir," Jonas replied.

"Enter the witness-box then," the squire said. And as the landlord obeyed, he inquired—"Now, what have you to declare?"

"I concur in all that has been uttered by the various witnesses in commendation of the lady claimant," Jonas replied, "and in much that has been affirmed concerning the gentleman. But he is not quite the pattern of conjugal fidelity he has been represented."

"Indeed!" the squire exclaimed. "What have you to allege against him? Speak out, man. Don't be afraid."

"Well, then, worshipful sir, since I must declare it —on one occasion I saw him walking in a sequestered place—a thick grove, in fact—with a young lady—a very pretty young lady—they appeared deeply interested in each other, and evidently desirous of eluding observation—and—and——"

"Go on," the squire cried.

"I saw him kiss her."

"More than once?"

"No—the salute took place at parting. Isn't it enough to condemn him?"

"Do you think you could point out the young lady in Court?" the squire said.

"I'm not sure," Jonas replied, looking round. "Paul Flitwick was with me at the time. It was rather dusk, and we didn't see her very distinctly. But she had a remarkably neat figure, as I observed to Paul."

"The young lady is much obliged to you for the compliment, Mr. Nettlebed," Bab said. "And as I happen to be the person you beheld, I think you will own there was no great harm in walking with a brother-in-law, or in receiving a parting salute from him.

At all events, my sister did not disapprove of the proceeding."

Loud laughed the Court, as the discomfited Jonas rushed down to hide his head.

" Are the Jury satisfied ?" the squire demanded.

"Entirely so," Simon Appleyard replied. "In our opinion, the present claim has been successfully maintained."

"The Court decides in favour of the demandants," the squire said.

Then occurred such a display of enthusiasm, as has rarely been witnessed. The whole of the assemblage arose, and, as with one voice, cheered. Handkerchiefs and hats were waved, and every possible demonstration was made of the heartfelt delight. Hands were stretched out towards the pair as if to grasp them, and those nearest them pressed eagerly forward, in spite of Will Crane's efforts to keep them back. All the ladies were greatly excited by the scene. Lady Fitzwalter seemed quite overcome by emotion; Mrs. Leslie smiled through her tears; and though Bab tried to laugh it off, it was plain she was affected like the rest—since, after waving her handkerchief energetically, she had to apply it to her eyes. Neither were Sir Walter nor the squire wholly exempt from the reproach of similar weakness.

But the expression of enthusiastic satisfaction at the decision of the Court was by no means confined to the interior of the Court House. The joyful intelligence had been communicated by the usher to the beadle, and by the beadle to the crowd outside :—and from them it ran on, with electrical rapidity, up to the gate of the old Priory Church. And the glad tidings elicited cheers and vociferations, which rolled on rapidly in the same direction ; and being sent back again with redoubled vigour, never ceased till they broke against the door of the Court House.

Young Fitzwalter and his wife could not fail to be deeply moved by this extraordinary manifestation. So overpowered by it was Rose, that she was obliged to hide her head for a few moments in her husband's bosom; and when she was able to look round again, and essayed to utter her thanks, the plaudits became more vehement than ever.

Silence being at last obtained, Alured said, in a voice of profound emotion,—"Most heartily do I thank you, my friends, for this expression of your good-will. That I have gained a prize, according to an Ancient Custom, instituted by an ancestor of my own, is a high gratification to me—and the pleasure is enhanced by your kindness. But as to merit I can claim none—unless to possess the best of wives be a merit. Good fortune I should rather style it than desert. Since I wedded Rose, I have tasted pure happiness. My wishes have been her wishes, my thoughts have been her thoughts. My heart has been lodged in her breast. This, my friends, and no other, is *my* title to the Flitch."

"And now hear me, my friends," Rose said, in her sweet, musical tones. "Like my dearest husband, I rejoice in our success, —and like him I disclaim all merit. He is not more fortunate than I am, for perfect happiness has been my portion since we wedded. That I have loved him with an ardour equal to his own I may venture to avouch—and that I have been a fond and true wife to him, as he has been a loyal and loving husband to me, I can, from the bottom of my heart, declare. This, my friends, is *my* sole title to the Flitch."

"You have both fairly won it, as all present acknowledge," the squire cried, as soon as he could make himself heard for the applause that followed. "And now let us proceed to the Old Priory Church, and conclude the Ceremonial."

V.

HOW THEY WENT TO THE OLD PRIORY CHURCH.

MARSHALLED by Roper, the Procession of the Flitch set forward to the Old Priory Church in the following order.

First marched Timothy Tipcat, the beadle, to clear the way, followed by Will Crane, Tom Deane, and Nat Smith, whose united efforts with two additional poles were required to bear aloft the mighty Flitch. Next came Juddock, strutting along, with a churchwarden's staff in his hand, and acting the part of drum-major to the musicians, whose pace and movements he regulated. The band, which followed the giant, had been augmented by some ancient instruments provided by the squire—such as a theorbo, a mandolin, a cittern, a cornemeuse, a couple of lutes, pandean pipes, and a triangle. These formed the first and second lines. In the third, there were drums, clarions, and hautboys. The band, under the guidance of Juddock, played lively tunes—and there was ever and anon a pause, during which the trumpets were alone sounded and the drums beaten. After the musicians came the Bailiff of Dunmow and the Burgesses, each with a white wand in hand; then Mr. Roper and his clerk Hopkinson; and then marched Doctor Sidebottom and Parson Bush, followed by Roger Bowes, the clerk. After these walked a large body of the squire's tenantry, six abreast. Then came Jonas Nettlebed and Nelly in the cart, still driven by Carroty Dick, and with Peggy in the back seat.

Jonas appeared to have got over his mortification, and bore all the jests made at his expense very good-humouredly; while his wife looked so pretty and amiable, that some people almost regretted she had not been successful. Then followed ten or a dozen coaches, in the foremost of which were Sir Walter and Lady Fitzwalter, with Mrs. Leslie. The coaches were succeeded by a numerous troop of ladies and gentlemen on horseback, making a very gallant show. Then came another mounted band of tenantry, mustered from amongst those provided with steeds. After them followed the Jury of Bachelors and Maidens, walking two and two, each youth holding a damsel by the hand. In the rear of this pretty train rode the squire, with his daughter Bab; and at the young lady's side rode Montfichet.

The time had now come, the young baronet thought, when his fate must be decided, so as they came to a momentary halt, he brought his horse quite close to Gipsy, and feigning to pat her glossy neck, said—"You promised to give me an answer when the Flitch had been won, Bab. Am I to have a chance of winning the prize with you?"

"You would never win it with me, I tell you fairly," she replied. "I've not been brought up at the same school as Rose. Papa has spoiled me dreadfully, as you know. Besides, you're not at all like Alured."

"Try me," Sir Gilbert cried. "I have no misgivings of happiness with you. Why should you have doubts of me? I love you to distraction."

"Come, come—don't let the lad break his heart, Bab," the squire said. "Take him—and make him happy."

"Do you really think he would make a good husband, papa?"

"On my faith, I think so," the squire answered—
"an excellent husband."

"What shall I say to him, then?"

"Why say you accept him, to be sure—or, I'll say
it for you, if you had rather.—She is yours, Sir
Gilbert."

"Will not Bab confirm my happiness with her own
lips?" Montfichet cried, transported.

"Well, I consent—if nothing else will satisfy you.
I never disobey papa."

"That's right, Bab. An obedient daughter is sure
to make an obedient wife—so I think you have some
chance of the Flitch, Sir Gilbert, after all."

The three suitors, who were close behind, and who
had caught something of what was passing, now pressed
forward.

"Are my hopes annihilated, Miss Monkbury?" Grub
cried.

"Is it all up with me?" Chip exclaimed.

"Am I to blow out my brains?" Clot vociferated.
"By the Lord Harry, I will—if I'm rejected."

"I hope not, colonel," the squire remarked to the
last speaker. "Better all dine with us at Monkbury
Place, and drown your griefs in a magnum of claret.
Pshaw! man; there are finer fish in the sea than ever
came out of it. As to you, my worthy Grub, and you,
honest Chip—take my advice, and think no more of
this little hussy. We shall have plenty of pretty girls
at Monkbury to-day, and it'll be your own fault if
both of you don't find a wife among 'em. So cheer up.
And do you cheer up, too, brave Clot. I've got a
buxom widow in view for you—lots of money, and no
incumbrances—so put by your pistol till she rejects
you."

With this, not wholly unsuccessful, effort to console

the desponding suitors, the good-natured gentleman
rode laughingly on. He pretended to take no notice
of Bab and Sir Gilbert—the latter being now in a
seventh heaven of delight, and wholly unconscious of
the many curious eyes fixed upon him. Bab, too,
appeared just as heedless as to what might be said or
thought of her—and everybody set them down as what
they were in reality—engaged lovers—beginning to
look forward to another procession of the Flitch.

And here we may as well mention, though they
never did claim the prize, that within a week of the
event we are now describing they were spending their
honeymoon at Stansted House, and that their married
life was but a succession of honeymoons. Besides
Montfichet's, many and many another happy marriage
dated from the day when Alured and Rose claimed the
Flitch. Of the Bachelors and Maidens composing the
Jury on that occasion, not one was a bachelor or a
maiden within three months of it. But though we
have searched the register for the purpose, we have
been unable to ascertain whether Carroty Dick was
wedded to Peggy, and rather think he was not.

The procession was closed by the loving couple, who
rode to the church as they had ridden to the Court
House; and who were greeted on their way with congratulations as heartfelt, and blessings as audible, as
those which had previously attended them.

The bells ceased to ring, the vast concourse now
gathered together on the green in front of the ancient
lane, or drawn up in the churchyard, became silent,
and only gentle strains from mandolin and lute were
heard, as the pair dismounted at the gate.

VI.

HOW THE OATH WAS TAKEN, AND THE FLITCH DELIVERED.

THE path from the gate to the church porch, as well as the floor of the sacred fabric, have been thickly strewn with rushes. Ropes of flowers and wreaths hang across the footway from the upper branches of the little avenue of lime-trees. As Alured and Rose enter the gate and take their way, hand in hand, towards the church porch, they are preceded by a little troop of rustic maidens, attired in white, with baskets in their hands; and those maidens scatter roses and gilliflowers and other sweet-scented flowers and herbs before them. A flag rustles in the breeze on the summit of the little spire. Just outside the porch stand Will Crane and his comrades bearing the Flitch; and beneath it, ready to receive them, are the vicar, the squire, and the steward.

And now the pair pause for a moment. The vicar advances a few steps; signs to them; and they kneel down.

They kneel down on the self-same spot, and on the self-same stones, where, more than four centuries ago, Reginald Fitzwalter and his wife knelt when they craved a blessing from the good prior.

Benedicite! fond pair! Ye deserve holy priest's blessing as well as those who have knelt there before you.

Bow down your gentle heads as the reverend man bends over you, and murmurs a prayer for your welfare.

All who hear him breathe a heartfelt response.

Now ye may look up. He is about to recite the Oath, and ye must pronounce it after him.

The Oath is uttered.

Yet hold a moment, ere you quit your kneeling posture. The youngest and fairest of the flower-girls approaches, and she will place a garland of lilies on the brows of one of you, and over the neck of the other she will cast the ancient silver chain, which has been given to her by the steward.

It is done. Ye may rise, and the Flitch shall be delivered to you.

The Flitch—the guerdon of your love!

Hark to those thrilling shouts! The people exult in your triumph.

Bells ring—drums rattle—trumpets resound. The other instruments strike up.

All is not over yet. Ye have to be placed in the antique chair, and according to usage, borne on men's shoulders, round the boundaries of the old Priory, which in the days of your predecessors stood hereabouts.

And see! the chair is brought out for you. It is decked with rich though faded tapestry, woven with armorial bearings, which ye must know well, since they are your own, and with a device, which each of you may apply to the other—*Toujours Fidèle.*

And now ye are seated. Now ye are raised upon eight stalwart shoulders—and again the Procession is formed to lead you on.

Not so numerous now as heretofore, for only those, who have rightful part in the Ceremony, may join it. But the Flitch shall be borne before you, and the gentle lute and mandolin, and the shrill pipes, and the loud hautboy shall precede you, and gladden all hearts with their strains. And the reverend man, who has just blessed you, shall walk in front. And so shall the Lord of the Manor, who has yet a dearer title to your love and honour, and who calls one of you daughter. And so shall another whose title is the same as his, and who calls the other son. And the worthy steward who has watched over you shall be with them. And the flower-girls shall hang garlands upon the chair in which ye sit, and sing simple songs in your praise. And the Bachelors and Maidens shall follow after you, and join in chorus. And much people shall attend you, shouting. And hundreds shall look on, and cheer and bless you as before. Thus escorted, shall ye trace out the precincts of the once vast and stately edifice. That done, the Ceremonial will be ended.

Then shall you go home lovingly as you came, and shall take with you hundreds and hundreds to enjoy the unbounded hospitalities of Monkbury Place. Many a cup shall be drained to you—and ye shall make merry and rejoice. And thus shall end a pleasant and memorable day.

And so, Fond Pair, farewell! All happiness betide you!

L'Cnbof.

A word more. Long and happily did our Loving Pair live together. Nor were they separated at the last, for the same blow chilled the hearts of both— realising what Rose herself had sung of her husband's progenitors.

To the other candidates for the Flitch, whose unsuccessful attempts to gain it have been here recorded, might be applied the couplet which old Chaucer has put into the mouth of the merry Wife of Bath—

> The Bacon was not fet for them I trow,
> That some men have in Essex at Dunmow.

THE END.

A. Bonner, Printer, 1 & 2, Took's Court, London, E.C.